He's her rock n'roll fantasy, but could he ever be more?

Half the year, Cassandra Geoffrey runs In The Pines Campground, and spends the other half alone on a West Virginia mountain. She's not completely happy with the situation, but she loves her wacky, close-knit hometown. Besides, the man of her dreams isn't likely to appear anytime soon—until Jason Callisto, lead guitarist for Touchstone, her ultimate fantasy crush, shows up. At her campground. It's gotta be fate.

After being dumped by his supermodel girlfriend, Jason has been impossible to live with. Now he's been exiled by his manager to West Virginia, before he breaks up the band on the eve of the Grammys. Clearly, Jason is Cass's adventure of a lifetime. To him, she's just an ego boost….Or is she? With so much at stake, can they take a risk and reach for more?

Visit us at www.kensingtonbooks.com

Books by Christa Maurice

Drawn to the Rhythm Series
Satellite of Love
Heaven Beside You

Arden FD Series
Three Alarm Tenant
Struck By Lightning
Spark of Desire

Weaver's Circle Series
Secrets Everybody Knows
Long Memory

One Ring to Rule
Melody Unchained

Published by Kensington Publishing Corporation

Heaven Beside You

Drawn to the Rhythm Series

Christa Maurice

LYRICAL PRESS
Kensington Publishing Corp.
www.kensingtonbooks.com

Lyrical Press books are published by
Kensington Publishing Corp. 119 West 40th Street New York, NY 10018

All Kensington titles, imprints, and distributed lines are available at special quantity discounts for bulk purchases for sales promotion, premiums, fund-raising, and educational or institutional use.

Special book excerpts or customized printings can also be created to fit specific needs. For details, write or phone the office of the Kensington Special Sales Manager: Kensington Publishing Corp.
119 West 40th Street
New York, NY 10018
Attn. Special Sales Department. Phone: 1-800-221-2647.

Kensington and the K logo Reg. U.S. Pat. & TM Off.
Lyrical Press and the L logo are trademarks of Kensington Publishing Corp.

First Electronic Edition: January 2015
eISBN-13: 978-1-61650-231-7
eISBN-10: 1-61650-231-2

First Print Edition: MONTH YEAR
ISBN-13: 978-1-61650-967-5
ISBN-10: 1-61650-967-8

Printed in the United States of America

To Def Leppard for the album Slang, which I listened to on repeat for most of the writing and editing of this book.

Chapter 1

Cassandra grabbed her phone before it rang a second time. Her printer spit out expense reports as she tucked the phone between her ear and her shoulder. "Hello?"

"Cass, I stopped at your parents and they said you'd gone up the mountain early."

"I have an off-season guest coming. Don't worry, Finn. I'll have my taxes to you in plenty of time." If only he had a body and personality to match that exotic name, but he'd spent most of his life training to be as boring as possible. The rest of the time he spent pursuing her. He never seemed to realize one goal was in total opposition to the other.

"Taxes? Oh. Good."

Good? He was her accountant. Timely submission of her paperwork should have been important to him.

"You have a guest coming? Now?"

"Don't worry, Finn. I'm not going to change my season." Cass glanced out the window for headlights. The guest's plane should have landed at Pittsburgh hours ago. He could be here anytime. If it was a he. The name J.P. Barnswallow didn't give much of a hint except that it sounded fake. The setting sun reflected off the snow, gilding the world. "This is my vacation, but the money went to my brain."

"Oh, well, if you need any help, I can come up."

"It's practically done now. That program you recommended is great. Thanks."

"Yeah, good." Finn sounded less than happy about his recommendation.

"Well, thanks for the call, Finn, but I want to get back to this and my guest should be here soon. So I'll talk to you in a week."

"Give me a call and we can have lunch at Ida's."

Cass cringed. Lunch with Finn? She could predict what he would have based on the day. Of course, all she had to do was tell her parents and they would show up to run interference. Paul would be there too, and the food would be excellent. "Sure, Finn. See you then."

Cass hung up and studied the computer screen. She'd been on the phone long enough for her screen saver to start up. Someday she had to grow up and take the Jason Callisto slide show off instead of continuing to update it. That day wasn't going to be today. She admired the shot from Aspen where he was wearing his long black wool coat, no skis in sight, and moved the mouse when it started to disintegrate. Three more reports, and she could clip everything together and stuff it in an envelope for Finn.

Lights splashed across the wall beside her. She jumped and peered out the window.

A black Cadillac pulled into the parking space closest to her door. The rental agency had either not known their car was headed into the mountains or had been too busy talking the customer out of a sports car. Hopefully the fault lay with the agent because she had no desire to deal with a difficult guest.

She pulled on her coat and tugged her hair out of the collar. Scooping up the cabin keys, she walked to the front door. How had she allowed herself to be conned into renting out a cabin during her off-season? Money notwithstanding, this was her vacation.

Cass stopped in the open door, letting all her heat out.

Her guest slammed the door of the rental car, stomping his feet to get the feeling back. She'd recognized his lean six-foot-one frame and long black hair before he'd stopped rubbing his eyes and confirmed he was indeed Jason Callisto, guitarist from Touchstone. He wore a long black wool coat just like the one he'd had on in the Aspen picture, black gloves and trademark black Converse sneakers, making him appear longer and sexier than she'd ever imagined. She didn't need to see his whiskey brown eyes to know it was him.

He squinted at her. "Are you the owner of this place?"

"Yes," she squeaked. Her breath log-jammed in her lungs around the vicinity of her heart, which wanted to pound right out of her chest.

The office booking the cabin should have warned her so she would have time to prepare. But how could they know she'd be more dumbfounded by the sight of Jason Callisto on her doorstep than anybody else in the world, past or present, real or fictional?

Okay, fictional might have thrown her, but she would have been able to breathe if Ishmael had appeared on her doorstep claiming to need a break from hunting the white whale. To be honest, preparation would have consisted of a lot of semi-hysterical gibbering. One does not prepare for the appearance of one's long term, unattainable lust on one's literal doorstep. One merely hopes not to make a fool of oneself in the impossible event it should happen.

Okay, time to stop squeaking, start speaking in complete sentences, and not let her knees unhinge.

"I guess I've got a cabin reserved here for the next two weeks," he told her, staring at the tall pines and firs surrounding the cabin. His voice was richer than she expected, like digital recording couldn't quite capture its depth.

Cass clutched her parka closed. She wasn't dressed to meet Jason Callisto. Her usual ensemble of baggy jeans and faded sweatshirt did not suit the guest. And she didn't own a red carpet or anything.

She swallowed. "Sure, I've got your keys here. It's the one with the shutters off the windows." She was missing something but couldn't place it. What was it? Give him the keys, show him his cabin...one more step. Five years of campground ownership and suddenly she couldn't remember her job. "Oh, I need to have you sign some papers."

"Can we do it inside? It's fuckin' cold out here." He started toward the door.

Cass stumbled backward, holding out the keys like she would a cross to ward off a vampire. Bringing him into the office would almost be like letting him into her house. Could she invite him in without serious repercussions? Or was it too late for that? What would those repercussions be? She hadn't cleaned the office since fall. It was dusty. Did he care if the office was dusty? "Here's the cabin key. You'll see it, it's the only one open."

"The one with the shutters off the windows. I remember. Thanks." He snagged the keys without touching her hand and dropped them in his pocket as he followed her through the door. His dark eyes were smudged with something weightier than simple fatigue and the corners of his sensual mouth drooped. At least, compared to magazine pictures.

Cass turned to the counter where she'd laid out all her paperwork in anticipation. Good thing too, she'd have never remembered what she needed if it hadn't been. "Normally I would have a schedule of events, but there aren't any this time of year. It's just you and me up here," she babbled. "There's some stuff that goes on down in town if you're interested."

"That's okay, I'm not really fit company right now anyway." He skimmed the rental agreement.

Cass pushed her hair off her face and wondered what his comment meant. She'd gotten past her shock enough to hear his tone of voice. He sounded worn out and miserable. Adding that to the darkness in his eyes and the cant of his mouth, the sum came up unhappy. People often showed up at her door tired and cranky. That was why they went on vacation. If his idea of a vacation was hiding out on a mountain in January, then the crowded airport was way more than he could handle. Especially since he couldn't be cranky without having it wind up in *People* magazine. "Long flight?"

"Long two years," he answered, signing the papers.

Last spring, Touchstone had released a blockbuster album heralded as their comeback. His band had spent all summer and fall touring. The summer before that, they'd been on hiatus and he'd released a solo album, which had been pretty awful.

Cass bit her lip. *People* magazine. Two years ago in the Valentine's issue there had been an article on famous love affairs. His three-year relationship with supermodel Stella Marina had been in the "*Over*" side bar. Stella had since been in several high profile romances. Jason had not. If Duke would move those magazines away from the checkout she wouldn't study them so religiously, but then she also wouldn't have a file of the best ones under her bed, including the fateful *People*. Should she say something, or pretend his life wasn't all over the gossip magazines? "Well, I'm sure I can put together a marshmallow roast if you're interested."

He smiled, but it didn't quite make it to his eyes. "I'll let you know. Right now, I just want to get warmed up. The heater wasn't so great in the rental."

"I turned up the heat in your cabin yesterday, so it should be nice and toasty. And there's a fire laid. All you need to do is light it and add wood when it gets going. There's a woodpile beside the cabin too. Should be enough to keep you for your stay." Cass wrung her hands.

"Great. What about dinner?" Jason ran his fingers through his hair. He'd probably intended to put it in better order. Instead he'd managed to make it even more mussed and sexy.

Trying to loosen her throat before she started squeaking again, she swallowed. "Dinner?"

"No dinner?"

Cass bit her lip again and his eyes followed the action. Before Stella, Jason had been quite the Romeo. He'd wined and dined the most beautiful women in Hollywood and every one of them had claimed he could melt them with a look. She didn't need any more melting. "Everybody brings their own food."

He cursed at the floor. "A little detail Jody left out. Does Domino's deliver?"

"We don't have a Domino's around here."

He raised an eyebrow. "No Domino's? Next thing, you'll tell me there's no McDonald's."

She shook her head. "Not in the valley. And you probably don't want to head down the mountain this time of night anyway. It's getting dark and it could be hard to find your way back."

"No McDonald's," he repeated.

"There's one off the highway but that's—"

"Thirty minutes away." He grimaced as if he were afraid of what might come out of his mouth if he opened it now. After a moment, he sighed. "Okay, this isn't your fault. I should have known Jody would pull a stunt like this. I guess I go hungry tonight."

"I've got a roast in the oven. It'll be ready in about an hour, if you want to come back over." She heard herself offer, but couldn't believe it. How would she eat with Jason Callisto across the table when she couldn't even breathe when he was in the same room?

"That would be great." He sighed. "I promise not to be a huge problem while I'm here, I just didn't know I had to bring my own groceries."

"You probably didn't bring linens either."

"Was I supposed to?"

Cass nodded. All of this had been in the confirmation letter she'd sent his office over a week ago, and she'd repeated the information to the secretary over the phone. Whoever Jody was, she'd pulled quite a stunt. "I've got some extras you can borrow. I'll get you a couple of towels now so you can shower, and have the rest ready when you come for dinner."

"Thank you." He bounced the keys in his hand. "The only one that's open?"

"The first one around to the right. The rest have shutters over their windows."

"So it's just you and me," he said.

She nodded.

This time when he smiled, it crept into his eyes, lighting them in a distinctly melting way. "That's not necessarily a bad thing."

Had it suddenly gotten hot in here? Or maybe it was uncontrollable shivering without being cold. It didn't matter; she was shivering all over. Even if he didn't mean it the way it sounded, her body whole-heartedly

Christa Maurice

believed the sexiest man alive was propositioning her. "I'll get you those towels." She tried to go up the steps backward and tripped on the top one then staggered backward a few steps before catching herself on the chair beside the mantle. Another two steps and she would have fallen into, and no doubt broken, the coffee table. She'd managed to attain the age of thirty with a modicum of dignity, but now that there was a cute boy in her house she'd dropped right back to puberty. Pulling herself up, she hurried out of the room.

* * * *

Fish in a barrel.

Jason set his suitcase on the floor beside the bed. He'd brought his guitars in first and left them in the living room. The bed was indeed a bare mattress. Leave it to Jody. She was still pissed because she hadn't made the short list when Stella dumped him. The fact that nobody had been on his short list didn't deter her for an instant. Of course, Jody wouldn't understand something purely physical. She wanted everything, up to the diamond ring. Pre-nup optional.

The cute little campground owner didn't have any of that predatory gleam. She had more than down-home charm. Something that looked suspiciously like honesty.

He glanced out the front window of his cabin at the owner's little Craftsman style bungalow. What was her body like under that puffy parka? If the legs were any indication, excellent. And every redhead he'd ever known had run a little hotter than average. If the way she'd acted a few minutes ago meant anything at all, her temperature was already rising. Getting that woman in bed was going to be like shooting fish in a barrel. Nothing spelled ego boost like a good sexual conquest. He needed the ego boost.

Stella dumped him in *People* magazine. Walking though the airport from the first class lounge to the gate last year, he'd kept seeing that fucking magazine in all the newsstands, but he'd avoided it. Then the goddamn attendant came around with the basket of reading material and instead of picking up something logical like *Forbes* or *Business Week* or the goddamn *New York Times*, he'd picked up *People*. If the airline had had better movies lined up on the in-flight entertainment, he could have been spared the news at least until he'd landed, but no, they had to have bought the Bruce Willis block that month. He'd been looking forward to settling in to their familiar New York apartment until the moment he'd flipped to that fucking sidebar. Leave it to Stella to use even their breakup to forward her career. Leave it to *People* to stick it in a sidebar. At least he hadn't had to face a half empty apartment unwarned when he'd arrived there. No, Candy had been on the phone with him seconds after the crew told them they were allowed to turn on their phones, pissed that her mole at *People* hadn't warned her ahead of time as she made sure he was okay.

It was the lousy reception that album had gotten. Thanks to the off album, their relationship no longer helped her career. He'd wanted to believe she loved him so much, he'd ignored how she'd used his fame to get her acting career going.

No, he'd sensed something, because he'd planned on asking her to marry him so she wouldn't leave. As if saying *I do* would have stopped her from jumping to a better gravy train.

Ditching the New York apartment hadn't helped. Releasing that shitty solo album made everything worse. Watching Bear find, court and marry his own one true love had been agony. Throwing himself into promo for the last album had worked because dropping into malls and small town radio stations during the tour not only boosted record sales and made him valuable to the rest of the band, it gave him something positive. He needed positive or he was going to get thrown out of the band, no matter how valuable he was.

Once the tour ended, Sandy strongly suggested going to West Virginia to sit on the side of a mountain for a while and cool his heels far, far away from where he could piss off the band more. "I want you back on your feet for the Grammys, boy," his manager had said. "You have two weeks."

In two weeks, he could seduce and thrill the sexy little miss and leave her with exciting memories while soothing his ego at the same time. A good bargain all around, right?

Maybe not. Guilt gnawed at the back of his mind. He knew what it looked like from the female side when Mr. Right turned out to be Mr. Right Now And Gone Tomorrow. He still knew the names of all the men and boys who'd broken his sisters' hearts even if they didn't realize he'd noticed. No way did he want to be that guy for any woman.

Still, she knew what the score was. She didn't have to bite. He showed up as Mr. Right Now. All alone up here all winter, sexy Cassandra had to have some time to kill, and judging by the way she'd reacted to him, she was inclined.

He checked his watch. Plenty of time to shower and shave before dinner. He opened his suitcase. Lots of black stuff, which suited his mood and his body. After ten years of being dressed by professionals, he knew what worked. With his swarthy skin and dark hair, black looked perfect. Blond Brian wore a lot of white and blue. Blond Brian, who was a husband

and father before he ever meant to be. Unfair, to say the least. Jason had always wanted to settle down. He wanted a wife and kids and a house in the country. Brian had all that stuff. Bear had it now too. Some days it was hard not to hate Brian and Bear, even if they were his best friends.

Jason threw a black shirt and black jeans on the bare mattress along with some underwear and socks. Then he sauntered across the living room to the bathroom and turned on the shower. The place was warm. Sexy Cassandra had made sure of that. The water spraying across his hand steamed. When Jody told him the proprietor of the In the Pines Campground was a woman named Cassandra Geoffrey, he'd envisioned a tough old bird with a buzz cut, built like a Marine and wearing a scowl that could scare tempered steel. He'd expected to spend his two weeks holed up in the rented cabin playing guitar and talking to himself. But the vision that had greeted him at the door had been more than welcome. That mass of curly hair made his hands itch to be buried in it, letting it twist around his fingers, and it was so red he wondered if cuffs and collar matched. From the shade of her eyebrows and eyelashes, they did, unless she dyed those too. Did women in the real world do that? He'd been living in LA too long. Seeing Jennifer Aniston in reruns and at the neighborhood Starbucks tended to warp the mind a little.

Jason stepped under the water, feeling himself thaw. Cassandra's sea-green eyes and lovely full mouth were pretty captivating too. And unlike most redheads, she didn't have freckles. Nothing wrong with freckles, but they'd always made him think of little girls, and he preferred women. No, her skin, what he'd been able to see, had been smooth and pale as sweet cream. Maybe it was like that all over. That led him back to wondering what her body looked like under the parka. The hint had been strong enough that he knew it wasn't bad, but how good was it?

He warmed to more than the water. It had been some time since he'd had much reaction to any woman. Getting dumped in the national press had sort of put a damper on things. He took a deep breath. If he didn't get himself under control quick, he'd have to stick his head in a snowdrift on his way to dinner, and she might wonder about him then.

He smiled, hoping she was wondering about him now.

Chapter 2

The tablecloth she'd spread on the table looked stupid. First of all, the very bright summery yellow did not suit the season. Second, it smacked of trying too hard, and she didn't want to fawn. Jason Callisto hadn't come to West Virginia to be fawned over. If he wanted that he would have gone to Aspen where the skiing was better, according to *People* magazine.

Yanking the tablecloth off, she folded it up before stuffing it back in the drawer. The roast had to go on the good platter because it was the only thing big enough, though she was not going to get much roast beef for sandwiches, which had been the point of cooking a big meal.

She checked the roast. It looked fine and would be ready on time. Good thing she'd done the full service carrots and potatoes.

In her bedroom, she surveyed the choices. If she didn't make up her mind, she would greet him at the door in her birthday suit, and that would put an entirely different spin on the evening. At least, she decided, they didn't do that in Aspen.

She picked up the jewel-tone purple sweater her mother had given her for Christmas. As yet unworn, but her mother had an unerring eye for color. However, it had a turtleneck. Hardly sexy. The other option was her tight black chenille with the low neckline. She'd bought it in the children's department, which is why it was so tight and low. That's also why almost nobody around town had seen it, but she felt voluptuous when she wore it around the house.

The dinner rolls had to get in the oven or they wouldn't be ready.

She pulled on a pair of black bell-bottoms—they accentuated her curves—and the purple sweater because it didn't make her look like a tart. A good trade off, under the circumstances. Then she hurried into the kitchen and, after wrapping an apron older than her mother over the ensemble, got the dinner rolls going and assembled her trifle.

Now, that was over doing it. Or looked like it. The pound cake and the strawberries were frozen and the pudding, instant. The whole thing took five minutes tops to throw together, but in a crystal bowl, it looked gorgeous and frilly. She turned the bowl. Did it even have a best angle? Every inch was bright, gooey and mouthwatering. Before she found one, the bell rang.

Jason stood outside, moody and seductive in his long black coat, like a member of the French Resistance who'd fallen out of World War II. Or a rock star who'd appeared in West Virginia to have dinner with a fan.

Because that happened all the time.

She pulled open the door and summoned up her normal speaking voice. Not an easy task when her tongue wanted to loll out of her mouth. "Hello, you're just in time. Come on in." She led him up the three stairs to her living room door.

Since she not only lived and worked here, but got stuck inside sometimes for weeks in the winter, the place was very cozy and warm. Dark wood floors, whitewashed walls, and overstuffed burgundy furniture facing the fieldstone fireplace, which she kept blazing most of the winter. Curtains blocked the view of her office. The TV sat where she could see it from the couch, but had a thick film of dust on it because she hadn't cleaned since she'd come back up the mountain after Christmas. On either side of the TV, bookshelves groaned with books and DVDs. It was nice. Not *MTV Cribs* nice, but nice.

He bypassed all of that and walked straight to the window overlooking the valley. She hadn't managed to set up her easel yet so there was nothing to block the view.

"Nice view," he said.

She felt obligated to go stand beside him. Because he was a guest and not because she couldn't resist the opportunity to be near him. Really.

Beyond her tiny side yard and across the access road, the ground dropped off for about five feet then resumed a more leisurely descent into the valley below. It gave the impression that her cabin was hanging on the edge of the mountain. The town below looked like a miniature in a snow globe, lit by a few lights from street lamps and houses, peaceful and sleepy. Across and down the valley, the new ski lodge did a brisk business, like an illuminated scar on the mountain. She hadn't minded it until they'd started with the night skiing. Then it ruined her pretty view and kept all the tourists on the slopes in the evenings instead of giving them time to go into town for dinner and shopping.

"Is that a ski lodge?" he asked.

"Yes." She kept her voice neutral. Finally, she'd found something to counterbalance his appeal. The ski lodge. She didn't remember any of his press saying he skied, but he might. Or he might be bored enough to take it up over the next two weeks. His rented Caddy wouldn't look as out of place in their parking lot. "Do you ski?"

"No, I don't. I just was thinking it looks funny lit up like that. Kind of ruins the view." He turned to her. "There. That's better."

"Better?" Her breath caught. So much for counterbalancing appeal.

"The view. It's much better from this direction," he said.

Cass glanced down to hide the blush she had to be sporting and realized she was still wearing her apron. And she'd been worried about what sweater to wear? "I should get the roast out."

She spun around and dashed for the kitchen. The roast was done enough to take out, the rolls were not.

Maybe he'd agreed with her about the ski lodge, or he was buttering her up. But how would he know he was agreeing with her? What would be the purpose of buttering her up? She shivered at the thought.

"Anything I can do to help?"

Cass jumped and spun around holding the serving fork like a weapon. Jason leaned against the doorway smiling lazily. He seemed less harsh than he had before. She cleared her throat. "I suppose if you want a job, you can get this out of the roaster and start slicing while I make the gravy."

"Gladly." At the exact moment she lost her grip on the fork, his fingers brushed hers and she would have dropped it if he hadn't been holding it. She fidgeted behind him while he moved the roast. "You look like you know what you're doing."

"I get a lot of practice. When the roads get bad up here, they can stay that way for weeks sometimes. I could probably get down the holler, but there's no guarantee I'd get back up." She took the roaster out of his hands and turned away to make the gravy.

"Couldn't you stay with someone in town?" Jason asked over his shoulder. He'd picked up the knife and begun slicing.

She tried to stop imagining Jason's long fingers wrapped around her serrated knife. "I could stay with my parents, but nobody wants that." She poured the gravy into a stoneware gravy boat. Overkill again. When she ate alone, she dumped what she needed into a coffee mug.

"You don't get along with your parents?"

She wondered if the question was more than idle curiosity and then dismissed that idea as a figment of her overactive imagination. Even if he was, as she sort of hoped and sort of feared, trying to seduce her, why would he care about her relationship with her parents? "Sure, as long as they're in the valley and I'm up here. I usually spend about three weeks with them between Christmas and mid-January. About the end of that, we're all ready to say our good-byes until summer."

"What happens in the summer?"

"Dad gives nature walks and Mom does craft classes."

"A real family affair."

"Half the town does something. I've got a storyteller and another craft teacher and an astronomer, and a historian who does tours of local sites. There's even a guy who comes up about once a week to show old movies on a sheet strung between the trees." Speaking of which, she had to get started scheduling. It gave her something to think about that wasn't Jason Callisto slicing roast beef in her kitchen.

Shiver. Jason Callisto slicing roast beef in her kitchen.

She took out the dinner rolls. Double batch. They would freeze fine. Unless Jason ended up liking them and ate the lot.

Jason glanced at the rolls and raised an eyebrow. "You've got enough campers in these cabins to support all that entertainment?"

"Oh no. There's two lots of RV hookups down the road and a couple of tent camping areas. I can have up to two hundred people here on an August weekend." She cradled the gravy boat in her hands to keep them busy.

Did he think it was hokey and provincial? It was kind of, but it was nothing to be ashamed of. When she'd bought the place, every cabin, including this house, needed extensive work. The town had been hanging on by a thread, full of older people who had nowhere else to go and half the shops had been closed. She'd done a lot with this place, and for the town below. In a way, the stupid ski lodge was her fault. She'd been so successful, she was surprised a McDonald's and a Domino's weren't sitting side by side in the center of town by now. "I want to build a rec hall next year so we can do more stuff and have someplace for tent people to go if the weather gets bad."

"So why aren't you open in the winter?"

"Too cold. Who wants to go camping in the mountains in the winter?"

Jason shrugged. "I didn't think it was too cold. My cabin's nice and warm."

"Wait until your fire goes out and you don't notice until morning." She carried the gravy boat to the table, trying to focus on extending her season and ended up thinking about Jason anyway.

"In the middle of the table?" Jason asked.

She jerked and sloshed gravy over the lip of the boat. "That's fine." She scraped the escaping drop from the side of the boat and licked it off her finger.

He set the platter on the table, but she caught his gaze skittering away from her mouth. "My manager's cousin vacationed here a few years ago and really liked it, but I guess it was smaller then. He didn't say anything about all those activities you talked about."

"It gets bigger every year. I just got my RV hookups for last season and I'm running out of room already." She ducked back into the kitchen for a deep breath and grabbed the potatoes and carrots and the basket of rolls at the same time. "What about you? All we've done is talk about me."

"There's very little about me that hasn't been printed up in a tabloid someplace," he muttered as he settled into a chair.

How true was that? Many of those tabloids were tucked in a box under her bed. Maybe she could check tonight after he left.

If he left. Hmm. "I'm sure that isn't true," she lied. "How about your family?" Father deceased, mother still living, four sisters, she thought.

"I have four sisters, all older than me. My mother still lives in Illinois and two of my sisters are close by her, the other two live in California near me. My father died when I was a kid. That's about all there is to tell."

"Are you close?"

He shrugged and served himself some potatoes. "Sure."

"I'm not interviewing you."

He looked up and met her eyes. For a moment he stared, then he grinned, making her breath catch. "I guess not. Sorry, habit."

"I understand." Her heart pounded in her throat. Photographs couldn't capture that grin, somehow rawly sexual and endearing at the same time.

"So what do total strangers talk about over dinner?" he asked, that gleam never leaving his gaze.

Cass smiled. Steamy eye contact or not, this she excelled at. She spent so much time chatting with total strangers, she hardly knew what to say to people who knew her. "What's your favorite movie?"

"Boy, current or for all time?"

She laughed. This would make things easier. Talk about neutral subjects, then she wouldn't have to wonder what his lips would feel like against hers.

"You know, I've always liked *From Here To Eternity*." He raised an eyebrow.

"Really? I've never seen that one." Not all of it, anyway. Everyone had seen the beach scene. The stars rolling through the surf kissing. How was it everything led back to kissing? She should be relieved he hadn't picked *Fatal Attraction*, the way she was headed.

"You should. It's a classic. Maybe one night while I'm up here we can rent it." He bit down on the piece of meat on his fork.

Cass watched his white teeth sink into the tender meat. Her mouth felt like parchment. He had such beautiful, full lips. "It is something I've always meant to see," she managed to say without her jaw unhinging.

"Do you have Netflix or a Red Box in town?"

"Red Box? No, but we have a little video rental place. I can call Walter and see if he has it, if you like." Cass picked up her fork. If she didn't start eating, he would wonder. She had to attempt to act normal. Not easy, under the circumstances. This was every high school fantasy she'd ever had. Her favorite rock star, sitting across the table from her chatting and making flirtatious motions. At least she hoped they were. She wanted them to be.

"No hurry. We have two whole weeks. What about you? What's your favorite movie?"

Fortunately, she had a pat, but true answer ready for that question. One that had nothing whatsoever to do with kissing. "*The Haunting*. The original black and white one with Claire Bloom."

"The original? I thought there was only one." He reached for another roll, pausing with his hand over the basket, and looked at her. He liked the rolls. Cass suppressed an irrational desire to giggle.

"No, the one with Catherine Zeta Jones was a remake. I've got the original. Widescreen. It's very scary and everything is done by suggestion." To distract her gaze from his hand on the rolls, she glanced at her DVD shelf. She'd gotten the DVD for Christmas and hadn't even opened it yet.

"If that's an invitation, I accept. After dinner?"

She nearly dropped her fork. Bad enough to have him for dinner, but to have him sitting in her living room, on her couch all evening watching a movie? She'd have to make popcorn—did she have any in the house? In separate bowls, it would help her tone down a little bit. Might ruin his appetite for the trifle though. Maybe if she kept making food for him, her mind and hands would be too busy to embarrass her. "If you like."

"Great, but is it going to scare you to watch it now?" He studied her across the table as he split open a roll. His eyes seemed darker than she remembered from pictures. Concern or invitation? Did he want to cuddle during the movie to keep her from being too scared?

"No. Why?" His foot lay under the table right next to hers. Accidental or intentional?

"I would have thought watching scary movies would be the last thing you'd want to do up here on the mountain by yourself." He smiled. "You must not scare easily."

"Oh, I scare." She was scared silly right now. That he was flirting with her and that he might not be. And really, really terrified, either way, she would end up humiliating herself. "I can't watch *The Shining* anymore. And forget about those *Sleepaway Camp* movies."

He laughed. The husky quality of it raised the hairs on the back of her neck. "I can see that. I wouldn't want to find you writing *all work and no play makes Cassandra a dull girl* all over the walls."

"It doesn't match the decor."

He laughed again, but this sounded a little less seductive and a little more mirthful. She relaxed and tried to eat. Maybe she would have leftovers like she'd planned. Her appetites had focused on something, someone, else.

"So what do you do up here all winter?" he asked. "When you're not writing on the walls."

She smiled. "I read, and watch movies, and I paint."

"And cook. It's very good, by the way." He waved his fork around the table, managing to take in everything, including herself. "Thanks for inviting me."

"You're welcome." Cass looked at her plate. She needed another noncommittal topic of conversation to steer her mind away from the eight hundred pound gorilla across the table, but couldn't think of anything else. Over the years she'd had her share of guests flirt with her, but this time he didn't come with a wife and kids in tow, and he wasn't a burgeoning mountain man looking for a comfortable place to spend the winter.

Jason Callisto had no wife and kids, and she'd been dreaming about him her entire adult life.

"What kinds of things do you read?"

Cass let him steer the conversation. For a man who didn't know what total strangers talked about over dinner, he did a dandy job of coming up with topics. They spent the rest of the meal on books, as he said he spent a lot of his time on tour reading or watching television series. Toward the end, the conversation drifted to books that had been made into movies, which is what they were talking about when the phone rang.

Annoyed by the interruption, she grabbed her plate and headed for the kitchen. She'd become neutral enough her head wasn't spinning, but like walking a tightrope across the Grand Canyon while juggling fine china, any lapse in concentration would be the end of her. "Hello?" she answered the phone.

"Hi, sweetie, we just wondered if your guest made it."

She grimaced. Only her mother could call with such deadly accuracy.

"Yes, Mom, he did." Cass closed her eyes. She had to get her mother off the phone before her concentration lapsed. She couldn't work on two fronts and her mother could just about read minds. "Listen, Mom, I have a dinner guest."

Her mother missed a beat. A sure testament to how odd that was. Let the mind reading begin. "A dinner guest?"

Jason tapped her shoulder. "Do you mind if I put on some music?"

"Go ahead," she said, and then she felt the blood rush to her face. She hadn't hidden her Touchstone CDs. He would see the whole collection in chronological order and think she was a freak, or worse, a groupie. But instead of going into the cabinet, he picked one up from the sideboard and popped it in. Nat King Cole from her Christmas pile. The soothing tones of the CD filled the room, but somehow managed to leave her unsoothed.

"I see." Mom could pack more meaning into fewer words all the time. Soon she'd be communicating solely through expressions.

"I shouldn't keep him waiting."

Jason began clearing the table. He'd located the dish soap and started filling the sink with steaming water while he carried the plates to it. If she stayed on the phone long enough, he might pack up the leftovers and wash the dishes. He walked past her with a damp rag to wipe down the table. "I'll call you later."

"I'll wait up. 'Bye, sweetie." Mom hung up before Cass could counter. Seriously, very soon the phone would ring and she would, upon hearing nothing, know it was her mother *and* what was meant by the expressions being made at the receiver on the other end. Nothing would need to be said because her mother would be able to read her mind. They might skip the phone altogether. Her mother could stare up the holler, communicating telepathically.

"You didn't have to do all that," Cass protested.

"All what?" Jason strolled back into the kitchen with the towel. "If you get started putting away the leftovers, I'll work on the dishes and we can get to the movie. Do you have any rubber gloves?"

She found the pair of too big rubber gloves she'd bought by mistake and pulled out a few pieces from her large collection of Gladware. He'd eaten heartily, which balanced out that she hardly ate. There would be plenty for sandwiches and she wondered if she should pack up some for him to take to his cabin. But then, he wouldn't have any reason to come back over. She put all the leftovers into her fridge, taking out the trifle to make room.

"What's that?" he asked, a stoneware plate in his hand suspended halfway to the drainer.

"Dessert?"

"Wow. If I knew that was coming, I'd have saved room. It looks fantastic." He set the plate in the drainer and crossed the kitchen for a closer look. "And you do this all for yourself all winter?"

Cass coughed. Caught in the act of trying to impress. "Sometimes," she lied.

"I might have to visit here more often." He turned, his face inches from hers, giving her a look that made her dizzy from lack of oxygen. Body heat radiated off him.

"We have to finish the dishes first," she croaked.

"Yes ma'am," he said with a very low husky voice. A promising smile curled his lips.

As he turned his back to her to finish the dishes, she shivered. She had to try not to get so close to him again. When she did, she stopped breathing and got all woozy and stupid. Unfortunately, with the leftovers put away, she had nothing to do but help him with the dishes, which would require standing very close to him. She hoped she wouldn't break too many.

"So what do people in the valley do all winter since they're not working here?" he asked in a much more normal tone when she joined him at the sink.

"The library runs a couple of reading groups and there's a pretty good amateur hockey league around the valleys." Cass swallowed. He was too close and her body was stuck in overdrive. She stacked the dishes on the others in the cupboard. "Just about everybody goes to the high school basketball games and the high school and middle school plays. And the Presbyterian Church holds weekly dances to raise money for a mission in Africa someplace. They do that all year."

"Dances?" He brightened. "Do you dance?"

"I can." Her mouth dried up further. How soon would this level of emotional madness kill her?

He set the last dish in the drainer and pulled off the gloves. "Will you dance with me?"

"Now?"

He smiled and lifted the glass out of her hand. Then he took her right hand and rested her left on his shoulder. She thought she might go totally boneless when he put his right hand on her hip. A shiver of delight coursed through her. He waltzed her out of the kitchen and into the living room. The song ended, but that didn't seem to bother him. The next song started. *Let it Snow*. Cass closed her eyes to imprint the whole experience directly on her brain. A rich baritone overlaid Nat's voice with a melting harmony. She opened her eyes to discover Jason singing along.

She'd heard him sing before on CD, but it bore no resemblance to the voice singing in her ear now, like the smile didn't show in photographs. The extra edge might be the fact that she felt the words vibrating through her chest.

He waltzed her around the living room, still singing along. His hands were sure, guiding her. She wanted to pursue that thought, but couldn't allow herself to with him here, holding her. Later maybe. Let it snow, let it snow, let it snow.

The song had to end, and much sooner than she'd have liked, the music faded away. Jason didn't let go and continued swaying with her.

"The song's over," she pointed out.

"I noticed."

"You're still dancing."

"So are you," he countered.

"Can you dance without music?"

He smiled, making her shiver again. "Do you like pina coladas? And getting caught in the rain? If you're not into yoga, if you have half a brain."

It took her a moment to catch on to what he was saying, or rather, singing. She hadn't heard "*The Pina Colada Song"* in years, and suffered a momentary stab of disappointment that he was singing lyrics, not asking questions.

"And there's something here I forget. And then something about champagne," he sang to the tune. "Do you like making love at midnight, and something I don't know."

"Sorry, I don't remember it either," she whispered. Now she understood why fires roared up when stoked. She felt thoroughly stoked.

"Doesn't matter. The important part is the making love at midnight." He released her and took a step away. "Would you like to watch that movie now?"

Cass stumbled backward and caught herself on the couch, hoping it was less obvious this time that she couldn't keep her feet around him. "Okay."

"You get the movie going and I'll turn off the CD player."

She found the movie and set up the DVD player. Her hands shook, trying to tear off the plastic. It came off in long thin strips that stuck to her hands. He had to be hitting on her. There wasn't any other logical explanation. Unless he did this to every woman he encountered. She'd read his press. He was a Romeo, a well-known Romeo. Up until the last girlfriend, he'd played the field with relish, and a large field it had been. In that sport, he would have been on the All-Star team if there had been one. He'd said it had been a long two years. Maybe he was warming up to play again. Did she want that? Sex was supposed to signify something. Something important, not just a chance to score.

Or he might be hitting on her because he was attracted to her. She preferred that story. Though being bush league wouldn't be all bad. "Are you ready for some of the trifle?"

Jason grinned and followed her into the kitchen.

Chapter 3

"Well, it's probably getting late for you." Jason stood and stretched.

He was so lean and gorgeous and stretched out right in front of her face. Any second he would turn around, catch her staring and what? Wink? Roll his eyes? Frown because she was acting like a hopeless fangirl when he really wanted to be on vacation? Time. What time was it anyway? Eight thirty? Late? She would have let him stay all night, if he wanted to.

What was she thinking? Even if she desperately wanted him to be flirting with her, he dated supermodels and starlets. What interest would he have in a campground owner from West Virginia? "I suppose so." She faked a yawn for color and to hide the disappointment she didn't want to be feeling.

"I thank you for the wonderful dinner and the fantastic dessert." He bowed, causing an unwanted giggle to rise in her throat. He'd attacked the dessert like a man who'd never tasted sugar but had heard stories, demolishing half of it.

"You're very welcome. I need to go to town tomorrow, if you want to come along and pick up some groceries." Down the holler tomorrow? Since when? But what the heck? How often would she get the chance to take a rock star grocery shopping?

"That would be great." He stopped inside her living room door. "And didn't you say you had some bedding I could borrow?"

Bed. How might he be encouraged to change direction and lead the way to her bed, which he had no doubt glimpsed through the fireplace since it opened on both rooms.

"Oh, yeah. It's out in the office." She reached past him and opened the door. Cool air swept around them. It should have helped to cool her off, but only caused greater personal atmospheric disturbances. Wrapped in a black garbage bag, the bedding awaited on the counter. "Right here. I gave you a pillow, sheets and two comforters. It gets pretty cold at night and the furnace can't keep up."

"I'll make sure I keep good and warm." He smiled as he gathered up the bag.

She managed to smile back. This was an active pass. It had to be. At least he would be sleeping on her sheets tonight. She might never wash them again.

He shifted the bag in his arms. "So I'll see you tomorrow then? What time did you want to go?"

"Time?" she croaked. "Oh, time is pretty flexible on the mountain. No rush, if you want to sleep in. Around lunch, I guess."

"Good. Then I'll be able to buy you lunch in return for tonight. Provided there's a restaurant in town."

"There's Ida's." The thought of Jason in Ida's made her want to break into a cold sweat. Half the town was in and out of Ida's on any given day, most of them having nothing better to do than call each other to discuss what they'd seen with the half who hadn't turned out. This was a spectacle in the making.

"Great." He reached for her hand. For an instant she thought he might pull her close and kiss her, but he lifted the back of her hand to his lips and kissed it instead, his lips soft and hot. Her knees wanted give out right there in the doorway and the chill in the office turned into a steamy summer night. "I'll see you tomorrow then." He gave her hand a little squeeze before releasing it and walking out the front door.

Trying to back through her living room door, she tripped over the top step again and landed hard on her derriere. Too dazed to even shout, she kicked the door closed and lay back on the floor. He had been hitting on her. He'd enjoyed their dinner, offered to take her out to lunch, kissed her hand, flirted. Things like this didn't happen to girls like her. Girls like her stayed in their small towns, married reliable men like Finn Runningwater, had kids and watched them fly the nest to go anywhere that wasn't Potterville, West Virginia.

But she hadn't married Finn, she didn't have any children, and she'd tried to fly the nest once already. It hadn't worked.

That didn't mean she should get involved with a transient rock star, no matter how many boring college lectures she'd spent fantasizing about him, how many paintings she'd done of him for college projects, or that they were alone up here where nobody would ever have to know. He would leave town and she'd be more alone than she'd ever been before.

She looked at the back of her hand, surprised she couldn't see where he'd kissed her. How was she supposed to bring herself to wash that?

Cass sat up and rubbed her face. Maybe it was madness to resist him. Or was it more crazy to give in? Not that he'd really offered anyway. So far, all she had was speculation and fantasy. Regardless, she had to call her mother, who would probably know everything and the outcome before Cass said hello.

"Hi, Mom."

"Hi, honey. Did your guest leave?"

Cass heard her mother turn away from the phone to check the kitchen clock. No matter how old she was, her mother always wanted to know if she'd gotten in by curfew. Comforting, and annoying at the same time. "Yeah."

"How did you end up cooking him dinner?"

"What makes you think it was a him?"

"Because you said him when I called earlier, honey. How did you end up cooking him dinner?"

Cass rolled her eyes at the phone. Her mother had always been far too observant. "He didn't realize he had to bring his own food and didn't have any dinner. I didn't think it was a good idea to send him down the holler in the dark."

"That was neighborly of you."

Cass shivered. It hadn't felt neighborly, more like foreplay. "I'm gonna be down in town tomorrow. He's got to get some groceries and I need to check my mail and talk to Sue about the schedule for summer."

"You just got your mail yesterday and you could talk to Sue over the phone," her mother pointed out.

Far, far too observant. "I could, but he needs to get groceries anyway and I know where everything is."

"So we'll get to meet him."

If her mother saw Jason, she'd know everything. Definitely a fate worse than death. In person, her mother could communicate with expressions while carrying on other conversations. A very scary talent, indeed. "Oh, I don't know. I don't know if he wants to go around meeting the whole town."

"We're not the whole town, honey. We're your momma and daddy."

Cass closed her eyes. She'd never realized there was a fate worse than death. "I'll ask him." In a tone somewhere below a mumble that he would never hear. She'd assume no response meant no.

"So who is this mystery man? Anyone we would know?"

"He's a musician."

"Oh?" Her mother waited. She had more patience than most saints ever dreamed of possessing.

"Jason Callisto," Cass admitted.

"Wasn't he in that band you liked?"

Liked? She'd had their posters up in her dorm room in college and brought them home, hung them in her room every summer. Bought their albums the first day they'd gone on sale if she didn't have them on pre-order. She and three friends had driven two hours to see Touchstone, stood in the predawn March cold for another three hours to get twelve people from the door when the show had sold out. *That band she'd liked.* "Yes, he is."

"How nice."

Nice? Cass dropped onto the couch. If the next two weeks were anything like today, it would be pure hell. "Yeah, it'll be great."

"You should call your friend Gretta. She'll be so excited."

Whoa. What a great idea. Cass licked her lips. She and Gretta had been inseparable in college but afterward had grown a little more separable every year, to the point where they now exchanged only Christmas and birthday cards. She didn't even have Gretta's email. Gretta had been one of the three friends in the car who'd gotten twelve people from the door. She understood the therapeutic value of a package of Double Stuf Oreos and a gallon of milk. Gretta would understand...all this. "I probably should."

"Well, it's getting late. I should let you go. You have a big day tomorrow. Good night, sweetheart."

"Good night, Mom." Cass hung up the phone. Call Gretta who shared her fascination with Touchstone and Jason Callisto in particular. She lived in another state and wouldn't have told a soul in town if she'd lived next door. Who had served as a steady conscience all through college. Cass hoped the number she had was still accurate.

* * * *

Jason finished making up the bed. Maybe not up to military standard, but he didn't plan to bounce quarters on it. He didn't plan on bouncing anything on it. What he had in mind was more of a slow, rhythmic rocking motion with some heavy breathing and moaning thrown in for good measure. The fire popped and he jumped. He'd never realized how empty silence could be. Hopefully he would be able to get his hands on some speakers in town, or borrow some. The open, airy cabin swallowed up any volume his phone was capable of. All he could hear were the fire and the sound of wind in the trees outside. Unnerving.

He sat down on the edge of the bed. What it lacked in audio equipment, the In the Pines Campground more than made up for in comfy furniture and attractive company. He peered through the fireplace to the living room. Hers opened into both rooms too. He'd been able to see her lush bedspread reflecting in the fire. Not that this bed appeared less cozy now with the two comforters, but he'd rather be in hers. Sliding between those sheets and making love to her in the glow of the firelight. The flames would glint in her brilliant hair when she arched her white neck and cried out his name.

Well, enough of that. He stood up. Over the last tour he'd been mobbed with groupies who knew he was single and not a one of them had appealed even a tenth as much as Cassandra Geoffrey wearing a vintage apron over a turtleneck sweater, which made no sense at all. The groupies had dressed to flaunt their attributes. Cassandra seemed to be showing off her culinary skills. And she cooked, very, very well. A definite bonus. If she cooked half that well in the bedroom, this exile wouldn't be so bad.

He went back into the living room. His cellphone lay on the coffee table between the couch and the fireplace. He'd left it behind so he wouldn't be interrupted by anyone trying to make sure he'd arrived. Now, he called Brian's house.

"Hey."

"I made it." The familiar chaos at Brian's came through the phone. He had a two-year-old and a five-year-old. One of them was squalling.

"How is it?"

"Rustic, but the owner is something else." Jason fidgeted with a tan couch pillow trying to define *something else* so it would cover this scenario. Brian probably wouldn't believe him if he said it meant she made his hands sweaty and his groin tighten in ways he hadn't felt in years, even if that was true. Rock star Jason Callisto should be too jaded to feel like this. He'd seen it all and had it all too often to be so turned on by a woman in a vintage apron, no matter how good her dinner rolls tasted. When he'd picked up his baggage at the airport, he must have forgotten to grab the box marked *Jaded*.

"She's a cow, isn't she? She looks like that woman in *Misery's* less attractive cousin," Brian said. He had been less than inspired by Sandy's solution to the problem Jason's continuing grouchy behavior presented. Of course, Brian's solution—getting him drunk and setting every groupie in Chicago on him—hadn't been the greatest either. Especially after they'd found him locked in his hotel bathroom the next morning because the girls couldn't get to him there.

Jason could almost see his best friend's buoyant grin through the phone. Blond, beautiful Brian was his polar opposite, and Jason wondered why he didn't punch him out. "Nope."

"Then she must look like what's her name in *The Shining*, Olive Oyl."

"You read so much Stephen King, you could try to remember the characters' names." Jason smiled. Brian had been the only one able to bring the slightest smile to his face for the past two years. Even the groupie incident had been funny later that day. He was also the one person in the world Jason harbored a burning jealousy for, and most of the reason was wailing in the background.

"So what's the verdict?"

"She's really hot. Really, really hot." Once again, the usual terms didn't cover the current situation. Hot? He'd have felt cooler standing in the fireplace. Plus, being on fire might have distracted him. Not much though. He'd missed most of the movie because he'd been focused on her sitting in the chair behind him. Even when he couldn't see her, she had all his attention.

"You do her yet?"

Jason flinched. He didn't think of Cassie in terms of 'doing her.' The first phrase that came to mind with her was long, drawn out, passionate lovemaking. The tension in his lower body notched up at the thought. "I seem to be on the phone with you," he pointed out.

"You used to be pretty fast. I thought maybe you were done."

Being fast wasn't something he prided himself on anymore. "I've matured."

Brian laughed until he snorted. "So what's the plan for this one? You've only got two weeks."

"I'll make the most of it."

A child piped, "Daddy, Daddy, Daddy, Daddy," in the background.

His lust for Cassie gave ground to the overwhelming jealousy for Brian's home life. It wasn't fair. Brian had stumbled into marriage and fatherhood. Jason had wanted to settle down and have kids years ago, Paul and Linda McCartney-style. One woman, a couple of kids, 'til death do us part. Maybe with somebody who knew how to cook a roast to perfection, made mouthwatering desserts and wore vintage aprons.

What was he thinking? This trip was for getting over Stella, not jumping back into the deep end.

"Hush a minute," Brian was saying. "So does this mean you're over the Stella bit—uh—lady?"

"What's a bitlady?" Brian's little girl asked.

"Hush, sweetie," his friend said to his daughter.

"I don't know." Jason knew what Brian meant. 'Stella bitch' was Brian's affectionate term for Jason's ex. The woman who was supposed to be The One. Depression snuffed out his jealousy, though lust lurked in the background. No groceries meant no bourbon, his depression medication of choice. All he had to drink was water. Did Cassie have any alcohol? It wouldn't take much to run over and check. She might already be in her nightgown. A long flannel nightgown with a ruffle at the throat, or an old T-shirt, or footy pajamas. Somehow, the thought of her in footy pajamas with her long hair spilling across her shoulders was intensely appealing. Or Cassandra in a white ruffled flannel nightgown with her hair pulled back in a demure little bun that he could unravel. Anything would work, really. He might find a better cure for depression. The lust surged, pushing his depression back where it belonged.

"Well, take it easy. You don't want to get sucked in again. You're a world class drag when you're depressed."

"Thanks, Bri."

"Anytime. Say good night to Uncle Jason."

"Good night, Uncle Jason."

Jason's chest tightened. Why couldn't that little girl be his? "Good night, sweetie. Make sure Daddy checks the closet and under the bed for monsters. I heard there's some bad ones in your neighborhood tonight. It was on the news."

"On the news?"

"Thank you, Jason. Goodbye. Honey, there are no m—"

The connection cut, and Jason grinned. Eventually Tess would stop believing him when he told her about monsters, but until then he intended to use it to its fullest and little Brian, better known as Bubbie, was about ripe for those stories too. He could see Brian, now forced to inspect every inch of Tess's room, cursing his name, while Tess stood at the door wide-eyed.

Stella hadn't wanted kids. She'd said it would ruin her figure and given him references of supermodels who had no careers once they'd had children. She had hinted she'd think about it once she passed her modeling prime, and Jason had been stupid enough to believe her. He'd believed a lot of things about beautiful, blond and cool Stella. Like she loved him and she hadn't loved any of those other guys she'd used as stepping-stones for her career. That she would marry and settle down with him, and had participated when they'd had sex. No surprise that she'd gone after an actor this time. She'd gotten a lot of practice acting like she loved him.

Jason peered out the front window. Cassie had a light on. She was still awake, and might have something to drink. Once she'd had a few drinks she might be willing to share that big bed with him.

Disgusted with himself, he tossed the phone on the table. It skated across the surface and clattered on the hardwood floor. Plotting to bed Cassie like this wasn't much better than what Stella had done to him, and he didn't have it in him to be that big a jerk. If she was willing, then something would happen. He wouldn't force or manipulate her. And she'd have to know being with him was a temporary thing.

He'd just get himself a nice glass of cold water, pour it over his head and go lie in the cozy bed Cass had provided and stare at the ceiling until morning.

If he had a glass.

* * * *

Cass huddled in bed late the next morning trying to get some sleep. The number she had for Gretta wasn't hers anymore and the person who'd answered had been annoyed. The Internet hadn't yielded any useful information either. She'd settled for writing a long letter to the last address she had for her, which she intended to send overnight when she picked up her mail. With luck, Gretta would call in two days.

If Jason Callisto kept acting like he had last night, though, how was she going to last two more days?

She heaved herself out of bed, slid her feet into fluffy slippers and pulled on her thick terrycloth robe. Before trying to make the bed, she tossed a log on the coals. The furnace kept the place habitable, but the fire was necessary to keep it warm. Damn. She hadn't told him how to bank the fire for the night. She'd have to go in and lay a new one for him. Although, he might have been tending it most of the night. Every time she'd gotten up last night, shadows had been moving across his front window that couldn't be attributed to the flames. Could he have been thinking about her?

No. She wasn't that special. Popping a slice of bread in the toaster, she made herself a cup of tea. It was already nearly eleven. If she intended to go down the mountain around lunchtime, that would be now. Instead she ate before dressing in jeans, a sweatshirt and a parka, resisting the impulse to dress up for him, and went outside to look at one of the trees in the circle.

The tall, thin oak down near Cabin One wanted to fall over. How she knew this she couldn't explain, just accepted that she did. The first winter up here, she'd thought a tree was about to fall and ignored the intuition, only to have it crash through the roof of one of the worse-off cabins. The cabin had been a complete tear down. She'd never ignored that particular hunch again.

The oak was small enough, she could cut it down herself. However, they'd get back too late today. It would have to wait until tomorrow.

"Hi. Is it time?"

Cass turned around. Jason stood on the porch, dressed in black again, with his arms wrapped around his chest against the cold. Cass forced herself to speak before she forgot how. "Oh, anytime. Do you want a bite before we head down?"

He shook his head, and was shivering hard. "I'm okay. I'll get my coat."

Cass peered up at the tree again. If she didn't cut carefully, it would fall through a roof. She was going to have to put it down in the road and block both of them in until she'd cut it up. The big oak in the center of her circle of cabins was about to lose some branches too. That job would require climbing equipment and a spotter, but could wait.

"What are you looking at?"

Cass jumped. She hadn't noticed Jason stroll up beside her. What she had taken for a black turtleneck from the distance was in fact dark gray. It contrasted with his black wool coat. Her heart throbbed in her throat, nearly cutting off her ability to speak. "This tree. It has to come down or it'll fall down. Will I bother you if I use a chainsaw tomorrow? I need to take it down before I get a heavy snowfall that takes it down for me."

He smiled. "Whatever you want."

Cass shivered, almost certain he wasn't talking about the saw. "We can get going. Just let me get a better coat." He couldn't see her wearing this ratty parka all through lunch. She went into the house through the garage and dug through her closet for her peacoat. At least now she'd look like she'd made a stab at fashion. It felt that way. This coat wasn't nearly heavy enough. The cold fingers of winter would find their way through the fabric the moment she stepped out. Maybe it would help cool her off. She grabbed her purse and the box of envelopes she needed to take to the post office.

Jason waited in the garage next to her beat up pick up. He didn't seem at all fazed by the twelve-year-old vehicle or its mismatched doors.

"I bought it from a friend cheap," she said. "I'm sure you have a much better car."

He shrugged, climbed into the passenger side. "It probably handles the mountain roads better than any of my cars. What's in the box?"

She nestled the box between them on the seat. Having a box wedged against her thigh reassured her more than the thought of nothing at all between them. "Confirmations for summer. Some people like to schedule early." The heater blasted them with cold air and the cab was still cramped and overheated. As Jason reached down and flicked it off with his long fingers, she couldn't take her eyes off his slender fingers on the switch. He had thick calluses right on the tips. What would they be like against her cheek? Her throat...her breasts?

When she managed to look away it felt like she'd stared for a long time, but Jason didn't seem to notice. Not that he was a great judge. He spent most of his waking hours being stared at.

He seemed quiet on the drive down the mountain. Maybe he was lost in thought. Could be, too, he worried about them making it down the mountain's steep, winding rutted road. She didn't need to concentrate on the road as much as she needed to not obsess about him. Was he tired this morning? Maybe she hadn't been dreaming when she thought she'd seen him in the window. No. Even if he had been standing in the window mooning, it didn't have to be about her. There were plenty of women he could have been thinking about last night. Models and actresses and heiresses. He didn't even have to be thinking about a woman. Anything could have kept him awake.

She pulled into the grocery store's parking lot and stopped, the nose of her truck nudging the wall of the diner. He could have been up all night pondering the state of the environment and climate change, for all she knew. She should have been lying awake worrying about how he would perceive the wacky charms of Potterville, West Virginia. The grocery store, for instance.

When she was growing up, that Potterville didn't even rate a decent chain grocery store had bothered her. Henderson's had cracked floor tiles, sagging, water stained ceiling panels and never had anything exotic like she'd read about in magazines. After her return from New York, she'd decided she liked Henderson's better. They didn't lack, they just didn't have a bunch of stuff she never used. If she decided she needed chipotle peppers or basmati rice, she could drive to Gaitherberg and buy them at the chain store or order them over the Internet. Henderson's had added wine recently, too. She might be the only one who bought it though, because it had all aged since the display went up, but it was for sale.

She looked back toward Jason. He was pondering the cement blocks on the wall in front of him as if they were terribly important. "Jason?" she whispered.

Jason didn't move.

"We're here," she said louder.

He started and turned to her. "Sorry. I was thinking."

"I thought we should have lunch first. Then you can get your groceries and I can run my errands." She put her hand on the door handle. Was she out of her mind letting Jason loose in this town? Or was letting the town loose on Jason maybe the worse crime?

"You're not coming to the store with me?"

"I have to stop in at the post office and see somebody at the travel agency."

"What should I get?"

Cass raised an eyebrow. He'd been twenty when Touchstone released its first record. Was it possible he'd never grocery shopped? "You don't have a crumb in the cabin. You need enough food to last you two weeks."

He frowned. "I don't even know where to start."

"Three meals a day times fourteen days. If I were you, I'd start in the canned soup aisle. And remember, you do have a small microwave." She climbed out. "We'll discuss it over lunch." She headed for Ida's. The cold wind cut through her coat. Her parka had been so warm. The snow under her feet crunched like Styrofoam. She rushed through the door with Jason on her heels. Only because it was cold and his coat wasn't built for this weather either. Couldn't be because he wanted to be closer to her.

"Cassie, don't you look pretty today," Ida said, grinning, as the door banged closed behind them. "What are you doing down the holler already and who is your scrumptious friend?" She tapped her long hot pink fingernails on the cash register. "Hey, Paul, come on out and get a load of Cassie's new friend."

Cass froze. Paul.

Chapter 4

The cook at Ida's Diner was her staunchest defender. Her greatest protector. The best friend a girl could have. Cass wanted to fall through the floor. Maybe there was still time to shove Jason back to the truck and hot rod right back up the mountain. Paul was a trial by fire.

Spatula in hand, he stepped out of the kitchen and took a long, simmering look at Jason. "Ida, I believe we are in the presence of greatness," he announced. "Do you know who this is?"

Ida shook her head and none of her Day Glo orange dyed hair moved.

"This is Mr. Jason Callisto, lead guitar player in the band Touchstone, which I believe is up for a Grammy for Best Album this very minute." Paul drew a deep breath. "Well, I'll just have to make something special." He disappeared into the kitchen. Then he poked his head out the kitchen door and narrowed his gaze on Cass. "You're wearing your peacoat."

"Yes." She shouldn't have worn the coat. Everybody else in town might think she'd dressed nice today, but Paul knew what the coat meant and why she hadn't worn it since she'd gotten back to Potterville. "What about it?"

"It just looks nice," he said. Then he grinned. "I know exactly what to make for this kind of special occasion."

Ida looked Jason over again. "Well, you'll have to have a good seat then. Sit here out of the draft." She gestured them to a booth toward the back. "Would you like a cup of coffee? I'm sorry, I don't have none of that cap-pu-ccino."

"Coffee will be great." Jason smiled. As soon as Ida had walked away, he leaned across the table and whispered, "She's playing up the down home thing, isn't she?"

A note of panic had come through in his voice. The town could be like *Deliverance* in the wrong frame of mind. She nodded and tried to look comforting. "The tourists eat it up. She has a cappuccino machine at home and she can certainly pronounce it."

"Local color?"

"Comes free with the food."

"So what can we expect from lunch?"

"If at any time you've stated a favorite food in a magazine and Paul has the supplies, he'll make the best you've ever had. He's really too good to be here."

"Why is he?"

"He was my neighbor in New York and when I came back home, he followed. He can make an old pair of leather tennis shoes taste like filet mignon." Cass glanced at the kitchen door. Paul's cooking had saved her on many dreary days. "He hides a world class chef under that short-order cook's apron. You see the old gas station next door?" Jason followed her pointing finger and nodded. "It's used for outdoor seating in the summer. They put the doors up and set tables on the lot and in the mechanics' bays. People even come in from other towns to eat here because of Paul. They have to hire waiters and bussers during the season."

"Thinkin' about hiring a girl to seat people, too," Ida added, pouring coffee into their mugs. Cassie's had her name on it. Jason's had a black bear. He examined it. "Like it?" Ida said. "I've got one for everybody in town. See?" She gestured to a cabinet next to the register. It was full, floor to ceiling.

"More local color?"

"We like our local color and we wouldn't have it at all if it weren't for Cassie."

"Oh, Ida, I didn't—"

"Sure you did." Ida hushed her with one hand while focusing on Jason. "She's a real find, our Cassie is. So talented, and yet here she is, saving our little town from extinction."

"I didn't—"

"If she hadn't come home and brought us Paul, why, I think it'd be me and old Ben at the post office and a couple of others left. She came back home, bought that abandoned campground and started having ideas people travel thousands of miles for." Ida leaned toward Jason. "We had a couple here last summer all the way from Germany. Why, they could have gone to Disney World and they didn't. And she's so pretty, too. Cassie, I haven't seen you in that coat before. Is it new?"

"No," she muttered. An amused smile played around Jason's lush mouth, but she felt as though she were on an auction block. "Are you getting any business from the ski resort?" she asked to distract Ida.

"Precious little. Those people don't mix with us. Least it brought a couple of jobs. Which wouldn't be here at all if it weren't for you. They could have opened up in any of these valleys around here, but since we have you here we have the infrastructure to support that kind of tourism." Ida slid into the booth beside her. "Did you hear Maddy and Spencer Wegman are thinking about opening a bed and breakfast in the old funeral home?"

Jason flinched. Cass had heard the rumor, but hadn't reflected on how strange a B&B in a former funeral home sounded. However, as long as Ida wasn't trying to sell her, Cassie wanted to keep the conversation headed that way. "What have you heard?"

"They're serious enough to talk to Paul about breakfasts."

"To do what? He doesn't have time to cook breakfast for them."

"They want him to teach Maddy how to cook like he does."

Cass put her hand over her mouth. The whole town was getting delusions of grandeur. "But Maddy can't boil water in a microwave." She turned to Jason. "We all joke about the Wegman Diet. If Maddy does the cooking, their guests will have to survive on toast and cold cereal."

Ida snorted. "Toast? You want Maddy burning the town down, trying to operate a toaster?"

"What did Paul tell them?"

"I told them to hire someone," Paul said, grinning, as he appeared at their table. "Junie Keyes is a very good short order cook and her mother is the best baker in town. That kind of talent doesn't skip a generation. Tapas." He set the loaded plate in the center of the table, turned on one heel and strode back into the kitchen.

Tiny triangles of Melba toast bearing combinations of cheese, olives and sardines were arranged across it. Hopefully they didn't spell anything from the other side of the table. "I think it's going to be Spanish."

Jason picked up one of the tapas and popped it in his mouth. "Great. I like Spanish."

Ida labored to her feet. "I should get to my other customers. People talk if I start favoring one over another, even if he is a cute young stud." She pinched Jason's cheek before strolling away from the table.

The floor really could open up anytime. Cass put her hand over her face. "I'm sorry. She's just like that."

Jason shrugged. "It's okay. I don't mind. She slips out of character occasionally though."

"No, it's all the same character. Ida has owned this diner for thirty years and before that waited tables for the last owner. He died the year after I was born. They say she could have gone to college with a full ride scholarship, but she wanted to stay here. When the mines petered out and the logging went west this place started to die, but Ida refused to let go."

"But you came along and saved it."

"I didn't save it." How could he think this was anything but corny? But he didn't sound like he was being sarcastic. "I was in the right place at the right time. I just used what was here."

Under the table, Jason slid his foot across hers and hooked it around her ankle. "You were the one to do it."

His touch and the admiration in his tone made her tense. "I'm trying to disprove what they say about New York." Could he hear that she was nearly breathless because of the way he made her feel?

"Which is?" He traveled up the back of her calf with his foot, creating ripples of pleasure.

"If you can't make it there, you can't make it anywhere." That wasn't it. Dammit, she couldn't even summon up a tired cliche. Her distracted, sluggish brain kept telling her *yeah, yeah, but Jason's touching us*. "Or is it the other way around?"

"You couldn't make it in New York?" His voice had dropped into a husky tone.

"I'm here, aren't I?" Where had all the air gone? There used to be air here. She licked her lips. Jason's eyes followed the motion, which only increased her distraction. Every resolve she'd decided on last night melted under his steady assault. About now, she'd do anything he wanted. Including hang out all her dirty laundry for his inspection because he'd kept his wits enough to ask questions.

"What were you trying to do in New York?"

"Cassie, honey. What are you doing here?" her mother said, standing beside their table.

Jason's foot vanished.

Cass glared at her mother with a look that said *you know exactly what I'm doing here*. She smiled. "Having lunch. And here you are, saving us a trip."

"A trip?" Mom asked.

"A trip?" Jason echoed.

"We were going to stop at the house before we went back up the mountain. How did you know we were here?"

Paul walked out of the kitchen with two bowls. "White chili. The beans are canned unfortunately," he informed them. "If you had called me ahead of time, missy, I could have done it right. I'll get two more bowls for Shirl and Andy."

"Oh, we didn't mean to interrupt," her mom, Shirl, said, sitting next to Cass. "We just decided to come out for lunch." Mom patted her leg and started her interrogation. "So, Mr. Callisto, how are you enjoying your stay?"

Dad sat next to Jason and grimaced at Cass. *Hi, swee'pea*, he mouthed. The idea to ambush them here had been Mom's. Her father was usually an unwilling participant.

Paul reappeared with two more bowls and set them in front of her parents before vanishing again.

"Very well so far. Once I found the place." Jason smiled at Mom and frowned at Cass almost at the same time.

"It is a bit hidden up there," her mother replied. "There's a sign at the foot of the mountain, but it blew over in the storm we had over Thanksgiving and there's no point in putting it back up until spring. Did you enjoy your supper?"

"Yes, I did. Your daughter is an excellent cook. She must have learned from you."

Jason's foot brushed against hers again. Apparently being interrogated by her mother didn't bother him much.

"Oh, you," Mom said, blushing. "Maybe you can come around sometime while you're here and find out."

"I'll be sure to fit that in." Jason gave her mom a jokey faux come-hither look

Cass searched for the sarcasm in his comment, but found none. He shifted her foot so it sat on top of his. Then he leaned forward. His fingertips brushed her knees.

"Oh, you kidder." Cass's mom blushed deeper.

Jason slid his fingers around her knees and hooked behind them. Cass jumped at the shock of him touching such a sensitive place. Her mother looked at her.

Cass smiled, trying to process the electric touch of Jason's fingers with the familiar diner and her mother sitting next to her, somehow unaware despite her extrasensory perception. This went a little beyond Jason maybe but maybe not flirting with her and straight into liking pina coladas and making love at midnight. Ida really needed to check her furnace. It was getting mighty hot in here and nobody else seemed to notice. Cass shrugged off her coat, shifting at the same time, but not dislodging Jason's fingers. She didn't want to lose them, but him touching her right in front of her parents felt a little too naughty.

"My little girl does run a nice place up there, doesn't she?" Shirl leaned across the table toward Jason, still seeming unaware anything was amiss. Her ESP must be broken. "Do you know, when Cassie first came home and bought that place she organized the whole town to help her?"

"Mom."

Jason sat back, pulling his fingers away from her knees. "Really? She's quite an entrepreneur."

Cass shifted again, sorry he'd moved his fingers. She put a hand to her cheek to see if she was blushing, but couldn't tell. Hopefully if she was, her parents would attribute it to what they were doing and not guess that Jason had done something. Then he twisted his foot around her ankle again.

"She did," Mom said. "Why, she took all of that creative energy of hers and came up with all sorts of things. That old campground used to bring in a few dozen families over the summers but it closed up years ago. Cassie wanted to have a full-service campground and make sure her campers had something to do when they weren't lookin' at the trees. She talked to the church about holding programs in their hall and then to Sue down at the travel agency about putting together a newsletter for the events, so people would know. A couple of the other businesses in town joined in, offering special things for tourists."

"Like box lunches on the hikes," Ida added from the counter, the incorrigible eavesdropper.

"Just like that. Even the school is participating now," Mom continued.

"The school is participating?" Cass asked. This should alarm her but she didn't know how to carry on any coherent conversation with Jason playing footsie with her under the table. He gave her a sly little smile.

"I nudged them a little," Mom said.

"You nudged them how much?" Jason's other foot joined the dance, cradling her left foot between both of his. He seemed so good at this. A chill she couldn't attribute to the cold passed through her. He'd practiced this. He was famous and he'd seduced far more experienced women than her.

"Just a little." Her mother preened. "I know how you want to build that new building next summer so you'll need to be booked solid all summer, and if you have lots of events going on, you'll be booked."

"Lots of events?" Between trying not to think about what Jason was doing and how he'd gotten so good at it, she needed to cling to the subject at hand with both clenched fists.

"Well, some." Her mom bit her lip and looked at the table. "You haven't been to Sue's yet?"

"No. Am I going to be surprised?"

Mom gave her a smile, eyes sparkling. "Well, you might."

"Is it going to be a good surprise or a bad surprise?" Cass asked.

Shirl stared into her bowl. "I didn't know you could make chili without tomatoes. I wonder if Paul will give me the recipe."

Her dad snorted then gave Cass an apologetic look. Well, there was the answer. When she'd been growing up he'd often said, "Nothing stops your mother when she gets a-going. Best just to get out of the way." Jason seemed to share her mother's determination, judging by the expertise with which he manipulated her foot under the table. She was the goal, and whether she wanted it or not, his determination raised her body temperature.

Cass looked at the table. She had never even managed a nightmare this bad. Exactly how much worse could this get?

"Hello, Cassie," Melinda said. Crap.

She met Jason's eyes. He was watching her. She dragged her gaze away and ended up looking at her mother, who also observed her, but for a different reason. Her ESP must have kicked in. Her father consumed his chili like Paul might take it away before he finished. By the time Cass got to the end of the table, Melinda was shuffling from foot to foot, wringing her hands.

Cass thought her head might explode. "Hi."

"Everything okay?" Melinda bit her lip.

Okay? Unlikely. She couldn't imagine what she looked like, but her mother shifted like a toddler with a hand still in the cookie jar and her father wouldn't take his eyes off the chili bowl. Ida had a world-winning smirk on her face, while Jason grinned like the cat who'd found the cream. "Sure. Great."

"Oh." The well-worn crease in Melinda's forehead deepened as she continued. "Dan will be happy to hear that. He said he didn't see you over Christmas. He thought you were mad at him."

Christa Maurice

Cass looked across the table for some confirmation of the insanity of her situation and found Jason, part of the insanity, still watching her. He moved his feet, reminding her that he still had her foot. She turned back to Melinda before her head did explode. "I'm sorry. I did miss him over his break. I had to get back up the mountain early because I had a winter guest coming. Melinda, this is my guest. Jason, this is Melinda Pierce. Her son Dan works for me in the summer."

"A pleasure." Melinda nodded and turned back to Cass. She had bigger fish to fry than meeting the visiting rock star. "So you're not mad at him?"

"Why would I be mad at him?" At the moment, she couldn't even remember what Dan looked like, let alone what he might have done to make her angry.

"He just really likes that job and wants to come back next summer."

"Isn't Dan graduating this spring?" Ida asked.

"He is, but he does want to have one more summer at the campground before he gets a real job." Melinda looked like she might start pleading if Cass didn't say something quick.

Paul came out of the kitchen bearing a tray of dishes. "Hello, Melinda. Are you joining the party?" He set the tray on a neighboring table.

"No, I—"

"She wants to know if Dan still has a job at the campground this summer," Ida explained.

"Of course he does, if that's what he wants. Isn't that right, Cassie?" Paul put a plate in front of her. Tamales, beans, salsa and ramekins of corn pudding.

"Of course." When had she lost control of her business? Her mother ran it, Paul ran it, and now the local school system, with her mother's encouragement, seemed poised to take a cut of the operations. She just showed up May first and smiled for six months. This must be how it felt to live in a soap opera. Someone handed out script pages and the actors did their thing.

"Besides, Melinda, if she's a good girl, she might need somebody to run the place full time," Paul said, serving plates to Jason then Cass's parents.

"What?" she nearly squeaked. Did they think she was going to run away with Jason? That idea appealed, even if it was complete fantasy.

Jason was watching her with a less devilish expression than a moment ago. And, he'd stopped dandling her foot. He still had more control over it than she did, but wasn't wielding that power now.

He smiled at her and gestured with his fork. "It's good," he murmured.

It felt like he'd whispered in her ear. Heat crawled up her cheeks to her hairline.

His smile turned dark and he winked at her.

The bell over the door rang, and as the crowd turned to see who'd walked in, she caught a glimpse of Finn arriving. Now the madness was complete.

"Bill Wernick is talking about selling that property that adjoins yours," Paul continued, seeming oblivious to what took place inside their booth. "It would almost double your grounds. You'd need somebody up there full time to help you then. You really need to call me, little girl."

"Bill wants to sell his high pasture?" her father asked, setting down his spoon. His eyes glazed with longing. "It's a beautiful piece of land, Cassie. There's that high valley up there with the pond and the waterfall."

"I'll talk to Bill about it," she said before her father could start waxing poetic about the land. He knew the mountain like no one else, and had taken her all over it when she was a child. High up and commanding a view of the valley, that land would be a great place for more cabins and tents below, but she'd have to look at her insurance and find out what his price was. Her rec hall would have to wait another year at least.

"So you think you might be able to hire Dan full time?" Melinda asked.

"Let's not get our hopes up yet."

"About what?" Finn asked, stopping at the edge of the table. He glowered at Jason in what amounted to a challenge, but Jason was too busy scraping the last of the corn pudding out of its ramekin to notice there'd been one issued.

Then Jason twitched one foot and looked at her through his eyelashes. The motion so startled Cass, her finger slipped off her fork and plunged into her refried beans. He'd noticed the challenge and blew it off. Someone must have given him the script pages with the background story, and he knew he had nothing to worry about from Finn's direction.

"Cass might buy Bill Wernick's high pasture," Paul told him.

"You should talk to me about these things before you make a decision, Cass. I am your accountant," Finn whined. He must have noticed his challenge had been dismissed, too.

Cass tried not to flinch at the possessive way Finn spoke to her and opened her mouth to snap that she'd just heard about it.

"Paul, this is excellent," Jason cut her off, announcing over everyone else. "I haven't eaten this well since the last time I was in Europe. Thank you."

"Oh, well, it was nothing." Paul turned a shade of red that competed with Ida's hair for wattage.

Cass stuck her thumb in her mouth to clean it off, hoping no one would expect her to speak. However, if she needed to intervene she would have food in her mouth and wouldn't be able to. Decisions, decisions. Jason watched her draw her thumb out of her mouth the way he might watch the first day of creation. His hand tightened around his fork, and he licked his lips. Oh dear.

"What's the matter, swee'pea?" Dad asked.

"Nothing," she said. "My thumb slipped."

"Are you going to buy this land, Cass?" Finn demanded.

"Paul," her mom asked, "could you find it in your heart to give me the recipe for that chili?"

"Well, if he gives all his recipes away, why would anyone bother to eat here?" Ida retorted.

Cass resorted to wiping the rest of the refried beans off her thumb with her paper napkin so she could observe the rest of the table for signs they had picked up on the interchange between her and Jason a second ago. Paul's gaze turned from her to Jason, innocently devouring his lunch. Two and two were rapidly becoming five, possibly six. Paul was a great cook and an excellent mathematician when it came to human algebra.

"Cass?" Finn demanded again.

"Oh, Finn, leave it alone." Paul elbowed him. "You know, Shirl, it isn't that hard if you have the right cilantro."

Paul started talking about the food. He must have picked up on her discomfort. Maybe she could speak with him about Jason flirting with her. Ugh, bad. Paul made an excellent information hub but a lousy confidante. Her father and Finn debated her ability to buy and improve the pasture with her current income stream. Finn was against it, felt she couldn't take the financial risk. Her father, in a typical knee-jerk reaction, thought she could if they were careful. He'd never been very fond of Finn. Maybe that had something to do with her lack of interest. Melinda asked polite and pointed questions, trying to ascertain the added workload the extra land would entail. She would be for anything that might keep her son in town.

"Well, the other customers are getting jealous," Ida said eventually, and wandered off. Melinda left behind her, seeming confident about Dan having a summer job and potentially a permanent one right here in town. Paul had meals to cook. Beneath the pressure of her father's barrage, Finn took his Wednesday turkey and Swiss on rye back to his office to eat.

There. Now she could breathe normally. She returned to the conversation. Her parents were talking to Jason. Actually, her father and Jason were discussing cars. Safe enough, so she let it go.

Cass finished her meal. Jason had not recommenced playing footsie since she'd stuck her thumb in the beans, but neither had he relinquished his hold. Paul delivered the recipe to her mother, gave Cass one long significant look and vanished into the kitchen. Based on the way Mom had focused on the recipe, she apparently thought she would have to memorize it and eat the card before she left the building. Hah! Everyone else might believe her mother was studying the recipe. She was really studying Jason.

"So is everyone full?" Ida asked, coffeepot in hand.

"Yes, it was excellent," Jason said. "My compliments to the chef."

"Oh, don't you dare. His head's already big enough." Ida cackled.

"I'll take the bill," he told her.

Mom and Dad objected, and Ida over rode them. "There's no bill."

"Really?" Cass asked.

"Are you kiddin'? This was an excellent opportunity to suss out what else that boy can make." Ida grinned. "We might be having us a Spanish special one of these nights. The tourists'll love it."

Dad stood and grabbed her mom's hand. "Well, I'm not looking a gift horse in the mouth. Nice meeting you, Jason." He pulled Cass into a bear hug and used the opportunity to whisper into her ear, "Nice boy."

Mom held out her hand to shake Jason's and when he kissed it instead, giggled like a girl. Still giggling, she hugged Cass. As Mom stepped back, a blush brightened her cheeks. Dad helped Mom into her coat. Cass turned back to pick up hers and found Jason already holding it open for her. Over the collar and past Jason's arm, she saw Paul simpering from the kitchen door before she turned to step into it. As she adjusted it around her shoulders, Jason scooped her hair out of the collar. The backs of his fingers brushed her neck. She had to bite back a moan of pleasure. The outward ripples of delight threatened to roll her eyes back in her head an instant before they nearly unhinged her knees. She kept her expression neutral through force of will, but her mother's gaze sharpened on her face anyway. It was hopeless.

Chapter 5

"When I'm done, I'll come help you." The cold wind sliced through her. She hugged herself, trying to get a little more coverage out of the inadequate coat. The cold at least encouraged her parents to hurry home.

"I still don't know what to buy," Jason protested. "Why don't I go with you, and when you're done, we can do my shopping together?"

Stars and birds should be circling her head from the cartoon anvil that just fell on it, but she refrained from looking. She needed a few minutes away from the too tempting Mr. Callisto to get her head back on straight.

But her father approved of him. Dad, who disapproved of the accountant, thought the rock star was dandy.

Her father must be getting senile.

"No, I just have a couple of quick stops anyway." She unlocked her truck and grabbed the box of mail on the seat. "Look for stuff you can eat without cooking, or heat and eat. I'll come find you as soon as I'm done."

"I'll be waiting." Jason shifted from foot to foot beside the truck like he was being abandoned.

Cass shut her door and set off for the post office with her box, not looking back to check if he was watching her.

The town commercial district consisted of two blocks along the imaginatively named Main Street, with lesser businesses off Maple, Pine and Willow avenues. Apart from the cars parked on the street, it looked like a movie set for the Depression. The town hall sat at the center of town with a statue of a Civil War hero on his horse in front of it. Every year the high school graduating class pulled a prank involving the statue. Last year they'd dressed the poor man in a flowered dress and straw hat. Cass's class had mummified him and his horse in torn sheets.

Beside the town hall was the post office. Cass pushed through the door and breathed deeply. The post office always smelled of wood, paper and coffee. Sanity itself, something in short supply after that lunch.

"Well, hello, Cassandra," Ben, the postmaster greeted her. "I didn't expect to see you in town already. And dressed up so pretty today. I heard you got yourself a winter guest."

"Hi, Ben." Cass set her box on the counter. She should have known the whole town would know about Jason even if they didn't know who he was. How had she not considered that when she'd offered to drive him down for groceries and lunch? "I do have a guest, but he didn't pack any food so I volunteered to bring him in to the grocery store."

"Good girl," Ben told her, his white walrus mustache quivering. "Got some things to go, do you?"

"Yeah." She took the letter she'd written to Gretta off the top of the box. "I need this one to go overnight."

Ben raised an eyebrow. "Truck's already been."

"I just want it to go out as soon as possible."

"I think that's doable. I'll take this and get you your mail."

Ben shuffled into the back room. He'd been the postmaster here all her life. The post office was only open a few hours a day and those were apt to change if he wasn't feeling well. Years ago, everyone in town started picking up their mail because they worried about Ben trying to deliver it. He didn't even try any more. The only way anyone got their mail was to pick it up themselves. Another thing she'd hated about Potterville before she'd left that hadn't seemed so bad when she returned. So the mail didn't show up at her door on a daily basis. Nothing coming that way needed to be dealt with all that fast anyhow.

"Here you are, my girl. You should be needing stamps next time, too, if I count these right." He winked. "You should dress up more often, Cassie. You look very pretty today."

She forced a smile. She'd worn a nice coat, and he'd be on the phone the moment she pushed out the door. Within half an hour everyone in town would know she'd come down to town all gussied up with her guest and had a special lunch at Ida's with the guest and her parents. They wouldn't go so far as to dress her in a ball gown, but the off-the-rack peacoat would have morphed into a designer coat she must have bought in New York City. By the time this seven-day wonder had petered out, she'd be wearing a Chanel coat and carrying a Coach bag.

And her father approved of the rock star over the accountant.

She hefted the refilled box from the counter and hurried out the door. The sooner she finished her errands, the better.

"Hey! Hey, Cassie! What's your rush?"

Christa Maurice

She stopped. How had she managed to forget she'd have to pass Finn's office to get to Sue's? She didn't want to deal with Finn right now, or ever really. Not that she didn't like him, she just didn't like him as much as he did her, and it never failed to make her guilty. As she turned to deal with this albatross, she tried to compose herself. "Hi, Finn."

"So that was your famous guest," he stated, wrapping his long arms around his chubby body. He must have been in such a hurry to hunt her down, he'd forgotten his coat. A blob of mayonnaise also clung to the corner of his mouth. If she had any romantic leanings for him, that sight would have been adorable. As it was, she only wanted him to go finish his lunch.

"It is."

"Are you sure it's safe to be up there on the mountain with him?" Finn asked. "I mean, I saw how he was looking at you and it didn't look like… look like he had good…intentions."

He wasn't worried about her safety as much as her virtue, what remained of it. She couldn't resist pushing him, and widened her eyes. "What intentions would he have?"

"You're all alone up there with no one to protect you. News said a storm's coming. What if you get trapped? What if he becomes a sex-crazed maniac and attacks you?" Finn blushed. Then his teeth started to chatter.

"It's pretty unlikely. Word would get out. There might be a trial or something. Go on back to your office before you freeze to death out here." He'd been after her since high school, and she'd never once felt the slightest spark of attraction for him. Repeated explanations of this fact didn't hinder him in the least, though it left her mildly annoyed. If she could settle for Finn, her life would be so much easier.

"I'm just trying to help." Now he verged on whining.

"I can take care of myself. Remember two years ago, when that bear decided to hang out around my house? I survived just fine. And those five years I lived in New York? Still alive. It's amazing really." She folded her arms. He started shivering and didn't seem inclined to go where it was warm, like Angela Costi's arms. "Finn, go back to your office. I'll bring my taxes by next time I come down the mountain and we can talk about them over lunch, okay?"

He smiled through his chattering teeth. "That would be great. We can talk about your property. I can help you, Cass."

"I know." Finn could always help her. He set up her computer, did her taxes and her financial planning, worked out legal and fiscal details she hadn't even considered, and occasionally appeared to help her clean up her camp sites after the winter. He wasn't so bad looking, even if the desk job and winter had him a little chubbier than ideal. Any woman in her right mind would leap at the chance.

But her father disapproved of the accountant and approved of the rock star, so madness might run in the family.

"You look nice today, anyway," Finn said, breaking into her thoughts.

"Thanks, now get inside before you freeze to death." She turned and walked away from him. He wasn't stupid, just obtuse. She'd lain awake nights wondering if she should be mean to him so he'd get over it. The small amount of friendliness she gave only served to encourage him. She did like him as a friend, and he was an excellent accountant, but maybe in order to help him, she had to hurt him. She just couldn't bring herself to do it.

She pushed through the door of the travel agency and Sue looked up with the wild look of a woman with too much coffee and too little company.

"Cassie! Did you hear?"

At that volume, Cassie could have heard her from across the street. "That the school is planning on doing some events this summer?"

"Small potatoes. Small, small potatoes." Sue waved her hands in the air over her desk. "You will never guess who I got a call from. Trish, the marketing director from the ski lodge. They want to distribute our schedule, and gave me their events and activities list to add to ours. They want to join in. This is big. This is huge!" She flailed her arms, knocking over her oversized coffee cup. Coffee splashed up the wall behind her. "Even better. Well, you heard about the school."

"I did." Cassie bent forward to watch coffee continue to dribble down the wall. "Don't you need to clean that up?"

"It's fine. I was going to call you. I figured out how to put the schedule online. We can advertise to a whole new segment. This is really getting big." Sue leaned over the counter conspiratorially. "Have you heard about the Donaldson Funeral Home? Wegman's are going to buy it and make it into a B&B."

"I heard."

"I hope Maddy doesn't poison anyone. But you came in to get the stuff to do the schedule, right?" Sue started shuffling through the piles of papers on her desk. She snatched up a red file folder, rifled through it, picked up a couple of papers off her desk, jammed them in and held it out. "This is everything. Absolutely everything."

And it would be. Under that chaotic and hyper exterior hid an organizational genius.

"Thanks, Sue. I'll send you the schedule as soon as I get it worked out." Cassie backed through the door, slightly exhausted by the encounter.

Outside, she paused to investigate what her mother had started.

The music teacher at the high school had a full schedule of evening concerts in the pavilion on the town hall green. Nothing could be more divine than listening to an out of tune, out of sync high school jazz band playing under the stars while being attacked by mosquitoes the size of helicopters.

Not to be out done, the drama-slash-English teacher offered plays, different ones every month for the whole season, Friday and Saturday nights. Their own little taste of Broadway in the high school gym yet, where the scent of floor wax, sweaty sneakers and chalk dust could complete the experience.

The middle school gym would be used for nightly dances, and Irma and Bob Tompkins were giving dance lessons in the afternoons. Irma and Bob were lovely people, but they could hardly walk anymore, let alone dance. Their daughter, the middle school principal, was probably behind that.

The shop teachers were organizing their own robot wars for Sunday afternoons on the football field, which made her wonder how the football coach felt about having his field torn up, or if perhaps they had misrepresented what robot wars involved. Of course, the football boosters were selling refreshments so maybe he knew.

And the PTA planned a rubber duck race for Labor Day Weekend. She really should start going to the school board meetings. Something was going on with those people.

She leafed through the rest of the papers. The usual suspects: nature walks, Civil War site tours, star gazing, church dances, a quilt show, etc.

The guests would love the out-and-out Mayberry-ness of it. Then they would go home and tell all their friends about this little gem of a town. She'd be booked solid by March, and the Wegmans, too. And the townspeople would have a blast.

Crap. Today was Wednesday and she'd sent Jason to the grocery store unescorted.

She jammed the folder in her box with the mail and sprinted down the sidewalk. She tossed her box in the back of the truck before running inside.

Jason was under siege in the canned vegetable and soup aisle in front of the cream soups. Nobody at the register, in the office or in the deli. All three employees surrounded him. Mr. Henderson hadn't noticed yet, but he might be sleeping in the warehouse. There was no telling how long Jason had been stuck like this.

His eyes lit up when she rounded the chip display. "Cassandra, *bella*," he called.

She almost stopped and looked behind her. He couldn't be talking to her. Beautiful Cassandra? "How's it going?" she asked, hoping to pass off the heat on her cheeks as windburn.

"Well—"

"Mr. Callisto said you made him dinner last night, but you're leaving him on his own for the rest of his stay." Cori Gwynn pouted her too-pink-to-be-natural lips. She'd been Homecoming Queen last year and now rang register. A pretty far drop. "I said I'd come cook for him." Her voice had dropped to a sultry tone that left nothing to the imagination. The clingy fuchsia sweater she wore didn't either.

"And I told her she'd have him poisoned before the weekend." Kady Stern smirked. The Prom Queen. Both of them seemed to think it still mattered. Kady worked in the office by virtue of a letter grade difference in high school business math. She held that over Cori, too. Her sweater wasn't skin tight, but her skirt was about an inch from obscene. And they hadn't even known Jason would be coming.

"Oh, Mr. Callisto, you don't want that kind." Sweet round face clouding with worry, Angela Costi picked up one of the cans in Jason's basket and put it back on the shelf. "It takes milk. You want this kind. This you just put in the pan and heat up. You do have a pan, don't you?" Angela had the imagination of a block of wood, but she was passionately in love with Finn Runningwater, who didn't seem to notice she was alive, and the only one concerned about what Jason would eat for the next two weeks.

Jason looked at Cass. He seemed terrified by the attention. She couldn't imagine why. Most of his life looked like this. "Do I have a pan?" he asked.

Cass sighed. She should have known better than to let any eligible man walk into Henderson's Grocery unescorted on a Wednesday, let alone one as wildly eligible as Jason. "I can loan you one. Listen, Kady, Cori, if Duke catches you out here there's going to be trouble." Using Mr. Henderson's first name felt awkward, but did the trick. They both paled. "Angela, why don't you go back to the deli and slice up a pound of ham, a pound of turkey and a loaf of Italian bread for Mr. Callisto?"

"Oh, that's a good idea, Cass," Angela said. "I'll get some potato salad and broccoli salad, too. Would you like that, Mr. Callisto? It'll keep to the end of the week at least."

"Great." Jason managed a smile. He hadn't moved from his defensive position against the cream soups.

"Oh, and some cheese. We have some really nice cheese." Angela hurried away, signaling the other girls to leave, too. Under the guise of discussing Jason's grocery basket, they sniped at each other as they disappeared around the Grandma Shears chips.

"It was like a scene from *The Birds*. All the sudden they were everywhere," he whispered. He moved out to the middle of the aisle and peered around the corner.

"Sorry, I forgot about them. Do you really plan to eat canned soup for two weeks?" In his basket were twelve cans. She couldn't possibly let him sit alone and eat canned soup for two weeks.

Her carefully-cultivated distance was shrinking. She'd thought running down the street to get her mail and the events from Sue would have been enough time out of Jason's gravity that she wouldn't have gotten sucked back in so fast. Her heart rate said different.

He shrugged. "I haven't gotten to the frozen food aisle yet. I'm really not very good at this. I eat out a lot."

She met his eyes. Familiar heat spread through her. His face softened. He shifted his grip on the basket so it hung at his side. The view changed, and she couldn't understand why until she realized she was leaning forward. The pulse in his throat throbbed inches from her face. Her body matched his beat. His dark eyes seemed darker, inviting. He licked his lips. Her stomach tightened in anticipation.

"Cass," someone said.

Jason and Cass leaped apart. His basket banged against the canned vegetables shelf behind him, knocking a can of peas on the floor. She reached back to steady herself, nearly pulling down half the Campbell's soup display. When she'd gotten her feet under her, she turned to meet the voice's owner and tried not to look like she'd been caught stealing something. Duke Henderson didn't seem to realize he'd interrupted.

"What are you doing down the mountain already? Didn't we stock you up well enough?" he bellowed from the far end of the aisle.

"Oh, I'm fine, but my guest needed some supplies so I brought him in."

"Ah." Duke stopped in front of them and looked Jason over. "Well, welcome to town, son. Hope you enjoy your stay. Next time, you give us a call in advance and we can send a delivery up to you."

"You can?" Cass blurted out. Duke scowled at her. Her nerves still sparked as if she'd been caught *en flagrante delicto* on the grocery store floor. But she had nothing to hide from Duke Henderson and nothing to prove to him either. She focused on the imprint of corrugated cardboard on his cheek above his whiskers. He had been sleeping in the warehouse. "When did you start that?"

"Oh, about ten minutes ago. I was thinking about your little campground up there and I realized I could get some business by delivering groceries to your campers. Have to hire a boy to do the driving in the summer. A service." He hooked his fingers through his belt loops and rocked back on his heels, quite pleased with himself for this inspiration.

Cass wanted to bury her face in her hands. "Of course, Mr. Henderson. Is it all right if I put that in my confirmation letters?"

"Now, that's a very good idea. Going to get fax soon. You can put that in there, too. I'll get the number to Sue for you."

A fax. Wow. "Wonderful," she whimpered.

Duke looked at the basket in Jason's hands, frowning. "You're going to need a cart, son. Can't get two weeks' worth of food in a basket." Then he turned and walked away, whistling.

"What was that about?" Jason asked.

"I've been trying to get him to deliver since I opened, and he always said it was a pig in a poke. Suddenly it's his brilliant idea. All's well that ends well, I guess." At least, Duke hadn't commented on her coat.

Jason been about to kiss her. He'd licked his lips and leaned toward her. He would have. He'd been through the beauty queen rivalry and met her parents as well as a few select townspeople who seemed intent on selling her to him, and he still wanted to kiss her. Probably wanted more than kisses, but they were in public. Why would it be bad to kiss him again?

Cass rubbed her face. Jason still needed food and the better she stocked him up, the less likely he would need to come back here for more supplies. Or worse, to have them delivered. She could imagine what would happen if Kady and Cori got hold of that order. "Come on. Let's hit the frozen aisle and pick up your deli stuff."

"I liked your parents. They seemed like nice people. I didn't realize you had planned on stopping to visit them," Jason said, following her past the detergent aisle.

"I didn't. I'd hoped to duck them." Cass dodged into paper products. She should have known she'd never get in and out of town without her parents catching her. Even if she did, they would have come up the mountain. She grabbed a package of paper plates and a mixed bag of plastic utensils. When she turned back, he stood behind her, so close she could feel his body heat. She clutched the plates against her chest.

"Why?" he asked.

"Why?" Cass bit her lip. "I didn't think you'd want to meet my parents. It's not like we're dating."

His lips curled into a slow smile. "I see. I suppose you're right."

She thrust the plates and utensils at him. "You'll need these."

"Thanks." He plucked them out of her hands and paused for somewhat shorter than a heartbeat before stepping back and allowing her past him.

As she turned the corner, she glanced down to make sure she hadn't put on high heels at some point. No, still wearing tennis shoes. Maybe the floor had become more uneven with age. Or maybe West Virginia was having its first earthquake since the Cretaceous. At the end of frozen foods, she stopped before she stumbled into a freezer case. "Okay." She tried to cough the squeak out of her voice before trying again. "Okay, here you are. Every frozen food known to Potterville, West Virginia."

Jason peered down the long aisle of lit cases. "Anything you recommend?"

"I don't eat many frozen dinners."

"I guess not. I wouldn't either if I could cook like you."

He was gazing at her again, and Duke Henderson wouldn't be interrupting this time. She should thank Jason for the compliment, but didn't think her mouth would work.

"I was hoping you'd bend your rule about not cooking for the guests at least one more time," he murmured, and reached for her hand. The callused tips of his fingers scraped across her palm.

A sigh built in the back of her throat. Her vision seemed to be filled with Jason. In Henderson's. Henderson's Grocery, where every Pottervillian bought the bulk of their groceries. Where anyone could see her and know, or assume, she'd fallen for her famous winter guest, giving them one more thing to feel sorry for her about. She drew her hand away. "I'll go get your deli order. Tombstone pizzas are supposed to be good."

She turned and walked away. Where had she gotten the willpower to pull back? When it came to a quart of mint chocolate chip ice cream, especially if hot fudge were involved, she never had that much willpower.

Jason was premium mint chocolate chip with homemade hot fudge, whipped cream and a cherry.

Much more than she could handle. She was a generic ice cream girl; premium would be too rich. Jason had been not just around the block, but around the city...the country. Around the world. He knew good from better from best, and if he had some idea about her, then maybe she didn't want to ruin it by letting him know the truth. Plus, it was a small town and word would get around. The way things were around here, the grapevine would buzz anyway and she'd be at a distinct disadvantage to denounce it if it were true. So what, if he made her pulse do a Zydeco beat and her fingers twitch uncontrollably to coil through his hair? If he did have some crazy notion about dropping back to the minor leagues for a little fun with her, well, she didn't have to start thinking she had any chance of moving up to the majors with him.

Of course, other people managed to have flings. She'd had campers who met their lovers for one-week stands and then went their separate ways. During one memorable new age retreat, neighboring cabins had combined into one and the resulting couple had stayed on for an extra week before going back to their regular lives. When Cass had spoken to the woman at the end of the second week as she turned in the keys, she'd discovered they hadn't even bothered to exchange addresses or phone numbers. Up there on the mountain by herself, the town would only have her word as to whether their speculations were true or false.

So involved debating the whys, with and without nots, she nearly went face first into Irma Tompkins's shopping cart in front of the Ragu spaghetti sauce display. Before joining the older woman's collection of flour, sugar, and produce in her basket, she skidded to a stop. "Hello, Mrs. Tompkins."

"Oh, Cassie." The old woman beamed, revealing a whole new set of wrinkles in her wizened face. "How nice to see you. Have you been to see Sue yet? Bob and I are going to give dancing lessons."

She sounded so excited, Cass smiled back. "I heard. That should be fun."

"Oh, we think so. I met Bob at a dance you know. He was going to the war. He wrote often, but right before D-Day his letters stopped and I thought he'd found someone else. Then I found out they weren't delivering the letters so the Germans couldn't find out where the troops were going." Irma looked back at the bottles in her hand. "You know I wish they had just stuck to plain old Ragu Spaghetti Sauce. There are too many choices now."

"I thought you canned your own sauce, Mrs. Tompkins," Cass said.

"I do, but every once in a while I like to walk on the wild side." She grinned again as she set down the two jars in her hands. "Maybe next time. Goodbye, Cassie."

"Goodbye, Mrs. Tompkins." Jarred sauce was a walk on the wild side? Irma had no idea. In the frozen foods aisle, the wild side was probably picking out pizzas at this very moment.

And he wouldn't be going on sale every other month. He was very much a once in a lifetime event.

"Cass?"

She blinked back to the present. Angela stood next to her with a shopping cart. She'd piled Jason's deli order in the child seat. "Yeah?"

"I thought Mr. Callisto might need a cart. Once I got all this stuff together, and I remembered he had all that soup, I thought he might need one. Do you think he does?"

Angela was going to think herself a hole in the floor. "You know I bet he does." One pound of ham, honey cured. One pound turkey, roasted. One pound loaf of Italian bread, sliced thin. Half a pound of cheddar cheese. One quart each of potato salad, macaroni salad and broccoli salad. A small jar of mayonnaise and a small bottle of mustard. Picnic food. If she didn't relent and have him over for dinner he was going to be eating picnic food, soup and frozen pizza his entire stay.

If she did have him over, it would mean spending another evening alone with him just a few feet away from her bed. The Zydeco beat started up again inside her. "He's in frozen foods. Let's go find him."

Jason was perusing pizzas. He had a small pile of Healthy Choice meals at his feet. At least he was trying. As soon as he heard them walking toward him, he looked up and gave her one of those smiles that made her hot and cold and slightly insane. Beside her and still pushing the cart, Angela sucked in a sharp breath, apparently believing the smile intended for her.

"Hello, Mr. Callisto, I brought your deli order and I thought you might need a cart," Angela muttered.

Cass folded her arms and took a step back.

"Thank you, Angela, I guess I do. Are these any good?" He held up a family size meatloaf meal.

"Oh, it's okay I guess. I make my own." Angela clenched her hands in front of her until the knuckles went white.

"I'll bet you do. You're probably a wonderful cook." He smiled at Angela, turning up the wattage on his charm.

Should she be jealous about this? Hmm. Well, she wasn't, which was a good thing. If she were, that would mean she felt proprietary toward him, and she didn't want that.

"Oh, I don't know about that." Angela giggled. "I suppose I'm okay. I could bring you a meatloaf dinner if you wanted."

"You don't have to," Jason and Cass said at the same time. He'd made it sound like an invitation. Despite herself, she'd made it sound forbidden.

Angela looked from one to the other, bewildered.

"Think what would happen if Kady and Cori found out," Cass added.

"Oh." Angela frowned.

"And Finn might get jealous." Jason glanced Cass as he said it. Did he somehow know about Angela's unrequited love for Finn or was he needling her? Why would he want to tease her about Finn anyway?

"Oh, yeah," Angela said, and turned to Cass. "Do you think he would?"

"That's just a better reason to do it as far as I'm concerned," she said before she'd thought it through.

"Really?" Angela brightened. "Would you like me to, Mr. Callisto? I'm off tomorrow. I could make everything and bring it up to you in the afternoon."

Jason put his arm over Angela's shoulders. "That sounds divine." He kissed her temple.

Angela made a sound that was probably meant to be a giggle, but came out hysteria. Jason released her and Cass hoped Angela wouldn't collapse in an overwhelmed heap at their feet. That would really annoy Duke.

"Don't tell Kady and Cori until after Jason leaves town, okay?" she told Angela. "I don't want them showing up on the mountain. Jason's here to relax, not to be harassed by the locals."

"Oh, I know. I won't say anything until he leaves," Angela whispered. "I'll see you Friday afternoon. And I won't tell a soul."

Angela rounded the corner, transformed. She'd always been a dowdy, nervous girl, even in elementary school. One peck on the temple from Jason, and she glowed. She even looked prettier.

Maybe everybody could see that in *her*, with the intense attention Jason had been giving her over the past day. Or did she just know what to look for?

Having put back the meatloaf dinner, he dropped the freezer door closed. "This should do me," he announced, setting his basket in the cart.

No way did he have enough food to carry him for two solid weeks, but she wanted out of the town with him as quickly as possible. "Okay. Let's go."

Chapter 6

At the checkout, Cass noticed Cori had opened the top three buttons of her smock, allowing the edge of her lacy bra to peek out. She was also rather cold, based on her physical reaction. Cass considered getting Duke out here to keep a lid on the proceedings, but that would mean leaving Jason alone while she went for reinforcements.

"Did you find everything okay, Mr. Callisto?" Cori asked in her best Marilyn Monroe impersonation.

"Yes." Jason smiled.

Kady had some urgent filing to do on this side of the office, except she didn't seem to be looking at what she was filing because she was too busy staring holes in the back of Cori's head.

"You know my offer still stands." Cori slid soup cans past the scanner with automatic efficiency. All the better to keep her limpid gaze trained on Jason.

"Offer?" His voice had all the personality of the electric company's phone tree.

"To cook for you." Cori put such subtle emphasis on the word *cook*, Cass winced and Kady dropped the entire stack of papers. Cass seized the grocery bag Cori seemed intent on filling to bursting and moved it to the cart.

"Oh, thanks. I think I'll be fine."

"Mr. Callisto is here for some peace and quiet," Cass pointed out.

"Yeah," he agreed, and gave Cass a look that heated the air around her. "Peace and quiet."

Before she spontaneously combusted, she managed to break his gaze. She grabbed a bottle of Jack Daniels and dropped it into the bag then hefted the bag into the cart.

"You know, I turned eighteen last summer," Cori volunteered. "Everybody says I look younger though."

"Oh? Happy birthday," Jason said. His tone could have been applied to a six year old.

Cori's face froze. Her hands were suspended over the scanner holding a Healthy Choice meal. Kady snorted, clapping her hands over her mouth, and then disappeared behind the office counter. Cass turned away, biting her tongue. At least now she knew what it looked like when Jason wasn't interested.

"That'll be fifty-one seventy-eight. Oh here, let me."

Cass spun around in time to see Cori pluck Jason's credit card out of his hands and run it through the machine. Then she held the card against her lip as she pressed the appropriate buttons without looking. No doubt her gaze was supposed to be a seductive, but the duck lips she'd pulled ruined the effect. She ripped off the slip and handed it to him with a pen. Jason took the pen and slip without touching her. When he handed everything back she used the pen to write her phone number on the back of the receipt.

"You can give me a call if you change your mind," she said, tucking a loose lock of bleached-blond hair behind her ear. In the last thirty seconds, she'd acquired a faint Southern accent. She still had the credit card in her hand and close to her mouth. It had to be a plan.

Cass reached across the belt and snatched away the card. "Thanks, Cori. Say hi to your mom for me." She held the card out to Jason, expecting him to take it back. Instead he closed his fingers around hers and raised her hand to his lips.

"Thank you, *cherie*." His eyes held hers as he pressed his lips to her knuckles and slid the card from between her fingers. Cass thought she heard one of the girls gasp. This was going to be all over town by dark.

Jason straightened and flashed a professional smile at Kady and Cori. "It's been nice meeting you," he said. Then he pressed one hand into the middle of Cass's back to propel her out of the store. As they walked through the front doors, "Slut," came from behind her, but she had no idea who it was directed at.

Her head started to throb in time with other parts of her body.

"They were fun," Jason commented as they hurried across the parking lot to the truck. At least she was hurrying, he didn't seem bothered by the fact that it was twenty degrees out.

"Fun?"

"Sure. It's fun to watch those kinds of girls lurch around." He grinned.

"I see. You weren't interested at all." She parked the cart next to her truck.

"No, not once I knew what was going on. They took me by surprise at first, but I'm not into little girls."

Cass lifted his last bag into the bed of the truck. "I didn't realize they were little girls."

"They aren't women yet. I'm interested in women exclusively." He put his hand under her chin to make her look at him. "Grown women."

Funny, wasn't it cold a few seconds ago? "So is that why you kissed my hand?"

"Maybe."

The parking lot of the grocery store, she reminded herself. Right next door to the diner. A more public place could not be found this side of live television. At least not in Potterville. "Maybe you should take the cart back while I start the truck and get the heater going."

Jason released her and grabbed the cart.

Cass leaped in and started the engine. She pressed her forehead against the steering wheel. Kady and Cori had gone into a feeding frenzy over tourists before, and caused a few screaming fights between husbands and wives in the parking lot, but they'd been in rare form today.

And Jason had dismissed them. However, Angela, who could be found in the dictionary under the headings low self-esteem and wallflower, he had put his arm around and kissed. After a couple of murder mysteries, Cass would have assumed Jason was a predator looking to take advantage of Angela's weakness, but that didn't fit when the beauty queens were throwing themselves at him. Was he just being nice? Did he sense Angela needed a boost, and if he could give it to her in return for a meatloaf dinner, what was the harm? So how did that explain the attention he'd been lavishing on her? Did he sense she needed a boost or was he really interested? Nothing in his press ever talked about his interest in the emotionally less fortunate.

"So the accountant, what was his name?" Jason asked, opening the door and climbing in.

"Finn Runningwater." She sat up. Her box of mail was in the bed of the truck, leaving the seat open between them.

"Interesting name."

"He's a very nice man."

"I'm sure he is."

Why did she have to defend Finn to Jason? He was leaving in a few days. Finn would be here forever. Jason would forget all of them. She lived here, and liked it, even if the town was populated with kooks.

"He didn't seem to like me much."

"You noticed?"

"Am I interrupting something between you two?"

"You're a guest."

"Doesn't mean he doesn't think I'm cock-blocking him. Am I?"

A snort escaped before she could stop herself.

Eyebrow raised at her, he said, "That's some answer."

"You just don't realize what a question it was." She shifted into reverse. "So tell me."

The possibility was, this would lodge in Jason's mind and become a song. Finn would never hear it, though. He only listened to light jazz. "Finn has had a crush on me since seventh grade, but I never felt more than a low-grade friendship with him. I like him well enough, just never could summon up any passion for him."

"You make that sound difficult."

She glanced at him. "Summoning up passion for Finn?"

"No, summoning up passion."

"That's pretty easy in the right circumstances."

"And what are those?" he murmured.

She'd wandered into deep water, and wasn't sure she remembered how to swim. Her heart pounded, and she had trouble focusing on the road. Jason would be leaving. She didn't mean anything to him. Might even be a charity case. She wasn't the kind of girl who hung on the arm of the actor at the Tonys. Or who had flings with the award-winning actor.

Musician, she corrected herself. Go to the Grammys, fling with the famous musician.

Fling with the famous musician?

Her mouth went dry. What would it matter? Up on the mountain alone with him. No one would ever need to know except her and the walls, and the walls hadn't revealed any secrets yet.

"Finn said there was a storm coming through," she said.

"What does that mean?"

"Depends on how bad it is. Regular bad, we'll be plowed in for a day or so. Real bad, you might not be able to get out of the cabin. Make sure you take in lots of firewood tonight."

"I did notice the change of subject, Cass."

"Did you? That's nice."

His low, husky tone tickled the hair on the back of her neck. "What are you afraid of, Cassandra?"

"I'm kind of leery of spiders. Not really afraid exactly, but I don't like them. Especially the ones in the firewood, but if you give the cord a good kick they usually make a run for it."

"You know what I meant."

He'd twisted sideways against the seatbelt and sat studying her with those dark eyes. All the hair on her body tried to stand on end in the hopes he would want to smooth it down. She felt herself getting warm and slick. It had been so long, so very long, since anyone looked at her with desire. "Why are you flirting with me?"

"Because you're a beautiful woman."

"That's all it takes?"

"My standards are very high."

"So it's a compliment?"

He reached over and brushed a lock of hair behind her shoulder. "I can see that you're attracted to me and you're not involved with anyone else."

A shiver skittered over her skin. "How do you know?"

"If your accountant, who you have had no interest in since seventh grade, is chasing you so hopefully, then there must not be any one else."

Her chest tightened. "I need to pay attention to the road."

Jason turned back in his seat, folding his hands in his lap. "The fire has gone out in my cabin. I must not have done a very good job of tending it."

"I forgot to tell you how to bank it last night. I'll show you how to build one when we get back."

"And I still owe you a lunch since I didn't get to pay for today's."

"That's okay. You can send me a gift certificate later. You have the address." Wasn't he going to pursue it any further? Why not? One look out the window might have made him decide she did need to watch the road. On the passenger side, a low stone wall separated the road from a sharp drop. Her margin for error wasn't great.

Only two weeks wide.

When she'd pulled into the garage and shut off the engine, he turned to her again. "You are a beautiful and intriguing woman, Cassandra Geoffrey."

"Thank you." Intending to flee into the house, she took the keys out of the ignition.

"I hope you'll give me the opportunity to know you better."

She kept her eyes fixed on the wall at the back of the garage. Just like she'd read the subtext of Finn's possessive comment at the diner, now she could hear the invitation in Jason's. What would happen then? Jason reached across the seat and touched her chin, guiding her face to his, paused inches from her lips. "Will you let me?"

The question left too many openings. Her body screamed, *Yes!* not caring what the real question was. Her brain locked up and refused to budge. He took her lack of answer as agreement and leaned forward, brushing his lips across hers.

Her whole body felt the kiss. Every inch of skin seared with contact. Everything else melted away, leaving only the light touch of his lips on hers. Her mind spun in senseless circles, unable to form thought, let alone reason out why this was happening. And she didn't care why, only wanted it to continue.

* * * *

Jason pulled away. He wanted to devour her. To pull her across the seat into his lap and kiss her dizzy and breathless. Pick her up, carry her into the house, lay her on the floor in front of her fireplace and make love to her while the firelight played across her creamy skin.

If he hoped to do any of that, he had to give her space now.

He sat back. She looked blissfully dazed, which was how he wanted to leave her. "Thanks for the ride," he said, stepping out of the truck. He scooped up his grocery bags and headed for his cabin. When he stopped to unlock the door, he glanced over his shoulder. She'd gone inside, but left the garage door open. She'd mentioned needing to cut down a tree tomorrow, maybe she wanted to get started today. Or, in her daze she'd forgotten to close it. That was promising.

He went in and put away the groceries. His body felt pleasantly tight, but needy. He hadn't wanted a female this much since high school, and that cheerleader had been better in fantasy than in reality. Which is why he'd kissed Cass now. He needed to know if fantasy would match reality. So far so good. Listening to them talk in the diner only increased his desire. Watching her deal with Angela and the girls in the grocery store had nearly led him into a fatal error. She was clever, creative, mature and sexy. The first three had been in short supply in the women he met. The girls at the store highlighted that nicely. Even Stella had been more shrewd than clever.

He poured himself a shot of whiskey and carried it to the living room window. No sign of her yet. Her place had been so warm and inviting last night. He could have stretched out on the couch and fallen asleep, if he hadn't wanted to climb into her bed so much.

It even looked warm and inviting from the outside. He walked away from the window to stop torturing himself by staring at her house, and gazed out the back window. The snow wasn't very deep under the trees, but it lay on the branches like white velvet. The forest stretched on forever. Where was the pasture they were talking about? Further this way or on the other side of the road? How much land was it? How much would it cost? What would she say if he offered to invest with her, to give her the money to buy the land? He didn't know anything about running a campground, but she did, and it would give him an excuse to linger in her life.

Which would give him more time to seduce her.

He went back to the front window. The garage door was closed. Maybe she wasn't coming out again today. Frustration clawed at him. Only two weeks. One more night seemed too long to wait. Not knowing how to start a fire on the cold hearth was a perfect excuse to call her, but it felt like cheating. He wanted her to come on her own. Knocking on his door, dark eyed and breathless. His ego was out of control. He turned away from the window and poured himself another shot. Still no music. He'd forgotten about it in his pursuit of Cass. If he wanted any, he'd have to make it himself. The silence rang through the house. She was right about needing a fire. The cabin had a chill about it. Or maybe he was overheated.

* * * *

A chainsaw roared outside. Jason lunged out of bed. He hopped into jeans and a sweater as he crossed the bedroom headed for the living room window. He hadn't slept well. Visions of Cassandra kept invading his dreams until he was too hot even without the fire. She stood at the foot of the tree she'd been looking at yesterday in her parka, hacking at the base. He grabbed his coat, pulling it on as he rushed outside.

Snow dropped on her as she worked, but she didn't pay any attention. She'd tied back her hair and put on a pair of plastic work goggles. They made her seem very cute and small, like a child playing with her father's tools. After a few minutes, the tree cracked with a sound like a gunshot and fell along the road, blocking it.

Without shutting off the saw, she worked her way up the trunk, cutting it into foot long pieces. By the time she stopped and turned off the motor, she had only the top section. When the thunderous sound faded, Jason clapped.

She didn't react.

Jason stopped, wondering if she was ignoring him, but then she took off her goggles and pulled out earplugs. Smart woman. He clapped again.

Cass spun around, alarmed. Her face glowed pink. "Did I bother you?" she asked.

"No, I just have a thing for chicks with chainsaws." Jason grinned. He didn't yet, but if they looked like Cass, he could develop one pretty fast.

She blushed a deeper red. Coils of bright hair stuck to her forehead. He wanted to brush it back and keep going until his fingers tangled in those skeins of fire. "I'm done with the loud part." She propped the chainsaw against her shoulder. "I'll clear the road."

"Do you want some help?" He came down off the porch.

"No." She stepped backward. "I can get it." Setting the chainsaw on one of the logs, she started hacking off smaller branches with an ax and tossing them onto the sled behind her without looking.

Jason looked around. She was slipping away. He couldn't stand another night watching her dark window, wondering. He couldn't even stand the rest of the morning wondering. But all he had to work with was snow. What could he do with snow?

He scooped up a handful, packed it, and threw the snowball at her back. It landed with a satisfying smack in the middle of her parka.

One eyebrow raised, she looked at him over her shoulder. Before he could see what she'd done, she'd scooped up some snow and thrown a snowball in one graceful motion. It landed in the middle of his chest. Then she lobbed a second one at his shoulder, laughing and diving for cover.

Howling outrage, he tossed another one, hit the tree she'd ducked behind. He pulled his coat closed, which made the snow stuck to his sweater melt faster. The cold water did nothing to cool him off. The sound of her laughter goaded him. Another snowball thudded on his chest as he ran for where she was hiding. He tackled her, but she swung their bodies around so when he landed, she sat astride him. Her left hand had fallen onto the middle of his chest while her right dug into the snow.

The laughter died on her lips, and her legs tightened around his hips. Jason bit back a groan. She licked her lips, leaving them slightly parted. Her damp lips hovered above him, just out of reach. He felt helpless, waiting for her to choose him. Then she traced his jaw, and her fingers should have been cold against his skin, but her touch made him warmer. He trembled.

She leaned down and touched her lips to his. A small moan escaped her. Her hand pressed his chest as though she wanted to push away, but couldn't. As he searched with his fingers for the hem of her parka, he only felt her warm mouth on his. Her tongue brushed his lips.

He shuddered, plundering her soft mouth, invading her warmth, drinking it into himself, feasting in her sweetness. He couldn't control himself. Better than the fantasy, so much better. Trying to touch her bare skin, he dug under her parka. He wanted to roll them over so he could press her into the snow and open her parka to feel her against him. She moaned again and the sound vibrated through him, flooding him with heat, and she slipped her hand from his chest to the back of his neck. Now she seemed to want to pull him closer. As he arched up to her, he drew her against him. He throbbed to move inside her. Her small body slid against him with a sweet friction. His mind spun desire into an elaborate cocoon. It didn't matter that he lay in six inches of snow, he wanted to undress her and make love to her now.

She pushed away from him. Her eyes were dazed but rapidly focusing. More rapidly than he could follow. A distance built between them even though she still straddled him. She looked wildly at him then struggled to her feet.

"What?" he asked thickly.

She almost ran back to the downed tree. "I'm sorry. I shouldn't have led you on." She grabbed her chainsaw and hurried toward her garage.

"Come again?" Jason struggled to his feet. Snow melt soaked through his sweater and a crisp wind blew into his open coat. He hurried after her.

"I didn't mean—"

"I did." He followed her though the door. As she hung up the chainsaw, he got behind her, crowding her and cutting off her escape routes. She turned and took a step backward, pressed herself against a worktable.

"Listen, you can't start something like that and then leave me out in the cold."

"I have to." Lips pursed in a prim line, she'd gone colder than the icy wetness soaking his chest. "I've been down this road before and I didn't like where it ended."

"What road? The next two weeks?" he demanded. "I'm not asking you to marry me or live with me or give up your life, I just want this." He reached for her hand. Thwarted desire choked him. The need to beg her not to abandon him burned, but the words wouldn't come out. "I want you."

Chapter 7

Softened, swollen from his kisses, her lips still tingled. Every inch of her skin seemed to be sparking with delicious sensation. She gripped the hem of her parka with both hands. For years she'd dreamed about making love with Jason Callisto. Ever since he'd appeared at her door, she'd been thrumming with a low throb of desire. He wanted her, and oh God, she ached for him.

Ever since he'd shown up, she'd also been seeing where sex with him could lead, and it resembled a road with a washed out bridge. A jagged strip of asphalt that dropped into a raging river on the other end of his stay.

But he was giving her a warning sign. A nice orange and yellow sawhorse with flashing red lights and a big reflective sign saying *Jason Will Be Leaving in Two Weeks*. This time if she knew, maybe it wouldn't be so bad, she didn't have to believe it would be 'til death do us part only to find out boredom was an equally good separator.

Cass forced her left hand to relax its hold on her hem then turned it and curled her fingers around his. She was warmed by his breath on her face. Her heart still wanted to leap out of her chest, but the reason had changed. She didn't fear a relationship with him would lead to abandonment. It would. In two weeks, he would leave and she couldn't change that. She just needed to learn to live with it. Now she only had to worry she couldn't live up to what he wanted. She hadn't been good enough in the past. "I don't know. I'm just—"

Jason put his finger over her lips. "Hush." He pulled her close and kissed her.

All her fears evaporated with that kiss, as he slipped his hands expertly under her coat, ran them up her sides, driving her higher. She clung to him, helpless as he devoured her. Pent up need she hadn't known she'd had shivered through her.

"Do you want me?" he whispered against her cheek.

"Yes." She couldn't imagine any other answer.

"Why don't we go inside?"

Her hand shook as she opened the door. He seemed taller in the hall. That or, in the tradition of Wonderland, the hallway was shrinking. He pulled the door closed behind them. Before she could come to any kind of decision about the size of the hall, he'd unzipped her parka and pushed it off her shoulders. He shrugged out of his coat, leaving it on the hall floor with hers.

What should she do next? She felt like a virgin. It had been so long, this might as well have been the first time.

Jason wrapped his arms around her waist and carried her into the bedroom. She hadn't made the bed this morning, leaving the covers thrown open, and kissing her, he laid her down on it. If she'd thought his kiss was intoxicating before, she hadn't understood the word. Her body flooded with heat and she heard herself moaning. As he shoved her sweatshirt up, he moved down to kiss her stomach. When his hot mouth touched her skin, she shivered with delight. He pulled the sweatshirt off and threw it across the room. It caught on the window crank. Kissing her scorched flesh, making her moan louder, he kissed up her body.

He fell on her mouth again, ravenous, and she reveled in the heat of his lips on hers. So soft, and yet so hard. Driving her to clutch him, digging her fingers into his shirt. His fingers laced through her hair were stopped by her hair elastic. He tugged at the elastic for a minute then lifted away from her. "Your hair. Take it down for me. Please," he asked huskily.

With trembling fingers, she tried to pull the elastic out, but it tangled in her curls. Jason sat back on his heels, watching her with dark eyes as he pulled off his shirt. His lean chest was scattered with wiry black hair and his nipples were dark and rigid with anticipation. Whimpering, she tugged at the elastic until it slipped free without taking too much of her hair with it. A hand buried in her hair, he kissed, pressed her into the bed. She skimmed her hands along his back. Iron beneath smooth skin, his muscles tensed at her touch. A groan escaped him. He slid his hand behind her back and unhooked her bra, yanked the material away. The air in the house felt cool against her skin, but everywhere he touched her was hot.

"So lovely," he murmured, stroking along the side of her breast.

"Please..." She couldn't have articulated what she wanted if he'd asked, she only wanted more. Suddenly, her loose jeans were too tight and binding.

"Oh, I plan to, *bella*," he told her, the low purr of his voice making her belly clench. He leaned down and captured one taut and aching nipple between his lips.

The throbbing now became a steady pounding beat. She arched her head against the pillow, mouth open, trying to draw enough breath. As he tugged, his tongue rasped across the tip. One of his hands rested on her waist, and curling it around to her back, he slipped one finger under the waistband of her jeans. She put her hand on his shoulder, wondered what she should be doing to please him, but she couldn't seem to get a message out. A hurricane raged around her, and she could only feel and react.

Jason pressed his face between her breasts, inhaling her scent. His hot breath fanned her. She stroked through his long hair, cradling his head. He shivered. Then he took her other nipple in his lips. She arched up to meet him. It wasn't enough. She wanted more. She reached for her jeans, but he caught her hand.

"No, *bella*, let me." He shifted onto his side and reached down, unbuttoned her jeans.

Cass took the opportunity to press her hand against his chest, sought and found his tight nipples, making him gasp. "You like that?" she asked.

"Very much."

She pinched his nipple lightly as he worked her zipper down. "If you lay back I can do more."

He smiled at her with hazy desire. "I'll bet you could. But first I'd like to remove your jeans." He knelt at the end of the bed and pulled off her jeans. Her panties went with them, leaving her naked. Laying a hand on her bare calf, he said, "You are an incredibly beautiful woman, Cassandra, *bella*. Do you know that?"

Cass had no idea how to answer him.

Jason leaned down and kissed the inside of her knee, then forward and kissed her inner thigh. She closed her eyes as his fingers slipped into her most sensitive spot, couldn't move, couldn't think. A rush of pleasure coursed through her. Her skin tingled maddeningly. He kissed the inside of her thigh again, higher this time. Cass shuddered. "It's so good."

"It gets better."

Then his lips closed around her, and as a surge of greater pleasure tore through her, she wailed. She reached down to touch his head. His hair brushed against her legs, making her nerve endings crackle. His tongue tasted her expertly, bringing her tighter and tighter until she could stand no more. Her body clenched and released in a flood of pleasure.

She fell back against the bed, ashamed. Groupies could probably hold out longer. They knew well enough to serve him first. "I'm sorry, I—"

Jason sat back, licking his lips. "For what?" His voice dropped lower. "I'm just getting started, *cherie*."

Still charged with his touch, hungrier instead of sated, she trembled.

Eyes on hers, he reached into his pocket. Then he frowned, digging deeper into the pocket. "Shit," he said, on his knees and looking in both front pockets. "Hold that thought," he told her, climbing off the end of the bed.

Cass watched him walk out to the hall and pick up his coat. He must be looking for a condom. Hopefully, he wouldn't have to go all the way to his cabin for one because she didn't own any. She'd opened her mouth to tell him to forget it, they could do without this once, when he dropped the coat and returned to the bed. He was tearing a condom's foil packaging open with his teeth.

"Did you hold that thought?" he asked as he opened his jeans. Then he shoved them down his legs. Everything about him was long and lean and powerful. Gorgeous, naked. Feral and beautiful. His skin had a tawny cast everywhere. Smiling at her gaze, he kicked away his jeans.

"I did my best."

He crawled onto the end of the bed. "I'm getting the impression that you didn't manage to hold on too tightly, but I'm willing to start over if I have to."

"Sounds good to me." Her breath caught. Then his body stretched along hers and any dissipation of her passion vanished. Before he'd even touched her, her skin tingled. One hand sunk into her hair, he urged her lips to his. She could taste herself on him.

"Am I starting over?" he murmured against her mouth.

"What?" Her voice sounded thick, as if she were drunk. Yeah, she was. On him. Because wherever his body touched, hers burned with acute pleasure. Even his hand in her hair was a thrilling agony.

"Good. I don't think I could hold out." Jason shifted between her legs.

Her breath stopped in her throat and mouth went dry with anticipation. He seemed to hang above her forever, looking down at her face. The room grew impossibly hot. The fire crackled. She touched her fingertips to his chest, watched his flesh pebble under her fingers. With a groan, he thrust inside her.

She cried out as her body contracted around him. He pulled back and thrust again. Digging her nails into his back, she dragged him down on top of her. Face pressed into the curve of her neck, he moved harder and faster, making her gasp. Her legs were wrapped around him, but she spread herself as wide as she could to bring him further and further in, even as her ankles locked behind him to keep him there. The moments drew out into eternities. Clutching him to her, she rode each thrust, hardly aware of the passionate moans she made. Like thunder on the mountain, rolling and pounding, vibrating everything, the climax took her with it. With a shout, he collapsed on her.

For a few moments, all she could do was lie still, getting her breath back. Jason didn't move either. Reaching over, she pulled the blankets around them. Sex had never felt this amazing before. Hopefully it had been as good for him. She put her arms around his shoulders, wishing she knew the words to tell him how wonderful he'd made her feel.

But what if he was disappointed? He'd worked hard to get her. What if she wasn't enough? He seemed quite spent. Did that mean she was good enough for West Virginia? She didn't want to disappoint him.

"I must be crushing you," he murmured.

"It's all right."

He rolled off her. Cass missed the weight of his body. She sat up, staring at a patch of wall. His silence worked under her skin like cold fingers of wind under her peacoat. Had he worked so hard for nothing? Behind her, the sheets rustled as he propped himself against the headboard. As he traced her spine, the calluses on his fingertips scraped her bare skin, making her shiver. That she could feel so good had her reeling. She wanted it again.

He probably didn't. Was likely sorry he'd gotten involved with her in the first place. *Mediocre on a good day*, Michael had said. Had today at least been a good day?

"I'm sorry," she offered. She pulled her knees against her chest and pressed her cheek against them, biting back tears. She'd offered herself to him like a groupie and hadn't measured up.

"For what?" Jason asked, and tugged her hair.

"I'm not very experienced."

He laughed. "Cassa *bella*, if you were any more generous and enthusiastic a lover, I'd be dead right now."

When she peeked over her shoulder, he was smiling and sweaty. She twisted to face him. "Really?"

"Baby, you just about gave me heart failure, but if it had been my time, I would have died a happy man." He pulled her against his chest, stroked her hair. "You must not be experienced, or some guy would have snatched you up a long time ago and locked you in his bedroom."

Cass listened to his heartbeat. Beneath her ear, it hammered. Michael had always told her she was a boring lover. Could he have lied about that, too? She'd never slept with anyone but him before now. Of course, Jason could be lying, too. She was the only woman for miles and he was lonely. He could be thinking better this than nothing at all.

Fine. She was lonely, too. In two weeks he would go back to his fabulous life and she would stay here. End up a spinster or married to Finn Runningwater. For two weeks she could have great sex, and for the rest of her life she'd have great memories.

She moved her leg across his and pushed herself upright. "That good?"

"That good."

"Mmmm." She smiled. "Maybe you should give me another shot at that heart attack."

He grinned back. "Now I know what you're capable of. You won't be able to spring anything on me."

"So I'll have to try harder next time."

"I hate to disappoint you, but next time might take a while."

Cass brushed her lips against his. "How long?"

"You making up for lost time?"

"Maybe."

"How much?" He trailed his hand down her back, and the pulsing excitement low in her belly returned.

"Five years. You?"

Jason hesitated, and she wondered if she'd been too nosy. His lips thinned. "Two years," he said.

Stella. Famous rock star Romeo had been solo since Stella. Cass traced her finger across his chest. His breaths shortened. "So what can I do to wipe out the memory of that gap?"

"You're doing a good job right now."

She leaned down and touched his now tense nipple with the tip of her tongue. He sucked a breath through his teeth. Cass felt herself speeding down hill. This was so wanton and wild seducing him this way, but she wanted him. Her whole body ached to have him inside her again. She played her hand across his hard stomach. He gasped and his penis stirred against her leg. He buried one hand in her hair. The other rested in the middle of her back. As she slipped her hand between his legs, testing his thickening flesh with her fingers, he groaned. He arched his head on the pillow, rolling his eyes closed.

"Cassandra, *bella*, you are a temptress." He moaned.

"Thank you," she told him, moved her hand across his belly, brushing the sleek skin covering his tight ab muscles. She'd never held a man in her thrall the way she held Jason now. He seemed unwilling to stop her, maybe even helpless, and when she scattered kisses on his chest, he quivered at her lightest touch.

His hand tightened against her back. He shifted toward her, trying to lay her back again, met her lips with hot urgency. She resisted, moved and straddled him. As she knelt across his body, he looked up at her with dark eyes. His gaze said he could wait and that he wanted her now. Slowly he moved his hands up her thighs, then curled them around her waist.

He filled her, hot, shocking, deliciously, as she impaled herself on him. She rocked against him, absorbed him deeper into herself. Jason sat up, pressed his face between her breasts. The deep-throated sounds coming from him vibrated through her chest. She let her head loll. Her hair hung down her back and across her buttocks.

Jason took one of her nipples in his mouth again. He matched her rhythm with the sweet tug of his lips. The sensation spiraled away from her, sweeping her down and lifting her up at the same time. With every shuddering sensation, she rocked against him harder. She pulled his face up to meet hers, dipped her tongue into his mouth, and explored every hot secret place, wrenching his ecstatic groans into herself. Their sweat-slicked bellies rubbed together. She was suspended on the cusp of climax. He had to feel the same way. Tight and aching. She dug her fingers into his hair, holding him close to her. Hands curved around her buttocks, he clenched her against him, faster and harder.

He shuddered.

Like a lightning strike this time, the climax hit her then sent ribbons of electricity through her. She shuddered and cried out, lost to the sensation.

When she came back to herself, she lay across his chest. She didn't remember lying down or curling her arms around his neck.

Chuckling, he held her close. "And I thought I knew what was up with you. If you had unleashed all that on me the first time, you really might have killed me." He kissed the top of her head.

She giggled. Every fiber of her hummed with passion, but her eyes wanted to close. As he settled the blanket over them, he shifted her so she wasn't resting on him, but still lay tangled around him.

"Rest, my little sex fiend. You worked hard today." He kissed her head.

"Will you be here when I wake up?" What if he slipped away while she slept? He could have his car packed and be gone before she woke up.

"I will, I promise. I have two weeks before I need to go back to the real world." He cuddled her closer. "And you're too good to let go any sooner than I have to."

Eyes closed, she let the world slip away. She could only hope, if he did sneak away while she slept, that this would be enough.

* * * *

When she opened her eyes, the setting sun washed the room in shadows and gold. Jason lay wrapped around her, sleeping. They'd missed lunch, but she'd thrown something into the Crock-Pot for dinner before going out to cut down the tree.

The tree, which still blocked the road.

She eased out of his arms. In sleep, he looked younger. Less worn. Sitting beside him, she studied his face. She hadn't realized how tense he'd seemed before. There were hundreds of pictures of him under her bed, but somehow, when he was on her doorstep, she'd forgotten what he looked like. He'd said it had been two years. Could he really have been alone since he and Stella broke up? Was there more to this story? Did she have any right to know?

She stood up. Probably not. She unhooked her sweatshirt from the window crank and folded it up. Different clothes and a shower were in order. She still felt sticky and slick from their passion. Never once when she'd had sex with Michael had she been so sweaty. In fact, she didn't remember ever breaking a significant sweat with her ex-husband.

She stepped under the warm water and washed off quickly so she didn't wake Jason or use all the hot water. When she turned off the shower, the cold air pebbled her skin.

God. She'd just slept with a man on the first date.

Maybe second date. They'd had dinner together two days ago and lunch yesterday. That might count as two dates. Three, if each day counted.

Either way, she'd never been that kind of girl, even if he was a famous, sexy rock star. Cass toweled off. She was the kind of girl who ended up a spinster on the side of a West Virginia mountain. No one would ever know in town. It wasn't their business. Well, Paul would know because he was nearly psychic about these things, better than her mother. But without confirmation, he would settle for significant looks and a nice chocolate mousse when Jason left town and wouldn't breathe a word to the populace. He knew he was a blabbermouth, and if somebody didn't tell him something, even if he'd guessed, he wouldn't speculate out loud.

She didn't plan on giving him confirmation.

Passing the bedroom door, she looked in on Jason. He'd burrowed under the covers and lay with her pillow in his arms. She doubted he even realized she had gotten up.

He hadn't left, she realized with a start. She'd been convinced when she'd fallen asleep that he would be gone when she woke up. But there he was curled up in the middle of her bed, sleeping. *Too good to let go of any sooner than he had to*, he'd said. Maybe he'd been telling the truth. Possibly, she would get her two weeks of bliss before her normal life came back to roost.

She checked the Crock-Pot. Dinner should be ready in about an hour. Taking several leftover dinner rolls out of the freezer, she set them on the stove to thaw. She still felt warm and languorous from Jason's touch. All her joints were loose and everything had a hazy, rosy tint.

She hurried down the basement stairs. In the root cellar she had apple butter she'd made last fall as well as some cherry pie filling. Growing up, she'd always sworn she'd never have a root cellar, but here she had the best stocked one in town because she couldn't rely on getting to a store all the time. She could be trapped up here for a month without running out of food. Cradling a jar of cherry pie filling and the apple butter, she ran back up the stairs.

The phone rang as she walked into the kitchen. "Hello?" she answered it.

"Cassie, I just got your letter. Are you serious?" Gretta demanded.

"Totally."

"Oh God, I hate you. Did you— Have you—"

"Yes."

"I really do hate you. What happened? What was it like?"

"He's here now."

"So you can't talk." Gretta whined. "Okay, call if you need me. This is so exciting. My best friend sleeping with Jason Callisto."

"'Bye, Gretta."

"'Bye."

Cass hung up the phone and turned to the pie she'd decided to make, hoping she wouldn't need Gretta. She didn't want this to end with the washed-out bridge and the sobbing long distance phone calls. Was a fond farewell and sweet memories too much to hope for?

As she was rolling out the crust, Jason slipped his hands around her waist. "You weren't in bed when I woke up," he murmured, kissing her neck.

"I thought you might like to eat some dinner at some point."

"Dinner?"

Cass felt him looking around the kitchen. The Crock-Pot on the counter, the rolls on the oven, apple butter beside them. The pie shell she was laying in the tin. She trimmed the extra crust and debated rolling out a lattice top. It would be showing off and he probably wouldn't notice the difference, but she would know. She knew too much. Like right now, he wasn't wearing a shirt. And she thought she could get him back into bed if she wanted to. Would he notice when she turned down the Crock-Pot so it wouldn't overcook while she seduced him again?

"Wow, looks like you have something special planned."

"Not really. I put the chicken a la King on for myself before I went out to cut down the tree. I got out extra rolls because I thought you might be hungry since we slept through lunch. The apple butter was in the root cellar, and when I went to get it, I saw the cherry pie filling and thought it might taste good." She laid the crust over the pie. Judging by his tone, he was impressed already. She pinched the crust closed and turned in his arms. Yup, no shirt and barefoot. He'd pulled on a pair of jeans, and that looked to be about it. She brushed her fingers down his chest. "Does that sound special?"

"Everything about you sounds special." He leaned down and kissed her.

Cass's body went limp as an overcooked noodle. As he pulled her tighter, lifting her off the floor, she reached behind her and shoved the pie back then stroked across the soft skin of his shoulders. Groaning, he settled her on the counter. Her legs seemed inclined to wrap around his waist.

"Too many clothes," he muttered, opening the buttons of her flannel shirt. "Could you arrange to be naked for the rest of the trip?"

"Maybe, but it means that you'll have to go get more firewood."

He chuckled, which made the hair on the back of her neck rise. She shivered. "I can't keep you warm enough?"

"Would you like to try?" she challenged. She looked down at him, watching his eyes grow dark. Instead of answering, he put his hand behind her neck and kissed her hard. Cass tightened her legs around him and he groaned. He hardened against her, and reached under her shirt and unhooked her bra. Then he pushed her shirt and bra off her shoulders. Cass gasped. He took one of her nipples between his lips. Tangling her hands through his hair, she leaned her cheek on the top of his head. Her hair hung around them like a curtain. She hadn't thought she could be hungry for him again so soon, but she was. She ran her hands down his back.

"Oh God, I have to stop," Jason muttered. He leaned his head between her breasts.

Tension thrummed in her like a high power wire. "Why?"

"I don't have another condom." He panted. "My God, you are tempting."

"What do we need a condom for?" She lifted his head so she could see his eyes. They were so deep and dark.

"Are you on birth control?"

"No."

He put his hands over hers. "That's why we need a condom. I can't leave you pregnant."

The window hadn't blown open just then, so this chill was all hers. All the ardor she'd felt a minute ago, drained away. *I can't leave you pregnant.* She'd moved past a little racy and into flagrantly irresponsible, and of all people, Jason was being the responsible one. So much for his love 'em and leave 'em reputation. But then, paternity suits could get expensive.

"You're right." She slid off the counter and turned away from him. Turning down the Crock-Pot hadn't even been necessary.

"What are you mad about?"

"I'm not mad," Cass lied. She was, just not at him. Why wasn't she being more responsible, more mature? Instead, she was acting like a hormone-driven high school girl. With shaking hands, she put her pie in the oven.

"Come on. I'm pretty good at knowing what mad looks like and it usually looks like this. Is it because I wouldn't have sex with you?"

She slammed the oven door and turned back to him. He stood in the middle of the kitchen barefoot and shirtless, still incredibly sexy, mouth hanging open. Well, she wasn't that far from baffled either. "No. Because I would have."

Jason folded his arms. "Okay, that almost makes sense."

Cass folded her arms too and remembered she was also shirtless. Her shirt and bra lay on the floor in the doorway behind him. "I should be old enough to know better. I don't know where you've been. I don't even know why you're so interested in me. Could be I'm just the only woman handy."

"Where I've been? What am I, used Kleenex?" He scowled, which also looked sexy. Only now he looked very, very angry, and sexy and shirtless and barefoot.

"No, but you might be a little cold here on the mountain," she snapped.

"Not hardly. I think I can last a couple of celibate weeks."

"Really? I haven't seen it. You had me within forty-eight hours."

"I didn't hear you protesting."

Cass adjusted her arms. She hadn't protested. She'd hopped into bed at the first opportunity and acted like some kind of whore. "No, you're right and if I remember correctly that's why I was mad in the first place."

Jason ran his hand through his hair. "I don't need this. I came up here to de-stress, not make things worse." He stalked down the hall.

"Where are you going?"

"Back to my cabin." He grabbed his coat off the floor and pulled it on then yanked open the door and as he left, slammed it behind him.

Cass picked up her flannel shirt and watched him walk back to his cabin, barefoot with his coat flapping behind him. The tree still blocked the road and it was getting dark. She'd have to get it after dinner. If she could get herself to do anything after dinner. Right now the best course of action seemed to be curling up in a ball on the floor and sobbing, but that hadn't helped when Michael left so she doubted it would be any more successful this time. She needed to do something. Move on. Take some sort of action. She checked the time. Dinner should be ready soon. It was at the very least, a place to start.

Chapter 8

"Shit." Jason slammed the door behind him.

Halfway to his cabin he'd realized he wasn't wearing his shoes. Another four steps, and he'd remembered he wasn't wearing a shirt either. By the time he'd reached the door, he was shuddering against the cold and wishing he was in Cassie's warm house, in her warm bed.

In Cassie's warm arms.

Why had he stormed out?

Jason poured himself a generous whiskey and slammed it back, coughing and sputtering when the liquid scorched his throat. He wiped his mouth with the back of his hand and poured another. Then he slumped on the couch and stared into the dead hearth.

From the moment he'd noticed the dinner, he'd become alarmed. A large chicken casserole, rolls, apple butter, cherry pie. People didn't put together a meal like that unless they expected company. Therefore, she'd expected company. Him. She'd baited the trap, and like a big dummy, he'd walked right in and said, "Oooh, cheese!"

But she'd been cooking a roast when he'd shown up, hadn't known who was coming or that he wouldn't have his own dinner.

He took a more appropriate sip of his whiskey and leaned his head against the back of the couch. The alcohol warmed his mouth, reminding him that nothing else was warm. He hadn't even taken off his coat.

It had been a memorable afternoon. The snowball fight followed by that incredible kiss in the snow. Then the incredible sex in her bed. He wasn't without a standard of comparison, but he hadn't yet met a woman he'd wanted to dive into and never surface from the way he did with Cass. She was hot and sleek and genuinely responsive.

His feet started to itch from the cold. He could fix the problem by taking a hot shower but that involved too much effort. Instead, he shrugged off his coat and threw it across the back of the couch. The chill helped clear his sex-deprived brain.

Maybe she hadn't been so genuinely responsive. Maybe it was all part of an elaborate ploy. He'd experienced plenty of ardent pursuit since he'd become rich and famous. Some of them were after the rich, others, the fame. All had wanted the guy they thought he was. The famous guy. Sometimes they fooled him, but never his sisters or his mom. When they all hated Stella on sight, he should have known something was wrong with her. He needed to get one of his sisters out here to look Cass over.

Jason stood up. He did not need one of his sisters to check out Cass because this wouldn't be any kind of permanent relationship. This was supposed to be an affair. Short, sweet and to the point. If she thought she could manipulate it into something more, was she wrong. He picked up the whiskey bottle, carried it back to the couch and refilled his glass. Besides, he had what he wanted. He'd gotten her twice in one afternoon and they'd been headed for a hat trick in the kitchen until he'd remembered his one and only condom had ended up in the trash beside her bed. If he'd been a rat about it, he could have been eating her food in her warm house after another nice session in her soft bed.

But besides the legal implications, he didn't do that kind of thing.

Her comment about where he'd been stung. Although, he didn't have any right to be upset. She was right. They didn't know each other well enough to get in too deep, despite his natural inclination to do just that.

His sister the lawyer, however, could dig up most of the dirt he needed. He picked up his phone and hit her preset. While he waited for her to answer, he emptied his glass.

"Hello?"

"Tessa, my favorite sister." The alcohol was beginning to flow through his veins like antifreeze. He couldn't even feel his feet anymore. He reached for the bottle. Already half empty. If he didn't slow down, he'd have to risk those girls at the grocery store again to resupply. He set the bottle down without refilling his glass.

"What have you done, Jason?"

"Nothing. I just wanted you to get some information for me."

"I see."

Knowing her, she indeed probably saw everything. Guilt settled in his gut. "Her name is Cassandra Geoffrey. She owns this campground I'm at."

"Surprise, surprise," Tessa said. "Do you want me to send you the information there or will you call?"

If a FedEx truck appeared at Cass's door with a package for him, she probably wouldn't assume it was a dossier on her. Still, he didn't like the idea that she might guess something was up. "I'll call you. She lived in New York City for a while."

"Well, that will definitely make her easier to hunt down," his sister retorted.

"Tessa, you're my favorite lawyer."

"I hope so. You bought the degree. I'll tell Mom you made it okay. This shouldn't take more than a couple of days. Give me a call Monday. Take care, little brother."

"Thank you, Tessa. See ya." He tossed the phone on the table and stood to stretch. A hesitant knock at the door interrupted him.

It might be Cass. She might have decided she wanted to give him a second chance. Or she remembered that she'd promised to relight his fire, which would give him a chance to relight hers. Almost willing to admit to excitement at the prospect, he yanked open the door.

Outside, Angela looked like she might flee. "Mr. Callisto?"

Jason stared at her for a minute. Why wasn't it Cass? What the fuck was the least terrifying grocery store girl even doing here? Then he noticed the plastic grocery bag clutched in her hand. She had promised to bring him dinner tonight. "Hey, Angela, you're here right on time. Call me Jason." He stepped back from the door to allow her in, but she stayed rooted to the porch.

"There's a tree in the drive," she pointed out.

Beyond her, the tree still lay there. Cass must be eating her dinner or something. He hoped she was eating dinner. '*Or something*' took in a whole range of messy female emotions that made him guilty. Guiltier.

Angela wasn't looking at his face, but focused on a spot over his head. The effort canted her head back at an unnecessarily obvious angle. Her blush could heat the living room. Probably the shirtlessness. "Come on in and make yourself at home while I get some clothes on."

"Okay," she muttered.

As he walked through the bedroom door, he glanced back. He hoped moving away would give her the breathing room she needed to step inside and close the door. She managed to get the door closed, but that seemed to be it.

Sorting through the clothes he'd brought, he found the raggediest, dowdiest sweater he owned. Angela had known Cass a heck of a long time. Tessa could get Cass's tax returns, but Angela handled her groceries. The government knew a lot, but the grocer knew more. Between them he could have a very detailed picture of Cass. In return, he could give Angela a huge ego boost by being nice, and from the look of her, she needed it. However, not leading her on while still being friendly would be tricky.

When he reentered the living room, she stood poised for flight in front of the door. She'd never even taken off her coat.

"I put it in the oven," she said. "You can take everything out in a half an hour. It'll be hot and ready then. Just give the dishes to Cass. She'll get them back to me."

The words *hot and ready* didn't have the same meaning with Angela. "You're not staying for dinner?"

"Staying for dinner?"

"Sure." He lifted her coat off her shoulders and tossed it over the back of the couch with his. "You did all the work of cooking, you should enjoy it. Would you like something to drink?"

Angela eyed the whiskey bottle on the table. "I don't drink."

"Yeah, don't start. It's a bad habit." He scooped up the bottle from the table and stashed it in the kitchen.

"Your fire's gone out," she said.

"I know, but I don't know how to start a new one."

"Oh, I can do that." She went to the hearth and peered in the wood box. "Your wood box is almost empty."

"Why don't I go outside and get some more wood while you get it going?"

Angela set to work before he'd gotten outside. On the top step, he remembered that he'd left his shoes in Cass's house. He glanced in that direction. What did he expect to see? Her curtain twitching as she spied on him? The tracks from the snowball fight earlier ranged around the center, his own footsteps leading from her house to his and Angela's leading around Cass's to his door, and the tree. Frowning, he gathered up an armload of wood from the pile beside the house.

Why did it matter? He'd had her. Why did he need to know about her tax returns and her groceries? Why did it really matter?

"It just does," he muttered to himself as he walked onto the porch and went inside. "This is a nice little town," he said to Angela. "Have you lived here all your life?"

"Oh, yeah. I never really wanted to go anywhere else. Not like Cass. I'd be afraid to live in New York."

"I didn't know Cass lived in New York," Jason lied, sitting down in one of the chairs.

Angela started stacking wood in an elaborate pattern in the fireplace. "Yes, she did. She lived there for five years before she came home. She was some kind of artist. She paints these great pictures that she sometimes sells to the tourists in the summer. She's really good. Maybe you could have her paint one of your album covers."

"Maybe." Jason smiled. Angela hadn't required much prodding at all. "She probably doesn't have a lot of time to paint. She's probably pretty busy with boyfriends and stuff."

"No," Angela said, pulled a lighter out of her coat and lit a twist of newspaper that she'd inserted in her wood sculpture. It caught, and she turned away. "She hasn't had a boyfriend since she came back from New York. Unless she's hiding him for some reason. She dances with about anybody who asks at the church. Finn always asks her to dance." Frowning, she looked at the coffee table. "Is that your cellular phone? It looks like one of the new ones."

Jason blinked. He'd been expecting her to start waxing poetic about Finn Runningwater, something he didn't especially want to hear. "Yeah," he said, sitting forward.

"Can I look at it?"

"Go ahead."

Angela picked up the phone and turned it over in her hands like it might bite. "Kady has a cellphone, but she won't let us touch it. She says we'll break it. It's out of service a lot because of the mountains."

"That makes sense." Settled back in his chair again, he said, "You're older than Kady and Cori, aren't you?"

"Way older. I graduated high school before they were even freshmen. But there's nobody from my class left in town. They all went to college or joined the army. Except Mike Bittner, he's in the Navy. And Oz Coontz up the holler. Oz is a little slow."

Maybe Angela was a little slow, too. She didn't seem stupid, just a bit behind the learning curve socially. The phone rang in her hand, and she jumped, dropping it. She went pale. "Oh God, I'm sorry. I didn't mean to break it."

He reached forward and scooped it off the floor. Brian. "I got it. No harm done. Just a call."

"I better check dinner." Angela rushed into the kitchen.

Jason answered the call.

"Hey, what's up?" Brian said.

"I'm having dinner with somebody."

"Cassandra Geoffrey?"

"No. Somebody else."

Brian snickered. "I thought you'd matured."

Jason left that hang for a moment. There wasn't any reason for Brian to not think he was on the trail of another willing female. Except that for the past two years Jason hadn't managed to summon up even passing interest in any of the hordes of willing females he encountered on a daily basis. Angela started setting the table with paper plates and plastic utensils as if he'd supplied fine china and silver. "Was there a reason you called?" he asked Brian.

Angela looked at him wide-eyed. As soon as she realized he was watching her, she flushed a more brilliant red and all but sprinted back into the kitchen. He only hoped she didn't think he was hitting on her.

"Tessa called and wanted to know if I knew anything about you and this campground woman. She said you had her fishing in the public records."

Jason walked to the window and looked out at Cass's cabin. She thought she lived in a small town. He lived in a much smaller town that happened to be spread out over a good portion of the United States, much of it within the county limits of Los Angeles. How had he ever managed to keep a secret from any of them? "I do."

"Any reason why?"

"Simple curiosity." Jason doubted Brian would accept this answer. His mother, his sisters and his other band mates wouldn't accept this answer either. He had to stop answering the phone. Except, then he would never get the dossier on Cass.

Smoke coiled out of Cass's chimney. He wanted to be in there, and simple curiosity had nothing to do with it.

"Yeah. Whatever," Brian said.

"Look, somebody's waiting for me."

"And you have a lot of time to make up for. Try not to break every heart in West Virginia."

"Don't make me call your kids and tell them about closet monsters again."

"Hah. See ya."

"See ya." Jason hung up and tossed the phone on the table.

Angela stood in the kitchen doorway, poised for flight again, and this time she appeared willing to go without her coat. "I'm sorry, I didn't mean to eavesdrop."

Jason beamed. He still needed to pump her for information. "Don't worry about it. Is everything ready?"

It took him an hour and twenty minutes and fourteen gallons of premium charm to get slightly more information than he'd figured out over that lunch at Ida's. According to Angela, Cass was nice. Very nice. She'd gone away to college in Philadelphia, married right after graduation and moved to New York with her husband. The wedding, to which most of the town had been invited, had been nice. Angela didn't know what the husband did for a living. He had seemed nice, but if Cass had divorced him he must not have been very nice. Cass's closest friend in town was Paul. Who, Angela informed him in a stage whisper despite that the only person within a mile was Cass, was gay. He'd followed Cass here from New York, where he had been a chef. Despite being a gay New York chef, or maybe because of it, Paul was also very nice. In fact, everyone in town appeared to rate on Angela's scale as nice or very nice with the exception of Finn. Finn was really sweet. At least Angela hadn't gone all mushy over the potato-shaped accountant.

By the time she became aware that she'd been alone with Jason for a very long time and bolted, he had a headache. She was, in her own words, nice, but he'd been hoping for some hard facts. He still wasn't sure why.

* * * *

The next morning, Cass pulled a sled across the snow to the tree. She had hardly eaten dinner, and her pie had gone into the refrigerator uncut the night before. Most of the evening had been spent tossing twigs across the coffee table into the fire while she washed her sheets, twice, and pondered whether anything more than dinner had occurred between Jason and Angela during the eighty-six minutes the other woman was in his cabin.

She'd followed Angela's progress along the road and around the tree to Jason's door, carrying a plastic grocery bag in each hand. He'd answered the door bare-chested. Surprisingly, Angela had not keeled over on the spot. Cass was torn between happiness that Angela seemed to be getting over her shyness and sick horror that it had to be happening now, with Jason. Michael had warned her she wasn't cut out for that life. He must have been right. She couldn't even manage a decent one afternoon stand with Jason Callisto without going insane.

This morning she'd been up before dawn and made herself a farm hand breakfast that would have put a real farm hand into a food coma. She'd inhaled it and started eyeing the pie. After several minutes' deliberation, she'd decided she didn't want to eat everything in the refrigerator because that would necessitate a trip to Henderson's, where she'd have to see Angela and speculate, while everyone else in town speculated about her.

Instead, she'd suited up against the cold and headed out to finish dealing with the tree.

She stacked some of the wood on the sled and dragged it to her woodpile. On her second trip to the tree, Jason's door opened. Her heart leaped to her throat. Maybe he wanted to talk to her. It would give her time to apologize.

"Hey, Cass," he called.

"Yeah." She dropped the sled's rope. He had no shoes on, she noticed. She probably had the only pair he'd brought with him in her hall.

"Yesterday, you said you'd start a fire for me and you haven't."

Her throat tightened. She'd dropped from "*my God, you are tempting*" to hired help in less than a day. "I thought Angela lit it for you last night." She bit her lip against the unintended double entendre.

"It went out again." He folded his arms across his chest. From this distance, his expression was cold and uncaring.

"Sorry. I forgot. I'll take care of that in a minute." She loaded a log onto the sled, trying to keep her eyes on the task. Looking at him stung.

"I'd appreciate it if you did it now. It's pretty cold."

Cass dropped another log onto the sled. Did she imagine that sharpness in his voice? "All right." Wading through the snow to his cabin, she could still make out the prints from his bare feet in the snow. At least his visitor last night had been Angela. Anyone else would have leaped to exactly the right conclusion. Angela would have just gone on dreaming about Finn.

Jason stepped away from the door to allow her in. Dreading going inside, she hesitated on the threshold. They'd gotten along well over dinner and he'd enjoyed the trip into town. Sex had been pretty fantastic, by her standards. His, too, if he'd told the truth. Then they'd hit yesterday afternoon. She didn't want it to be this way, and wasn't sure what way she wanted it to be, but this turn of events seemed wrong.

He now stood on the far side of the room watching her. He'd obviously tried to light it himself this morning. Three logs were stacked on top of a sheet of charred newspaper.

"You have to start with more paper and smaller pieces of wood," she said, stepped inside and closed the door behind her. Her cabins had often been described as spacious, especially on her web site. They were pretty large. Whole families slept in them comfortably. Now it felt no bigger than a standard closet. Though he was across the room, he might as well have been next to her. She could almost feel the heat of his breath on her skin. "Listen, about yesterday—"

"Forget about it. It was nothing," he said.

Cass steeled herself against a flinch. Her entire life was a wasteland compared with those short hours yesterday, and to him it was nothing? "Okay," she mumbled.

She started crumbling paper to line the grate. Her eyes burned, which she couldn't explain because she hadn't gotten any smoke in them yet. Scattering some twigs across the top of the paper, she built a lean-to of thicker branches and thin sections of split logs. Then she looked around for the long thin lighter she supplied each cabin with. "Where's the fire lighter?"

"On the mantle."

Cass stood and looked across the mantle. There wasn't anything on it. Her throat hurt and her eyes wanted to overflow. She had to get out of here. "It's not here." Her voice sounded tight. Michael had always hated it when she'd cried, and claimed she was manipulating him.

"Oh, sorry. I stuck it in my pocket."

She held out her hand behind her, turned and looked down at the hearth, trying to get herself under control. Unwilling to even touch her work gloves, apparently, he dropped the lighter in her open palm. She heard him walk back to his place on the far side of the room as she fitted the lighter in her hand. Crouching, she lit the paper. It caught quickly. Slivers on the inside of her lean-to blackened and curled. Then edges of the split logs began to char.

"You should be okay now," she said without turning to look at him. "Let this get good and hot before you add any larger logs and tonight when you go to bed, rake the ashes over the coals. That'll keep them glowing until morning when you can add more fuel." She swiped at an annoying tickle on her cheek, like a fly landing on her face.

"Cass, are you crying?" Jason asked. The floor creaked as he stepped forward. "Why are you crying?"

Another tear escaped and followed the track of the first. "I got some smoke in my eyes." She faked a cough.

He lifted her face to meet his. "You're crying."

Though she hadn't heard him cross the room, the touch of his hand rang from the ends of her hair to the tips of her toes. "I'm not." She sobbed. Her knees stopped working and she collapsed forward into his arms.

Jason caught her and held her tight, whispering. He stroked her hair, calling her *bella* and *cherie* and telling her everything would be fine. She closed her eyes. His heart pounded against her chest. When her weeping

had receded to a shivery trickle, he asked, "What's the matter, *bella*? Are
you upset about our little spat yesterday afternoon?"

She nodded. Any second now he was going to get defensive. He would
tell her she was just trying to make him apologize when it wasn't his fault.
That it was unfair to use tears against him like this. "I'm sorry. I didn't
mean to cry and I didn't mean to insult you. I was just so—so—"

"I know, *cherie*. I was feeling a little like that myself. I shouldn't have
started something I couldn't finish. I think I got us both too wound up."
He stroked her cheek with his thumb. "You're too tempting for my good.
Am I forgiven?"

"Of course. It wasn't your fault. I'm the one who went all crazy," Cass
protested.

Jason put his finger over her lips. "Let's call it a mutual mistake and
chalk it up to our first fight, brought on by sexual tension."

His forgiveness tasted like ambrosia, and as she kissed his finger, he
drew a deep, shaky breath.

He cupped the back of her head in his hand, pressing his lips to
hers, and with his other hand, opened her coat. Then he slipped his arm
around her waist, pulled her tight to his body. "You know I can finish this
time, right?" he murmured against her mouth. "You don't want to start
something you don't want to finish now."

"Believe me, I want to finish."

He was backlit by the window. His long hair fell forward, brushing his
jaw and casting his face into shadow. She couldn't be sure, but he seemed
to be smiling.

"Good, can you take the gloves off? Or would you rather fight some
more?" he asked with a soft purr that made her skin ache for his touch.

Now he wasn't making any sense, and he wasn't kissing her. Both bad
things.

Jason laughed and kissed her forehead. "Let me." He took one of her
hands off his shoulder and peeled off her work glove, kissed her palm. "I
can't believe how much I want you."

"I want you, too," she whispered. Though she quivered with
anticipation, she was lying. This was more than just wanting or simple
lust, but if she told him, he might leave. Or it might sound like a lie and
he would leave anyway. She had two weeks. She had to make the most
of them.

Jason picked her up. "Then let's move some place more comfortable."

He carried her into his bedroom and undressed them both and laid her
down on the bed. Cradling her, touching her while kissing every inch of

her flesh, he lit all the nerves in her body one by one. Cass melted into the bed as he explored her, laying her soul bare. Outside the wind picked up, howling through the eaves, reflecting the swirl of passion inside her. He touched her everywhere, and her core coiled into a hot, tight ball of ecstasy. The whole room filled with her cries.

And then he entered her, shattering the world, leaving her wrung and gasping, clinging to him as he clung to her.

Chapter 9

"You are something else," he told her, when he'd caught his breath. Propped up on his elbow, he looked down at her.

Still too loose and relaxed to speak, she could only smile. With an unsteady hand, she brushed his sweaty hair off his face. He caught her hand and kissed her fingers.

"How was your dinner last night?" she asked.

"Dinner?" Jason frowned. "Oh, Angela. Good enough. I'd have rather been with you." He stroked with his fingers through her hair. "Were you jealous?"

"Angela's meatloaf is famous around these parts."

"She gave me the leftovers. I was going to eat them for breakfast." Jason raised one eyebrow in challenge.

"You haven't had breakfast?"

"I've had you." He kissed her cheek.

It was a joke, and wasn't supposed to mean anything. None of this meant anything. "I'm not in any of the food groups."

"Then I suppose the whiskey I had earlier doesn't count, either."

"Whiskey?"

"I got up this morning and the fire was out again. I thought about calling you to start it for me. Then I started thinking about yesterday afternoon and got so pissed off, I poured myself a glass and tried to light a fire. I thought about pouring the whiskey on the wood to see if that would help, but the way things have been going, I figured I'd end up burning the place down." He placed his hand on her stomach, weighting her to the bed. "I really am sorry about what happened yesterday. I should have just run over here for another condom. I was too wound up to think straight and wanted you so much, I latched onto the first thing that would let me blow up."

"No, it wasn't you. It was me. I'm the one who insulted you."

Jason pulled her on her side, spooning her against him. "You won't even let me apologize."

"I'm sorry."

He chuckled, and the husky sweet sound of it shivered down her spine.

Eyes closed, she basked in the sensation of warm skin and hard muscles pressed along her. She had never been so close to anyone, so attached. He felt like an extension of her soul.

But he wouldn't be here long. Two very short weeks at the beginning of a very long winter. She wanted to wake up like this with him every morning of the little time they had. "Why don't you bring your things to my house?"

"What?" He sat up and looked down at her.

Choosing to ignore the note of panic in his voice, she said, "Just bring your things over to the house. I have some dinner left and I never cut the pie."

"You want to live together?"

"Why not? It's only a little while."

He frowned. "It is only two weeks. Are you trying to make sure I don't have whiskey for breakfast too often?"

"It was part of the plan," she said, swinging her legs off the bed. She wanted him ensconced in her home as quickly as possible. "Come on, I'll help you carry and then I'll cook you something healthy for breakfast."

* * * *

Settled like this in the overstuffed chair in her living room, his guitar in his lap, Cass doing something at the window behind him, being in her home was way too pleasant. She didn't hang on him like he'd worried she might. Instead she'd gone into her little office at the front of the cabin and worked at the pile of mail she'd gotten from the post office, leaving him to noodle on his guitar, sift through her movies and books, and study her music collection. He should have known a woman who spent all winter in solitude by choice wouldn't become clingy the moment there was a man living in her house temporarily.

That she had all his albums didn't surprise him because she had a lot of other contemporary stuff, too. The amount of hillbilly and blues music he'd never even heard of had startled him, though. When she'd come in for supper, he'd been crouched on the floor in front of the CD player sampling a Smithsonian collection of scratchy recordings from the twenties.

After dinner, cuddling on the couch, they'd watched movies from her large library, then gone to bed and made love again. All night, they'd slept tangled around one another. He'd woken up, warm and rested, with Cass nestled in his arms as if she'd always been there. After she'd thrown another log on the fire, they'd lain in each other's arms, talking and laughing until the house warmed up and hunger drove them to the kitchen in search of breakfast. Working around her in the kitchen while she made pancakes, he couldn't remember what waking up alone or with Stella had been like. Or rather he could, but the memory had a surreal quality, as if it hadn't happened in his life. More like a TV movie he'd once seen with a vaguely familiar plot. This felt right for him, like he'd come home after a long absence.

That made him nervous.

He'd never belonged anywhere. Not like this.

The vise of anxiety in his chest tightened further.

"So why did you leave New York?" he asked. Angela had been less than helpful on that point. All he'd divined was, a husband had been involved. Angela didn't seem to understand why anyone would want to leave Potterville, especially for some place as huge and noisy as New York City. She had no yearning to see what happened outside the valley at all. Had Cass suffered a brief wanderlust before returning to her spawning grounds or did she resent being sucked back here by circumstance? Had she gone there just to be close to her beloved? And most importantly, had she carried this feeling of hominess with her or was it something about this cabin on the mountain?

"My husband left me and I was broke."

"You were married?" One more question to add to the list. Did she still miss the ex-husband? Was that why she stayed here alone? His sister Connie had never recovered from her ex-husband's infidelity and their subsequent divorce. Everyone suspected his eldest sister Eleanor had never loved her husband because she'd never gotten broken up when he walked out. And his mother… His mother never seemed to notice there were other men available. She'd married once, and once was enough.

"Yup."

That didn't sound like the answer of a heartbroken woman. Jason looked over his shoulder. She was locking the legs of an easel in place. "Why did he leave?"

"He just did."

There had to be more to the story. As she set up her work space, the line of her shoulders and body language revealed nothing. Whether she'd struggled to save her marriage like Connie, or shrugged and changed the locks the way Eleanor had. Cass wasn't telling. Her movements were focused on the paints and brushes she'd spread across a small table next to the easel. "What were you doing in New York?"

"I was going to be a famous artist."

She had her back to him, and the painting on the easel was a picture perfect image of the view out her window. The colors showed late fall instead of midwinter. He blinked in surprise. It looked as though she'd placed another window beside the first, a window on another season.

He set aside his guitar and went over to examine it. Up close, the painting was even more realistic.

Angela's definition of good covered as much territory as her definition of nice.

In the immediate foreground, he could make out the veins on the leaves that probably hung in front of Cass's window. In the valley, most of the buildings were hidden by multicolored trees, but the church spires and the town hall with its statue and green identified it. A gold dragon circled the valley, sailing on an updraft from the mountain, sunlight glinting off his scales.

"Nice dragon."

"I started it last fall, but didn't get to finish before Christmas."

He couldn't see any flaws. "It's not done?"

Cass gestured with the end of her paintbrush. "I need a little yellow on the underbelly and in the trees here by the river. Then it'll be done. I think next I'm going to do an alien invasion."

"Done a lot of these?" He couldn't stand being near her without touching her, so put his hands on her shoulders. They fit neatly into his palms. The scent of shampoo and the wood smoke clung to her hair.

"I usually manage about three a year."

Jason laughed. She'd said it as if painting the same little town over and over again wasn't odd. "What do you do with them all?"

"I do at least one straight one every year, and it'll sell over the summer. The odd ones sell, too, but I don't show those to everybody. I have one in the closet with a Big Foot sitting on the edge of the cliff eating a banana, but it's never sold. I do other paintings, too. It's my retirement fund." She dabbed her brush in the yellow and made tiny strokes on the dragon's underbelly.

"Why couldn't you get work?"

"I had work for a while. I colored comic books."

"You what?"

She turned to him. "I put the colors on comic book pages. It's not one of the world's most common professions, I guess."

"What happened?" Jason coiled a lock of her hair around his finger. He didn't know a lot about art, but he could see she had more skill than most.

"Politics. One of the editors took a hate for me and blacklisted me."

Sounded like sour grapes. Lots of people who couldn't make it decided somebody had it out for them. That usually meant they weren't good enough or reliable enough. Cass had amazing talent, though.

"One particular editor decided to hate me, and she was powerful enough, the other editors wouldn't hire me." Cass shrugged. "I was never late and my editors were always happy with my work, but one day I couldn't get any jobs. Then Michael left me, so I came home."

"He was a fool to leave you," he said, giving her shoulders a squeeze.

Another shrug, but she didn't say anything as she touched some yellow to the leaves. "There. Now to dry and I can start on the next. Do you want some brandy?"

"Sure." The painting could have been a photograph taken out her window of the town being attacked by a fire-breathing dragon. Looking closer, he picked out the grocery store and Ida's Diner.

"Who ruined you?" she asked, handing him a snifter.

The snifter was crystal, and nice quality. He sipped. Rich, orange amber apple brandy. A bottle he hadn't noticed before sat on the sideboard in the dining room. Laird's Applejack. Mentally, he added classy to her long list of qualities. "Stella."

Cass nodded.

"She dumped me in *People*."

Cass raised one eyebrow. Now he knew what he'd looked like when she'd told him she'd been blacklisted.

"I went out of town thinking nothing was wrong and picked up a *People* magazine in the airport on the way home to find myself listed in the 'over' column." Swirling his brandy, he watched the color thin against the glass. He also now knew why she'd shrugged. It still hurt, but there wasn't anything anyone could do. At least he hadn't lost his career and his relationship at the same time.

"She wasn't good enough for you," Cass offered.

"I thought she was. I wanted to marry her." He pursed his lips. He'd never told anyone that. No one. Wanting to surprise Stella on Valentine's Day, on his trip out of town, he'd bought the ring. It had been in his pocket when he saw the magazine, and he'd been so relieved he hadn't popped the question.

"I'm so sorry."

"You're right. She wasn't good for me." Letting the chair mold around him again, he pulled the guitar into his lap. Music had been his only hope at the time. His lifeline. He'd played guitar until his fingers ached. "I had to compound it by putting out that lousy solo album."

"I didn't think it was bad. I bought a copy."

"Then I owe you fifteen bucks."

"Twelve ninety-nine plus tax. It was on sale." She moved aside her finished painting, leaning it on the wall below the window, and set a clean canvas on the easel.

"Add it to my bill." He picked out a few notes. "At the time I thought I was creating a work of tortured genius. Something like an album-long *"I'm Looking Through You,"* Paul McCartney wrote it when he was breaking up with Jane Asher. I should have just gotten permission to record that."

"She hurt you that badly."

"She dumped me in *People* magazine," he snapped. Immediately, he wished he could take the words back. Cass didn't deserve being snapped at because he still felt a little too raw two years later. "I'm sorry. It's not your fault."

"No, but I understand hurt. At least you didn't marry her." She turned back to him. "Try getting a divorce from another state neither of you were born in. Very messy. And when you're fighting with a weasel, it doesn't help. He tried to get a piece of this place."

"Why did you marry him in the first place?" What kind of a guy would screw with somebody as sweet as Cass? How difficult it would be to track Michael down so he could deck him? Tessa would probably include some info on him in her dossier.

"We went to college together and we both wanted to go to New York when we graduated. We got along well. It seemed right at the time." She drew in a deep breath. "He was a charming scoundrel, and I discovered too late he was more scoundrel than charm."

"I can understand falling for that. I did."

"Stella was a charming scoundrel?"

"In a way. I went for the pretty face and didn't notice the snake underneath." Snake was a good description. The way she'd slithered into his life, taken over and slithered out when she was ready. Stella had suggested they live together, and insisted on the New York apartment. She'd decorated their homes, even directed their vacations. She'd run everything. He'd just accepted it as part of being famous. It made for great album sales.

"Ouch." Cass perched on the arm of the couch. "So what do you want for lunch?"

"I don't care." He watched his fingers picking out notes on the strings. Stella. The sun rose and set at her direction. The apartment in New York was an expensive pit thousands of miles away from where he needed and wanted to be, but she was there, so he'd lived there. Jet set vacations to Cannes and Sundance because she wanted to go. The press with her on his arm was great. She always made best dressed lists, and lived for movie premieres. He'd seen a lot of movies because she'd finagled an invitation to the premiere so they could be photographed on the red carpet.

"What about the situation in the Middle East?"

He mumbled, "Nothing." It wasn't his press. She hadn't been worried about his press, but hers. She'd gotten herself connected to all the right people to help her career on those vacations and she'd gotten herself into while with him, photographed in lots of magazines on his arm. *People* magazine would never have thought to talk to her before she was his girlfriend and the new sucker would have never met her if she hadn't flirted with him in Cannes.

Cass took his guitar out of his hands and laid it on the couch.

"What are you doing?"

She straddled his lap. "I'm making you forget about her for a few minutes." She kissed him, running her fingers through his hair.

Her warm, sweet mouth obliterated everything in his mind. Soft and fragrant, her hair hung around them in a red-gold curtain. There was an exclusive resort on St. Tropez he'd gone to with Stella. He wanted to take Cass there. The water would match her eyes. He'd lace tropical flowers through her brilliant hair and walk down the white sand beach hand in hand with her.

Grasping her hips, he shifted her higher, pressed his face between her breasts, and the sound of her happy sigh bound him to her. She pulled her shirt over her head, allowing him access to her sweet pale skin. It felt like velvet under his hands. As he stroked her back, her quiver made him smile. Always so eager for him. Not eager like a groupie, but a woman. Cass responded to him every time. She didn't lie back and acquiesce. She burned bright all the time.

He nibbled along the line of her bra, tasting her soft flesh. With a hand on each of his cheeks, she turned his face to her again, explored his mouth as if she had never kissed him before. He unhooked her bra and slid it off, dropped it on the floor and cupped her breasts. Her hands clutched his shoulders. One of them moaned, though he couldn't tell who. It didn't matter. Nothing mattered.

"Shit," she hissed.

"What?" Now she was pulling away from him. This was not the time for her to be leaving. He reached for her, but she turned, hopped to her feet.

"Someone's coming."

"Coming?"

"Someone's driving up the road." She picked up her bra and struggled into it on as she ran to the office window and peeked out the curtain. "Shit. It's Finn. I need you to hide."

"Why?" Jason stood up. Her tension was contagious and he couldn't think straight. He wanted her now. Whoever was outside could go hang. But he didn't want her to be mad at him either, and this kinda felt like mad. "Couldn't we just pretend not to be home?"

"He knows I'm home. All he has to do is look at the tracks in the snow. He can't find out you're here. Christ, if he looks around the other side of the house, he's going to see our footprints."

"Why?"

"Because I can't let Finn know what's been going on. Please, Jason, this is a small town and I have to live in it." She pulled her sweatshirt on inside out. "If he finds you here, he's going to put two and two together. It's going to make a lot of trouble for me. Just hide in the bedroom and I'll get rid of him." She picked up his guitar and pushed it into his hands.

"Cass, you're an adult," he protested as she shoved him toward the bedroom.

"I know, but I'm an adult living in a small town full of people with nothing better to do than snoop in each other's private lives. Please, Jason," she pleaded, pushing him ahead of her.

"All right." He stopped in the bedroom doorway. "But you have to promise to pick up where we left off."

A car crunched through the snow in front of the house.

Some of her anxiety must have disappeared, because her eyes sparkled and she smiled. "Do you really need a promise on that?"

"I guess not." He kissed her. She was leaning into his arms, drawn into his embrace when the knock came at the door.

Blushing, she leaped back. "Just a minute," she called, then said to him, "Stay in here and be quiet. And stay away from the fireplace, he can see right through."

Jason stood in the corner of the bedroom, listening to her walk to the door. They hadn't bothered to make the bed this morning. The blankets were still thrown around invitingly. Remembering waking up with her in his arms, he smiled. Hopefully tomorrow morning would be like that, too.

"Finn, what are you doing here?" Cass said at the front door.

"I wanted to warn you that storm I told you about is on its way. Sounds like a really bad one." The needy whine in Finn's voice made him sound like a desperate mosquito.

"You could have called." A nervous laugh came from her.

Jason looked around. Cass hadn't closed her top dresser drawer all the way this morning. Something scarlet peeked out.

"I didn't like to think about you up here alone with him if you got snowed in," Finn said.

"I'm perfectly safe with Jason. Callisto," she stammered.

Jason reached into the drawer. Silk. Scarlet silk? In her underwear drawer? This could be fun.

"I brought an overnight bag with me."

"Why?"

"So I can stay here with you and ride out the storm." Finn's mosquito whine had become louder.

"And where did you plan to do that?" Cass snapped.

"Why are there two glasses of brandy out?"

A tug, and a scarlet silk nightgown drifted into his hands. He held it up to the light. Floor length, and designed to show off every luscious curve. What would he have to do to convince her to wear it for him?

"Oh, is that where that is?" Cass again. "I knew I poured myself a glass and couldn't find it."

"On the coffee table?"

"I was working by the window. Thanks for the warning about the storm. I'll let Jason know."

But if she had been single so long, why did she have a silk nightgown? Who was it for?

"I'll stay up here and sleep on your couch."

"Finn, you are not spending the night. What would people say?"

"Then I'll stay in one of the cabins."

"None of them are warmed up."

Frowning, Jason dug further into the drawer and discovered another negligee. A white velvet teddy. And beneath it, a royal purple silk short nightgown trimmed with white feathers. Also very new. Three negligees.

Why did Cass have sexy underwear when she claimed she'd been solo for five years?

"So we'll warm one up."

"And we can all be trapped inside our cabins alone when we get four feet of snow."

"I just don't like the idea of you alone with him."

"I'm fine alone with him."

Jason folded the negligees back in her drawer the way he found them. Stella used to tempt him with this stuff whenever she thought he was losing interest. Would Cass try that trick on him, too? Drape herself around him, whispering sweet lies he would believe because he wanted to?

"Cassie, this isn't right. You shouldn't be alone with him. What if he tries something?"

Cass laughed sharply. "Like I have a hope in hell of that."

She made a very convincing liar. She'd suggested they move in together and made him feel so at home. Maybe it all been part of the plan, and his instinct this was a trap had been right. Had she reserved the silky stuff for a last resort?

"Well, why don't you come down the holler then? There's got to be someplace we can put him up. He can stay at my place."

"No. He's come here for a rest, not to bunk at your house. We're both perfectly safe."

"There's a tree blocking your truck in."

"Oh, that. I cut it down yesterday and it got dark before I was done. I just forgot to get to it this morning. Look, I'm busy. Next time you come up, you should call first."

A very convincing liar. Jason closed his eyes. He'd fallen right back in again. Straight from one woman who'd used him for his fame to another one who wanted to use him for some other undiscovered purpose. She probably missed New York and planned to use him to lever herself out of her small town. Or she was tired of scraping by with her little campground and had an eye on his money.

"I'll help you clear it."

"Finn, I don't need help."

"Are you sure?"

It didn't matter. He didn't have to fall for it this time. They had two weeks. For two weeks they could have a good time and then he could go home a happier man. Then he would know what to look for next time.

"I'm sure, Finn. Thanks for coming up to warn me. But I'll be fine."

"Do you have all the supplies you need? What about him?"

"We'll both be fine."

"There's no smoke coming from his chimney."

"His fire must have gone out again," Cass said. "I'll go check on him before I finish that tree."

"I'm worried about you up here alone, Cassie."

"You've never been worried about me before."

"I was, I just never thought I had to come up here to protect you. You seem to be getting sloppy. You left that tree blocking the road and you're wearing your sweatshirt inside out."

"I don't need protecting, but since you're here, can you drop these reservations at the post office? That would be great."

Heart pounding hard, Jason closed the drawer. How much of the comfort here had been a set up? Had he been chasing her or had she been luring him? If he searched through her bookshelf would he find a copy of *The Rules* with dog-eared pages? And a copy of Machiavelli's *The Prince* right beside it?

The front door clicked shut. Outside, a car started up and crunched across the frigid snow. The car's engine faded down the road, and Cass pushed open the bedroom door. "Okay, it's safe." She brushed her hand through her hair. "Thanks. I can't let this get around, or you might find yourself the guest of honor at a shotgun wedding. What's wrong?"

Jason realized he'd been staring at her. He couldn't mesh the conniver he'd just discovered with the woman he'd been enjoying for the past four days. "Did he say there was a storm coming?"

"Yeah. Sounds like a bad one. Why?"

To cover his turmoil, he smiled. That she might be playing him made his gut sicken. He wanted this all to be real. For her to want to stay with him. "We have to make sure we have enough supplies."

"We've got lots of food and fuel. I stock up for these things." Her brows were knitted, making her cute nose wrinkle.

"But we're about to run out of condoms."

"Oh, well then, we must make a run to the other side of the mountain." Her eyes lit up. "That's an essential. If you help me clear this tree, we can get going. We'll run up the interstate, where they won't know either of us."

"Let's go, then." She looked so open and honest. Maybe he was wrong. God, how he wanted to be. Wanting to be wrong had gotten him in trouble last time, though.

Chapter 10

Clearing the tree didn't take long. Cass cut while Jason hauled. Then they had a quick peanut butter sandwich, and she drove them down the other side of the mountain, dropped him at the drugstore, went on to the grocery store. Since Finn's arrival, he'd seemed distant and odd. Being shoved into the bedroom like a teenager who had to hide from Mom and Dad could do that to a man, but on the way down the mountain, she'd started to wonder if it was something else. He was too quiet and seemed to be watching her.

She tried not to even let her questions formulate. With feet of snow and blistering cold winds imminent, she didn't have time to wonder what was going through his mind. Supplies and firewood were top priority.

She had supplies. Before coming up after Christmas, she'd stocked up, and between the wood she had and the cord she'd had delivered for Jason, there should be enough fuel for weeks.

Snowed in with Jason for weeks? That she could handle. She might even come out of it better than she went in. He made her feel beautiful. Desirable. She'd never felt so sexy, and this glow wasn't just because he was famous, her all-time fantasy.

She parked at the Gaitherberg grocery store and headed inside. A little treat was in order if she wanted to keep his attention and she knew just the thing.

The way he looked at her, as if he was simultaneously undressing her and putting her up on a pedestal. Like he wanted to worship her and every word she spoke was a gift.

Maybe she'd damaged that. When she'd heard Finn's car on the road, she'd been too panicked to think straight. Jason said he understood, but how could he? He hadn't grown up in Potterville, endured their pitying looks after Michael walked out. If they found out about Jason, she'd have to live through that again. She couldn't do it. Or survive Jason walking out on her before her two weeks was up.

And she couldn't decide which would be worse.

She pulled up to the curb outside the drugstore where she'd left Jason a few minutes earlier. He waited, blowing into his hands to warm them. People in heavy coats with hats pulled down over their ears hurried past him, unaware that the man in the black coat was famous. They might not have cared, had they known. In the cold, with a storm bearing down, they didn't have time to gawp at famous people who were underdressed for the weather. "All ready?"

"I got the big box."

She smiled, and checked traffic then pulled out. "So we're planning on going through the gross size package, are we?"

"I'm going to try. What did you have to get?"

"A surprise." She'd tucked the bag behind her seat where he wouldn't see it.

"Am I going to like this surprise?"

"I hope so."

"When am I going to get this surprise?"

"When you least expect it and need it most."

"Sounds intriguing." He leaned back in his seat. "Is that why you took the guitar out of my hands?"

"What?" A glance showed he stared straight ahead, but one quick look wasn't enough to read his expression.

"Before Finn showed up. You took my guitar out of my hands and climbed in my lap. Was it because I needed it most?"

Her throat tightened. He'd drifted away from her, then. She recalled sitting on the edge of the couch, listening to him leave. Not physically, but emotionally he was out of the room. Out of the state. Wherever he'd gone, it didn't look like a good place. Between the panic that he was unhappy and the jealousy of him distancing himself from her, she'd jumped at the first notion. Maybe that's what had happened to cool him toward her. What if Finn hadn't been the reason at all, but that she'd taken his guitar away? "You had started to play *"I'm Looking Through You."*"

After a moment, he said, "I guess I was." He reached across the bench seat and put his hand on her leg. "I'm pretty hard to derail once I get on a track like that."

A sigh of relief shivered through her. She'd been struck with an urgent need to make him feel better, and the only thing she'd been able to think of was sex. She'd rather not be a Band-Aid, but if that's what he needed, she would do it. Even if she felt a little dirty about it.

A lot dirty.

Going all the way to Gaitherberg for condoms so it wouldn't get around town? Shoving him into the bedroom so Finn wouldn't catch them? Was it unwillingness to be pitied or huge, blinking neon signs of shame? Turning up the road to the mountain, she realized she'd even gone out of the way so she wouldn't pass any of her neighbors.

"It's starting to snow," she said turning onto the drive to her house. Big, fat flakes floated down, doing their best to look harmless, but she could see the heavy gray clouds coming over the mountains, bringing all their kin to camp on her doorstep.

"Pretty," Jason commented.

He still had his hand on her leg. Regardless of how guilty she felt about carrying on this affair, she wanted him. His hands all over her followed by his mouth. Or vice versa. Emphasis on vice. "Wait until it's all on the ground so deep, we can't open the doors."

"Will it get that deep?"

"I was snowed in for a month up here the first winter. If that happens now, you'll miss the Grammys."

"And we'd run out of condoms. I think that's a bigger tragedy." He slid his hand up her thigh to where it met her hip.

Her stomach coiled at the touch. A flush of heat swelled between her legs. She hit the garage door opener. "Should I be insulted, or pleased that you'd rather be with me than at the Grammys?"

"Definitely pleased." His hand slipped between her thighs, to the center of her heat. "The Grammys are a blast. You get all dressed up and you see your girl looking pretty, and if you're lucky you get to go up on stage and take home a shiny trophy."

"It does sound like fun." She felt breathless and light headed. He must know the way she throbbed for him, with his hand pressed right in the center of her. She managed to park the truck before she drove through the back of the garage.

He leaned across the gearshift. "I'd rather be here with you."

"Your stay can be extended, if you like. Just tell the campground manager."

Pressing his lips to hers, he tasted her greedily.

Dying for his kiss, she moved into it. He tried to pull her into his lap, but the gearshift and the steering wheel stopped him. Instead, he opened her coat and caressed her breast through her sweatshirt. Her skin ached to be touched directly.

"How do you do this to me?" he murmured, kissing her jaw. "I can't even wait to get you in the house."

"Witchcraft." God help her, his touch lit her on fire. A whimper of need escaped her as he slid his other hand around her waist and pulled her against the gearshift. She unbuttoned his coat.

"Must be," he said, brushing his thumb across her erect nipple.

"We're going to have to let go if we want to get any closer." She ran her hands down his chest, feeling the muscles tense and shiver under his sweater.

He responded by kissing her neck, and suddenly she only wanted him inside her. The need to touch him tingled through her. She would do it. She would have sex with him here on the seat of her truck because she couldn't wait to move the twenty feet to her bedroom. The windows were steaming up. "Race you to the back door."

She pushed away from him. His momentary confusion allowed her to slip out the door and race around the back of the truck. He met her at the door to the house, and they tumbled inside together.

Holding her against the wall with his hard body, he devoured her with kisses.

The rush of need overwhelmed her, made her cling to him. His hot breath skimmed across her neck followed by his lips, and he lifted her off her feet. Between her legs, his length pressed, hard and throbbing, and she reached down and stroked it. He shuddered.

"You're a terrible tease," he whispered, nibbling her earlobe.

"Isn't teasing not giving you what you want?" She pressed harder against him and he moved under her touch. "I plan to give you what you want." She unbuttoned his jeans. "Is this what you want?"

"Yes," he groaned.

Unzipping him, she slipped her hand inside his underwear. He was hot and thick in her hand, making her slick with wanting him. He opened his mouth against her throat, and as she tightened her grasp, the harsh, lusty sound he made shivered through her. "Is it good?"

As she moved her hand up his length, he shuddered. His shoulders kept her against the wall.

"I want to feel you inside me," she whispered. Still stroking him, she used her free hand and opened his jeans.

He eased her to her feet and took her mouth with his, pushed her jeans down until she kicked them free, and pressed a condom into her hands.

Her fingers couldn't seem to grasp the foil and tear it open at the same time. She groaned, fumbling the packet in her hands, aching for him to move higher. To slide inside her. She turned her face away from him, breaking their kiss so she could look at the condom package.

"I want you now." Jason growled. He tried to bring her face back to his, but she put the packet between her teeth and tore it open before he could capture her mouth again. Deprived of her mouth, he bit her neck at the curve of her shoulder, sucked hard on her tender flesh.

She slid the condom over him. "Now."

He lifted her off the floor and thrust into her in one smooth motion. She gasped. Her fingers tangled through his hair as he pounded into her against the wall. The wall behind her felt cold against her hot skin. Her body opened to him. His hot panting ruffled through her hair. She heard herself sobbing for faster, harder, more, forever. He responded, thrusting harder until she shook apart.

"Cass!" he shouted. Then his knees buckled and she found herself sliding to the hall floor, wrapped around him, filled with him.

They lay in a tangle for a long time, still wearing their coats. His jeans were wrapped around his ankles, hers lay in a heap against the back door, her shoes stuck in the legs. She trembled with the aftermath of release.

"I think you were right," he murmured, trailing his fingers along her cheek. "It's got to be witchcraft."

Trying to focus her eyes, she stared at the door. "I don't know who's enthralling who. I do know I'm never going to look at this house the same way."

Jason looked around. "I suppose not. Are you ready to move?"

"I suppose the wood won't carry itself in." She sat up. Her body still shook. "You know my view of the house isn't going to be the only thing changed when you leave."

"Oh?"

He sounded hesitant, but she didn't know why. What did he have to be afraid of? She'd be the one left behind with the memories. She touched the wall behind her. How would she walk past this wall everyday without remembering?

She didn't want to drag the moment down. To frighten him away with her fears. She wanted to remain cheerful so on those rare occasions when he did remember her, it would be good. "I'm going to be bowlegged."

"We could experiment, if you're interested. There are a couple of positions that wouldn't leave you so bowlegged." Grinning, he stood, pulling his pants up.

If this storm snowed them in for a month, she'd be willing to do all kinds of experimenting. "I have to bring in more wood."

"I'll give you a hand." He reached down and helped her up, but pulled her back into his arms. "I wasn't blowing smoke before. I've never known a woman who turns me on the way you do. You're amazing."

"I'm flattered. The competition is stiff." Cass shifted out of his arms so she could pull on her jeans. Stella. Beautiful Stella. She must not have pushed Jason's buttons. Unless he was lying. No real reason for him to, though. He had her in whatever way he wanted so didn't need to flatter her into bed.

But now they needed wood. Outside, she held her coat closed while crossing the garage to the door leading to her woodpile. She should have brought the carrier, but in the sudden need to be away from Jason, had forgotten it.

The snow was falling faster. If clearing the tree had taken much more time, they wouldn't have gotten back up the mountain. By dark, their tire tracks would be covered. If it kept up like this, they would have to fight the front door open in the morning.

She loaded up her arms and turned. Smiling, Jason stood behind her. The urge to frown at him overcame her, and she didn't know why. "Grab an armload and we won't have to come back out tonight."

"Will this be enough?"

"Yes."

"For all night?"

Cass stopped in the doorway. She'd picked up more than she could hold and didn't want to drop it right now. It hung in her arms like lead. Her shoulders ached. "I've lived up here for five years. I know how much wood we'll need to get through a night." She shoved past him.

"No reason to get snippy," he called after her.

Inside, she stacked the wood in the box by the fireplace. The fire had died down, but there should be enough embers to bring it back up. She was being snippy. It welled out of her like oil seeping from the ground. She set a small split log on the embers. If she wanted to chase Jason away, this would do it. Have great sex with him and then snap at him. It was becoming a pattern.

Balancing a huge armload of wood, Jason walked in, looking wary.

"Here, let me get some of that." She stood up and took the top pieces off his stack. "I'm sorry. This is not something I normally do."

"Snap?"

She felt herself turning red. Sleeping around probably didn't seem like a big deal to him, but she'd seen *Almost Famous*. He lived it. "Have affairs."

"I didn't think so. If you had, some smart guy would have grabbed you up by now." He eased the rest of the wood into the box.

Cass put another piece of wood on the fire. A joke. That's all this was to him. A joke and a passing fancy. Anger welled up again, and she needed to cap it before it got away from her. This should be light, not an ugly scene. She needed to stop making this more than casual sex between consenting adults. He was not going to fall madly in love with her and decide to take her away from all this, and she had to stop herself from falling in love with him. "I'm going to go take a shower before I get dinner."

"Sure." He frowned, but didn't say anything else. As she walked into the bathroom she heard him noodling on his guitar. He wasn't playing *"I'm Looking Through You,"* so she felt safe enough to step under the water.

* * * *

After her shower, Cass brought out the hanging grill for the fireplace. Jason's eyes lit up when he realized how she planned to cook dinner. While eating his hamburgers and baked potatoes cooked in the fireplace, he acted like a big, happy kid. Afterward, they sang campfire songs for a while, then put in a movie and cuddled on the couch. While she lay back in his arms, he seemed comfortable, just watching the movie and holding her. Michael had never wanted to do that. He'd either critiqued the acting and directing or told her the movie was a waste of time, and wouldn't she rather go see a play? Not until her first winter on the mountain had she been able to watch movies again. That first long winter, when she'd discovered she could stand on her own.

"Why do you call it In the Pines Campground?" Jason asked as she took the DVD out of the player.

"I named it after a song my dad likes."

He brightened. "Can you sing it?"

"I'm sure I have it on a CD here someplace."

"I want to hear you sing it."

Her father had sung it to her since she was a baby. The words should be encoded in her DNA. "In the pines, in the pines where the sun never shines and you shiver when the cold winds blow. True love, true love, won't you write to me, not even your mammy knows." Then her mind went blank. She was singing for a singer. Her down-home, untrained, amateur voice sounded fine around a campfire, but he knew how to sing.

"I forget the rest. Something about being in jail, I think. Maybe getting married. Those were the popular themes. My dad could sing it for you."

"Sing the tune for me again." He picked up his guitar.

She snapped the DVD back into its keeper case.

"Come on, you've been singing all night," he encouraged. He picked out a couple of notes. "In the pines, in the pines where the sun never shines…"

Because she had no choice, she sang the small bit she remembered so he could pick out the tune on his guitar. He played the bit again. "I could call my dad and ask him what the rest of the words are," she offered.

"Ah, but then he might catch on," Jason said. "I don't want to be the guest of honor at a shotgun wedding, remember?"

"True."

The notes spun into the air as he started picking the tune out again. "I'll track it down. I just wondered. I'm not much for tree watching, but I know a pine when I see it, and you don't seem to have any."

"No, it's mostly elms, oaks, beeches and maples around here." His fingers had played across her skin the same way they now strummed the strings. Masterfully, confident…almost lovingly. Remembering it, everywhere on her tingled. Her phone rang, startling her. She darted across the room and got it on the second ring. "Hello?"

"Cassie, are you all tucked in for the storm?"

"Oh hi, Mom. I am." Cass leaned against the wall. At times, her mother seemed psychic. When she was a child, she'd been sure of it, but later realized she just lived in a small town with lots of eyes. Times like now she wasn't so sure it was only nosy neighbors who clued her mother in to her wrongdoing.

"How about your guest?"

"He's fine."

"I wish you weren't having this storm while he was up there. I don't like to think about novices in this weather."

Jason was playing something softly and note perfect. Her mother probably assumed it was a CD. "I'm sure he'll be fine. I'll keep a watch on him," Cass said. Without missing a note, Jason looked over his shoulder and winked at her.

"Your father and I were just talking about you taking winter guests. If you had good weather, it wouldn't be so bad. You know, Sue could get you a pack of guests in the winter. She always has people clamoring for her retreat things, and those folks always want to be left alone anyway. But I worry about this weather."

"I guess this will make a good test run." Head down, eyes closed, Jason had turned back to his playing. Cass doubted she would be treating the regular guests the way she treated him. Or anyone, actually.

"I should warn you, Finn Runningwater is just wild with jealousy."

"Why?"

"He's sure something is going to happen between you and your guest."

Cass rolled her eyes, and for once her mother didn't seem to hear it.

"Not that I would blame you."

"Mother!"

"Oh, honey, you're a grown woman and I must tell you, that Jason is quite nice to look at."

"Dad isn't around, is he?"

Jason turned around, frowning curiously.

"No, he's watching television downstairs, but he did defend you to Finn. He told him it was your choice what you did and he, Finn that is, had no claim on you."

"When did this happen?"

"At Ida's this afternoon. We went in for lunch. You know, I don't think Paul likes Finn much."

Cass put her hand over her eyes. Ida's, which meant Ida had been there as well as Finn, her parents and Paul, and an assortment of townsfolk. As far as they knew, nothing was happening on the mountain, but they were making something up anyway. Heaven help her if they ever found out what was going on. "Why don't you think Paul likes Finn?"

"Well, they got into it today. Paul said you knew what you were about and Finn should keep out of it, and Finn said if you'd gone off with Michael then you must not know what you were about so somebody had to keep watch over you. Well, you know Paul and Paul was right there with you. He just about went through the roof."

Paul rarely controlled himself when he could go full hissy fit, and if her mother said 'through the roof' it must have been Paul classic, complete with broken dishes. The town would be talking until spring.

"Paul told Finn he had best keep his opinions to himself because he wasn't there and didn't know what happened. He said he doubted even you knew all of what had happened between you two." Shirley paused for a beat. "What do you suppose he meant by that?"

Her stomach lurched. Living next door to her and Michael in New York, Paul had gotten a front row seat to every fight, heard every slammed door. He'd also seen their comings and goings, and who with. Michael didn't think she'd known how often he'd held private rehearsals with the beautiful and exotic Sasha, whose real name was Sarah, and who worshipped Michael. Sasha's number had appeared often on Michael's phone, but Paul no doubt knew Sasha had been in their apartment many times when she hadn't been home. And about the other women who'd come and gone, whose names were still a mystery. Huh, Paul was a better secret keeper than she'd given him credit for. "I have no idea," she said, and hoped it fooled her mother.

"Oh, well, you know how dramatic Paul is."

Growing up, Cass had thought dramatic meant homosexual. In college, she'd learned dramatic and homosexual were synonyms only in her mother's thesaurus. No way to tell if her mother was referring to Paul's sex life or his penchant for screeching and giving people the hairy eyeball.

"He broke Finn's mug."

So, broken dishes, after all. Apparently her mother was using the theatrical sense of the word. "Is that so?"

"He did. Paul just snatched that mug out of the case and threw it against the wall. Ida told him, Finn that is, not to worry about it."

"Mom, I'm amazed at how you all can take nothing and turn it into high drama."

"It's a gift, sweetheart. We talked to Bill Wernick today, too."

"Did he get to witness the mug smashing?"

"Yes, he was there. We asked him about that pasture."

Though not keen on her parents running her business, if it got her mother off the subject of what might be happening on the mountain, she had to encourage it. Besides, she wanted to know what was going on in Bill's mind. "And he said?"

"You know he'll decide in the next few days. He's getting so old, Cassie, and the price of mutton is just bottoming out. He said he might wait until after lambing and sell the flock and that pasture. His daughter wants to move home to take care of him, and her husband has a horse stable where he rents horses to tourists. They thought it might be a good thing around here, and they're getting squeezed out, where they are. Too many other people in the business. Plus, his daughter would be right on hand to take care of him in his infirmity. We told Bill that he had to give you first crack if he did sell. He said he'd call you after the storm passed."

"Good, as long as the lines don't go down, I'll be right here."

"If the lines do go down, you'll be right there, too. Do you have your cellular phone charged up?"

Damn. In all the arguing with Finn, running down the mountain for condoms and having sex in the hall, she'd forgotten to check her cellphone. "No, I didn't. I'll go get it right now."

"Okay, honey, I just wanted to make sure you were all right."

"We're fine." Cass bit her lip at the slip. We? As if the whole town didn't already have her trysting with Jason.

"That's good. You keep warm and don't forget about your cellular phone."

"'Bye, Mom." She hung up and headed for the dining room cupboard, where she kept the phone.

"What's the big news?" Jason asked.

"Oh, Finn is wild with jealousy about you being here on the mountain and he got into a fight with Paul about it at the diner today, probably while we were working at that tree. Anyway, Paul smashed Finn's mug, which is sort of like being banned from the diner."

"Sounds like a tribal ritual." His lips thinned. Paul wasn't the only one who didn't like Finn.

"Sort of. Paul made an unfortunate comment to the whole world about me and my ex-husband." She plugged in the phone on the sideboard. When she turned around, Jason stood behind her. He looked furious.

"What did he say?" His eyes narrowed to match his thinned lips.

"He just said he didn't think I knew everything that went on between Michael and I. Paul lived next door, so he got to hear and see a lot. There was another woman or two." Cass looked down. Michael's cheating still humiliated her. She could read all the books she wanted on how it hadn't been her fault, but if that were true, whose fault was it? If she had been a better wife or a better lover, Michael wouldn't have had to go looking, would he?

"Your husband cheated on you?" Jason stood up.

Biting her lip, she nodded.

"What a bastard!" he shouted, which made her flinch. He put his hand on her shoulders. "Cassie, why did you let him do that? Why didn't you kick him to the curb?"

"I wouldn't say I let him." She'd only left the apartment for hours, told Michael when she would return. When he'd straggled home after "late rehearsals" with cat hair on his clothes and the smell of cigarettes in his hair, she just hadn't asked.

She'd just never stopped him.

"Cassie," Jason said, "how could he?"

"Maybe he was missing something at home." Cass gnawed her lip.

"What? Great sex? Home cooking?" His voice hitched. "Companionship? Come on. Cassie, as much as I know you, I know he had plenty of that with you. Did he tell you he was missing something?"

She shook her head.

"You can't make a promise like marriage and not mean it."

"I meant it," she snapped. She'd stood at the altar, sworn to love and honor through sickness and health, for richer or poorer 'til death, meaning every word.

"You did, but he didn't. He can't have ever loved you. If he didn't want to try and if he didn't talk to you about what he wanted, then he didn't fucking try."

"He said I wasn't cut out to be married to an actor."

"Why?"

"I hated parties. We had to go to a lot of them to socialize and I hated it. He would leave me alone in a booth, and I'd spend the whole night miserable."

"Why did he leave you alone?"

Cass opened her mouth and then closed it. She'd never wondered why Michael left her alone, he just had. While he networked, she nursed a Shirley Temple and talked to people who felt sorry enough for her they sat with her for a little while. "Didn't Stella leave you alone?"

"We're not talking about Stella, and no, she didn't. She wore me on her arm like a giant piece of jewelry. The point is, I wouldn't have left you alone. No gentleman would. He was a jerk, Cass. You're better off without him."

"Why do you care?"

Jason let her go and turned away. She waited for a long time, hoping he would turn around and say something stupid about how he'd fallen madly in love with her and wanted to take her away from all this. Or he wanted to stay here with her forever. Or just how he'd fallen madly in love with her. They could work out the details later. He walked to the fireplace, and leaning on the mantle, watched the flames. Moments passed, then he said, "I guess because I have four sisters. Two divorced. I learned all the names girls call rotten guys, and pretty much had it beaten into me that being one of those wasn't acceptable."

"I don't think you are."

He snorted, but continued to stare into the flames. Cass laced her fingers together. Maybe he was thinking about Stella again. Should she do something about it?

The set of his shoulders warned her off. He'd put up a barrier she couldn't cross, one she couldn't bear to live with for another moment. "Jason?"

"What?"

Good question. "Are you mad at me about something?"

"No."

He sounded angry. "Are you sure?" Sweat drenched her palms, and she felt kind of sick that he might be angry because she hadn't worked hard enough to save her marriage. There were things she could have done. She could have been more social at parties and more discerning about her taste in movies and plays. Made herself sexier. Confronted Michael about the other women and asked him what he got from them that she didn't give. She could have learned to be the kind of woman Michael wanted even if that woman wasn't her.

Would Jason want her to become someone else to please him? Or would he be happy with who she already was? Would great sex, home cooking and companionship be enough for him? Since he wasn't staying anyway, none of that would probably matter.

"I'm not angry at you."

He muttered something else under his breath, but she couldn't summon the courage to ask him to repeat himself. "Well, I've got some work to do." She shuffled into the kitchen and located the index cards. Working on the summer schedule would at least distract her. The papers together, she set everything on the dining room table. He was still standing by the mantle staring into the fire. The air crackled with tension, which could be coming from him, or her worrying about him.

She sat down. Michael used to give her the silent treatment, and it always made her feel small and worthless. Picking up the first blank card, she stared at it. She'd done this for the last three years yet couldn't remember how to start. Sinking into a small dark place where all she could do was struggle not to cry was all too familiar, though.

"Stop it."

Chapter 11

Cass was on her feet listening to the chair bang into the cabinet behind her before she realized she'd shouted. Jason whirled around, eyes wide and mouth open. Her chest heaved with unshed tears. For a long moment, nothing moved but the fire.

"Stop what?" he asked.

"Shutting me out. You said I didn't do anything wrong, but you're not talking to me." Tears spilled down her cheeks. This wasn't supposed to happen. She knew how to roll over and be quiet, how to avoid a fight. Screaming and knocking over furniture wasn't avoiding anything. He would leave. Pack his things and go, much sooner than she could stand.

Hide. She needed to hide. From him, from her life, from everyone. Wasn't that the point of being here on the mountain? That's why she'd never told anyone why her marriage came apart. But then she'd gone and invited the whole world in, in the form of Jason Callisto, and allowed him to see her mistakes. To judge her. Condemn her.

Dodging through the kitchen, she headed for her bedroom, where she might be able to hide, but Jason caught her at the hall door. She tried to pull away, but he dragged her against his chest.

"I'm sorry," he whispered into her hair. "I didn't realize what I was doing. I was trying not to take it out on you. I was angry, but never at you."

At last her tears dried and she relaxed into his arms. He didn't seem upset about her crying. What was he trying not to take out on her? The thought of getting an answer frightened her. Everything seemed so nice right now and she didn't want to screw it up again. He tilted her face up to his. His jaw flexed as he studied her face.

"I'm sorry, Cassandra, *bella*, for everything."

"It's not your fault I married badly."

He winced. "Let me make it up to you." Leaning down, he captured her mouth in a sweet, gentle kiss. Before she had time to recover, he'd lifted her in his arms and carried her into the bedroom.

Kissing away the last of her tears, he laid her on the bed, tangled his long fingers through her hair. Slipping her hands under his shirt, she caressed his warm bare skin. He sighed and moved away a little, pulled his shirt off. Then he captured her hand, guided it across the tight muscles of his abdomen and up his chest to his lips.

"So beautiful," he murmured, pressing his lips to her palm. "So sweet. Cassandra."

The low, intimate tone of his voice went through her and settled warmly inside. She still felt dried out and jittery from her tantrum, but he smoothed across her body, taming her nerves even as he pulled them tight. He began unbuttoning her shirt, kissing each new exposed bit of skin. When he reached her belly button, he dipped his tongue into her. Unable to gather breath, she clutched the bed. Heat welled through her. They'd had sex before, so why was this so dizzyingly new?

Jason unbuttoned her jeans and then lowered the zipper. Sliding up beside her, he slipped his hand inside her clothing, laid it across her stomach.

"Let me make love to you, *bella*," he whispered. His hot breath caressed her ear. "I want to kiss every part of you. I'll show you what a woman feels like when she's with a man who loves her. Lie still and let me do everything." He covered her mouth with his.

Eyes closed, she allowed herself to just feel. He inched her jeans over her hips and down her legs, dropped her jeans off the side of the bed, then knelt at her feet and rolled her onto her stomach. She pressed her face into a pillow as he kneaded her feet with his strong hands, rubbed each toe with exquisite care. Then he licked her instep, and when his mouth closed over her smallest toe, she couldn't hold back a moan of pure delight. He suckled it as he massaged her ankle. When he shifted his mouth to her next toe, he moved his hands to the bottom of her calf. He worked across each of her toes and up her calf to her knee. She barely remembered how to breathe.

"Is it good?" he asked, setting her foot down.

Trapped between agony and nirvana, she could only reply with a whimper. Her feet felt lopsided, like one was jealous of the attention the other had received. Her heartbeat slowed to a languorous pace.

Her other foot, he rubbed with the same attentive care, then sucked each toe as he kneaded her calf. When he'd finished, he kissed the back of each knee, exploring the dips and grooves with his tongue. Cass dug her toes into the loose sheets, and as he started working his way up her thighs, clutched the edge of the mattress. He dug into the muscles, squeezing and releasing until she wasn't sure she had muscles anymore. A low feral growl built in the back of her throat when he reached the tops of her thighs, in anticipation of his skilled fingers touching between her legs, massaging her, filling her.

He reached up and pulled her shirt off her back and unclasped her bra, allowing it to fall loose. Lingering for a moment, he traced her spine, then shifted forward, leaned down and kissed her buttocks. Just when she thought she couldn't stand not feeling him against her anymore, he rested his body along the length of hers, keeping most of his weight on his knees and elbows. He kissed her shoulders. "You know you're beautiful, don't you, *bella*?" he murmured. "You know you're completely intoxicating? You're irresistible."

Jason's words made her breath catch in her throat. *Beautiful. Intoxicating. Irresistible.* His bare chest pressed her back. His jeans chafed her massaged, weak legs. His penis nudged, hard and erect, against her buttocks. One small movement, and he could slide inside her, fill her, pushing away this sweet inertia for a much sweeter arousal. She arched her hips upward.

His chest moved against her as he drew in a sharp breath. "So utterly intoxicating." He pushed himself upright and began massaging her back. His thumbs in her spine were deliciously accurate, and her muscles uncoiled at his command. She lay helpless as he worked away years' worth of tension. Randomly, he would place kisses on her back as he continued to manipulate her with his fingers. When she thought she might dissolve into the bed if he continued for one more minute, he stopped.

He rolled her over, pulled her slack bra away and tossed it on her jeans. "You don't, do you?" he asked, brushing her hair off her face. "You don't know how beautiful you are."

Nothing in his expression revealed the lie behind the terrifying sincerity in his voice. The look in his dark eyes weighted her to the bed, fixing her like a butterfly in a case, and he roamed down with a hand and cupped her breast. Eyes on hers, he licked his lips as if he wanted to say something else, then leaned over and took her nipple between his lips, traced it with the tip of his tongue.

Wrung out with pleasure, she didn't know how she would endure another minute, how she would survive having it end. Tears of frustrated desire leaked from the sides of her eyes. Aching. Throbbing. A vast emptiness he seemed in no hurry to fill swelled in her and she seemed unable to communicate her need.

He turned, devoting equal attention to her other breast. First licking and then suckling with a maddeningly slow rhythm. Cass clutched his back, distantly aware of her short fingernails digging into his skin. When he lifted his head, a small smile played around his mouth. Then he reached for the condoms on the bedside table. When he turned back, he leaned down and kissed her while he unfastened his jeans. She grabbed for the packet, but he closed his hand around it.

"I want to do everything, *bella*," he murmured, shoving his jeans down his hips.

With the same agonizing slowness, he entered her. A sigh came from her, and she sank her nails into his skin. She couldn't remember anything. Nothing. Her life shrank to this pinpoint of time. The beat of her heart picked up pace with the pulse of his thrusts. Climax came over her like the tide, ever increasing crests of pleasure until one crest obliterated her.

Gasping, she clung to him as he shifted them so her head rested on his chest. He stroked her long hair, murmuring. She never wanted to move again. Every part of her body was warm, loved and exhausted. Her eyes drowsed closed, and she took a deep breath, imprinting the scent of Jason's skin on her mind.

So this was how a woman felt when she was with a man who loved her.

Hours later, she woke, and reached for Jason, but the other side of the bed was cold. Through the view in the fireplace into the living room, he sat on the couch, long legs propped on her coffee table, warming his feet in the fire and staring at the dying embers.

When had it gone wrong? She'd screwed up, but when? At some point, however, she'd gone and fallen in love with him. She hadn't meant to. Been trying not to. This was supposed to be a little affair she could remember into her old age. Two weeks of passionate sex with no strings. But somewhere along the line she'd gotten tangled up in invisible strings. Was it three days ago when they had their snowball fight, before he'd even offered his proposal? This afternoon when they'd talked about Stella? Today when they'd come home from Gaitherberg and he'd wanted her so much he could hardly wait to get inside the house? When he got so angry about Michael she'd imagined he would have loved her too much to hurt her that way?

It didn't matter. She'd made the fatal mistake of falling in love with the transient musician and now she had scores of winters in her future to remember it. Cass pressed her face into her pillow and let silent tears fall until she fell back to sleep.

* * * *

Jason stared at the glowing orange embers. How had he allowed this to happen again? He'd gone into this cheap, short run relationship, everything up front, wanting to get Stella out of his system. He'd done that all right, but he'd managed to replace her with Cassandra, who wanted to use him to escape this little town. And to make the whole mess perfect, he felt guilty because he wouldn't be her savior. He couldn't be her savior.

Her ex-husband had done a number on her, teaching her to doubt herself. Jason could imagine what she must have been like before Michael, based on the small miracles she'd worked after him. She'd turned around an entire town almost on her own. She burned brighter than all of them.

She certainly heated him up.

He'd never known a woman who turned him on so easily and consistently. She was always warm, willing and fantastic. Hell, he could go in there right now and be in her before she woke up, and she'd still be ready and enthusiastic. Two years of celibacy behind him, and she was scorching that out of his system fast.

What would it have been like if he'd met her before Stella? In those few months between her divorce and his fatal error. He wouldn't have seen the trap for what it was—the wronged woman, the siren ready to smash him on her rocks—and he'd have fallen for her without looking back. He'd have been really, really happy for however long it took Cass to get what she wanted. Happier than he'd been with Stella.

But in the end, when she had what she needed, she'd have gone. Just like Stella. They always left. This time, he had to be the one who left first. He couldn't be fooled by her false love.

He loved her.

Not lust. He knew the difference well, and while there was a fair amount of lust in this three-day-old relationship, it certainly wasn't founded on that. He'd been smitten with her the day they'd gone into town and he saw how proud they all were of her. Then watching her surefootedness, dealing with those two vixens in the grocery store. Once upon a time, he'd have lapped up the kind of attention those little girls threw at him, but one night of Cassie's sweet company spotlighted how empty it was. Every moment he spent in her company confirmed it. He'd been right the first night, thinking he could curl up on her couch and fall asleep. If only he'd stopped there.

He stood and stretched. Should try to get some sleep, or barring that, get some time wrapped in Cassie's arms. Too soon he'd have to leave, and he wanted to get as much of her as possible before the inevitable.

* * * *

Cass sat at the dining room table doing something with index cards and frowning. Jason had discovered a deck of cards on the video shelf and was trying to remember how to play solitaire. He hadn't slept well. Once in bed, he'd wrapped his arms around her and lain in a half-awake twilight zone, feeling her body curl against his in the darkness, warm and heavy with sleep.

Nothing had been said about the night before. If she'd woken up while he'd sat on her couch beating himself up, he didn't know, but he'd noticed tear stains on her pillow this morning. He wanted to believe she had been crying because of the argument. The devil on his left shoulder, though, kept whispering that she sensed her opportunity slipping away.

They had cuddled in silence until hunger drove them to the kitchen. Breakfast had been quiet, but not strained. She'd started working on her project as soon as they'd cleaned up. He'd watched TV for a while before finding the cards. Now staring at them, he couldn't focus on them because all he could think about was how to get more time with her. He didn't mind sitting in the same room with her, not talking or touching, only being together. Liked it, in fact. There was no pressure to be entertaining or entertained. This, he could live with. Forever.

If it was real. It felt real. It looked real.

But his judgment wasn't reliable on that subject. Stella had looked real, too.

The phone rang. Cass shifted out of her seat and picked it up on the second ring. "Hello?" She brightened. Jason wondered sourly if Finn was calling before coming up this time. "Oh, hi, Bill. Did you weather the storm all right?"

Bill? Did she have somebody else on the line? No, Bill was the guy selling the land. He smiled down at his cards. Good. Not another guy. But what right did he have to be jealous, anyway? Was she trying to make him jealous?

That didn't make sense. If she were, wouldn't she dangle Finn in front of him, instead of a guy who was selling land?

How was she dangling anybody, when Bill had called her?

Maybe this was what a nervous breakdown felt like.

"How much are you looking to get?" she asked.

Cass was quiet for too long for the price to be good. He wondered what kind of negotiator she was. He'd never been good at it, which was why he had an talent manager, a business manager and a lawyer.

"I hear your daughter is moving back with her husband," she said. "Are they bringing their stable, too? It would be awful good for their business if my business was good, wouldn't it?" She looked at the floor, nodding as if Bill could hear her nod through the phone line. "Well, at that price I'll have to think about it. Do you mind if I take a drive over there?"

How far away was this pasture? Would she try wading through the snow to get there today? The Weather Channel said it would warm up, but a lot of snow had fallen overnight.

"I don't think it'll take me that long to decide. Thanks for giving me first crack, Bill." She turned back toward the kitchen, but her voice carried through. "Well, thanks anyway. Maybe I'll take a ride over there as soon as the snow settles. 'Bye, Bill."

Cass hung up the phone and leaned on the wall, and he waited.

"The pasture?" he asked without looking up. Maybe he was playing it too cool. Or not cool enough. He supposed it depended on whether she was genuine or fake. "How much does he want?"

"Too much."

Jason nodded. He didn't have any idea what land cost out here, and only a passing idea what land cost in LA. "Is it worth it?"

"To me it's worth about half what he's asking. To anybody else, I can't imagine it's worth even that. Unless somebody from DC decides to build a little country house here." She sat down on the couch next to him. He relaxed more than he'd realized he'd tensed up. "That black seven can go over here."

"Oh, thanks." He moved the card, revealing an ace. "So what do you do now?"

"I'll go take a look and then I'll ask Finn to barter him down some."

He should have known Finn would enter into this somewhere. Finn had his fingers on the pulse of everything. Or maybe just her pulse. Or maybe he was over thinking it. "Why Finn?"

"Because he does books for both of us so he knows what position we're both in." Cass studied his cards.

"Isn't that unethical?"

She shrugged. "It's the way things have always been done."

"And if he decides you're in a better position than Bill is?" Maybe Tessa, his sister and lawyer, would be willing to give Cass a hand with this purchase. How would she feel about his sister stepping in? Tessa would get a good deal and then Cass would owe him a favor. She might be grateful. Very grateful, depending on the quality of Tessa's deal, and his sister was known for the quality of her deals. That was a nice thought.

"He won't."

"Because he's madly in love with you?" Jason tried not to let the venom welling up his throat leak out, but the thought of her grateful to Finn made him want to break things.

"No, because he does our books. He'll check the market value and both our finances and come up with a deal that's fair for both of us. Finn doesn't put me on a pedestal because he's attracted to me. Your two of diamonds is up." Cass hooked her hand through his elbow.

"What's fun about that?" What kind of a would-be-beau was Finn, if he wouldn't work on Cassie's behalf just because it was hers? That was the point of being with her. Why would Finn even want to be with Cassie if he couldn't be on her side, making sure she got the best deal, the nicest table and the sparkliest jewels? He moved the two of diamonds onto the ace of diamonds. "You'd look good on a pedestal."

"Thanks, but that's not the way Finn thinks. He takes his position as the town's only accountant very seriously. Sometimes I think it's not so much me he's attracted to as the fact that our seasons don't conflict." She leaned her cheek on his shoulder.

He took a deep breath. Her cheek on his shoulder and her long hair coiling down his back felt good. Almost as good as having her hair trailing around him as she straddled him. A shiver of desire rose, and he suppressed it. He didn't want her to think he just wanted her for sex, which didn't make sense because this whole relationship was built on sex. Wasn't it? "Your seasons?"

"Tax season and camping season."

Jason made a face. Finn didn't know what he was dealing with. Cassie would burn him out in one season. Tax or camping. "What a romantic." He kissed her forehead and was rewarded with a smile. "Did you know your boyfriend was so dull?"

"Yeah. That's why he's not my boyfriend. I think it's the last name. He got teased mercilessly in school because of it, and I think it made him get as dull and normal as he could."

"Didn't he have some Runningwater relatives around?"

"Not really. They were sort of stereotypical drunken Indians. Nobody's even sure where they came from. They'd just always been here. Finn is the last one. His mother ran off on the back of a motorcycle when we were just kids. He was mostly raised by other kids' moms including mine.

His father died of cirrhosis just before he graduated high school. That probably sent him over the normal edge."

"Oh, the dark secrets of a small town." Just because he felt bad for the guy didn't make Jason any less contemptuous of him. Finn had known Cassie all these years and hadn't managed to snag her because he couldn't be what she wanted. Finn could have protected her from Michael. She didn't want anything extraordinary. Or he might be falling for her story. Jason flipped over his last card. "I lose."

"You're giving up?"

"I don't have any more moves."

Cass reached around him and started shifting cards. "One of the great things about long winters trapped on the mountain is you become a world-class solitaire player." She finished sorting cards into their correct piles and dropped the last king on the top.

"How did you do that?"

She grinned at him. "Sheer genius."

He kissed her. Her mouth always tasted sweet and wild. Her body quivered as he pulled her closer. Did he want to make love to her now or later? Correction. He wanted to make love to her now, he just wanted to be sure if it would be better now on the couch or later, after the anticipation had built up a little, in her bed. He stroked her curls, lifting his lips from hers. Later. He liked a little anticipation, and in the last three days he hadn't allowed himself any. "I still think it's witchcraft."

"You think whatever you want, mister."

He brushed his fingers through her curls again, loving the way her hair wrapped around his fingers like silken chains. If he could be sure the chains she offered were all like this, he wouldn't mind being locked up at all. "So when can we go see this marvelous pasture?"

"Maybe tomorrow, if it warms up enough. I'd like to see some of this snow melt off before I try to drive up the path. Why do you want to see it?"

"The curiosity is killing me now." By her smirk, he knew he'd pulled off a light tone, but he was serious. This was important to her and it was close. The thought of going into business with her hadn't left his mind. It would keep her near him and give him the upper hand. He tried to smirk back, but something real must have slipped through, because she gave him a funny look.

"Well, I'll make sure you see the pasture before you go." She stood up and walked back to her task.

Jason watched her go. She'd dressed in baggy jeans and an oversized flannel shirt and pulled her hair into an untidy ponytail. It was the least seductive outfit he'd ever seen and yet he wanted to rip it off her and make love to her on the floor in front of the fireplace. He smiled and had to duck his head when she reached the table where she could see him. He shuffled the cards. Wouldn't she be trying to seduce him more actively if she were trying to get something out of him? He'd asked her to go naked, and she hadn't done that. Most women he'd encountered would have leapt at the chance. She hadn't jumped through any of his hoops.

Could it be she wasn't trying to seduce him and trap him? That he'd fallen ass backward into something real?

He set aside the cards. She had index cards printed with her neat handwriting spread across the table. Standing behind her chair, he looked over the orderly mess. He ran his fingers down her ponytail.

"You shouldn't do that unless you mean it," she said, setting a freshly filled out card aside. In neat capital letters she'd written *Star Gazing Wes Wednesday 10:00.*

"I mean it." He wrapped a bright curl around his finger. "I wish I'd had more time to court you before we made love."

"Oh?" Her shoulders relaxed. She stacked another card on the first. This one read *Star Gazing Wes Friday 10:00.* The handwriting on this one looked a little less neat.

"It would have been nice to tease and touch, knowing I had to wait."

"You want to wait?" Her voice sounded warm.

"I would have liked to taste you slowly," he said, trailing his fingers down her soft neck.

"Just me?"

"Just you, *bella.*" He leaned down and kissed her warm flesh. "Just you."

She shivered. Her pulse throbbed against his lips. Closing his eyes, he ran his tongue along the vein.

"Mmm," she hummed. Right now he could lay her down on the floor and she would welcome him. His groin tightened, but without the needy feeling he'd had three days ago. Her breath came in shallow gasps that matched his. Her pen clattered on the table. He ran his hands down her arms until he could lace his fingers though hers.

"Cassandra, *bella*, I have to let you go now."

"Why?" she wailed.

"You want to let the anticipation build, don't you?"

She shivered.

He stood up, still holding her hands.

"You just want to torment me," she complained, releasing his hands.

"That's the plan." He smiled and stepped back so she could stand.

"Hmm." She looked up at him through her lashes. "This sounds like a challenge."

"A challenge?" He loved the way this woman's mind worked. Not a passive lover, in any sense.

"Sure. To see who breaks first." The corner of her mouth curved.

"Are there rules to this challenge?"

"Like?"

Jason looked down into her eyes. Just the thought of a challenge had him feeling hotter. He knew he should have something since he'd brought it up, but the sexual tension in the air muddled his mind. "No wardrobe changes," he said.

"Fair enough."

That was too easy. She stood in front of him with a small smile playing on her lips, as if she knew something he didn't. She probably did. Like, that he was incapable of resisting her for long. "Aren't you concerned about what you're going to sleep in tonight?"

"Oh, I'm pretty sure it'll be the same thing I've slept in since you got here. Nothing. I just want to know what I get when I win."

"When you win?" He'd intended to sound saucy and dubious, but it came out thick with sexual tension. Perhaps he'd already lost this bet.

"I expect to." She walked past him toward the kitchen. "And I expect to do it well before bed time," she tossed over her shoulder, shooting him a steamy look.

He followed her. Everywhere on him felt unpleasantly tight now. If he hadn't introduced this stupid challenge, he would have had her against the wall by now.

She filled a mug with water. "Cup of tea?"

Chapter 12

Jason blinked. "What?"

She looked at him over her shoulder. "Would you like a cup of tea?"

"Oh, yeah." She was cool enough to make tea? He already wanted to cave on the whole challenge.

"You never did say what I would win." She filled another mug and got out two tea bags. When the microwave dinged, she took her cup out and put his in. "If it is a challenge, there should be a prize."

"Sex with me isn't enough of a prize?"

"It is, but I'll get that anyway." She dropped a tea bag into her cup. Then she started tracing the lip of the mug with the tip of her finger. He couldn't stop staring at her finger on the white porcelain. "So what will I win?"

"What would you like?" Hell. If he'd handed her a blank check she could do less damage. Did she know that?

"Oh my. Anything I want?" She licked her lips. That distracted him from her finger on the edge of the mug, but didn't help any. The microwave dinged, so she took out his cup and put in the tea bag. Then she started adding milk and sugar to the first cup. "Oh, I should have asked if you wanted this one. Do you want it?"

Was she doing that purr intentionally? It didn't matter. It felt like fingers running up and down his spine. "No. I—it— I'm going to take a shower."

"A cold one?" She gave him a slow smile.

Yes, a cold one. He summoned some self-control. "I haven't shaved yet and I want to be nice and fresh when you crumble."

"Is that so?" She stepped across the kitchen and traced with her finger along his jaw. "Funny, how I didn't notice you hadn't shaved yet."

Why had he tried to lie? She'd seen him shave this morning when they got up. Dammit, how was she keeping so cool? He closed his hand around hers. "Well, I want to be nice and fresh for you."

"What about your tea?"

Her body brushed against his, she stood so close, and the scent of her lingered in the air. It was maddening. "I can heat it up later."

"All right. Have a good shower." She turned away, and her hip brushed against his groin, nearly making him groan. As if unaware of the contact, she went back to her tea.

"No sneaking in on me."

"Is that one of the rules, too?"

"It is now." He walked out of the kitchen, passing close enough, he patted her rear.

She squawked and then laughed. "You're still going to lose, Callisto," she called after him.

Jason stood under the cold water until his skin hurt and his erection shriveled away. He heard her go out to the garage, which made him wonder what she had up her sleeve. She'd bought something yesterday, and in the chaos, he'd forgotten. It had to be something pretty titillating, but he couldn't imagine Gaitherberg, West Virginia, having anything kinky. Cass was pretty creative, though. Maybe she was going to MacGyver a sex toy out of gum and an index card.

By the time he came out, she was sitting demurely at the table, talking to someone on the phone, shuffling her index cards. It sounded like event stuff. His skin, pebbling with cold, added to the heat inside, combining into a storm front. While he warmed up his tea, he glanced around the kitchen to see if he could figure out what she'd brought in.

A grocery bag poked out of the top of her bag of bags. What the hell could she have gotten at the grocery store?

Wondering how he'd ended up on the defensive, he took the tea to the living room and looked over her bookshelves for the least erotic thing he could find.

She didn't own any novels that couldn't be construed as erotic to his fevered mind, so he ended up reading a tree identification guide. It sort of worked, although puns about wood kept popping into his thoughts. Meanwhile, she made half a dozen phone calls related to the events and her little stack of index cards grew.

"Are you hungry?" she purred, next to his ear.

Jason jumped. He'd dozed off in the middle of the birches. "Hungry?"

"For lunch."

"Oh." He rubbed his face and then reached out and pulled her down on top of him.

"Hey!" Cass fell into his arms. "Are you giving up already?"

"No. I'm just getting an appetizer." He seized her mouth, drawing her lower lip between his, and she shuddered, encouraging him. Slipping his hand under her shirt, he cupped her waist and stroked her velvet skin with his thumb. She plastered herself against him, burying her hands in his hair. Her nipples strained at the cloth of her shirt. Shifting, she ground herself into him. That small motion unleashed a fresh maelstrom of desire. He twisted, trapping her under him. Cass wrapped her arms around his shoulders, arched up and kissed him then nipped his lips. He kneed her legs apart, rubbed against her heat.

She laughed. "I thought you weren't giving up."

"Giving up?" Desperate to taste the satin skin between her breasts, he unbuttoned the top button of her shirt.

"The bet."

Before his lips met her flesh, he caught himself. The bet. He'd meant to tease her, but somehow he'd lost the upper hand. Again. He looked into her eyes, which right now looked smoky. She was close to losing control. "I'm not giving up. Are you?"

"No." Her voice was breathy.

"Then I guess the bet is still on." He stood up and hauled her to her feet. Before she'd gained her balance, he pulled her against his chest, kissed her hard on the mouth and released her. "So what's for lunch?"

She licked her lips, blinking. "Roast beef leftovers. Do you want them hot or cold?"

"I like everything hot." He leered.

Obviously in control again, she shrugged. "Okay, open face roast beef sandwiches it is." She walked back into the kitchen.

He hoped he looked as in control as she did, because his hormones were still drag racing through his veins. Now he needed another cold shower. No way would he have lasted through a long courtship with her. Even as he watched her assembling lunch through the kitchen door, she was too sexy.

After their heated session on the couch, she did seem perfectly cool.

A chill came over him. Maybe it hadn't affected her the same way, and this was all part of her plan to ensnare him with sex. She might not be as turned on by him as he was by her. With that in mind, it might be easier to win this bet, but he wondered what he'd lose.

* * * *

Christa Maurice

Cass thought she covered her shaking hands pretty well while they ate. She'd almost given into him, even if it meant losing the stupid bet. All through lunch, she'd been throbbing and trying not to spill anything. He, however, seemed cool and collected, like a hunter waiting for his prey to exhaust herself.

Water ran over her hand. She'd chosen to take a bath to give herself a little more time settle down. If he could do it, so could she. She intended to sit in the water until her skin puckered, and she'd brought a good book along to help.

The water swirled into the tub creating mounds of bubbles.

She liked her bathroom. It had dark wood paneling half way up the wall, even around the bathtub. The walls above were painted light blue to match the delft patterned tiles around the tub and on the back splash of the sink. It would be a thoroughly unsexy room, if she could stop remembering Jason had been naked in it a few hours ago.

She sank into the water, opened her book and tried to forget that image.

Two hours later, desire successfully blunted, she was waterlogged and had read the same three chapters three times because she'd kept losing her place.

This wasn't working.

Cass hauled herself out of the tub and looked out the window. Darkness hadn't even fallen yet. She'd been saving her big guns for after dark, but she doubted she could hold out that long. Actually, she was surprised she'd held out this long. If she'd been able to resist needling him, she could have won on the couch earlier.

She smiled at her reflection in the mirror. No one had ever made her feel as sexy as Jason did. He made her believe she was the most beautiful woman on Earth. It was worth a little guilt to feel this glorious.

A lot of guilt.

A whole lot of guilt. That was why she kept lashing out at Jason after sex.

She'd only slept with two men in her life and been dumped not a few times because she wouldn't go all the way. Once, she'd given a boyfriend a bloody nose because he hadn't caught on to the meaning of no in a timely fashion. That relationship had been over before he'd stopped bleeding. She'd only slept with Michael after they were engaged, and she'd felt guilty until they got married.

All Jason had had to do was smile, and she'd just about leaped into his bed. Her bed, actually. And from the very beginning, she'd known what the deal was. This was a fling.

She sat down on the edge of the tub and pressed her face into her hands. He made her feel so good in so many ways, but it was all wrong.

A knock at the door startled her. "You okay in there?" Jason asked through the door.

"Uh, yeah. I'm okay." Her voice sounded funny. She hoped he wouldn't hear it.

"I thought you'd gone down the drain."

"I'll be out in a minute." Cass stood up and looked at herself in the mirror again. She needed to pull herself together. She only had a little more event stuff to deal with, and needed something to do. Paint maybe. Or sit around pining about how she was losing Jason in a few days.

At least she wouldn't have to worry about the bet anymore. Jason would break before she would in this mood.

He'd told her if she won she could have anything she wanted. All she wanted was him, and he wasn't part of the deal. The bet did not supersede the original contract.

Bare feet propped on the armrest, he lay on the couch in the living room, still reading that stupid tree identification guide he'd found. "You got a couple of calls while you were in there," he told her. "They're on the machine."

"Okay." For a moment longer than necessary, she stood in the kitchen door, watching him. She still wanted him. Her bath and her guilt had dampened her desire, but hadn't extinguished it. Nothing would ever do that. Which increased her guilt. She turned to the answering machine and pushed *Play Message*.

"Hi, Cass, it's Donny. Hey, the weather says we have another storm brewing for tonight, so do you want me to plow you out now or can you wait some? Just call and leave a message on my machine, okay?"

Cass paused the machine and called Donny's. "Hi, Donny, it's Cass. We might as well wait until tomorrow if we have another storm coming in. I hope we don't have to dig again. I'll see you tomorrow, I guess." She hung up and started the machine again.

"Cass, this is Finn... Um, I hope everything's going well up there. You weather this storm, okay? Um, I hear Bill gave you a high price on that land of his. I can help you with that if you want. He's got it in his head that you've got money to burn with this fancy winter guest of yours and he wants near the fire. Give me a call when you're ready to talk about it. Or I guess I'll see you when you come in for your mail. Unless you're coming down the holler for the dance at the church the day after tomorrow. Give me a call."

Poor Finn. For some reason, years of her resistance and refusals hadn't brought home the idea that she didn't love him, but Jason appeared, and he knew. Maybe she needed to give Angela a call.

"Hi, Cass, it's Paul," was the next message. "You probably know already about the argument I had with Finn. I feel terrible about it and I wanted to tell you how sorry I am. I wish I'd never opened my mouth, but that man makes me so angry. He thinks you're his right as a citizen of the town. He votes, he pays taxes, he gets Cassandra. Anyway, would you please call me? I just can't sleep, thinking you might be mad at me."

Cass picked up the phone. Paul might be dramatic, but he was dramatic through and through and he really wouldn't sleep until he talked to her. At best, he would start baking and not stop until the sugar ran out.

"Who are you calling?"

She jumped and spun around. Jason leaned in the kitchen door like he'd been there all along. His gaze trailed down her then rose and met her eyes. Heat coiled in her belly. "Paul," she managed to say.

"Oh. I thought you were calling Finn."

Cass shook her head. Her knees shook, too. Her guilt receded to the dim recesses of her mind, driven there by the desire in his eyes. "Paul, he'll worry until he hears from me. He's very sensitive."

"Then by all means, call him." Jason smiled. "I'll just watch."

Her hands were so sweaty, she had to adjust her grip on the phone. What was Paul's number? It was in her phone book. What was his last name? Where was her phone book? She wondered what Jason would exact from her if he won the bet. Free camping every winter for the rest of their lives? Gosh, wouldn't that be terrible. "I can call him later."

"We don't want him to worry."

She'd never come up with the number now, and so hung up the phone. Not with him looking at her like that. "He's lived this long. Another hour or more won't hurt him."

"What do you plan on doing for that hour?" Jason's smile turned wicked. Shivers tumbled down her back.

Cass licked her lips and watched him watch her do it. She'd had a surefire plan a minute ago. Where had it gone? "Ever made s'mores?"

His salacious grin disappeared, and he blinked. "What?"

"S'mores. We make them around the campfire all the time." Cass crossed the kitchen and opened the cupboard. "You toast a marshmallow and put it between graham crackers with some chocolate. It's like a dessert sandwich. You've never made them?"

"I didn't go camping when I was a kid," he said.

"Well, we'll start with lessons on how to toast marshmallows." Having stacked the bag of marshmallows, the box of graham crackers and the package of Hershey bars on a tray, she opened her utensil drawer. "I thought you might not have. I have some skewers that should work. Here they are." She held up the long handled skewers.

Jason looked befuddled now. "Okay."

Cass carried the tray past him into the living room. As she settled in front of the fire, she felt willful and wild. She'd never purposely provoked a man into seducing her, and wasn't sure how she planned to do it now, but a hot fire and some sticky food should provide inspiration. Desire thrummed through her as he sat down beside her. She stuck a marshmallow on a skewer and handed it to him. "There are two schools of thought on the toasting of marshmallows. One says to let them catch fire and eat them when they're completely charred on the outside."

"And the other school?"

His frown, brows drawn down, confirmed, yes, he was truly bewildered. Obviously the idea of a hot, sticky food wasn't working for him yet. "The other school leans toward a slow roasting so the inside melts."

"Hmm." He smiled. "I think I like the second school."

"Until you overcook one and it falls in the fire." Eyebrow raised, she watched a flush rise up his neck and spill across his cheeks. Turned to the flames, she held her marshmallow just above the glowing coals while she arranged a piece of chocolate on a graham cracker with her free hand. He had thrust his marshmallow in the flames. It caught fire, and he started turning it so all sides would char.

"I thought you liked the second school," she said.

As he blew out his marshmallow and pulled it off the skewer, he captured her gaze. "Baby, I've been on a slow burn all day." He popped the whole thing in his mouth.

"You forgot the rest of your s'more." Cass hoped she sounded like herself, but the sight of him licking melted marshmallow off his lips had her feeling hot and melty like her slowly roasting marshmallow. She forced herself to look at it instead of him.

"I thought I should investigate all positions first." He skewered another one.

So far hers was browning nicely. If only her plan wasn't backfiring. He seemed to be in complete control while she might spontaneously combust. Her marshmallow flamed, and she blew out the flames before sliding the oozing mass onto her chocolate. Perfect. Gooey all the way through and beginning to melt the chocolate. A good approximation of how she felt at this moment. She looked at the tray to see where the condom she'd prepped had gone. The way things were headed, she was going to cave in a few minutes and she wanted to know where it was.

"Your turn," Jason murmured.

Cass turned and he pressed a scorched marshmallow to her mouth. The charred skin crackled across her lips. Her eyes closed as she caught his hand and leaned forward to draw his fingers into her mouth. As she licked the sticky sweetness from his long fingers, he trembled, tangled his free hand tangled through her hair. He drew his fingers out of her mouth and eased her back onto the floor.

"You win," he murmured as he slanted his mouth across hers. His demanding hands tore at her clothing, undressing her in moments. She shuddered at his raw need. Everywhere his hands were not, she felt his mouth, his lips, his tongue, as if he wanted to devour her. He struggled out of his jeans and cursed.

"Here." She grabbed the condom and pressed it into his hand.

He laughed. "You had this all planned, didn't you?" he whispered as he entered her. Cass arched under him, only aware of his long powerful strokes filling her. She clutched his shoulders as his lean, hard body slid against hers. The heat of the fire beside her seemed distant and cool compared to the heat in her belly. His friction increased until she over wound and released, uncoiling in his arms.

His thrusts slowed, but didn't stop. Face buried in the curve of her neck, he breathed hard. "Come for me again, *bella*," he whispered. His lips brushed the shell of her ear, sending fresh shivers down her spine. Incredibly, her body tightened around him. She dug her fingers into his back, and his mouth closed over hers as she came in a shattering crescendo. He groaned against her lips and collapsed.

For a long time they lay twined together. Her legs wrapped around his waist and his head between her breasts, just breathing.

"That's the most foreplay I've ever had," she said, trying to sound light even though she wanted to sob. She had promised herself this short affair would leave her with sweet memories, but suspected they'd be bitter as well because they would only be memories.

Laughing, he sat up and helped her up. "You are certainly full of surprises."

Cass forced a dry chuckle.

Jason watched her face. She tried to plaster on a convincing happy expression, but it cracked at the edges. After a moment's study, he picked up her flannel shirt and draped it over her shoulders. "You better put this on," he said. "It's kind of cold in here."

* * * *

When she called, Paul was predictably distraught. From the sound of things, he'd gone into a round of guilt-induced baking which would make the Baptist Church dance a real treat the day after tomorrow and next week as well. Cass leaned on the kitchen counter watching Jason play cards, wishing she could go. Bill, Finn and Angela would all be there, offering the chance to wrap up several problems at once, but Jason's presence would create more. As she watched, Jason picked up a card and flicked it into the fire. It went past too fast for her to register what suit, but it was either diamonds or hearts and a face card. He made a few more moves and then flicked another card into the flames. This time she saw what it was. The king of hearts. She finished her conversation and hung up.

"Throwing cards in the fire will make it more difficult to win," she commented.

He looked up and the chill in his eyes nearly made her stagger. "I guess it will." He scraped the rest of the cards together and dropped them in the fire, but not before she noticed the queen of diamonds missing. "I'm coming up all spades anyway. I guess you'll have to add a deck of cards to my bill."

"I've got a computer version if you promise not to throw that in the fire."

He glowered at her and this time she did step back. Half an hour ago they'd been making love on the floor and now he was glaring and tossing cards in the fire. The king of hearts and the queen of diamonds yet. Why? Was he thinking about Stella again?

"I'm going to take a walk," he announced, startling her.

She nodded. "Okay. Stay within sight of the cabin though. There's another storm coming up and you might need to get inside quick."

He grunted and stalked down the hall.

Once she heard the garage door open, she dialed the phone. "Hello, Gretta?"

"Hey, honey, did you manage to spare a few minutes from having hot sex with Jason Callisto to give me an update?"

"Something's not right."

"What's the matter?" Her tone had shifted from cheerful to deadly.

"He's acting funny. He just threw the cards in the fire." Cass's throat closed. She didn't want to panic Gretta and Jason to walk in on her crying, but everything seemed to be headed there quick.

"What cards?"

"My deck of cards. He threw them in the fire."

"Is he scaring you?"

If she said the wrong thing Gretta would have state troopers on her doorstep in twenty minutes, storm or no storm. "You watch too much TV, Gretta. He's not going to kill me. He's just moody and he withdraws from me." She'd been trying to sound light, but still choked on the last words.

"Is he there with you?"

"He's outside." Cass pulled the phone to the window and looked. Jason stood knee deep in snow in the side yard, his black coat making a stark outline against the whiteness. "I think he's building a snowman. Oh God, Gretta, I've done something terrible."

"You did?"

"I fell in love with him. I didn't want to and I didn't mean to, but I did." Saying it out loud felt so good. It had been festering in her like a wound. In the air the secret might dry up and heal. Why did she feel like she had to heal from being in love with Jason?

"Surprise. It's not like you weren't half in love with him when he walked into your house. Cass, you've been hot for this guy since college. Hell, if he was walking around my living room, I'd be thinking seriously about my wedding vows even if he wasn't flirting with me."

"It's not just lust, Gretta. I really love him. Stella hurt him when she dumped him and I want to heal that. I love the fact that he snores a little in his sleep."

"He snores?"

"Very softly. I love the fact that he wipes up the last traces of his food with a chunk of bread, and the way he wraps my hair around his fingers. I love his playfulness. I love that he's building a pyramid in my yard."

"He's building a pyramid in your yard?"

Cass pressed her cheek against the window to get a better look. He'd found a shovel in her garage and was using it as a sculpting tool. "It might be an Aztec temple. You know, those pyramids with the steps. Hard to tell at this stage. I love that he balls his socks up and throws them in the corner at night."

"Oh, I promise you, that gets old real fast."

Turned away from the window, she leaned on the wall. "There isn't time for anything to get old. He's going to leave, and what am I going to do then?"

"You're going to do what you did before. You'll run your camp and be adored by your whole town," Gretta told her.

"That's the other problem." Cass slumped and closed her eyes. "The town. What if they find out what's been going on up here?"

"They'll assume you're a perfectly normal adult female who had a shot at the hottest male on Earth. Give them a little credit."

"Gretta, this isn't New York. This kind of behavior just isn't done around here. Not when you're a responsible adult."

"Can I remind you that when you were in New York, the best you managed to do was get drunk with a gay man and learn to cook better than Betty Crocker? Cassie, your little home town is cute and everything, but they're not totally stupid. They won't shun you or make you sew scarlet *A*s on your clothes." Gretta sighed. "Look, I don't want to burst your bubble, but you've given me no choice. Repeat after me—I am not in love with Jason."

"I am not in love with Jason."

"I don't have to be in love with a man to have sex with him. Especially not if he's Jason Callisto."

Cass repeated after her. Gretta was right. That's why she'd called her. She'd known Gretta would be right.

"I deserve this and I'm not going to ruin it with a bunch of emotional horse shit." Gretta said.

"Horse shit?" Laughing, Cass looked out the window. Jason had gotten out a trowel. His pyramid now stood about five feet tall with a flat top and he seemed to be adding tiny steps.

"You heard me. Let it be what it is. If you want to make him feel better, do it by being the rebound relationship and envy the heck out of the next girlfriend."

Cass twisted the phone cord around her finger. "So how do I make myself stop feeling like…like…"

"A whore?"

"That's a little strong, but kind of. I just feel cheap about the whole thing."

"How so?"

Shame clawed at her chest. "I can't help feeling like he thinks he paid for me along with the cabin rental." She could see his cabin from her window, too. She should drain the pipes and close it up again.

"You can't pay for what's given freely. Were sexual services itemized on the bill?"

"No."

"Then stop being so guilty and relax. You've been half dead since Michael dumped you. So Michael didn't want you. Look who does."

Outside, Jason knelt in the snow, looking up at the third side of his temple. His shoes, gloves and coat weren't up to this kind of biting cold. She should warm a blanket by the fire for him. "Okay."

"And you call me if you need me."

"Yes, mother."

"Damn right. You take care of yourself first. Worry about what he thinks, and what the town thinks later or not at all. Preferably, not at all. If they can't handle the fire, they need to climb out of the Victorian Era already. And I've met some of those folks. They are not as uptight as you think. All they might be is really jealous. Then you have my permission to revel in it."

"Revel?"

"Sure, what good is other people's jealousy if you can't enjoy it?"

That made her laugh. Basking in the beauty queen's jealousy would be better than skulking around, guilty, for the next sixty years.

Chapter 13

Jason stood in front of the last side of his Aztec pyramid. It hadn't started out to be one, but once he'd found the shovel so he could make the sides nice and square and the trowel to carve out the steps, it had seemed appropriate. The Aztecs ripped out peoples' hearts on these things anyway. He'd been at the bottom of the third side, working with numb fingers, when he'd realized this whole mess was his fault.

He'd been sent here to get his head together.

Instead, he'd pursued her then teased and seduced her.

He couldn't expect her not to take advantage of the situation.

But, he was going home in about a week and a half after a short, torrid, very satisfying affair, and no law said he had to take her with him.

Jason looked for the trowel to carve out the steps. She hadn't torn out his heart, Stella had. Stella had been wrong for him. Cass had shown him what he wanted in a woman and a wife. Somebody to take care of him who would allow him to take care of her, who didn't expect to be entertained and wasn't trying to entertain. A woman who could stand on her own, but didn't feel like she had to do it all the time. Who thought about him and not just about what he could do for her. He would have to go home and find that woman. She had to be out there some place.

By the time he went inside, he couldn't feel his fingers and his feet were a memory, but his heart was somewhat less battered. He stamped snow off his shoes as he walked through the garage. About now, a hot bath would do the trick. Afterward he could lure Cass to bed and make love to her for the second time today. His appetite for her was insatiable. He hadn't had this much stamina at eighteen.

"Stop right there."

When he turned away from the door he'd just closed, Cass stood blocking the other end of the hall. A smear of paint smudged her cheek, and she looked deadly serious. A flash of fear hit him. The way he'd stormed out, had he hurt her? His temper had gotten him packed off here in the first place, maybe it had pissed off his refuge, too. "Listen, Cass, I'm—"

"Off with everything."

If she meant to seduce him, this was a really funny way of handling it. "What?"

"You're dripping wet and I don't want you dragging it all over my house. Take off all your clothes and hang them in the bathroom. Then come out here by the fire." She started to turn away.

"I was going to take a bath to warm up." Jason stripped off his gloves, hoping they weren't ruined. They didn't look healthy, all shriveled with half the fingers turned inside out. He'd forgotten how it felt to be unsure of a woman's reception. Most women fell all over themselves to please him.

Now she looked at him with one eyebrow raised as if he were a bug in her garden. "You'll burn yourself before you warm up enough to realize it. Come on. Get out of those wet things and come out here. I've got some blankets warming by the fire." She disappeared from the end of the hall.

Jason slunk into the bathroom, wondering how much trouble he was in. He'd treated her pretty badly, throwing her cards in the fire and stomping out. Even if she were trying to manipulate him, he didn't have to act like a jerk. He leaned on the wall and tried to untie his sneakers, but his numb fingers couldn't grasp the laces, so he sat down on the edge of the tub, hoping for a better grip.

"Aren't you out of those clothes yet?" Cass asked from the bathroom door.

Jason looked up. The snow was melting down the back of his neck. An icy drop slid down his spine and made him shudder. As the temperature of his body registered with his brain, his teeth chattered.

"Oh, look at you." Cass sighed. "You're hopeless."

She stepped forward, grabbed a towel from the rack, draped it over his head and rubbed his wet hair. Wanting to lean forward and let her minister to him, he closed his eyes. Quickly she dried his hair and tucked the towel around his neck. Then she knelt at his feet. "I'll get the shoes. You get that coat off. Just toss it in the tub. I'll hang it up in a minute. You should have taken a break to warm up. The snow will still be there." She tossed his shoes in the corner and reached for his sweatshirt.

"If I'm going to undress anyway, I know of something more fun we could do." Jason tried to grin, but his teeth were chattering in earnest now.

With a snort, she brushed his clumsy fingers away from his fly. "I don't want your hands on me until they're at least room temperature."

"Are you sure?" He reached for her and she leaned away.

"I'm positive. I'll take a rain check." She pulled him to his feet and pushed his soaked jeans and underwear down to his ankles, ending up at eye level with his erection.

"I think I like you there," he said, and patted the top of her head.

"I'll bet. You can still forget it." A pretty flush bloomed on her cheeks. Her breathing seemed a little shallow, too. Perhaps with a nudge in the right direction, she would change her plans.

"I promise not to touch you with my cold hands. In fact, I won't touch you with any of my cold parts."

"That's almost impossible." Cass stood up. "Every part of you is a cold part."

"Not all of them."

"Enough to make me not want you on top of me."

"That'll make it more interesting." Despite what she'd said, when he cupped his hand around her cheek and kissed her, she leaned against him, welcoming his cold lips on her warm, soft ones. Her sweater and jeans rubbed his cold flesh as her hands danced across his shoulders, and he eased a hand around her waist, under her sweater, on her hot bare skin.

Yelping, she jumped away.

"I thought you weren't going to touch me with your cold hands." She pressed herself against the bathroom wall.

"I already was."

"Well, not under my clothes."

"It's hard to resist touching you. What can I say?"

She stepped away, and he felt colder than he had before. The shivering returned with a vengeance.

"Come on, you need to get warmed up for real."

"I was getting warmed up for real," he protested, but followed her down the hall. It felt good to be naked in her house. He didn't like to leave his bedroom naked at home, but walking around her house seemed perfectly comfortable. There wasn't any chance of paparazzi catching him and putting him in *Playgirl* between Sting doing yoga and Brett Michaels doing Pam Anderson. The house was warm and, even though his feet felt like half frozen hams and his hands had started to throb unpleasantly, he liked the touch of the air on his skin.

"Here," she said as she draped a soft, warm blanket across his shoulders. The heat coming from the fibers enclosed him in a cocoon of warmth. "I warmed it in front of the fire for you. You sit down here and I'll wrap up your feet, and then I'll get some hot chocolate for you."

"Such service, you provide here. I'll have to tell all my friends," Jason said settling on the couch. He thought she flinched, but decided he was wrong.

"This service is special to you, my dear." With another blanket from the hearth, she wrapped his feet. Whether from the chill on them or the warm blanket, his feet throbbed to life. He closed his eyes and let the skirl of sensation run through him.

A beautiful woman tended to him without the usual demands for sex in return. Most women he met did things for him because they knew they would get some and could then go brag to their friends. Because she'd wanted to take care of him first, she'd turned down an invitation for sex. He'd have to add that to the list of things he wanted in a wife. Someone more interested in his well being than in getting the all-important notch on her bedpost.

"Here, drink this." Kneeling on the couch beside him, she cradled a steaming mug in her hands.

"What is it?"

"Hot chocolate." She settled the warm cup in his hands and brushed her fingers through his damp hair. "I'll have to remember to call you in when it gets cold outside. You've been living in California too long."

The hot chocolate tasted sweet and rich, and going down, was as comforting as the feel of her hand in his hair. "This isn't the cocoa mother used to make."

"Depends on the mother." Cass stood up. "Mine always put a shot of brandy in it when we got really cold." She walked out and he heard her in the bathroom, hanging his clothes to dry.

The fire on the hearth crackled, the flames leaping wildly around the log, pumping out heat. She'd built it up for him. Would she be interested in a mistress arrangement? He could come out here for a couple of weeks every year. Closer to the end of this trip he'd propose it and see how she took the idea. He leaned his head against the back of the couch and closed his eyes.

* * * *

Cass carried his shoes and mangled gloves to the living room. "Jason, these look like driving gloves."

Asleep. Setting the gloves and shoes on the hearth, she went over to rescue the half-empty mug from his lax fingers. She'd figured he would drift off, but hadn't realized it would happen so fast. While settling the blanket more securely around his neck, her fingers strayed up his neck, and she stroked his cheek. He was going to wake up sore and hungry. Maybe cranky, too, which made her smile. Somehow, as nervous as she became when he got moody, it was still endearing to watch. Gretta was wrong. This was not simple lust, and Cass was knee-deep in "emotional horse shit." Possibly deeper.

She downed the rest of the hot chocolate in three large gulps then turned to the shoes and gloves. Thin, leather driving gloves. If she'd known, she'd have insisted he wear Dan's work gloves. They would have been better suited to snow sculpting. These were for piloting a Ferrari with a good heating system. And the shoes. Canvas sneakers. Not that she could have done anything about his shoes other than force him to come inside and warm up every fifteen minutes. She arranged his things on the stone hearth where they would dry.

As she walked behind the couch to her easel, she couldn't resist running her fingers through his hair again. She'd have to keep the depth of her feelings under wraps until he left or he might leave before the two weeks were up. It was going to be a long enough winter after he left without hurrying that inevitability.

Out the window, the storm had started, blocking her view of the valley. It didn't matter. She could paint the scene from memory.

* * * *

The next morning they woke to another eighteen inches of snow sitting atop the two feet they'd had yesterday. The new snow covered Jason's ziggurat, leaving it looking more like an Egyptian pyramid. Over breakfast, he announced he wanted to build a life size Olmec head.

"Dan's gloves are by the front door in the basket, and don't forget to come in to warm up when you start to get cold," she reminded him as she handed him a coffee table book on archeology.

By the time Donny appeared in the plow, Jason had finished Olmec and three pyramids. He'd come in at lunch to warm up, eat and make love. As dusk shrouded the mountain in gray and purple, he came in for the day, eyes shining like a child's.

"Tomorrow, Easter Island heads," he announced, setting the gloves and his shoes on the hearth.

Cass laughed as she washed her brushes. She'd blocked in the background colors. Tomorrow she could start making the painting look more like a real scene and less like modern art. "There's a blanket by the fire for you."

"I noticed. Thanks." He stepped behind her and enveloped her in his arms, kissed her cheek. "I think I've done permanent damage to my coat. I'll have to bring a more suitable one next time." He released her and started out of the room. "And real boots."

Her fingers went lax and she nearly dropped her brushes. Next time? Would he come back...and could she cope if he did?

She threw all those thoughts into a mental box labeled "emotional horse shit" and shoved it to the back of her mind. "Paul is dying to know if you're going to be at the dance tonight."

His brows lowered in a wary, puzzled expression. "Why?"

"I think he wants to dance with you."

Jason roared with laughter. "Really? Would that rattle the whole town? Would he let me lead?"

"If you say please, I think he'll let you wipe your shoes on his back." Cass set her brush on the back splash to dry then stirred the spaghetti sauce she'd been simmering all afternoon. She must have been thinking of herself when that doormat analogy came to mind.

Now he stood behind her, a wall of heat and man, wrapping a curl around his finger. "Are you asking me to the dance?" he asked in a low tone that made the hair on the back of her neck rise in a good way.

"Technically, I think it was Paul who asked, but I'll drive if you like."

"Do you want me to go to the dance with you?"

"If you'd enjoy it." She measured out the noodles with trembling fingers.

"Do you want me to go to the dance?"

She turned around and pressed her hands against the counter behind her back. "Only if you want to go. I just thought I'd mention it."

Searching her gaze, he grazed her cheeks with his knuckles. "I'd like to dance with you. In public, where people will see us, but I don't want to cause problems."

Cass looked down, aware of Jason's tense breathing. He'd continued his trip down her cheek, slid his hand around her throat and tangled it in the hair at the back of her neck. She wanted to dance with him in public, too. For the town to see the way he looked at her. Then they'd know her marriage hadn't failed because she wasn't desirable.

But he was right. The town would spin a wild tale about her and her winter guest that would be entirely true, and she'd be the pathetic abandoned woman for the rest of her life.

"Or," he offered, "we could go to the dance and pretend to be nothing more than concierge and guest, and when we got home, we could dance together like we mean it."

Cass looked up. She doubted it hurt him half as much to make the offer as it had for her to accept it. "I think that's the only way. We don't have to go at all."

His grip tightened on the back of her neck, and he pursed his lips, frowning for an instant, then his smile lit his features. "I think it would disappoint the town if we didn't go."

She smirked. "Can't have that. Dinner will be ready in a few minutes. And my dad said if you'd like to learn some of the old mountain songs, he'd teach you."

"Really? That would be great."

"Just bring your guitar." Tears threatened, but she blinked them back. When she'd been with Michael, she'd gone to exactly one church dance, and felt like a giant wallflower. He'd flitted around the room charming everyone and left her to sit with her parents. Though she'd been comfortable at those dances, he'd made it such hell. Please let Jason not make the dance hell for her. "I guess I'll have to get something out to wear." The noodles needed at least seven minutes. Time enough, to check her closet.

"Is this a dressy thing?" Jason followed her to the bedroom and sat on the foot of the bed to watch her search.

"Only sort of. They won't refuse to let you in if you don't have a tie." In the depths of her closet, she reached for the nicer clothes that didn't suit her campground managing lifestyle, but she hadn't been willing to give up. Along with a few things in her underwear drawer, they were the last vestiges of her New York life.

"What's that?"

She turned toward him, holding a navy blue skirt. "What's what?"

Jason reached around her. His hand closed over a dry cleaning bag. He shook it free of the clinging clothes around it, pulled it out of the closet.

"Oh, that," she murmured. Heat rushed into her cheeks.

Oh that was a floor length, strapless, brilliant yellow silk sheath dress. He held it up to her, studying her and let out a low whistle. "Why don't you wear this?"

"To the Baptist Church Saturday night dance? I think I'd be overdressed."

"Will you wear it for me? Not to the dance. Later."

"Why?"

"Because I want to take it off you," he said in that voice that did the most delicious things to her insides, grinning.

She couldn't help but smile. "Then maybe I should wear the coat with it." She reached in the closet and pulled out another dry cleaning bag. This one held a long black velvet coat with wide lapels. The hem of the full skirt started at the knee in the front and curved to floor length in the back. A glittering brooch clasped the low neckline closed just below her breasts. "Or would you rather I wore this." She drew out yet another dry cleaning bag. This one held a white satin bolero jacket with a high Mandarin collar.

Jason pulled the bag off the dress, stroking the material as he dropped the gown on the bed. Then he took out the bolero jacket and laid it beside the dress. Last, he lifted the velvet coat from her fingers and removed the bag. He pressed the lapel to his cheek, breathing deeply. It had to smell like dry cleaning, but he didn't seem to care. "This one. Wear this one for me."

The thought of wearing those clothes again made her skin crawl, and she turned away. Looking was one thing, having those clothes on her flesh again was quite another. She wasn't sure why she hadn't left them behind in New York. He looked so excited. Why? He'd been on red carpets with women wearing much nicer things than this. If it made him that happy, though, she could bear to put them on again. "All right. I'll put it on for you tomorrow."

"Tonight."

She shook her head. "I'll think about it."

"Why do you have these dresses?" he asked, sinking onto the bed beside them.

"For Michael. We had to go to parties sometimes, and I needed formal wear. I didn't want to buy a whole bunch of dresses I couldn't afford, so I bought one dress and two jackets. Sasha called them The Dress, Bride of the Dress, and The Dress Strikes Back. I think the velvet was The Dress Strikes Back." Cass scowled. "She thought it was tacky that I showed up for everything in the same dress."

"She probably thought it was tacky that you were married to her lover."

That about summed it up, but still, it made her flinch.

Jason's hands closed around her shoulders. She hadn't even heard him stand up. "I didn't mean that."

She patted his hand. "It's probably true."

Then she was turned, facing him, and he kissed her, sliding his hands down her back, urging her tight against him. Tasting the inside of her mouth with his tongue. Arms around his neck, she allowed him to lift her to her toes. Her pulse felt indistinguishable from his as he wove his fingers through the hair at her nape, sending a frisson of pleasure down her spine. He curved his hands around her buttocks, pulled her off her feet. With her legs wrapped around his waist, he carried her to the side of the bed and laid her down.

"Dinner will burn," she pointed out.

"Not if we turn it off first."

* * * *

The dance had been going for forty-five minutes when Cass parked the truck two blocks from the church. Based on the lack of spaces, the entire town had turned out. Holding the neck of her peacoat closed against the icy wind, she hurried to the doors with him. She hoped she didn't look flushed. Her lips still felt swollen from Jason's kisses. He'd sat on the bed watching her dress, disrupting any thoughts she'd had about last-minute instructions.

She'd meant to tell him to keep his distance at the dance so nobody would pick up on them, that they should leave at different times so it would look like they drove there separately and to warn him that Kady and Cori would be in rare form.

Jason opened the door of the fellowship hall. Faint Lawrence Welk wafted out into the night. She should have warned him about that, too.

Betsy Partrager looked up from the little table outside the doors and grinned. Behind the rims of her glasses, her eyes sparkled like aquamarines. A rhinestone studded barrette held her snow white hair away from her face.

"Well, now you're here," she said, "I suppose I can go inside and enjoy the fun myself." Her January pin glinted in the low light, a snowman acquired from Avon many years ago and missing a few stones including one red eye. Next month it would be a cupid whose arrow had broken during the Regan administration.

"What?" Cass asked.

"Well, the whole town is here, aren't they? If this was Election Day, I'd be dancing on my toes."

In a clearer mind, Cass would have snorted in response. Betsy made sure everyone in town voted, if she had to send her three sons out to get them and bring them to the polls. She'd even sent Donny up with the snowplow one March for Cass when she'd gotten snowed in.

"It'll be two dollars for each of you."

Jason handed her a ten. "Keep the change."

"Oh, well thank you, Mr. Callisto, and may I tell you, we're all tickled you decided to vacation here. I hope you're having a good time."

"I am having a wonderful time," he answered, smiling.

"I see you brought your guitar, are you going to play for us tonight?"

"Cass's father is going to teach me some old songs."

"Are my parents here?" Cass broke in before something unfortunate popped out.

"They certainly are. Everyone is. Even Kady Stern and Cori Gwynn, and the way those girls are dressed is just shameful. You would think they were in a disco, instead of a church."

Cass smiled through gritted teeth and glanced up at Jason. He seemed amused by the prospect of facing the girls again.

"Finn's here, too," Betsy said. "He was asking if you'd gotten here yet. I think he wants to talk to you about that pasture of Bill Wernick's."

If only the universe would stop throwing bricks at her. All her business seemed to be public record and her one dirty little secret was standing right next to her. When had coming to this dance seemed like a good idea? "I guess we should all go inside then, shouldn't we?" She pushed open the door and walked down the stairs with weak knees.

The hall did appear to be filled to capacity, and everyone in their Sunday best, with the possible exceptions of Cori Gwynn and Kady Stern. Cori wore a skirt so short and slung so low around her waist Cass thought she had tied a wide flocked ribbon around her hips until she realized the skirt, if it could be called that, was suede. Kady had gone for a pair of black bell-bottoms so tight, how she managed to walk in them, let alone move as fast as she was closing in on them—or rather, Jason—was a mystery.

"Cass." Finn appeared at her side like a genie. "I need to talk to you."

Cass stopped and Jason copied her. She wondered if he'd caught sight of Kady and Cori yet. In fact, she wondered if their mothers had caught sight of them. "What is it?"

Finn glared over Cass's shoulder at Jason. "If you don't mind, I'd like to talk to Cass privately. It's about business."

Wild laughter rose in her throat. What private business? Half the town probably knew her underwear size. "If this is about that pasture, he already knows, and if I'm getting audited, everybody's going to know soon enough."

"I'd prefer to talk to you alone." The tips of Finn's ears had begun to turn red.

"Oh, Mr. Callisto, I heard you were going to be here." Kady pulled up short of falling on Jason and tottered back on her high heels. Her top looked like it came from a bondage catalog. "Is this your guitar? Can I see it?"

"Mr. Callisto, I hope you're going to play something tonight," Cori purred, stepping between Jason and Cass and slipping her arm through his. "You've got to save us from this boring old people music."

"Listen, Cass," Finn said, "I've talked to Bill and told him his price is absurd. I think we can bring him down."

"We're going to have to bring him down a lot. I don't have that kind of money." Jason was being drawn away by Cori and Kady, but when Cass looked over her shoulder the whole group had been intercepted by the minister. The minister might be able to control things.

"Let's go talk to him. I'll get you a good deal." Finn put an arm around her shoulders.

His possessiveness hemmed her in, and she turned as if she wanted to look around the room, letting Finn's arm fall away. "Where is he?"

Within minutes, the crowd had swallowed up Jason. Cass gritted her teeth for negotiations. She ended up hardly having to say a word. Finn negotiated and Bill played hardball. Cass found herself sitting at a table with a cup of punch, watching the tennis match over her money. She spotted Jason dancing a few times, mostly with town matriarchs who looked elated, but once with Kady, who spent most of the waltz trying to grind her hips against his. Jason spent his time trying to keep daylight between them.

"Hi, swee'pea, Bill, Finn," her dad greeted them as he sat down in the chair beside her. He nodded to the men, but focused on her. "The minister says your boy is here, but I haven't seen him yet."

Finn wore a dark scowl, obviously because of the reference to Jason as *her boy*, but she didn't let it bother her. "Oh, he's here. Last time I noticed, he was dancing."

"When did you kids get here?"

She looked at her watch. "Almost an hour ago. You know how famous people like to be late."

All three men stared at her. What had she let slip? "Where's Mom?"

"She's in the kitchen, piping filling into lady fingers. Paul must have made a thousand cookies."

"Is he in the kitchen, too? I should go say hi," she said, rising.

"What about the negotiations?" Finn almost wailed.

"You're doing fine. Let me know how it turns out." Two steps toward the kitchen, and someone blocked her way. Jason, grinning slyly. The room contracted to nothing but him. The music and chatter faded to the distance. She found herself grinning up at him. His breathing sounded a little short, probably from the series of fast dances they'd played and evading Cori for four minutes twenty seconds. Or was it Kady? They were beginning to blur together, along with the rest of the townspeople.

"Hello there, Ms. Camp Director," Jason said.

The person he'd led off the floor had been Angela. The perfect antidote to Kady or Cori. Angela blushed bright red, beaming up at Jason.

Turning away from Cass, he brought Angela's hand to his lips. "*Cherie*, you are as light on your feet as you are beautiful."

Angela blushed so hard, Cass checked to see if her feet touched the floor anymore. A familiar feeling. When he turned on the full wattage of his charm, you could be hit by a train and not notice.

She glanced back at Finn. He looked like Lord Thunder himself. "Finn, weren't you going to ask Angela to dance?" she asked.

"Yes. I was." Finn stood so fast his chair fell over, but didn't seem to notice it as he came around the table. Cass couldn't tell whether he was angry about her, Angela, or Jason.

"What about the negotiations?" Bill protested.

"It's a dance. Let the kids have fun," Cass's father chided him.

"Dance?" Jason murmured. He didn't wait for an answer before he took Cass's hand and led her to the floor. Someone had found the church's only Beausoleil CD and landed on a rare slow song. He rested his hand on her waist and took her other hand in his, looking down at her with a faint smile.

"Are you having fun?" she asked. She wondered if everyone saw the way their bodies moved in concert so well, as if they'd had practice. Lots and lots of practice.

"A blast. Between the giggling old ladies and the groupie twins, I can't remember ever having so much fun. In public anyway." He smiled.

Cass wished she didn't blush so much. It was an easy signal for everyone to see. But the way Angela had been blushing when he led her off the floor, everyone would comment if she didn't, she supposed. "I should have known Cori and Kady would go full out tonight. I meant to warn you, but I forgot."

"It's okay. Kind of cute really. In a baby piranha way."

"Baby piranha will still eat you alive."

Jason raised an eyebrow. "Did you overhear what Cori whispered in my ear?"

A groan escaped her. "I'm so embarrassed."

"Don't worry about it. I've been promised worse. Besides," he said, voice dropped to a murmur, "you deliver better."

Doing her best to quell the delicious shiver that elicited, she tried to glance around casually. Nobody paid any more attention to them than they had been all night, and Finn, even less. He spun Angela in a tight circle, studying her face as if he'd never seen her before. He probably hadn't. Even across the room, Cass could see a new light to Angela's face. She looked prettier and brighter, still bathed in the glow of Jason's charm. "Thank you for dancing with Angela."

"Who?" Jason followed her gaze. "Oh, her. She's nice. Pretty girl and a good dancer. I thought Kady was going to break my toes in those stilettos."

"Probably because she was trying to climb up you."

Jason shrugged. "That might have been part of the problem." He spun her around and dipped her. Cass giggled. She had no choice but to trust him. He'd taken her too much by surprise to get a good grip. As he held her suspended above the floor, his gaze seemed to bore into hers. This time, she allowed herself to shiver. Then the notes signaling the end of the song played, and he lifted her upright and set her on her feet.

"I think Paul is waiting for his dance," she said.

Jason bowed. "At your service."

"He's hiding in the kitchen." Cass wanted to take his hand and lead him off the dance floor. It would show everyone he belonged to her.

But he didn't.

Her chest tightened. Why had she reminded herself? She'd wanted to pretend as long as possible, but she was far too much of a realist to let herself go for long. If she took his hand, announcing to the whole town they were a couple, she'd have to endure a lifetime of smirks and pitying stares when he left. So, brilliant smile dimmed by her thoughts, she went into the church's kitchen.

"Good Lord, Paul, is there a single pound of sugar left in West Virginia?" she demanded, surveying the room. Every surface seemed to be covered with cookie sheets piled with cookies. "Oooh, kolachi." She reached for one.

Ida, standing guard over the cash box, slapped her hand. "Fifty cents."

Cass was fishing in her pockets for money, when Jason handed Ida a five. At that moment she caught sight of Paul's terrified expression.

"Five gets you a dozen." Ida informed Jason, who made an appreciative noise looking over the selection.

"What?" Cass asked Paul, and wove around a prep table.

"Cass, I'm so sorry," he said, grabbing her hands, which coated them with powdered sugar. "I should have kept my big stupid mouth shut."

She shrugged. "It doesn't matter anymore." Last week, the most striking period of her life had been her marriage and desertion by Michael, but the moment Jason walked through her door, everything had changed. Her highs had gone higher and she suspected her lows were going to challenge the Mariana Trench. "Look, I brought Jason to dance with you."

Paul brightened. "Dance?"

"So, Paul," Jason asked from across the table. "Would you like to dance?" He had cookie crumbs on his lip, and though she longed to reach up and brush them off, she glanced away. Her mother, holding a pastry bag, watched her as if she were reading her mind.

Paul fluttered a hand to his throat. "I would love to."

"You have to let me lead," Jason warned.

"Anytime." Paul pulled his apron over his head, wiped his hands on it and crammed it in Cass's direction. Then he offered a newly clean hand to Jason, and to the accompaniment of Ida's cackling laughter, allowed himself to be led out of the kitchen.

"Cassie, you have eight cookies on account," Ida told her before turning to a new customer.

"Hi, Mom." Cass kissed her mother's floured cheek. "The mission is doing well tonight."

"The mission?"

"You know, that place that gets all the proceeds from the dance." More for the opportunity to get her soul out of her eyes than to peruse the heaps of cookies again, she looked pointedly around the kitchen.

"Oh, the mission. Yes, very well. Paul's baking fit hit before the right dance. There's more in the freezers. How are things going on the mountain?"

The tone was light, but her mother knew. In high school, everyone said you could tell when a girl lost her virginity by looking at the whites of her eyes. They were supposed to get brighter or yellower. She should have checked the whites of her eyes before she left home tonight. "Fine. He didn't seem at all bothered by getting snowed in. He's building snow sculptures." Great, now she had a burr in her throat...or was it the half-truth getting stuck?

"That's good. He's going to be here for what? Another week?"

"Something like that. He has to go back in time for the Grammys."

"And when is that?"

Though she didn't want to admit she knew to the hour when he was leaving and would be on the Grammys, she doubted she could keep that fact from her mother. "I don't know. I think it's the first weekend in February. You should ask Paul, he'll know."

Mom returned to piping cream into the ladyfingers. "I might have to watch them this year. Now that I'll know someone."

"Well, I'm gonna go out there, on the floor. I don't want to miss all of the big dance." Before her mother could learn more through osmosis, Cass hurried out of the kitchen.

The townspeople had cleared a space on the floor for Paul and Jason. Paul looked ecstatic, Jason amused. Everyone else seemed to think it was funny, but then most of the town thought Paul was funny.

Angela sidled up beside her. "Hi," she said. "Thanks for what you did."

The girl's face still glowed with shy excitement. "What did I do?"

"When you got Finn to dance with me. It was nice of you."

Oh that. It seemed to have happened on another plane of existence. "You seemed to be holding your own."

"Oh." Angela looked at the floor. "I don't know. I tried. Mr. Callisto told me I was pretty, and I tried to remember that when I danced with Finn. You know, if Mr. Callisto says you're pretty then you must be, right? I mean, he's seen lots of girls, hasn't he?"

Angela was going to hesitate herself right out the door. "You are pretty and very sweet. I don't know why Finn doesn't wake up."

The other girl sighed and stared across the room at the object of her affection. Finn didn't appear particularly amused by Paul and Jason dancing, but he couldn't be too happy with either man at the moment. "I just don't know what to do to get his attention."

Finn's expression was so dour. Too funny. It would serve him right to get it smack between the eyes. "You know what I think you should do?"

"What?" Angela asked.

"Do you work Monday?"

She shook her head.

"Monday, go into Ida's and pick up his lunch and then take it to his office in your coat."

"In my coat?"

Cass leaned forward and whispered, "With nothing on underneath."

Angela gasped and slapped her hand over her mouth. "I couldn't do that."

"Yes, you could. Just pretend you're Kady."

Angela's giggle sounded every bit like a little girl planning mischief. Her dark eyes sparkled. "Do you think it would work?"

"He noticed you tonight. If you show up in his office in the nude, he'll really notice you. Be brave and grab the chance while you have it. Remember, Jason Callisto thinks you're pretty."

"Yeah. Grab the chance." Bottom lip between her teeth, she looked over the dance floor.

"And you better take a condom. I doubt Finn will have any on hand in the office."

Her mouth curled upward in a wide smile. "He will when I get done with him."

Cass almost laughed out loud. She might have inspired Angela to a life-changing prank. If only she could come up with a simple answer for herself.

"He really seems to like you," Angela said.

"Who? Finn?" His crush on her was hardly a secret, had been common knowledge since high school.

The slow song had ended and a new song began. Her father had collared Jason and Paul was floating back to the kitchen.

"No, not Finn, Mr. Callisto. He seemed annoyed you were sitting with Finn and asked me if you guys had ever gone out. He asked me a lot of questions that night I had dinner with him, too." Glancing around, she said low, "I haven't told anybody about that."

"Good. I don't want Kady or Cori showing up unannounced." Especially now. She prayed Jason wasn't asking everybody questions. That would blow their cover as quickly as having Kady arrive while they were having sex on the living room floor. "Why don't you go ask Finn to dance?"

"Good idea." Angela set off around the hall.

Would she go to hell for encouraging adultery in a church? She shook her head. The way the week had been going, she was going to hell anyway. What did a couple extra millennia matter?

Chapter 14

Across the room from him, Cass had been talking to Angela. A second ago, Cass had been looking at him and he'd wondered what he was doing wrong now. "So, Paul, have you known Cass long?"

"Oh, not really. Not the way they count time in Potterville. We were neighbors in New York."

"So you're not from Potterville?" A little smokescreen was necessary or Cass would have reason to worry.

"Oh, no. I was born in Indianapolis."

"What brought you here?"

"Cassie. She's just the best friend a girl could have." Paul had gone into this weird Southern belle routine, but he was a much better dancer than either Kady or Cori. "I couldn't imagine staying in New York without her. If I were straight, she wouldn't be single."

Thank God Paul was gay.

Andy met them at the edge of the dance floor.

"Told a few people you wanted to learn some old songs," he announced. "Everybody's gone up to the chapel so we can play without interrupting the dance. You brought your guitar?"

"Yeah. The minister took it to his office."

"Thanks for the dance," Paul said. He almost giggled and then drifted in the direction of the kitchen.

"Come on then." Andy led the way. Cass started toward them.

"Are you all going to play now?" she asked when she intercepted her father and Jason.

"Your dad said a few other people brought instruments. It's turning out to be an old-fashioned jam." Wishing he could put his arm around her, but knew she'd panic, he looked into her eyes. Asking Angela and Paul a few questions hadn't been smart either, but he hadn't been able to resist. Angela was a sweet and charming girl and seeing Cass sitting forgotten beside Finn had driven Jason crazy. If Finn was so hot for her, how could he sit beside her and not try to touch her? And Paul knew a lot.

"Good. I hope you enjoy it." Cass stuffed her hands in her pockets.

Jason caught himself staring at the fall of her curls over her shoulder. He shouldn't be having the kind of thoughts he was having in a church.

"We're going to find Reverend Bell and have him open his office for us. Ben brought his fiddle." Cass's father, Andy, led Jason through the press of people. They found the minister in his office counting the door receipts. On the tattered couch beside Jason's guitar case sat Andy's guitar, a banjo case and a violin case. Andy picked up his guitar and the banjo, so Jason took the violin case along with his guitar. They carried the instruments to the worship hall.

He hadn't been inside a church in years, and the last one was a six hundred-year-old stone Catholic church in Italy. This church didn't look anything like that one. The walls were painted bright white and the carpet in the aisles brilliant red. The windows were clear glass and Jason could see the stars through them. It didn't take long before the owner of the violin appeared with the banjo owner in tow to claim their instruments. Then Cassie's mother came upstairs with the woman from the door.

They joked and played and teased one another about missed notes and out of tune strings. Andy had a clear, strong voice and bottomless patience for teaching. Ben added a couple of tunes and then Cassie's mother sang a haunting ballad *a cappella*. Jason wished he'd brought a tape recorder with him. He'd never remember all of this.

He also wished he belonged to this group. They were all so comfortable together, and even though Cassie worried about what the town would think, she knew they would be thinking about her. They all loved her. Jason loved his family and got along well with the other guys in the band, but he'd never belonged the way these people belonged to one another. They probably wouldn't be as shocked as she thought by what was going on at her house. The way they teased each other, they weren't prudes.

Cass appeared, walking up the aisle. Jason had a flash of vertigo and looked at his watch to cover it. It was late. Most of the older folks seemed to have filtered up here. Watching Cassie again, he had the same impression of her walking down the aisle to marry him. Why she would be marrying him in a navy blue skirt and purple chenille sweater, he couldn't say.

She stopped beside where he leaned on the railing in front of the pulpit.

"Hi, swee'pea," Andy said, plucking his guitar strings. He'd tried to demonstrate a finger picking technique and hadn't been able to get it right yet, much to the amusement of his cronies.

"Hi, Dad. Boy, it's turned into *Dirty Dancing* down there."

One of the women gasped and jumped up, sprinting down the aisle with Reverend Bell hot on her heels.

"Mrs. Stern. Kady's mom," Cass filled in when Jason looked up.

What would happen if he reached up, pulled her into his lap and kissed her? Would she freak? Would her parents? Would he regret it for the rest of his life or would it be the best decision he'd ever made? He gripped the neck of his guitar, half ready to set it aside and experiment. They were in the perfect location for a shotgun wedding. Somebody might even have a shotgun.

"It's getting late, and Paul said he would take me back home if you wanted to stay," Cass said. "I can leave you the keys to the truck." Her voice sounded cool and even as she held out the keys, as if she wouldn't care if he decided to bunk down in one of the pews for the night. A sick jolt hit him that he'd left her alone for a very long time with Finn. Had Finn managed to make a successful play for her? But if Finn had met with success, wouldn't he be taking her home?

"We could have driven him home," her mother volunteered. He still hadn't caught her name. Sue? Shirley? Sharon? He should have paid closer attention.

But he wasn't staying. This cozy small town environment wasn't his. He was just visiting.

"No, Paul wants to talk to me," Cass said.

"If you don't mind me taking your truck." Jason took her keys. As long as Paul was taking her home it would be okay, but how soon could he duck out of here without raising suspicion?

* * * *

Cass caught herself as Jason took the truck keys from her. She'd lifted her hand toward him and then changed direction, set it down on the railing. She'd been about a breath away from brushing her fingers through his hair and kissing his forehead. It had seemed like a natural thing to do. "Well, I guess I'll see you then. You have the number if you have any problems."

Jason nodded.

Before she did anything revealing, she forced herself to walk away. He looked so comfortable and happy, it nearly brought tears to her eyes. She'd been surprised to hear music coming from the worship hall as she'd headed up to find him. Her father told her he had roped a couple of other old fogies into playing, but she hadn't expected to find half the community in the pews singing along. Any lingering guilt about leaving Jason alone with her father vanished when she saw him sitting right up front, bright-eyed and smiling. Of all the photos she'd seen of him, posed and impromptu, she'd never seen him so happy. She hadn't wanted to interrupt, but had a plan to carry out and Paul did want to talk to her.

Paul apologized again for saying too much to Finn on the way home, but accepted her assurance that she didn't hate him this time. He even tried to lie and tell her he didn't know what had gone on at the end of her marriage, but didn't attempt to come inside when he pulled up at her front door.

Once home, she took a record-setting shower. Locating the correct underwear took longer than she'd planned. Some things she never wore were packed into a box under the bed, and that's where she found her fancy underwire and lacy underwear. She had to shove her collection of magazines out of the way. Probably she'd be throwing those away now. None of it was really Jason.

No time for that right now though. Well before she thought Jason might decide to come home, she shimmied into the dress, left the bolero jacket, and darted into the bathroom to fix her hair and face. Her makeup was so old, half of it was dried up. She was pinning her hair in place when she heard her truck pass the house. Leaning into the garage, she pressed the door opener before sprinting into the bedroom to grab her velvet coat. She heard him stomping snow off his shoes in the garage as she turned on her Nat King Cole CD.

Jason opened the garage door. "Hi honey, I'm ho—" He stopped at the edge of the hall, staring.

Cass tried to remain calm. She clasped her hands in front of her. Her palms were damp, waiting for him to say something. What if he didn't like it? Maybe Sasha was right and the dress really looked horrible on her. What if? What if?

He set down his guitar case, never taking his eyes off her. "It's— You're— Wow." He took a step toward her. "You have such beautiful hair, *preciosa*," he murmured.

Cass smiled. She hadn't expected him to be quite so stunned. Happy, yes, but not speechless. He cradled her cheek in his palm as if he thought she would break. His thumb brushed the underside of her lip, and she leaned into the touch. Her eyes drifted closed. The room felt charged. Jason caught her in his arms and waltzed her across the room. He stroked the velvet at her waist until he had his hand on the small of her back, pulling her tight against his hard chest. She leaned her head on his shoulder.

"I wanted to dance with you all night," he whispered into her hair. "I wanted to hold you close and sway with you, and show all those people how beautiful I know you are, but I had no idea." He took her lower lip into his mouth, traced with his tongue along the sensitive inside.

When she reached up, trying to crush herself to him, he eased back to a teasing distance, relinquished her lower lip and tantalized her upper lip. Cass laced her fingers through his hair. Every strand glided across her fingers like silk.

He unbuttoned the one button holding the jacket closed, released her and took it off. As he folded it over the back of the couch, he stroked the velvet one last time. Then he turned to her, drew a deep breath through his nose. "You know what this dress needs?" he asked, his voice thick with desire.

Cass shook her head.

"It needs a nice yellow sapphire necklace." He trailed the tip of his finger along the side of her neck to a point above the neckline and between her breasts. Her skin sizzled with sensation in its wake. "A nice-sized one, surrounded by diamonds, hanging right about here." He traced a small circle on her flesh, dipping below the neckline of the dress, following the silk. "Or a garnet."

The brush of his finger against her skin paralyzed her. He seemed to be in no particular hurry, and she wanted to cry out with frustration, but her mouth had gone dry. Outside, the wind howled around the eaves. Jason walked behind her, spreading his hands over her bare shoulders. The soft weave of his sweater brushed against her skin.

"Silk suits you, Cassandra, *bella*," he murmured, his breath caressing her cheek and touching her nerves. He trailed his knuckles down her spine to the zipper.

"Jason, please." Heat throbbed between her legs.

He kissed her shoulder, unleashing waves of pleasure. "I want to see your hair down, *bella*." Need cut at the edge of his voice.

With clumsy fingers, she reached back for the comb holding her hair up in the simple French twist. No sooner had she pulled it loose, than she dropped it. Running his fingers through her hair, he freed it from its heavy coil, draped it across her shoulders.

"You have such beautiful hair, *preciosa*," he said, in that same low, intoxicating voice, combing his fingers through it. "You're best dressed when you're only wearing your beautiful hair." As he pulled down the zipper and the dress fell in a bright puddle around her feet, the cool air added its touch to her skin, caressing as his fingers soon would.

Turned to face him, she stepped out of the material. Eyes wide, he took in her lacy bra and panties.

"Surprises within surprises tonight," he said.

Reaching out, she pulled his sweater over his head, and while he watched, leaned forward, kissed his chest and chase her tongue along his collarbone. She pressed her hands against the hard planes of his stomach, moved them upward until her fingers brushed his tight nipples. Then he rested his hands on her shoulders again, kneaded the soft flesh. She had to taste his skin again, that delicious flavor distinctly his, and touched his nipple with the tip of her tongue. A heavy groan wrenched from him.

Abruptly, he lifted her off the floor and carried her to the bedroom. He laid her on the bed and followed her down. His weight pressed her into the mattress, his mouth commanded hers. Straining at his jeans, his length insisted against her and her legs fell open for him. Instead of taking off his jeans, he slid down her body, kissing her skin. He unhooked her bra, pulled it away, and mounding her breasts with his hands, suckled her nipples with a sweet, slow pressure that had her sobbing with pleasure. His journey down her stomach continued, bringing heat that bordered on pain, which coiled and snapped in her as he traced her belly button with the tip of his tongue. When he thrust his tongue into her belly button, she arched to meet him.

"Please, Jason, I want to feel you inside me." Now she was panting, couldn't wait.

Jason sat back as he pulled her panties down her thighs, watching her with dark eyes. "You keep making me want you more, *bella*," he said in a tight, pained voice. "Just when I think I want you so much I could die, you make me want you more." Kneeling, he unbuckled his pants.

Her heart swelled as she watched him kneeling over her. The firelight glinted off the wiry dark hair on his chest and stomach that eventually disappeared into the open waistband of his jeans. His hair fell across his face, shadowing his eyes. He looked so beautiful. She wanted to give him everything. To make him happy and heal all his hurts. Make the world perfect for him. Glad to have at least thought to open a condom as part of her preparations, she took it from the bedside table, handed it to him.

"The lady thinks of everything," he murmured. He slid it on and stretched out above her, hanging for a long moment.

With a suddenness that brought a cry from her, he thrust into her. Then he drew back almost to the point of slipping out and paused, gaze intent her face. Tears in her eyes, she stared up at him and put her hands on his shoulders. He thrust into her again. She drove her mouth against his shoulder. His strokes were powerful, almost frightening. Wilder than ever before. Cass opened herself to him, allowed him to drive into her.

"Jason," she cried out, as the tension inside her reached a crescendo. "Oh, Jason, I love you."

* * * *

Afterward, hoping he hadn't heard her, she lay very still in his embrace. So far he hadn't given her any indication he had. He lay beside her, panting. He laced his fingers through hers. "It was a wonderful surprise, *bella*," he said.

The dress or her declaration? It had to be the dress. He wouldn't be happy about her declaration. "I thought you would like it."

"Is that why you left early?"

"Yes."

"So you had it planned all along."

She turned her head sideways so she could see his face. "Not all along. It occurred to me in the middle of the dance that I could get home in time to change before you got back."

He touched his thumb to the corner of her eye where her mascara had smeared. "Makeup and everything."

"I've been told I clean up nicely."

He pulled her close, rested her head on his chest. "You're not bad dirty. In fact, you're pretty good." He kissed her head and tangled his fingers through her hair. Within moments, his breathing evened into sleep. So far she was safe. She closed her eyes. Gretta was wrong. She did love him.

And it doomed her.

* * * *

Half an hour ago, he'd awakened and wanted her with an intensity that surprised him. He needed to be wrapped in her. Cradled, protected, loved. Not only that, he wanted to be in her life, have the right to wake up next to her and pull her into his lap in the Baptist Church worship hall surrounded by the entire town.

It terrified him.

So he watched her sleep, waiting for the first signs of wakefulness so he could banish his fears in the security of her arms. Her eyelashes fluttered.

"Good morning, *bella*," he murmured, brushing his lips against her ear lobe.

"Good morning," Cass gasped. She arched her back. Her sweet feminine body brushed against him, delicious curves and wonderful clefts opening.

"Did you sleep well?" He traced the shell of her ear with his tongue.

She shuddered, pulling him closer. "Please, oh please," she moaned.

"Please what, *bella mia*?" The same havoc he'd created in her surged through him. His whole body felt like a live wire. He could still remember the way she'd looked in her beautiful silk dress with that half fearful, half hopeful smile when he'd walked out of the hall the night before. Shyly eager to please him, not sure of his reaction. He'd never known a woman who could do this to him every time.

"Jason," she gasped, then caught his mouth in a mind bending, urgent kiss that seemed to touch him everywhere. Wrapping her hands around his shoulders, she tugged him until he lay on top of her. Wanting to sob from the welcome he found in her lush heat, he thrust into her as she matched his movements with her tongue, invading him. She fused to him until he didn't know where she ended and he began.

He went rigid, cradled in her body. A roar of ecstasy shook him and in the moment after, as he sunk against her, he remembered they hadn't used a condom.

His breath stopped in his throat. What if she got pregnant? She would be bound to him forever. He could marry her and lock her up in a golden cage. Then he'd have his family and his home like he'd always wanted. He could have all of it with Cass.

And she would have succeeded in her little plan.

He shoved himself away, almost lunged out of bed in his haste.

"What's the matter?" she asked, sitting up. As if he hadn't already seen every inch of her creamy white skin, she yanked the sheet up over her shoulders.

"I forgot to use a condom." He stalked across the room.

"Oh." She licked her lips. "Well, I probably won't get pregnant the first time anyway. I mean, what are the odds? That is what you're upset about, isn't it?"

No. "Yes," he told her, flipped open his suitcase and grabbed clean clothes. "I need to take a shower."

"Jason?"

Her forlorn tone stopped him. When he turned back, she'd drawn her knees up in front of her and wrapped her arms around them like a personal wall. Her curly hair fell like a molten curtain and the tears in her sea blue eyes seemed about to spill over. She looked like an abandoned child.

He was a heel. A monster. A greedy bastard.

He went back to the bed, dropped his clothes at the foot and gathered her into his arms.

"Don't worry," he murmured, sifting through her wild, enticing hair with his fingers. "If you are pregnant, I'll take care of you."

"No. I just don't— Are you mad at me?"

"Mad at you?" Jason leaned back to look at her white face. Her fair skin was blotchy and tendrils of hair stuck to her cheeks. He'd never loved anyone so much. So ironic, when he'd never meant to love her at all. "Why would I be mad?"

"I could have remembered the condom, too. It's my fault. It's all my fault." She put her hands over her face.

Jason petted her hair. Crap like this was why the band had exiled him here in the first place. Not that the other guys would have cried, but Bear punched him in Denver and Tyler poured a large Coke over his head in Oklahoma City on the last tour. He'd have rather had it the other way around because being punched by a drummer wasn't preferable, but he'd have gladly endured both again instead of seeing Cassie cry. Unfortunately, it seemed to be the only thing he was good at. He'd made her cry twice in less than a week. Maybe more, because she had taken a couple of marathon baths. He leaned his cheek against her head. "I'm sorry, Cassie. I'm a bastard and I'm taking it out on everyone around me. Maybe I should go."

"Go?" She looked up, a feverish fear in her eyes. "Go where?"

"Just away. The longer I stay with you, the more I hurt you."

"No," she protested, gripping his shoulders. "Please, no. I mean, I don't want you to go. You won't be here that much longer. Please, Jason, stay with me a little while longer."

"Cassie, I don't want to keep hurting you." Jason tried to pull away from her, but her fingers dug into his shoulders.

"Please, stay. You won't hurt me. I promise."

"Cass." As if he were prying a cat's claws from his skin, he removed her hands. "How can you promise I won't hurt you anymore?"

She drew a deep breath like she meant to get herself together, but her hands didn't relax. "Easy. I won't let it bother me when you get moody and quiet. I won't push you for anything." As he moved away from the bed, she climbed to her knees. "And even if I am pregnant, I won't ask you for anything. That first day you said you just wanted this. It'll just be this." She gestured at the bed, letting the sheet fall away from her. "You can leave here next week and never look back. I won't contact you for anything and I won't tell anyone what happened between us. I promise."

One eyebrow raised at her, he hid his turmoil behind a cool mask. Was this some grand master level of the con? "I think if you're pregnant, people will figure out what's going on up here."

* * * *

Cass wanted to crumble into a heap. When he woke her passionately this morning she'd been so happy. She'd thought he had heard her and didn't hold it against her. She'd even been outrageous enough to think maybe he shared the feeling. Obviously, she'd been wrong. How could the man who had touched her so lovingly stand at the end of her bed negotiating with her heart? "I can hide the pregnancy. I'll give the baby away."

A flicker of something dangerous crossed Jason's face then his mask slammed back into place. "If that's what you want," he said with a shrug, picked up his clothes and walked out of the room.

When the bathroom door closed she slumped sideways, too stunned to breathe. She couldn't ever give his baby away. What had possessed her to say such a thing? How would she have hidden a pregnancy anyway? She'd be due at the end of September when she still had campers. But she could keep the promise to not ask for anything. Let the whole town look at her with pity as she raised her dark-haired, dark-eyed child. Even if all she had left of him was his child, at least that she could keep forever.

The bathroom door opened, and he entered the bedroom, clothed and smelling oh so good. "I'm going to build more snow sculptures," he announced.

Cass had succeeded in getting out of bed and dressing in some clean clothes. If she'd been alone this morning, she might not have bothered with clothes. Or getting up. "Do you want some breakfast?"

"No. I'll come in when I get hungry." He picked up his coat and walked out of the bedroom.

Cass opened her mouth to say something, but before anything came out, the door closed behind him. She didn't understand. Last night he'd been happy. He'd enjoyed the dance and the jam session, even seemed amused by Kady and Cori's antics. The dress had wowed him speechless. Then, this morning he'd gone from loving to angry to guilty and back to angry so fast, she hadn't had time to register the change.

Sharp, stabbing pains originated from everywhere in her head, ricocheted around her skull. Her heart felt like someone was juicing it like an orange. She summoned the energy to put one foot forward. Once that was accomplished, moving the second foot came easier and she was able to totter to her living room. Her dress still lay in a puddle on the floor. The velvet coat hung over the back of the couch. She picked them up and carried them to the bedroom, draping both over the corner chair. Right now, she didn't have the energy to manipulate hangers. Instead she walked to the window and looked out.

Jason was busy digging in the snow. He hadn't left. When he got cold he would come in to warm up and eat something. She had to remember to take what he gave her and cherish it, because everything was a rental.

And the contract was nearly up.

Cass turned away from the window. She'd promised she wouldn't ask him for anything or let his moods bother her. They would her, but she'd have to learn to hide it. Which meant not wandering around the house like a lost soul. It was only a few days more. Not a lifetime.

She squared her shoulders. Her painting. It was something to do. Something very, very normal.

Cass strode into the living room. Paint. She could paint while the world ended and not notice except to wonder why her landscape wasn't sitting still.

Her bare foot came down on something hard, snapping it. Cursing, she hopped away.

The comb she'd used in her hair last night lay on the floor in two jagged pieces. She scooped up the pieces, stalked to the trash and tossed them in. Combs could be replaced at any drugstore in the country for less than a dollar. Just because that was the last of the combs that had secured her hair on her wedding day all those years ago, meant nothing. Should have thrown it away a long before now because it was damn bad luck. She slammed the lid on the trashcan.

* * * *

Jason surveyed his third Easter Island head. The first one had fallen over and split in half moments after he finished it. The second looked more like Olmec than Easter Island. This one's nose wouldn't stay on. He blamed the sculptor. His hands hadn't stopped shaking since this morning.

How could she consider giving his child away? How dare she?

That they'd only been unprotected once didn't matter and he didn't plan to repeat it. Somehow, in his mind, they had a child.

He wanted that.

Or he thought he did.

Didn't he?

He glanced back at the house as the nose plopped off again. Cass was what he longed for in a mate, except for the scheming. Imagining the rest of his life with her was easier than imagining the rest of his life without her. And she might be pregnant now.

He thought he wanted her to be carrying his child.

At the same time, the concept made him want to run screaming into the woods.

He glared at the last head. What made him think he could be a husband and father when he couldn't even raise a half decent snow sculpture? He stamped snow off his shoes, but the cold leaked up his legs. Was it possible to freeze to the ground? He'd have to stay then. "*Sorry guys, can't make the Grammys. Frozen to the ground.*"

She'd said she loved him, but that had been in the throes of passion. Women said stuff like that during sex. They were biologically programmed to, so she might not mean it.

At some point he must have wandered into *The Twilight Zone*. Wasn't there an episode where a train stopped in a perfect little town? What was the twist at the end? Potterville had an eerie perfection about it. The cute diner and the weekly church dances. Just the kind of place to settle down and raise a little family. A little family he might have started this morning.

Almost five, his watch read. Yesterday she'd called him in at least once an hour to warm up, but other than when she called him in for lunch he'd been out here all day. She hadn't looked peachy at lunch. Could be, she was inside struggling with the same questions, looking for the door to her personal *Twilight Zone*. Did she regret what happened this morning? She might regret telling him she would give their baby up. Or was she rubbing her hands together, thinking she'd caught him permanently like Bonnie had snared Brian? Was that a bad thing? Most of the time he was jealous of what Brian had.

Cass appeared at the open garage door.

"Jason?" she called. "Why don't you come inside and warm up. Dinner's about ready anyway."

"All right." He turned away from the heads. They didn't have any helpful advice tonight. In the morning he'd try them again.

Cass made chicken sandwiches and some kind of bean salad for dinner. They ate in strained silence the way they had eaten lunch. Afterward, he helped clear the table. His shoes were drying on the hearth. Next time he needed to bring more than one pair. In fact, he needed to invest in some real boots, not for fashion, but the kind built for winter hiking.

Wait. Next time?

Jason put the last plate in the sink and walked out to the living room. The painting she'd been working on looked finished and he admired it while she wiped off the table. She could have put it in the window and told people the scene was real and they would have believed her. A car drove down Main Street, like any day of the week. That was what he wanted to step into.

"Where's that pasture?"

"Pasture?"

"The one you were talking about buying. You said I could go with you and take a look at it."

Cass knotted her fingers. "Did you really want to go see it? It's getting dark soon."

He put his arms around her. She was beautiful, clever, sweet, thoughtful, kind. And had said she loved him. "How long will it take to get there?"

"Half an hour or so, depending on the road." She bit her lip. "It's only a little way on the other side of the mountain, but when you drive, it takes longer. Do you want to go?" She looked up at him, and he heard echoes of questions she wasn't asking.

"Sure. Why not?" He kissed her forehead and didn't move away immediately. This felt good. He could step off *The Twilight Zone* train at this stop and it wouldn't be so bad. "Can we go now?"

Chapter 15

She tried to relax. He might be acting a little more like himself, but she wasn't sure she could judge. She felt deranged from a day of painting and peering out the window wondering what was going on in his mind and worrying he was going to walk through the door and announce he had to go. Now. Immediately. Yesterday, if possible.

But he wanted to go to the pasture instead. "Okay, if you really want to. It'll be dark, but I think there's a full moon tonight." Her eyes lingered on his for a few minutes before she turned away. "Let me get my coat."

Cass started the truck and let it warm up for the long drive down the mountain and up the holler to Bill Wernick's. As she reached the last turn to his place, she stopped.

"Fence posts," she told Jason, and pointed.

Squinting through the glare of the headlights, he said, "Yeah, what about them?"

"They're new and too tall. He's putting up a sign for the riding stable."

"Why?"

Cass smirked at him. "Because he thinks it's going to be an entrance for my campground. That's why he offered right of way so fast."

"Well, if this is going to be an entrance, you're going to have to do something about the road."

Cass followed Jason's gaze up the single lane that wound between the trees and cursed under her breath. She had forgotten about the goat track Bill called a road leading to the pasture. It made the road so far look like an interstate. The wind normally blew harder on this side of the mountain, so she wasn't worried about deep snow, but she wasn't sure how deep some of the ruts might be. Getting stuck would be awkward, but she had her phone and she could come up with some reason for Jason being with her. She might even be able to tell the truth.

"Hold on," she said.

Starting up the lane, she watched for the first switchback, which at this time of year would only be visible by the presence of trees seeming to grow in the middle of the road. Jason ignored her advice and sat with one arm across the back of the seat, his long legs crossed at the ankles. By the third switchback, he'd shifted to a more cautious position, gripping the door with one hand, feet braced against the floor. She straightened the wheel as they turned out of the woods, and the truck slid sideways. The rear wheel dropped into a rut, halting the truck. Jason gasped as they jerked to a stop, but she couldn't be sure if it was because of the slide or the view.

The pasture opened in an oblong bowl shape between the sheltering arms of two ridges. It spanned the length of a football field at its widest and half again as long. In the center the wind had uncovered a long shallow pond reflecting the black sky and the stars overhead. By his expression, he'd been gasping at the view. His eyes were fixed on the waterfall.

The high ridge on the west side of the valley rose at a steep angle. The frozen waterfall spilled down the wall in lace ruffles of ice. A rocky pool caught the fall before allowing it to trail across the valley floor to the pond and then through a gap in the ridge.

"My God," Jason breathed. He fumbled with his door, popped it open and tumbled out of the truck. "It's beautiful."

Cass stepped out, enjoying his open-mouthed wonder. It was a nice valley. Sheltered and cool. Utterly peaceful. The full moon reflected off the snow, gleaming across the black ice in the center. "I'll have to take out the fence." She motioned toward the low fence Bill had installed to keep his sheep under control. "And I think I'll cut a road through from my end instead of using his right of way. Too many of my campers have trouble with my entrance. No trailers back here though. Even if they got them in, they'd be impossible to get out again."

"Would you build cabins here?" Jason tore his wide-eyed gaze from the scene before him and glanced at her.

"Sure. I could fit fifteen cabins here. The cabins up front are too close together. I'd like to spread these out a little more. And there's another little plateau below the eastern ridge where I could offer tent camping."

He sat on the front bumper with his hands between his knees, looking around the valley. "I'd love to build a house here."

Cass blinked. "A house?"

He turned to her with sparkling eyes. "Yeah. A nice two-story place right over there, facing the pool, but angled toward the waterfall. And the master bedroom, too. That would be right upstairs over the living room.

You'd have to be able to see the waterfall from the master bedroom. The driveway would angle around that way so it wouldn't interrupt the view. I'd put your painting studio on the second story over the garage so you could still see into the valley, and my music room would be across the hall."

Cass's chest tightened. "So you're building this house for us?" she asked as evenly as she could manage.

Jason stood up and gathered her into his arms. "Do you want me to build a house for you?"

She tried to laugh, but it sounded more like a sob. He was playing with her. There was no way he would ever stay in Potterville, West Virginia. This was not the kind of place people like him lived. He was building castles in the air. Maybe he was the kind of person who talked about these kinds of things without ever doing them. "Yes. I do. Maybe you could start construction tomorrow. There's plenty of snow to work with."

Laughing, he released her. He'd turned away, so he didn't see her stumble and catch herself on the hood of the truck. "I can see it now. Just like your bungalow, but bigger. A big living room with a fieldstone fireplace and floor to ceiling windows and a big warm kitchen with hardwood floors the color of honey."

And huge heating bills. Jason didn't think about things like heating bills. People who built castles in the air never worried about practicalities. She closed her eyes, holding in tears. She didn't need a house, she needed him. "So you approve then?"

"Approve? This is fantastic. I can't believe you'd waste it on cabins." He turned to her, grinning. "I'd keep it for myself."

A chill that had nothing to do with the weather had settled on her, and she wrapped her arms around herself. "It's getting cold. Let's head back." She climbed in the truck without waiting for him. As she turned the truck around to leave, he was plastered to the window, soaking in the view. He'd be overjoyed in the summer when honeysuckle and mountain thyme hung on the air like a balm and wild flowers grew everywhere. It would be a popular campsite, she thought, jerking the wheel too hard and making the rear end slide. She hit the gas to pull the vehicle out of the slide, but the wheels spun. Cursing, she slammed the truck into reverse and stomped on the gas. Nothing but noise.

"We're stuck?" Jason asked.

Dropping it back in first, she stomped on the gas again. The tires whined in protest, but the truck didn't move. She opened the door and looked back. In her haste to leave, she'd swung wider than she thought and sunk the truck into a trough up to its axle. She pulled the door closed and rubbed her face with her gloved hands. "We're stuck."

"Should I get out and push?" Jason offered.

"Only if you're about to turn into the Hulk." Cass patted her pockets, searching for the phone. Donny would come up and get her. She'd tell him Jason had been curious about the property because he'd heard them talking about it over lunch and he'd been a little cabin-fevered after the storm.

She patted her pockets again. If she could find her phone.

Damn. Before they'd left, she'd seen the phone charging on the sideboard and reminded herself to grab it, but apparently hadn't done so. She'd been too dazed by the idea that Jason wanted to do something with her. He'd been outside all day, and she'd had plenty of time to worry that he'd changed his mind. Not that her distraction was an excuse for forgetting. "You didn't happen to bring a cellphone with you, did you?"

"No."

Cass leaned her forehead against the steering wheel. She'd never done anything so careless and stupid in her life. Her phone went with her when she walked around the cabins during the off-season in case she got hurt and couldn't get inside. If the weather was heavy, she didn't even set foot out the door unless she had to. Her cabin was stocked with enough food to survive for months, if need be. She had spares, backups, and extras of everything she used at the cabin. She even had a shotgun in case of bears and wolves, but when she saw those, she stayed inside and shot pictures instead.

"It's not that bad. Is it?" Jason sounded uncertain, which reminded her that, in addition to all her other failings, she wasn't doing her campground director job and handling the situation.

"No, it's not." She sat up. "I forgot the phone so I can't call anyone to pull us out. The truck is stuck good so we're not going to get out on our own. I'll walk down to Bill's—"

"No."

Cass looked at him. "No?"

"You're not leaving me here while you walk for help by yourself. I'll go with you."

"You're wearing tennis shoes."

Jason shrugged. "It can't be more than a mile."

"Yes, it can. A bit more, in fact."

"I can manage." He reached over and put his arm around her. "It'll be fun."

"It's half a mile to my house through the grounds."

"Really?" His expression brightened.

"See that gap there on the far end of the valley? My farthest tent site is right on the other side."

"Good. We can be home in time for the news." He jumped out of the truck.

Scowling, she climbed out her side. The temperature had dropped earlier today when the snow stopped falling. The snow had a crisp crust she would have admired on a pie, but not on the ground. Snow masked the true edges of the pond and right now she couldn't remember how far it came out. This whole adventure already felt too much like Jack London's *To Build a Fire* for her to want to get her feet wet. Jason stamped his feet for warmth. The snow came to his knees and well over hers. What had she been thinking, coming out here today?

She hadn't been.

Since Jason had showed up on her doorstep and made that comment about the long two years, she hadn't been using logic at all. Sexy rock star, she could have handled. Even sexy flirtatious rock star. But sexy flirtatious wounded rock star had been too much to withstand. A quiet little tryst, leaving the emotions to deal with later, had seemed simple enough.

It had been like setting a devil's food cake and a gallon of milk in front of a chocoholic and walking out of the room.

And now she'd arranged a romantic double suicide for them. How sweet. Someone might find them next week if the wolves didn't get to them first.

"Jason, watch out," she snapped. He hadn't stuck by her side, but had set off in a straight path down the middle of the valley, heading right for the pond.

He froze in his tracks.

"Stay with me. I don't know where the edge of the water is, and if you get your feet wet you could get frostbite." She scowled as he backed up three steps and then walked toward her still grinning from ear to ear. "This is the most exciting thing that's ever happened to you, isn't it?" she accused.

"I wouldn't say that," he replied, and put his arm over her shoulders. "It's not even the most exciting thing that's happened to me this week, but it's pretty darn cool."

"I'm not sure what's so darn cool about being stranded on the mountain in the middle of the winter," Cass grumbled.

"I've never been out in the woods like this. It's amazing." He looked up at the sky, his face bright in the moonlight, and squeezed her shoulders. "I never went camping when I was a kid, and the only snow I had was pretty dirty after the plows went past."

"So has building snowmen been a lifelong dream?" Cass fought a smile, but the smile won.

"I didn't know what I was missing."

The wonder in his voice made her heart ache.

It was a pretty magical scene. The ski lodge was even hidden around the curve of the mountain. Almost a shame to put cabins here.

They stepped under the canopy of trees. The clearing of the last tent camping site was visible through the trunks. In the summer, she could hardly see it through the bushes. "You grew up in Indianapolis, didn't you?" she asked.

"In the projects. After my dad walked out, Mom didn't have much money, with five kids to feed."

That stopped her in her tracks. Walked out? "I thought your father—"

Halted two strides ahead of her, he turned back, his face still and pale, as if he waited for her response. "We tell everyone he died. He walked out when I was four. My mother told us he went looking for work. Then one day she got a letter, and she started saying he was dead."

"Are you sure?" Cass gasped. She felt stunted and weird, as if she'd been personally attacked by this piece of trivia and left bleeding in the snow.

"When I was twelve, I found the letter and it said he wasn't coming back. He had a new family he liked better." His face could have been made of marble, and he stood with his feet planted wide, as if the mountain might start moving under him like the deck of a ship.

Her knees gave way. She grabbed a slender birch for support, snapping off a small branch with her glove. She could envision him finding that letter at twelve, all long legs and squeaky voice, being told he wasn't a good enough for his father to want him. Her father had been such a constant in her life, she couldn't imagine living without him. He'd held her hand when she'd learned to ice skate, and when she got divorced.

A shadow fell across him, leaving him faceless as he straightened his shoulders.

"Jason," she whispered. "I'm so sorry."

"You didn't do it."

No words could bridge the distance that had grown between them. She reached out, releasing her hold on the birch, but her arms weren't long enough either, so she floundered forward to put her arms around him. His arms came around her, but he held her stiffly, as if he'd prefer to shove her away. Or he expected her to push him away. Squeezing her eyes closed, she pressed her cheek against his chest. His heart pounded. She longed to cradle him in her arms and tell him everything would be all right. That she could make it better.

But she couldn't. How could she fix his father walking out on him at four and rejecting him again at twelve, when she couldn't do anything about Stella dumping him in the national press? She couldn't even fix the fact that he was standing in the woods in the middle of January wearing shoes that probably still weren't dry. "I am so sorry, Jason," she whispered.

"I don't know why I told you," he muttered. "Nobody outside my family knows. Not even Brian."

She brushed a shaking hand through his hair. Why hadn't she made him wear a hat? She wasn't taking very good care of him at all. "I won't tell a soul. I promise."

On tiptoes, she kissed him. For a moment he resisted the pressure of her lips, then he relented slightly. She shivered so hard that she thought he must be, too. Clutching his shoulders, she tried to draw him to her embrace. She wanted to drag him bodily from his pain, but he wouldn't move. It hurt to hold him.

She broke the kiss, rested her forehead on his chest. Her breath came in long deep clouds that rose up around them, mingling with his over their heads. "It's getting colder by the minute out here," she told him. "We should get moving before we freeze to death."

Jason nodded, and for a heartbeat, didn't release her, clenched her against his stiff body instead. Then he dropped his arms. Cass swayed back, staying within reach, hoping he would pull her back against him. He didn't. Aching with a loss she didn't even understand, she moved away, but she reached back and took his hand, squeezing it until his fingers closed around hers.

"Do your sisters know?" she asked as they reached the mouth of the second RV campsite.

"Probably. We never talked about it."

She nodded, watching the ground. "Does your mother know you know?"

"I don't know. I happened to be hitting those awkward teenage years when I found the letter, so she probably thought the wearing black and not talking was part of growing up." Jason pulled his hand away and jammed it in his pockets. She let him go, and he walked behind her, almost in her footsteps.

"He hasn't tried to contact you, has he?"

"I don't think so. My office handles that stuff and nobody has said anything."

Walking along the ridge at the edge of the road, the snow wasn't as deep under the trees so she didn't have to bring her feet up as high with each step. Every part of her felt wrung out and tired. Next time she saw her parents, she'd have to hug them and tell Mom and Dad she loved them. In fact, she should hug Ida and Paul and Ben and select other townspeople, while she was at it.

Cass kept putting one foot in front of the other. She needed to get Jason home and warm. Get him where she could take care of him again, somehow. She could give him her body to blot out the pain of losing a woman he loved, but she could never replace his father.

A glance back revealed he walked with his head down, hands shoved in his coat pockets. That long ago letter seemed to float in the air above his head. What kind of man would have five children and walk out on them? What kind of man could not be proud of the man his son had become?

"Almost home," she said brightly. She reached back and hooked her arm through his elbow. "You want to make popcorn and watch a movie or do you just want to have sex?"

Jason blinked at her. "No. I think I'll go to bed. I'm pretty tired tonight."

"I don't have any blankets warmed by the fire this time."

"It's okay."

When they reached home and she'd unlocked the front door he went straight for the bedroom, while she checked her messages. Bill Wernick called saying he'd found her truck in the pasture and assumed she'd gotten stuck and walked home. The truck was in his barn with the keys in it, whenever she wanted to come get it. Her mother wanted her to call as soon as she got in because Bill had called them too. Cass heard Jason moving around taking off his clothes and getting ready for bed as she dialed her parents. He'd said he was tired. Too tired for sex. And the clock in the kitchen showed it wasn't even nine yet.

"Hello?" her mother answered.

"Hi, Mom."

"Oh, honey, we were starting to worry. Bill said he found your truck but not you. I was giving you another half hour before I called the state troopers."

"I got stuck and forgot my cellphone so I walked home."

"That's fine, honey. We just didn't know where you were. I started to worry you'd been attacked by wolves or something."

And people think I have an overactive imagination. Why would wolves attack me when there's plenty of deer around who don't look like they might be packing guns?

"You didn't have your rifle with you either, did you?" her mother asked in another show of mind reading.

"No, but it was fine." No sounds came from the bedroom. Jason must have already gotten under the covers. She wished she could do something more than hug him, but he didn't seem to want anything. His father had abandoned him. His *father*. She couldn't even imagine it. Both her parents had always been there. And Jason had been lying about his father all his life. He must have been too devastated to tell anyone. Why had he told her? Why had he started planning a house for them, when he didn't plan on staying past the end of next week? Why was he being so quiet?

"Honey, are you there?"

"Sorry, Mom, I was thinking about my cold feet. It was a long walk." Cass held her breath, waiting for her mother to discover the fib. She wasn't sure why she didn't tell the truth. Her mother had already given her blessing to the idea that Cass might sleep with her winter guest and she didn't know all the details. Probably if her mother knew about Jason's past, she'd be all for her doing whatever she could to make him feel better.

"Cold feet? You should get out the hot water bottle to help warm your bed up. Did you make sure your guest was warm?"

"My guest?" Terror struck her that her mother somehow knew her guest was in her bedroom warming her bed.

"Bill said he saw two sets of footprints. I thought your guest must have gone with you when you went to see the pasture. I can't imagine why. It's just a pasture."

Smiling at her mom's assessment, she crouched in front of the dining room cabinet, digging for her hot water bottle. *Just a pasture* had Jason open mouthed with wonder, bowled him over, and he'd been all over the world. The hot water bottle lay buried at the bottom of the cabinet, and she snatched it up. "He liked it. He heard us talking at Ida's and wanted to see it."

"He's probably not used to being cooped up by the winter like this, either. A man like that probably flies off to the Virgin Islands when the weather turns."

The hot water bottle slithered out of her fingers and fell on her overly tender, thawing feet. "Ow!"

"What's the matter?"

"I dropped something on my foot. I'm going to fill up this bottle."

"All right, sweetie. You get warmed up and make sure of your guest. Good night. Sleep tight."

"Thanks, Mom. Good night." She couldn't promise sleeping tight, or at all.

In the bedroom, Jason lay curled on his side facing away from the fire, buried under the blankets. Cass slid the now full hot water bottle under the covers near his feet. He wasn't anywhere near sleep, but seemed so intent on pretending, she didn't disturb him. It had been a long, cold hike.

She added two large logs to the fire. The fire leaped up, casting troubling shadows on the walls as she slipped off her clothes and draped them over a chair to dry. For a moment she hesitated, fingering the flannel nightgown she hadn't worn since Jason moved in. She would have welcomed the soft touch of the cloth against her skin now, knowing his sweet caresses would not be coming.

She turned away from the nightgown and walked around the bed to where Jason had dropped his clothes in a careless heap. The wet cuffs of his jeans had soaked his shirt and sweatshirt already. On the bottom of the pile lay his sopping wet socks. Holding them, she wondered if she should "wake" him and insist he dry his feet, but a glance at his shadowed face stopped her. His feet would dry well enough on the sheets. She draped his clothes on the chair with hers where they would dry and climbed into bed beside him.

Jason's familiar weight pulled her to the center of the bed. Usually he slept curled around her, his face buried in her hair. They fit together like two spoons in a drawer, knees and hips curved together, his arm draped across her stomach. Not tonight. How long would it take to learn to fall asleep without the whisper of his breath across her cheek?

She propped herself on one elbow and tugged the blanket over his shoulder, allowing her hand to trail across his back under the sheet. He didn't react. Normally he responded to her every touch, even if only to sigh in his sleep. She wished he would roll over and take her in his arms. His strong chest pressed against her back would feel so good right now. But something had torn between them tonight. She slid her hand around his waist as she fitted her knees behind his and curved her hips around his. She pressed her cheek against his shoulder. Breathing his scent, she closed her eyes.

Chapter 16

Jason opened his eyes in the dark room. The clock beside the bed said 1:30. The way he felt, he would have invited a hangover. His head rested somewhere warm, soft, and seemingly safe. Without moving and alerting Cass, he discovered he'd twisted around her in his sleep and now had his cheek resting between her breasts. She had her arm draped around his shoulders and her other hand on top of his head. Her knees hooked over his, trapping him. Getting out of bed without waking her would be tricky, and if he woke her, he'd have to talk to her.

He didn't want to talk to anyone now. He wanted to slip away and leave a cheery note saying it had been fun, but he had to get home to take care of some business. Never mind that business would be finding another hideout to finish out his exile and lick his fresh wounds.

The slow beat of Cass's heart pulsed under his ear. He'd watched her shadow as she'd undressed by the firelight last night, and for the first time, not been aroused. Even when she climbed into bed and lay naked against him, stroking his back, he hadn't wanted to roll over and take her.

He'd wanted to run then, too.

He closed his eyes, which proved to be a mistake. Eyes closed, he could see the letter in his hands.

He'd gone into his mother's room to find some money for milk. She'd been out working and had taken her purse with her, so he went through the pockets of her thin, ragged winter coat and torn raincoat. Finding nothing, he'd pulled down her church purse. Before he found the dollar bills she kept there for her tithe, he found the letter in a side pocket. The paper was soft from handling, the letter dated the day they'd told him his father had died. Every year on that date, Jason went to the church and lit a candle for his father's soul.

But according to the thick block letters on this page, his father wasn't dead. He'd found a woman in Santa Fe he liked better and they were expecting a baby. Too stunned to even tear the letter to shreds, he'd sunk to his knees, reading and rereading it until every inkblot had burned into his mind. His two oldest sisters had been at work, waiting tables to supplement the family income. Connie, the middle child, was out with friends. She wouldn't have her waitressing job for six more months. Only Tessa had been home, nose in a book, studying for a test. He'd tucked the letter back the way he'd found it and walked out of the house.

The police had dragged him home at three in the morning after a fight in a pool hall. The next day he'd gone to school with no sleep, two black eyes, and a split lip, and he'd managed to keep the truth from his family, the police, and the school counselor.

Jason shifted and Cass moved, moaning in her sleep. She rolled away from him and lay with one arm and one leg dangling off the side of the bed, facing the glowing remains of the fire. He sat up and looked at her. Her face in the firelight was flushed with sleep and tendrils of hair stuck to her forehead.

He trusted Cass. She loved him, but she wouldn't for long. Not now that she knew the truth. Soon she'd start wondering what his father saw that made him leave. He hadn't left when the girls were born. When the boy was born, he'd packed up and left.

She'd see what had made his father leave, or her father would. And by then, he would need her too much to lose her.

He slipped out of bed and picked up her yellow silk dress, draped over the chair in the corner, and pressed the material to his face. It still smelled like her. A faint scent of vanilla, ginger and hope. That night two nights ago had been one of the highlights of his life. The little church dance and taking a turn around the dance floor with the town's one gay man and most of the matriarchs. The hillbilly jam session in the chapel. He'd felt so much like he belonged here. And he wanted to. He wanted to watch Kady and Cori compete for the attentions of some man who wasn't him, learn Maybelle Carter's fingerpicking technique from Cass's father and memorize the words to that haunting ballad Cass's mother had sung. Most of all, he longed to dress Cass up in beautiful clothes just to have the right to take them off her. He ached to come home once in a while to find her standing in the living room looking so beautiful, his heart wanted to stop beating.

It wasn't fair. He couldn't have any of those things. If he tried, when Cass abandoned him for a better sugar daddy, he'd end up even lonelier. Or she'd figure out why his father rejected him and then she'd reject him too. It didn't matter. She wouldn't stay. They never stayed. Only his mom and his sisters would remain with him, and they depended on his money and his connections. The guys in the band needed him because he was a great guitar player. None of them liked him. His father was right all those years ago.

He knelt in front of the fire and fed a few small sticks into it. As he moved, trying to get closer to the heat, his foot caught on something poking from under her bed. Leaning down beside the bed, he tugged on the corner of the box.

The banker's box held carefully filed magazines. He pulled out one from the back and recognized his own smiling face from several years ago. Drawing out another, he saw himself again. Sifting through it, he found the infamous issue of *People* magazine. On page thirty-seven, he found a picture of himself and Stella, smiling on the red carpet of a movie premiere with an artful tear separating them. Cass had everything in that box. So it was a con. She needed him. Nobody could love him.

Something sour coiled in his stomach.

"Jason?" Her voice was heavy with sleep, but still so sweet.

"Yeah."

"What are you doing?"

"The fire was going out." He glanced up. Her eyes were closed, so he jammed the magazine back into box and shoved it under the bed. She'd studied her prey. Part of him wanted to keep being conned. Even if it only lasted for a little while, it might be worth the ride.

"Come to bed. It'll be fine." She opened one eye.

"I heard what you said."

"About the fire?"

He didn't want to continue and couldn't stop himself. "You said you loved me the other night."

Stiffening, she sat up, clutching the blankets over her breasts, looking impossibly small and fragile. Either she was really hurt or she was a really good actress.

"We weren't going to get involved."

"I know," she said. "I didn't mean to. I'm sorry."

"Are you?" Hardly aware he was wearing nothing, he stood. "After all, if you were to manipulate me into loving you, it would get you out of this little burg and you'd never have to worry about money again."

"What?" Her voice had no strength. "I wasn't manipulating you."

"Oh? The nice cozy dance, the little jam you arranged, the dress you surprised me with, the very convenient timing of your confession."

"I thought it would please you." Her voice tightened.

"You even conned me into telling you a lie to further soften what I thought was your soft heart."

She frowned, pulling the sheets higher around her neck. "A lie?"

"My father never walked out on me." He grinned cruelly, and hated himself for doing it. That story would be worth a lot to the tabloids if they got hold of it. She couldn't know he'd given her anything worth selling. "I can't believe you bought that. It works every time."

"Why?"

He shrugged. "Why not? You were conning me into believing you loved me."

"I wasn't." Cass bit her lip. "I do love you." Tears glistened on her eyelashes.

He sneered, fighting against the urge to gather her into his arms and hold her. That was what she wanted. "I have to go. This whole act is getting to me."

"Act?" She gasped.

He snapped on the light.

Blinking against the sudden brightness, she said, "What are you doing?"

"Leaving." He picked up his discarded clothing and dressed.

"Why? Why now? It's the middle of the night. You have another week."

He paused, searching for a sweater. "That is true. I have another week of your tender attentions."

Her face stiffened with fury. "Of course. You have paid, haven't you? If you are set on leaving tonight, maybe you'd like another tumble before you hit the road. After all, it's a long flight. Though one of the stewardesses might be willing to initiate you into the mile high club."

"I'm already a member," he snapped from the depths of the sweatshirt he yanked over his head.

"I don't doubt it. You'll sleep with anything that's handy."

"And I slept with you."

The look on her face stopped him. Some deep hurt cracked open inside her and spilled across her cheeks. Tears ran down the sides of her nose and across her lips.

He wanted to drop to his knees and apologize. Anything, to stop that pain. Instead, he picked up a pair of jeans, jammed them into the suitcase and snapped it closed. He stalked into the living room, picked up his guitar and carried it into the bedroom, where he'd left the case.

"Jason, please don't go," she begged. Tears ran down her jaw and neck. "It's late and you're tired."

"You sense me getting away, is that it?"

"No, it's—"

"I'm already gone." Hefting the suitcase in one hand and the guitar case in the other, he walked toward the door.

Cass lunged off the bed. Her legs tangled in the sheet, bringing her crashing to the floor. "Jason, please. I don't know what's wrong. I don't know what I did, but I'm sorry. I didn't mean what I said." She snatched up a robe and pulled it over her shoulders as she chased him down the hall.

"So now you don't love me?"

"That's not what I mean."

Jason shrugged on his coat. "When did you start planning, Cassie? Was it the minute I walked in the door, or later? You must have been so happy to see me coming. Your ticket out of here."

"I never thought that. Please. You can't go like this. The roads are bad." She grabbed his arm. "Just stay until morning."

He shook free. As he stomped down the garage stairs, he hit the door opener. Cass followed him.

"Can't we talk about this?" She sobbed.

"No," he said over his shoulder. He stomped around the roadway to his rental car. His head spun. The winter wind reached icy fingers into his coat as he dropped the suitcase and guitar in the trunk.

"Jason, be careful on the roads," she called.

Seated behind the wheel, he slammed the door and started the car, revved the engine. He reversed too fast and slid a few feet into deep snow, but when he put the car in drive and floored the accelerator, the car jerked free, fishtailed around Cass's house and shot down the drive. In his rearview, she stood on the road in her bare feet, clutching her robe closed against the cold, eyes round with shock. It was almost enough to make him stop and herd her back inside.

Almost, but not quite.

* * * *

Cass staggered into the house trying to get her breath. The house rang with silence. She'd once been a passenger in a car accident. A friend had been driving and lost control on a frozen road. The car slalomed into a tree and then bounced sideways into another. Neither of them had been hurt beyond bruises, but the feeling of the abrupt, slamming halt came over her again. Like every cell in her body had been slammed against something immovable, rattling her from teeth to toenails.

One hand on the wall to guide her, she made her way to her bedroom. All the blankets lay on the floor in a tangled heap. How had they gotten there?

Wait, she had fallen out of bed chasing Jason. She looked at her knees. They were red, but so were her feet. Had she hit her feet? She shook her head. It would come back to her later. The mattress still held the impression of their bodies. His pillow lay against the headboard. Hers was turned sideways and had been very nearly knocked off the bed.

As she stepped over the blankets, reaching for her pillow, her thawing toe bumped into something. For such a small injury, a hell of a lot of pain. She looked down.

Her box of magazines.

When she'd awakened to the realization Jason wasn't in bed with her, she'd heard him close by. She'd opened her eyes against the glow of the fire and seen his head bent over something.

He'd found her magazines. That stupid magazine collection she should have thrown out years ago, but instead kept adding to. *Manipulating. The act. The nice cozy dance, the little jam, the dress, the very convenient timing of her announcement.* He'd found her magazines and thought she was doing what Stella had done.

Cass seized the box. She threw it into the fire, nearly smothering the flames. The lid popped off and magazines spilled across the living room floor. She ran to the other room. Scooping them up, she dumped them into the flames. While watching to make sure they caught fire, she noticed her silk dress and velvet coat lying on the chair in the bedroom. Running, slipping on the floor and falling into the wall, she finally managed to propel herself into the bedroom.

She snatched both of them and threw them on top of the fire with a screech of rage and despair. The flames leaped up, consuming the paper and cloth. Chest heaving, she stared into the blaze as the glossy magazine paper curled and blackened and the velvet charred. She sank to her knees, sobs shaking her body. Hot tears streaked her face, blurring the flames into a wash of red and orange. Unsure why she bothered, she reached out and shoved an errant magazine off the wooden floor so it wouldn't end up burning down the house.

* * * *

Where the hell was he? His head felt like a dragon had attended a chili cook off and then died in his mouth. The rest of him more closely resembled a train wreck. He remembered charming drink after drink out of a plain, but kind, flight attendant. Later, she'd scuttled him out a back entrance at the airport and into a cab home to save him the humiliation of appearing drunk in *People* magazine.

Cassie standing barefoot in the snow.

He squeezed his eyes shut. How did he keep falling for these blood-sucking, gold-digging women? Wasn't there a woman in the universe who would want him for himself instead of for his money, fame or connections?

If Cassie were here, she'd be fussing at him to get up and drink some water because it was good for him. He rolled off the bed and stumbled to the bathroom. The harsh light was not flattering. His skin had the attractive pallor of rotting parchment and his eyes were so bloodshot, they glowed. He drank a glass of water, took a cold shower, and brushed his teeth. It didn't help.

Sitting down on the side of the bed, he looked at the clock. Eight thirty. Dark outside, so it must be PM. He'd misplaced a whole day at least.

He picked up his cell to check his messages. When he'd moved into Cass's house, he'd shut the phone off and hadn't bothered to turn it on again. With her, staying in contact with anyone else hadn't mattered. Everything outside Cass's mountain and the valley below didn't matter. It was a bad TV show about somebody else.

The messages ranged from "Hey, what's up?" at the beginning of the week to more frantic "Where the hell are you?" by yesterday. One near the middle from Tessa told him she had the dossier, what did he want her to do with it? She'd also left one of the later "Where the hell are you?" messages. Hopefully, they hadn't sent the cops to Cassie's looking for him, but if they had, at least he would know she was all right.

What an idiot. Why did he care? He had to stop that. Cassandra Geoffrey wasn't his concern. He dialed Sandy. "Hey, I'm back."

"Jason, you're back early. Feeling better?" Sandy said.

Jason squinted against the glare of his manager's cheer. "Different, anyway."

"I see." Sandy's cheer withered. "Well, you have three weeks before the Grammys. Let's try not to break up the band in the meantime, shall we?"

"I just wanted to let you know I was back."

"I understand, son." Sandy sighed. "You know I'm here if you want to talk about it."

"I don't." There was no reason to be a jackass. Sandy hadn't done anything wrong. If not for him, all of them would probably still be back in Indiana working crappy jobs and playing bars on the weekend.

Jason's hands were sweating against the receiver and he wanted another drink.

"Well, you should give Brian a call."

"Yeah." Before he said something worse, he hung up. His credit with these people was going to run out. He dialed Brian, and Brian's wife Bonnie picked up.

"Hi, are you back already?" she greeted him. "I thought you were going to be out there another week."

"I came back early," he grumbled. "Is Brian there or not?"

"Yes," Bonnie snapped. "Are you sure you don't want to go back to West Virginia? You don't sound like the week did you any good."

Without replying, he hung up. He rubbed his face. They were never going to forgive him. Sandy had asked him not to break up the band before the Grammys, and the best he could do was get himself kicked out. He should call Tessa and get his hands on the dossier. Then he would know everything about Cassandra Geoffrey and why she'd sunk her hooks into him. Instead, he stood to get another glass of water. The phone rang. Undoubtedly someone he didn't want to talk to. "Hello?" he answered the call.

"Hey, man, you called."

"Brian, this isn't a good time."

"I know. There hasn't been a good time for about two years now."

Jason ran his hand through his wet hair. "Yeah, I know. Listen, tell Bonnie I'm sorry I hung up on her."

"Already done. You hook up with the camp director?"

Jason smiled, remembering Cass standing in her silk dress and velvet coat in the living room. Her hair up, showing off her slender white throat. Beguiling and beautiful. All for him. "Sort of, but it didn't end well."

"Which explains why you're home early."

He still wanted to drape a big glittery yellow sapphire around her neck. To feel her fingers tangling through his hair. To see her smile. A groan escaped him.

"Jason, are you there?"

"Yeah, sorry. It was a rough flight."

"Wow, two sorrys in five minutes. This is some kind of record." This was why they'd been friends since they were nine. Brian was impervious to his moods. "Why don't I stop over tomorrow and we'll grab some lunch? The suits want to know when we're gonna get to work on the next record."

"Okay."

"Get some rest, man. You sound like shit."

"Thanks. See ya tomorrow." After he hung up, Jason lay back on the bed. He should get another glass of water and get dressed. That would make him feel like a human being.

Instead, he closed his eyes and remembered throwing snowballs at Cassie.

* * * *

When Cassie didn't come down for her mail for two weeks, her mother started calling. At the beginning of the third week, Shirl sat in her kitchen, listening to the phone ring. Andy perched across the table as if he wanted to fly through the line to their daughter's house and make her answer.

"Hello, honey. Everything okay up there?"

"Fine, Mom," Cass said.

"You know, Ben says your mail is piling up down here. I'll bet you've got a bunch of reservations in there. Your dad and I were thinking about driving it up to you."

"You don't need to do that."

"I know, sweetheart. We like to help out."

"I don't need any help."

"We have your truck here. Your father fetched it from Bill before it ended up with wool in the gas tank. He's gotten it all tuned up too. Do you want us to bring it up?" If they didn't take the truck up the mountain soon, Andy was going to overhaul the engine out of sheer frustration.

"No."

"You know your father really doesn't like you up there all alone without any transportation," Shirl said.

"I know. I'm fine."

Shirl wiped a crumb off the kitchen table. Cass sounded fine the way the Titanic had been fine after its encounter with the iceberg. Across the table, Andy leaned forward, frowning. He looked about to shoot out of his chair and head up the mountain at a run. Shirl cleared her throat. "So what have you been up to?"

"Stuff."

"Is the summer schedule done? Sue was asking."

"No."

"I heard something amazing just the other day. You'll never guess who's got engaged."

The line was silent.

Shirl licked her lips. Some days it was very hard to remember her daughter was no longer a teenager. Today it was hard to remember she wasn't a truculent toddler. "Finn and Angela. Isn't that a hoot? I heard she showed up at his office in nothing but a coat about two weeks ago and they've been just inseparable since. Isn't that nice?"

"Yeah."

"Your father says it's a good thing. This way he won't be following after you anymore."

"Yeah."

"Finn says he hasn't got your taxes yet."

"I know."

Shirl listened to the empty line. When she was growing up the phone lines had crackled, but now they were clear as a fine summer day. All the better to hear her daughter saying nothing, yet speaking volumes. "Are you coming down the holler anytime soon?"

"I don't know."

"Is there something you need help with?"

"No."

Shirl looked at Andy and shook her head. She'd have had to be blind to not see something had gone on between her daughter and the winter guest. Now she would have to be deaf to not hear something had gone wrong. Cass had sounded better when her marriage and her career had been falling apart simultaneously in New York.

Andy stood up and stalked out of the room. They'd agreed they liked the boy. He'd been pleasant enough over lunch the first day, but they had really enjoyed his company when he came to the dance. Just the idea that he wanted to learn some of the old songs had Andy wanting to adopt him. A blood daughter trumped a nearly-adopted son every time. "Well, honey, you just call if you need anything."

"I will."

She had the distinct impression Cass would sit there with her ear pressed to the phone until given further instructions. "Goodbye, sweetie."

"Goodbye."

The phone clicked in her ear, and Shirl hung up. She wished Cass was still five, when bad things were spiders and scraped knees she could fix with a well-placed shoe or a carefully applied bandage. Nothing here she'd use a bandage for, but she could think of a couple of creative uses for a shoe.

Andy walked into the kitchen wearing his coat and holding his keys. "Get your coat. We're going up there."

"Right now? She won't like it."

"No time like the present, and I don't care if she likes it," he said. "We'll take up her mail and her truck and bring down her taxes. It'll make a good excuse."

Chapter 17

Cass sat on her couch, wrapped in a blanket, staring at a movie. She'd been working her way alphabetically through her collection because she had no desire to make a decision about what to watch next.

The knock at the door would have startled her if she'd still been capable of that kind of emotional response.

Throwing off the blanket, she hobbled to the door, legs stiff from disuse. As she moved, her garage door opened on the other side of the house.

Her mother smiled as she stormed the house carrying a corrugated plastic post office tub. "You know, right after I got off the phone with you, we decided we should just run these things up and collect your taxes so you can get your refund." Her mother's practiced gaze took in the mostly empty peanut butter jar with a spoon sticking out of it on the coffee table surrounded by an assortment of mugs and glasses; the pile of DVDs scattered on the floor in front of the television; the blanket on the floor; the dead hearth. Her father walked out of the hall behind Cass.

"Your fire's out, swee'pea," Dad said, and dumped an armload of firewood in the wood box. "I'll shovel out the ashes and start you a new one." He knelt in front of the hearth, where she'd made s'mores with Jason. The magazines hadn't completely burned, leaving a hard ridge of charred pages in the middle. A scrap of yellow silk lay on the stones. Probably the hem of her dress.

"Have you been sick, honey?" Shirl pressed the backs of her fingers against Cass's cheek, looking for a fever or a chill, anything to explain her pale face and greasy matted hair. "You know, you'll feel a lot better once you've had a shower. Let me just brush your hair for you. Come sit at the table."

Obediently, Cass sat down at the table while her mother got a comb. Her mother clucked, working the tangles out of her hair. "You have such beautiful hair."

You have such beautiful hair, preciosa. You're best dressed when you're only wearing your beautiful hair.

Cass squeezed her eyes closed. So much easier to be numb.

"Where did this sweater come from? I don't remember you having one like this."

"He forgot it," she said. She rubbed the weave between her thumb and forefinger. When she'd found it in the gray dawn light the morning after he left, she'd put it on and had not taken it off since.

"You're coming home with us," Dad announced. "You're not well."

"I'm not leaving."

Though she hadn't raised her voice and her tone sounded weak, her dad turned away and started building a fire in the hearth without any more of a fight. Cass bowed her head, so her mother could reach the ends of her hair. It felt so nice to be touched. She wanted to cry, but there didn't seem to be any fluid left in her body.

"You've got a limb down out there," her father said, when the fire started crackling. "I'll go see to it."

The limb had fallen in the middle of the night two days after Jason's departure, cracking like a gunshot and demolishing two of Jason's pyramids. Then the wind knocked over the two Easter Island heads he'd gotten to stay upright. Olmec had merely sagged, looking more forlorn than he had in the first place. The wind had blown away most of the snow that had settled on the Aztec temple.

Mom stood back to allow Cass to stand up, and smiled at her. "You are such a pretty girl." Her mom patted her cheek.

You are a beautiful and intriguing woman, Cassandra Geoffrey. You know you're beautiful, don't you, bella? You know you're completely intoxicating? You're irresistible. So utterly intoxicating. You don't, do you? You don't know how beautiful you are.

"I'm gonna take a shower." Cass ducked her head and almost ran for the bathroom.

The hot water felt good pelting her skin. When had the house gotten so cold? After the fire went out? Or after Jason left?

She washed her hair, letting the stream run over her until the hot water ran out. For the first week after Jason left, it had been too much to move. She had not slept, hadn't eaten or bathed. When she had taken a bath four days ago, the desire to drown herself had been so strong, she'd been afraid to be around that much water again. Over the year both her marriage and her career disintegrated in New York, she had been miserable, but never so hollow as the past two weeks. The pain of that whole year had been distilled into two weeks.

She peeked out the high bathroom window. Her father attacked the tree limb. He'd successfully trampled the two crushed pyramids into nothing and had taken chunks out of the third. While she watched, he turned to the Olmec head and gave it a swift kick, which explained the earlier damage. If she didn't put on a better face for them, they would never leave. They, or someone else from town, would be up here every day on some pretext, and right now the last thing she wanted was company. She squeezed the water out of her hair and wrapped herself in a towel.

Her mother stood in the bedroom, pulling the sheets off the bed.

"What are you doing?" she shrieked at her mom before she could stop herself.

"Changing the bed. I thought I would start a load of wash."

"No. *No*." Cass dragged the sheet from the floor to the bed. Jason had slept in that bed, and she hadn't been able to sleep there at all, but she couldn't bear to change the sheets like she couldn't take not wearing his sweater.

"You know, if I didn't know better, I'd think you were thirteen again," Mom snapped.

"The bed does not need changed. Just leave it alone," she shot back.

Her mother pursed her lips and stomped out of the room. "I'll put on some soup, if that's all right with you," she shouted down the hall.

"It's fine." Cass tucked in the corner of the fitted sheet and replaced the pillow covers. One of them had a long black hair still clinging to it. She pressed the fabric to her face. It still smelled faintly of him. If she closed her eyes, she saw his face when he first woke in the morning. Smiling, reaching for her, his fingers touching her, the callused pads scratching. The soft moan of his breath, as if he couldn't stand to look at her without touching her, and he couldn't stand to touch her without making love to her.

She opened her eyes and dropped the pillow. Before drawing the blanket up, she dressed in jeans and a sweatshirt. She might never be able to sleep in this bed again. Might have to chop it up for firewood and buy a new one. Maybe then she could bear to have fresh sheets.

A lie. He said what he'd told her about his father was a lie. What else hadn't been true? That she was beautiful and he wanted her? That she was anything more than convenient?

Her mother stood in the kitchen, stirring soup with a wounded air. "You're looking thin. Have you been eating?"

"Some. Not much."

Her mother turned from the soup pot. "I'm not going to ask you, Cassie. You're a grown woman and you can make your own choices, but I don't like seeing you like this. And your father, he can't stand it. For his sake if not for your own, you're going to have to pull yourself out of this dive. Now, why don't you gather up your tax stuff so your father and I can drop it off on the way home?" Then she turned back to the soup.

* * * *

Jason stared at the clock on the DVD player. In ten minutes he had to leave to pick up Brian for a songwriting session. Being alone was killing him, yet he couldn't stand being with people. At home, the silence and his thoughts ate at him, but he hated being out too. Mostly, he hated being. He had the sneaking suspicion everyone else didn't think much of him either. Two years of this ongoing temper tantrum was too much, no matter how much the band needed him. Brian had been riding with him to act as a buffer. Yesterday Tyler had suggested using GarageBand so they could email material to each other.

Every morning for the last two weeks, he'd woken up sure Cassie was in bed with him. He'd believed he would open his eyes and be in West Virginia with her leaning over him about to kiss him.

Waking up was a nightmare.

Going to sleep was worse. When he slept, he dreamed of Cassie. Talking to her, making love to her. Christ, the other night he'd dreamed they were sitting on the couch watching a great movie. He'd told her he'd never seen it before, and she'd laughed and told him it was part of her witchcraft. She had special movies.

Then he'd woken up to the cold, empty bed, and he still couldn't remember the plot of the movie.

Standing up, he grabbed his keys. He had to get out of here before he broke something else. Last week he'd had to restring a guitar because he'd very deliberately broken every string. That made him wonder if he was nuts. He didn't even do stuff like that when Stella dumped him.

At Brian's house, his little daughter Tessa and son Bubbie sat on the steps with their chins on their fists. Bubbie was imitating his sister, but Tessa's irritation was genuine.

"What's the matter?" Jason asked, despite that Brian and Bonnie's yelling was quite clear from here.

"Mom and Dad are fighting again." Tessa pouted.

Brian and Bonnie fought all the time. Jason thought they did it as an excuse to have sex. They made up like pros. Jason checked his watch and decided they were going to be late, so he sat down next to Tessa. He didn't need to call. The other guys would guess why they weren't on time. There would be some snickering and good natured teasing until somebody said something stupid, and everybody would look to see if Jason was going to blow up this time. That had been the pattern over the last two years, and he didn't see it changing anytime soon.

"Why do Mom and Dad fight all the time?" Tessa asked.

Jason grimaced. He couldn't very well tell her what he thought. "They fight because they love each other."

"That doesn't make any sense, Uncle Jason," Tessa told him.

"Yeah, that doesn't make any sense, Uncle Jason," Bubbie agreed. Then he frowned, taking three pennies out of his pocket. "How many cents should it make, Tessa?"

"Dummy," she growled.

"Hey, be nice. That's not what she means, Bubbie. She doesn't mean cents like money. She means sense like reason."

"Oh." Bubbie smiled as if he understood, though Jason was pretty sure he didn't.

A door slammed inside the house.

"You never fighted with the pretty lady. Daddy says so."

Jason looked at the pads of his fingers. He and Stella had never fought about anything. He either caved or she went quiet. In one week with Cass he'd shared more heated words of all stripes than in three years with Stella. "I know, but she didn't really love me. That's why she isn't with me anymore."

The shouting had stopped inside the house. That meant, depending on how sorry they were, it would be fifteen to thirty more minutes.

"I still don't see why fighting means you love somebody," Tessa said. She looked at the door, but made no effort to go inside. On some small child level, she knew the drill.

"People fight when they love each other because they have something to save. If you don't care about somebody, you don't care if you hurt them and they can't hurt you so there's nothing to fight about." He remembered Cass lighting the fire in his cabin and claiming she had smoke in her eyes to cover the fact she was crying. He put his arm around Tessa's narrow shoulders. "People who love each other feel bad when they hurt one another, and they fight about it."

"It's stupid."

"Do you care about your brother?"

Tessa looked at her brother like she might survey a squashed toad on the road. "He's my brother."

"And what would you do if somebody was hurting him?"

"I'd beat them up."

Jason grinned. Bonnie's influence, not Brian's. "What if the person hurting him was you?"

Tessa's expression changed. She wrapped her arms around her brother. "I'm sorry I called you a dummy."

"Okay." Bubbie hugged her back, beaming.

The front door banged open. A very brief apology this time. "Hey, sorry. I got distracted." Brian bounded down the stairs, dropped kisses on both children's foreheads and headed for the car.

Jason settled into the driver's seat. He'd been aware of the lack of fighting with Stella. He'd told himself they had a very solid relationship and didn't need to fight. But maybe Stella hadn't bothered to fight with him because she didn't care. Or because she didn't want to piss him off. It was possible. Likely, even.

Cass had never hesitated to fight. With that fair skin and those open eyes, her every emotion was on display all the time. Never had she made him feel like he was playing chess with her, or even demanded any kind of winnings from their bet.

Though she had probably hoped to parlay that bet into some kind of promise, and when he'd stormed out she'd been caught off guard. She had been playing him, she'd been very good. He snorted out loud.

"What?" Brian asked.

There were some things you couldn't even tell a best friend. Revealing you were a huge sucker was on that short list. "Why do you have a kid named after my sister?" he asked instead.

"Bonnie liked the name." Brian flushed. "She's already pissed about the tour next fall. She's mad because I won't be home for Christmas."

"The tour isn't even planned yet," Jason protested, then realized what he was saying. "We'll be home for the day, but we will probably have to head out before New Year's. Can't she bring the kids to you?"

"She says it's not the same, which it's not." Brian pressed back into the seat. "At least when I come home this time, my kid will recognize me."

"Bubbie was just a baby." Jason frowned. When they'd returned from the first tour after Brian's little boy was born, he'd been old enough to walk and had screamed and run out of the room when Brian walked in.

Brian had missed the birth too. Getting the time off for him to be home when Tessa started school last fall had been a herculean effort.

If Jason somehow managed to catch Cassie and marry her, that was the life he'd be dragging her into. Part time, long distance relationship. He'd do almost as well just going out there for a couple weeks every winter.

If she didn't drag out that shotgun she kept in her office.

But he didn't plan on ever seeing her again because she'd been using him, right?

Frowning, he turned into Marc's driveway. The others were already there. In the downstairs music room, Tyler, Marc, and Bear stopped their tinkering to harass Brian when they walked in. Jason drifted to a corner and opened his guitar case. The same guitar he'd taken to West Virginia. The one Cassie had lifted out of his hands so she could crawl into his lap and make him stop thinking about Stella. He could feel the weight of her body across his legs and the taste of her lips on his. Her hair had curtained around them, inspiring him to take her to St. Tropez so he could put flowers in her hair and hold her hand on the white sand beach. Then she'd shoved him into the bedroom because Finn was coming. He'd never gotten her into that silk nightgown, but she might have been saving it for later.

The room was quiet.

The guys were looking at him sheepishly, and he had no idea what they'd said that should have set him off.

Marc coughed. "That's...ah...a nice tune. Is it something you've been working on?"

"It's a song I learned in West Virginia." Jason continued to play.

"Cool. What's it called?"

"*In the Pines.*"

"Hey, wasn't that —" Bear's question cut off when Brian shot him a look dark enough to have its own gravity. Bear coughed.

All of them went silent again. They stared at the floor, the walls, the ceiling, anything but him. They were all grouped on the other side of the room. Once upon a time these four guys had been his best friends in the world. They'd done all kinds of crazy stuff and talked about everything.

"Come on, guys, it's not like you have to walk on eggshells around me," Jason said.

"Yes, it is," Bear said. He caught dirty looks from Marc and Brian. Tyler had his hand over his face as if he didn't want to see a fight erupt. "Well, we do. Say the wrong thing to him lately and you might—"

"Have to punch him?" Tyler asked.

"You dumped a pop over his head," Bear said in a snarling tone.

Jason stood up. "Look, I'm the problem here. Maybe I should go so you guys can get some work done."

"You don't have to go." Brian stepped into the middle of the room. "Why don't we all go get something to eat and start fresh after lunch. If we don't get something down pretty soon, Sandy's gonna skewer us. Besides, you can't go. You're my ride."

Brian would have made an excellent sheepdog. He herded them to a restaurant they all liked and tried to maintain some kind of social conversation without touching on any of Jason's hot points. That pretty much left politics, the weather, and TV. They were halfway through their lunches, and embroiled in a spirited conversation about *The X-Files*, which they had been watching together last tour, when Brian looked up and groaned. Tyler cursed and Bear stood up and stomped away from the table, leaving the seat beside Jason open. There were only six people in the entire world Bear couldn't stand to be around, but Jason couldn't imagine which one of them might risk approaching the table. He looked around, bewildered, until he met the brilliant blue eyes of his ex-girlfriend.

"Hi, Jason," Stella said sweetly. "How have you been?"

"Good," he lied.

She slid into the seat Bear had vacated. "I've been thinking about you." Her seductive purr had all the sincerity of a bad porn actress. What kind of 'work' had she been doing?

"Really?" Jason asked. "The new guy dump you?"

Brian made a choking sound. Jason picked up his water glass and took a sip.

"I thought we had something," Stella said.

Sweat filmed her upper lip. She needed something pretty bad. Probably publicity. That was her drug of choice. "I'm taking my mom to the Grammys, if that's what you want."

"What makes you think I need to go to the Grammys with you?"

"Need? Isn't that more of a *want* situation?" Marc asked. Jason wanted to laugh. Warmed up, Marc could be brutal, and he'd been warming up for two years. Even when they hated him, they were still his friends.

Stella shot Marc a sour look then tried to marshal her charms on Jason again. "I only want to know how you were doing. Are you seeing anyone?"

Jason smiled. She had to know he wasn't, she followed gossip columns like religion. "Is there something you wanted, Stella? My lunch is getting cold."

She glanced at his salad. Crystal tears formed on her perfect lashes. "How can you be so cruel? We were lovers."

"You dumped me in *People*."

"In a sidebar, no less," Marc added.

"I thought you knew it was over. I didn't realize it would hurt you so much." She reached out and rested her manicured hand on his cheek.

Nothing. No flicker of desire or flush of heat. No urge to touch her back. How had he let this plastic doll mess him up so thoroughly for so long? He'd sooner find himself a mannequin and take that to the Grammys. His trip to West Virginia had served its original purpose. He was over Stella.

She realized he wasn't responding, and sat back. "Well, it was good seeing you again." She sobbed. Then she jumped up and ran away from the table.

"Oh, look. There's a photographer. Maybe you'll make *Us*," Tyler said, pointing through the restaurant window.

"*Just Like Us*." Marc framed a shot of Jason and the chair Stella had vacated with his fingers. "They fight in restaurants."

"I missed something good, didn't I?" Bear demanded, standing behind his chair.

"Did you ever. It was awesome," Marc raved.

Jason studied his plate. Stella touching his face only reminded him how it felt to be touched by Cassie's loving hands. The way she'd wrapped him in a warmed blanket when he came in from building his ziggurat, and rubbed a towel though his hair. She'd ordered him out of his clothes and then informed him she didn't want any of his 'cold parts' touching her. Around him, his friends were telling Bear what he'd missed. Bear lamented that nobody had taped it. "What do you think about *Crocodile Tears* for a song title?" he offered.

"Oh yeah," Brian shouted. "That would be perfect."

"Damn, I gotta call Maur and tell her. She's going to love this." Bear pulled out his phone.

Marc batted his eyelashes at them. "What makes you think I need to go to the Grammys with you?" he asked in a falsetto.

Jason laughed, and it didn't hurt as much as he thought it would. What hurt was knowing he couldn't tell Cassie about it.

* * * *

Cass put the final strokes on the canvas. Since her mother's lecture, she'd made an effort to pull herself together. She'd been showering and eating more or less regularly, and not all peanut butter straight from the jar. Although, what sleeping got done was on the couch. She was still watching her entire movie collection alphabetically, but she put them back on the shelf instead of leaving them all over the floor. She'd even managed to paint—she just hadn't meant to paint this.

She turned away from the canvas. Her whole body ached with an exhaustion almost indistinguishable from her gnawing loneliness. Paul had come by with a casserole three days ago and the next morning, a box of chocolate muffins sat frozen on her doorstep. She suspected the muffins came from Angela, based on the fact that they came in an old tax form box and Finn couldn't bake. When Donny plowed the road yesterday, he'd dropped off her mail, a basket from the Baptist church ladies containing a meatloaf dinner complete with mashed potatoes and green beans, a hand crocheted blanket and a DVD of *The Best Exotic Marigold Hotel*. He'd also said he was sorry she was under the weather.

Probably her mother had told the town she was sick.

And she was. All the food in her refrigerator made her queasy just looking at it. Hopefully, the series of storms the news predicted arrived soon, because then everyone would stay away for a while. She picked up the phone and dialed Gretta. All those people so worried about her, and she couldn't talk to any of them.

"Hi."

"Oh, honey, he left didn't he?" Gretta said.

"Shouting and stomping in the middle of the night almost three weeks ago." Two weeks, three days and sixteen hours ago. Cass checked the clock on the DVD player. Two weeks, three days, sixteen hours and thirty-seven minutes ago. Every minute felt like Chinese water torture. The digital display added another minute to the growing pool.

"Shouting and stomping?"

Cass rubbed the bridge of her nose. She seemed to have an ever-present headache. "He found my magazine collection and decided I was trying to manipulate him into getting married or something. He just went nuts. It was the middle of the night, and he packed up his stuff and stormed out."

"Oh God, how awful. What did you do?"

"For the first two weeks, not much. I sat and watched movies."

"You could have called."

Cass sighed. "Gretta, I could barely get off the couch. Answering the phone was hard enough. Dialing would have been impossible."

"I understand. So what got you off the couch?"

"My mother yelled at me. It got me moving, anyway. The whole town thinks I'm sick." Her stomach responded to the word, roiling ominously.

It had to be the stress. Having someone slam out in the middle of the night, shouting wild accusations could make a person sick, couldn't it?

"Are you?"

Cass hesitated. If she heard it out loud and it wasn't true, she'd be crushed. She didn't think she could stand another blow this year. "Some."

"Sick how?"

"Headache, tired, upset stomach. I think it's just depression."

Gretta breathed for a long time on the other end of the line. "Could you be pregnant?"

Now she'd heard it, and her heart grabbed the idea and ran. Pregnant with Jason's dark-eyed, dark-haired baby. A little piece of him, hers forever. "Maybe," she admitted. "We were careful, but we slipped once." And she doubted condoms were sturdy enough for multiple uses, which had happened more than once.

"Once is all it takes."

"But I wouldn't be sick already. It hasn't even been a month."

"A girl in my office was sick practically the next day."

Cass struggled to keep hope from blooming out of control. It might be depression, or subsisting on peanut butter and no sleep for two weeks. Or shock. She might have caught a bug at the dance and hadn't shaken it yet.

But please let it be a baby. Please.

"Listen, I know you can't get sensitive stuff in the mail, but how about Fed Ex?"

"The nearest hub is in Charleston. Nobody sees him even come over the mountain."

"I'm going to overnight you a pregnancy test. I want you to be thinking about whether you're going to keep the baby and whether you're going to tell him."

Chapter 18

Jason heard Cass, but he couldn't find her. By the time he crawled to the foot of his king sized bed, he'd hear her sweet laugh from the headboard and when he got there she was somewhere on the left side calling him with a seductive purr. It didn't help that the bed had grown to the size of a football field and he couldn't figure out how to get off his knees.

Then he woke up tangled in the sheet in the middle of the bed with one limb stretched toward each of the sides, hard as iron. Pushing himself up, he shook his head to clear it. Why was he always so optimistic that would work? Shaking his head just aggravated his headache. He'd never wanted a king-size bed. You tended to lose the other person in it. The acre of mattress had been Stella's idea, something about needing enough space to sleep. Cass had a queen-size mattress. Big enough to stretch out in, but small enough he could always reach her.

He'd finished off the brandy last night. On the way home from his encounter with Stella a few days ago, he'd bought a bottle. That night he'd needed one glass to put him to sleep. The next night it had been two. Last night he'd needed the rest of the bottle before his eyes started to droop. As far as building a tolerance level went, this was insane. By the end of next week, he'd be buying brandy by the case and mainlining it. Maybe he should take Sandy up on that therapy option. Self-medicating wasn't doing the trick.

He rolled out of bed and slicked sweat off his face with his hand. Waking up sweaty, hard and frustrated every day wasn't exactly a peak experience. The hangover never helped either. Stumbling to the bathroom, he drank two glasses of water then stepped into the shower.

Grammy day. He had to pick up his mom for hair, makeup, and wardrobe at two, then some dinner with the guys and their dates so they could be in their seats by five and sit around until at least seven before they got to the good awards. Good thing they weren't nominated for children's recordings or Best Incidental Music in a Commercial. Those poor suckers were already there. He staggered out of the shower and drank another glass of water.

Hopefully his mom had taken Connie with her when she'd picked out her dress. Designers could convince his mother of anything. Connie had an eye for style and wouldn't let Mom look bad. Thinking of which, what was his sister dressing him in tonight? When she called last week he'd told her he didn't care. She would make him look good, too.

He yanked on a tattered Metallica T-shirt and black jeans worn to an uneven gray. It wouldn't do to turn up looking decent. One had to torment one's sisters, even into adulthood.

He surveyed the look in the mirror. A couple of years ago, say, pre-Stella, he'd have been overjoyed by the thought of tormenting his sister with junky clothes. Today, it felt like an empty gesture in an empty house. This room, done in cool white with its king-size bed and gauzy white curtains, always made him feel like an unwelcome speck of dirt. He should have it redone. Connie might be up to the job, around her regular work doing wardrobe for television. Or Candy would know somebody.

The writing sessions were going very well. The other guys had been working on stuff independently. Thanks to the hillbilly songs he'd remembered snatches of, he could fake some contribution. His main contribution had been the title *Crocodile Tears* that Marc had run with.

Settled in the kitchen, eating a bowl of cereal, he decided he hated the color of the kitchen too. Claiming the color was good for appetite, Stella had picked out some screwed up shade of green that didn't exist in nature and shouldn't anyplace else. Though it was great for ruining appetite, he hadn't bothered to argue with her. It needed redone as well. So did the living room. From his seat at the table he could see his black leather couch. He had some thoughts on what he wanted for the living room. Hardwood with light finish. Burgundy drapes and furniture. Maybe a fake fireplace.

He flipped open the half-memorized dossier on Cass that Tessa dropped off the morning after he got home. She'd rattled him out of bed at ten thirty and handed it over amid disparaging comments about his appearance and work ethic punctuated by some Spanish she'd learned to make it look like she had street cred, but which impressed him not at all. The dossier didn't tell him anything he didn't know, but added some color and it was all he had. There was a picture from her driver's license and a summary of her old tax returns. Tessa had included the paperwork from her divorce and a copy of Michael's acting portfolio. Jason didn't ask how she'd gotten the portfolio. Tessa had probably called his agent for it and now the little creep thought someone in Hollywood wanted him.

Jason hoped so. He wanted to think the bastard was twisting in the wind, especially after the summary of Michael's attempt to steal part of Cass's campground in the divorce proceedings. That had made him want to attend Michael's latest performance so he could throw rotten vegetables at him. He also had a yen to buy Cass's old comic book publisher just to fire a couple of people. To pull that off though, he'd have to convince everyone he knew to invest with him, and make Tessa understand why it was a good idea. So far it seemed too daunting. Maybe next week.

For a guy who wanted to get as far away from Cassandra Geoffrey as he could, he certainly had a lot of plans to be her knight in shining armor. He missed Cass's kitchen, all finished wood and good smells. Maybe he should sell this ugly house and start over.

The only comfortable room was his music room in the back. Stella never laid a hand there. In fact, she'd never stepped in it. If she wanted to talk to him, she would stand in the doorway as if afraid the cables snaking across the floor would attack her.

Jason settled in the big comfortable chair in the corner and picked up his oldest guitar. It was the first one he'd ever owned, given to him by his mother and sisters for his thirteenth birthday. At the time, he'd been guilty about the cost even though it was the cheapest guitar available and never stayed in tune, but he'd paid them all back. Comforted by the feel of the strings and the slightly out of tune sound, he started to pick out notes.

The phone ringing almost startled him out of the chair. He ran to the kitchen and grabbed it, absurdly hoping Cassie would be on the other end. "Yeah?"

"Jason, where the hell are you?" Connie shouted. "It's two thirty. You were supposed up pick up Mom an hour ago. Everybody else is already here."

By the time on the wall clock, which took a second to figure out because it was some kind of nonfunctional artistic thing, he'd sat down to play over three hours ago. That didn't make sense. He wasn't drunk. People blacked out when they were drunk, not when they were stone cold sober and playing guitar. The tips of his fingers ached. "I lost track of time."

"Damn right you did."

"Look, I'm sorry." Jason set aside the guitar.

"Have you been drinking again?"

"No. Call Mom and tell her I'm on my way."

"Eleanor is bringing Mom. Just get over here. And you better not be wearing anything stupid." Connie slammed the phone down.

Jason hung up the phone and dashed for his car. Right after he'd gotten the guitar, there had been times when he'd gotten lost in it. He'd learned to play on Brian's, and when he got his own he could play *Stairway to Heaven* for hours. When Tessa threatened to beat him to death with his guitar if he played that song one more time, he'd embarked on learning every one of George Harrison's songs, including his Beatles and his Wilbury stuff. Consoling himself for three years with a guitar and a monumental goal made him one of the most proficient guitar players in rock. It also meant he lost track of hours.

As he swung into Connie's driveway, her little boy came racing out of the house. "Mom says you're late and you've got to get into a chair immediately." Colton seized his hand and dragged him to the house.

Connie took in his outfit and glared at him. "You never get tired of this, do you? Get that off. Put this on." She shoved a clutch of hangers into his hand and gave him a push in the direction of the bedrooms, which had been turned over to dressing rooms for the day. His mother sat in the makeup chair watching him. Burgundy trimmed in gold, the dress his sister had chosen for her made her look like an attractive older woman without making her look like a fossil. Connie had given him a burgundy shirt, black pants and a black jacket that was a little too short in the sleeves.

"Hey, Conjob, this is too short," he pointed out.

On her knees in front of Bear's fiancée, Maureen, adjusting the hem of her dress, she glanced over her shoulder at him. "Don't call me that. It's supposed to be that length."

"It's too short."

"No, it's revealing the cuffs of your shirt. Tonio is waiting for you."

Jason slumped into the hairdresser's chair. Around him everyone chattered, fidgeting with their dress up clothes and trying not to muss their hair or makeup. In this sea of happiness and excitement, he was an island of misery. He'd have cut off his right hand for the opportunity to sit on Cass's couch watching the Grammys with her leaning against him. There had to be some way to get a little bit of her. But if she wanted everything, she would never settle for some, and he couldn't let another woman dictate the color of his kitchen unless she was his sister.

Eleanor pulled a kitchen chair next to him and sat. In her jeans and t-shirt, hair pulled back in a ponytail, she looked as out of place as he felt. "I hear you met up with Stella the other day," she said.

"Bitch," Tonio snorted. "I worked with her on a commercial last year. I told her I'm not a plastic surgeon or a magician. It ain't happenin'." He snapped a Z in the air.

Tonio might like to meet Paul.

Eleanor smiled at Tonio's outburst before focusing on Jason again. "I hear it went well."

Jason shrugged. "Well enough."

Eleanor reached up to brush his hair off his face as she'd done when he was a little boy, and hesitated. She must have remembered where they were. "So what is it?"

Jason shrugged. He couldn't hide his face because Tonio had hold of him. "Nothing."

"You can't lie to me. Is it this woman you met in West Virginia?"

"How do you know about her?"

"Brian can't lie to me either. I used to babysit you guys. Tessa said you asked her to dig up dirt on her. Divorced, single, former artist. What's she like?"

He closed his eyes, and was with Cassie again. Bright eyes smiling, she laughed with him, that warm, husky sound that proved whatever he'd said, she thought it genuinely funny. Her hands were on him again, gentle, caressing. The clean, citrusy scent of her hair surrounded him and he could taste her salty sweet skin.

His breath hitched. Eleanor put a hand on his arm and the touch reminded him of Cassie. Those non-sexual, undemanding touches she never hesitated to bestow on him that made him feel loved instead of just desired.

"So you loved her?"

"I only knew her for a week," he said. He opened his eyes, ashamed to discover tears in them.

"Sometimes you know right away. What happened?"

"She didn't love me."

Eleanor nodded. "She rejected you."

"No, she manipulated me. She wanted to be the next Stella." The ever present vise around his chest tightened. All these people loved him. Three of the five members of his family were here, his best friend from childhood, his closest adult friends. He shouldn't feel so alone, like some important part of himself was missing.

"Are you sure?" Eleanor asked.

Jason thrust away from the chair, losing a few hairs to Tonio's comb. "Jesus, would you all stop it?" he shouted.

Utter silence, and everyone's eyes on him. Then Tonio's comb clattered to the floor. The front door opened a moment later.

"Hello! Have I missed anything?" Tessa barged into the living room wearing a neat pink suit and black pumps. Her gaze honed in on him, joining those already staring at him. "Oh. It looks like I'm right on time," she said.

"Jason Albert, you behave yourself!" his mother bellowed.

Jason turned away, putting his hands over his eyes. Someone behind him whispered his name with wonder. Probably Maureen. His middle name wasn't common knowledge, and she was new to the group. He hated it. Albert was his father's name. He didn't know why he hadn't changed it years ago.

"Jason, I'm sorry. I didn't mean to bring up a sore point." Eleanor rose and rested her hand on his arm.

Cassie had stood in the window behind him, painting, while with his back to her, he sat on the couch, playing his way through the Harrison catalog from memory. She'd stepped away from the easel to check to her work and lain a hand lightly on his shoulder. The touch had made him fumble a chord, and had felt so incredibly good. He wanted that again. Even if it was an act, he wanted it.

"Don't coddle the boy, Eleanor." His mother scowled. "Jason Albert, you are such an ungrateful little monster."

Dressed in a designer gown dripping in diamonds, she glared up at him, calling him ungrateful? Monster he could admit to, but he'd done his best to never be ungrateful. And he wasn't little.

"Just because your papa walked out on you when you were a little boy doesn't give you the right to act like a beast all your life."

The chorus of shocked sounds seemed to echo for a long time. His sisters didn't even flinch, but suddenly found fascinating points of interest on various walls. They must have discovered the letter, too.

"You don't think we didn't know?" Mom yelled. "Did you think your mother was stupid? Why do you think you got that guitar for your birthday? We had to use money from Tessa's college fund."

"Well, I paid it back. I put her through law school!"

"That's not the point," his mother shouted, louder than him.

"Please, stop," Eleanor pleaded. "There's no need to yell." She tried to step between them.

"Talking hasn't gotten through." His mother reached around Eleanor and shoved him back a step. "Your father hurt you. He hurt all of us.

You let that ugly, skinny woman hurt you. And now you won't see when someone really loves you because you have cold feet."

About to yell something even more unfortunate at his mother, he closed his mouth. Not only his feet were cold. No single part of his body felt warmer than it had when he'd been building snow sculptures in Cassie's yard. Why did everything come back to her? Cassie, who sight unseen, his mother believed loved him. "How do you know that? You've never even met Cassie."

"I don't need to. I can read you better than I can read a book. I see when the pain comes to your eyes and the tears you don't cry, the way you clench your fist. You aren't stupid, Jason. You know when someone loves you but just can't accept it. You push them away because you're scared. You reject them before they can reject you."

"Mama," Tessa put her hands on their mother's arms, trying to guide her to a chair, "you're going to hurt yourself."

Mom pulled against Tessa's hands as if she wanted to lunge at him. "No, I'm going to hurt my only son because he seems to think that's what he deserves."

Her words rang off the walls. Jason checked to make sure he was still standing. He should have been beaten into the fetal position by now. That, or this was the worst nightmare he'd ever had and he'd be waking up any minute now. Around the room, his family's expressions were grim, his friends, shocked. The other day he'd told Brian's daughter people fought because they had something they wanted to save.

"Why didn't you tell me, man?" Brian asked.

Unable to form a response, Jason shook his head. He'd been so humiliated to discover his dad wasn't there, not because he couldn't be, but because he'd chosen not to be. On some childish level, he'd been sure if his friends knew, they'd leave him, too. It had never gone away.

After he'd told Cass, she'd wanted to be with him. Even as he'd pulled away, she tried to comfort him, warm him from a coldness that had nothing to do with the winter hike.

"Son, you love this girl." His mother stepped toward him, twisting off the wedding ring she'd always worn. "Go to her. Give her this, and love her always," she said, and folded it into his hand.

The solitaire diamond was so riddled with incursions from hard wear, it was cloudy. Why hadn't he replaced the stone for her a long time ago? He laughed bitterly. "It didn't work for you, did it? He left anyway."

"Jason!" Eleanor scolded.

"He left me, but I never betrayed my vows." His mother lifted her chin.

A sob came from Bonnie. Marc's sister Becky, who had been doing her makeup, put her arms around her and hid her face in Bonnie's hair, destroying the perfectly coiffed arrangement.

"You could go now," Tyler suggested. "It's not like we can't go pick up the award without you, and this is kind of important."

Jason set his jaw. They didn't understand. It wasn't some baggage he had that was the problem. His mother wasn't all right. Cass didn't love him. She wanted to use him. Well, he could manipulate back. "Tessa, I need you to buy some property for me."

"What? Property? What are you talking about?"

"Potterville, West Virginia. It's owned by a guy named Bill Wernick and everybody calls it the high pasture. Just give him whatever he asks." Jason jammed the ring in his pocket and stalked out the door.

"Why?" Tessa demanded, hurrying outside after him.

"Because I need a bargaining chip."

"Jason, this is a really bad idea," Brian said. He passed Tessa in the driveway. "You really don't want to do that."

"It's the only thing I can do," Jason snapped, lengthening his strides as he neared his car. He pulled out his phone and dialed his office. "Jody, I need the first flight to Pittsburgh on any airline, any seating. I'm going to be at the airport in half an hour. I need a car in Pittsburgh, too, and snow shoes. Just do it." He shoved the phone back in his pocket.

"Jason, I have to advise you not to run off like this." Tessa trotted alongside him.

"Are you speaking as my sister or as my lawyer?"

"Both. What do you want this property for?"

"I'm gonna let Cassie use it as long as she…" Jason couldn't finish his own sentence.

"As long as she lets you use her," Brian said.

Tessa gasped. "Jason, you can't. It's illegal, it's immoral, it's totally scummy— Ow!" She'd stumbled as her heel caught in a crack in the drive and Brian caught her.

Jason jerked open the door of his car. "Just buy the property. I want to own it by the time I land in Pittsburgh." He slammed the door and revved the engine, peeled out of Connie's driveway.

Chapter 19

Cass sat on the couch, immobilized. Any progress she'd made at pulling herself together had been shot to hell by three massive blows.

Yesterday Gretta's package arrived. Cass had opened it, and set it on the table, unable to look at it or look away. She couldn't even summon the energy to open the one-pound bag of M&Ms Gretta had included.

Then, last night at sunset a massive winter storm had howled over the mountain, dumping four feet of snow in six hours. She'd called her parents before they got the state troopers to pull her out. According to them, a seven-foot wall of snow hid her road and the temperature drop after the storm had frozen it to a solid block of ice. It might require a backhoe to tear down. If she wanted out at all, she would have to climb. By that time her fire, unattended since the arrival of the package, was nothing but embers. When she'd fallen asleep in the middle of *Pinocchio*, the glowing coals were just ash.

This morning, she woke up already running for the bathroom. As she'd washed her face, she'd remembered today was the day of the Grammys, which brought on another round of dry heaves. She'd turned on the television, wrapped herself up in the blanket, stared at the screen and hadn't moved since. Now it was nearly ten PM.

The Grammys were leading up to the rock album of the year. She'd been studying the crowd shots, trying to catch sight of Jason. So far, she'd managed to spot Brian's blond head and Marc's brown hair, but not Jason. She felt queasy and light headed. If she still felt like this in the morning she was going to have to let them come get her. She'd managed to keep down only a glass of water and a slice of dry toast all day.

Outside, there were crunching noises. The bears should all be hibernating, and even the wolves weren't stupid enough to be out in this weather. Stupid wolves didn't bother her much. Rabid ones were a problem. A sick one might get enough height from the snow banks, break through one of the windows and attack. Could she deal with a rabid wolf in her condition? Doubtful.

She rolled off the couch and crawled to the office because she didn't think she could stand up. Her shotgun leaned beside the desk, and she kept the shells in the desk drawer. As she loaded the shells, she thought of another possibility. It could be a human predator. Everyone knew she was up here alone and trapped in.

Too much A&E. She had to stop watching those shows about serial killers.

She pulled herself to her feet and looked out the front window.

A person waded through the snow about twenty feet from her door. He was tall, wearing a parka with a hood that shadowed his face, and was equipped with snowshoes. As she watched, he gained another five feet. She could call the troopers, but it would take them forty minutes to get here. Instead, she shoved open the door, letting it bang against the side of the house.

"I don't know who you are, but I suggest you turn right back around and leave. I've got a shotgun here and I know which end is which," she shouted. She racked the gun and sighted down the barrel. All the strength had drained from her legs, so she leaned against the wall, bracing the barrel against the door jam. If she fired, the recoil would knock her on her ass.

"Cassie?" The figure floundered forward another step and stopped, shoved back his hood.

No wonder she hadn't seen Jason on television. "Jason?"

He held out a hand. "Look, I know you're pissed, but could you put the gun down?"

Cass lowered the gun as he continued to struggle toward the door. When he got to the step she reached down and helped him inside. She fell into his arms. He felt so warm and solid. Inexplicably here. He kissed the top of her head.

"Come on, let's go inside," he murmured.

All the grief, fear and anger she'd numbed herself against for the past three weeks spilled over, and she shoved herself away from him. "How dare you come here, after what you said? The way you left here. You should know you're not welcome. How did you even get here?"

Jason closed the door and bent, unlaced his snowshoes. "Same as last time, but I don't think the rental company is going to be very happy with me. There's a Buick LeSabre sticking out of a snowdrift at the end of the road. I hope nobody plows into it from behind."

Cass stomped up the stairs. "What makes you think you can even come here anymore?"

"I have an offer for you."

"An offer?" She walked across the room to the table and leaned on it to keep from falling over.

"I bought that land."

She frowned. Her head was pounding. "What land?"

"The pasture where we got stuck."

That land? "Why? Isn't it enough to ruin me emotionally, you have to ruin my business too?" she shrieked, which hurt her head, but she drew some satisfaction from the way it made Jason flinch.

"No, I have an offer for you." He closed the living room door behind him, glancing around the room. His gaze fell on the fireplace. "*Bella*, your fire's gone out," he murmured.

"Forget about the stupid fire." Twisting her features, she battled against tears.

* * * *

"You never let your fire go out." *Ruin me emotionally*, she'd said. *Ruin me.*

She looked awful. Her hair had escaped its braid and frizzed around her too-pale face. The expression in her eyes seemed almost feverish and the bones of her face stood out more than he remembered. Suddenly, every moment they'd shared, from the instant he'd set eyes on her, to walking through the door just now, flooded him. Every kiss, touch, every sweet sigh. The memories assailed him like a high wind peeling back layers of snow and rock, revealing the geological record of his soul. This information didn't match what he'd been thinking for the past couple of weeks. "And you're wearing my sweater."

"You left it here." She folded her arms beneath her breasts.

He'd never unpacked. The bag he'd brought home sat in the closet, where he'd dropped it.

"Is there something you came here for? Because I was busy."

Behind him on the TV, Steven Tyler announced nominees at the Grammys. "I see that," he said, narrowing his eyes at her.

"Are you going to tell me why you bought that property out from under me?" she demanded. She clutched the table behind her.

"Shouldn't you light a fire? It's cold in here." He shrugged off his coat and draped it across the back of the couch. Her place was a mess, and the air held a distinct chill not entirely due to the glare she'd focused on him. A nearly finished painting leaned against the wall sideways, like a window that had fallen over but kept displaying the same view. Her easel sat against the far end of the couch facing the dining room with a canvas on it.

"Shut up about the goddamn fire," Cass snapped. "I'm just not that worried about making you comfortable."

Jason's jaw tightened. He needed to pull out of this maudlin mood. This woman didn't love him no matter how much his mother thought she did. "I have a business proposition."

"Which is?"

"I'll give you the right to use the land if you'll just—" His throat spasmed. What if she said no? What if she threw him out at the point of that shotgun leaning on the wall behind him? What if his mother was right? "If you'll just keep pretending to love me the way you have been."

Her face went paler.

"I'll only come here in the winter," he said. "I won't interrupt your regular season. I'll be discreet. No one in town will ever know I'm here."

"Pretend?" she shrieked. "What do you mean, pretend? What is this, high school? Maybe you'd like to try going steady in secret?" She grabbed something out of the box behind her and threw it at him.

He flinched as the bag of M&Ms hit his shoulder and split open, showering candy around the room. "No, I thought it would be easier this way."

"For who? You want me to be available to you whenever you want to scratch your itch?"

"That's not what I want." He wanted things to go back to the way they were. Hanging out in her house playing at a relationship, but this time he wanted it to be real.

"You want me to be your whore," Cass screeched. She snatched something else out of the box and threw it at him. With a gasp, she tried to grab it back.

Jason grabbed for the small box. It bounced off his fingers twice, turning in the air over his hands like a slow motion camera shot, before he caught it. Cass darted forward and tried to whip it away, but he lifted it out of her reach. Her eyes looking up at the box were panicked. He opened his hands to see what she so desperately wished he hadn't caught and stared at the box stupidly. "This is a home pregnancy test," he said when he could understand the writing on the side.

"It's mine." She reached for the box, not meeting his eyes.

"The test or the baby?"

"There might not be a baby." An arm wrapped across her stomach in a protective gesture, she stared at him, looking utterly miserable.

"But you want to be sure. Is it mine?"

She slapped him, spun on her heel, stalked to the table and leaned against it.

The imprint of her fingers was probably as visible as it felt. He didn't know why he'd said anything so cruel. Of course it was his. Theirs.

He studied the slope of her shoulders as she huddled there, held up by the table. When Connie had been carrying Colton, she'd been sick for the first seven months. Pale and weak, throwing up every day. Eleanor hadn't fared much better when she'd had her kids. Annamaria had been lucky with her first, but two and three had been bad. His mother swore Callisto babies were hard on the body. Cass looked so pale and weak. He stepped behind her and put his hands on her shoulder. "*Preciosa*, are we pregnant?"

"We are not. I am. You never wanted my baby." She jerked away from him.

"You said you would give it up."

"Well, maybe I lied about that then. After all, you lied to me." She shuffled toward the hall and stopped. In front of her, a painting sat on an easel, and she tried to block his view.

He walked over to study it. The image looked so alive, he expected to see his fingers moving across the strings as he sat on her couch with his bare feet propped up to the fire. If he were sitting at the table, it would fit perfectly with the rest of the room and appear as if he sat on the couch, playing guitar.

Cass, who slumped in the kitchen door wearing his sweater, had painted *him*. Face turned to the side, she now studied the floor. *You aren't stupid, Jason*, his mother had said. *You know when someone loves you, you just can't accept it.*

"You love me, don't you?" he asked.

Cass shook her head, but wouldn't look up, and chewed her lip in a gesture he recognized well.

"I love you," he said.

Her head jerked up. "Do you love me, or are you avoiding a potential paternity suit? I'm not going to let you charm me and lie to me again."

"Lie to you?"

"About your dad. Oh poor pitiful me, my papa walked out when I was just a baby. Come to bed and make me feel better."

Jason cringed. He'd done a great job covering his tracks on that one. "Cassie, it was true. I was lying when I said I'd lied about it. I was afraid you'd sell the story to the tabloids. Nobody outside my family knew. Until today."

"What?" Her eyes looked a little too crossed to be healthy.

"My mother blurted it out in front of the whole band. My dad did walk out when I was a kid. I wanted to be completely honest with you, but as soon as I was, I got scared that you hadn't been honest with me."

"So the kettle decided the pot must be black." Eyes sparking with anger, she folded her arms.

He shrugged and stared at the floor. This was so far off the script he didn't know where to go next. "I made a lot of dumb mistakes. I can make up for them."

"Why?"

"Because you are everything I ever wanted. Exactly the way you are." He met her eyes. Her arms were hanging a little looser. Maybe in time they would open again to welcome him. He reached in his pocket. By some miracle the ring he'd dropped in there in Los Angeles had made it all the way across the country and up her driveway. "Will you marry me, Cassandra, *bella*?"

Cass swayed on her feet. Her eyes tried to focus on a point somewhere near the tip of her nose. Then she listed to one side and started to fall, making no effort to catch herself.

Before she hit the floor, he caught her. He carried her to the couch and wrapped her in the blanket. Fainting wasn't the response he'd expected. Good money was on her running for her gun to chase him out. He hadn't been counting on anything as absurd as a yes.

He set the ring on the coffee table. Before he returned it to his mom, he'd get that stone replaced. Right now, though, he needed to get a fire going.

The way Cass had taught him—paper first, small twigs, larger twigs, small branches, larger branches—he laid the fire. Over his shoulder, the announcers listed off the contenders for Album of the Year. All in all, he'd rather be here.

The guys on the screen had rearranged themselves so they were all sitting together. His mother sat next to Brian in the seat he would have had. She was holding Brian's hand.

He glanced at Cass. Her eyes fluttered open, so he dropped some good size pieces of wood on the fire and went to her, helped her sit up.

"How are you feeling?" he asked, brushing her hair off her face.

"Like I should be speaking in tongues," she said, groaning.

He smoothed his hand across her silken cheek. When she didn't smack it away, he took it as a good sign.

"And the winner is..." The announcer dropped the envelope and had to scoop it off the floor. "The winner is, *Bayonet Ball*, Touchstone."

"You won. Congratulations," she whispered.

"Thanks." Jason leaned back against the couch, settling her against his chest. This was what he'd wanted. Not what he really wanted, but what he'd asked for earlier. To be watching the Grammys sitting on Cass's couch with her leaning against his chest. Maybe with time he could make it up to her and make her love him again. He'd have to start all over. Be her friend for a while before trying to move things along. If she'd let him.

"We'd like to thank everyone who made this possible," Marc was saying. "Without the love and support of our families, our friends and our fans, this wouldn't have been possible."

Brian commandeered the microphone. "And to Jason, who couldn't be here tonight, we hope your personal project is going well."

Well? He'd come out here to bribe Cassie into a sham of a relationship, ended up asking her to marry him, and wrecked any hope of happiness in the immediate future. *Well* wasn't the term he'd use.

"Yes," Cassie said.

"What?" She'd said something about speaking in tongues; maybe nonsense was considered a tongue.

"You asked me a question." She turned in his arms. Her eyes were bright with unshed tears but her smile lit her face. "The answer's yes."

Nothing spelled happiness in the immediate future like her yes to his marriage proposal. He crushed her against him and pressed his cheek to the top of her head. Yes.

Epilogue

With what would have appeared to the untrained eye to be a smile, Cass leaned over and whispered to Jason, "If one more person asks me when I'm going to have this baby, I'm gonna punch 'em."

"I don't think that would be a good idea, sweetheart," he said. He'd already decided, Cass pregnant was a master's program in patience. Between temper and illness, Cass's mother's ferocious protectiveness, his sisters' well-meaning if smothering concern, and Mom's conviction that he couldn't be patient enough, he was developing a near psychic ability to know when to be patient and when to go to ground until the worst was over.

Then there was his mother's dating. He hadn't developed the ability to cope with that yet. Laughing, she now whirled past in the arms of the Potterville postmaster, who was not as gimpy as everyone had supposed.

"Do you think if I hit someone," Cass asked as if he hadn't spoken, "the excitement would be enough to induce labor?"

"I doubt it." Jason tightened his arm around her shoulders. This was one of those be patient, hold on and keep quiet times. Last week, when she'd merely been due any minute, he'd made the mistake of saying he wished he could help her carry the baby. She'd whipped a plate at his head and then cried when it smashed on the wall.

"Well, Cass, look at you." The middle school principal stopped in front of them, smiling. "I hope this isn't a trend for your child. Being tardy isn't a good habit."

Angela, on Cass's other side, laughed. "Marla, your instructors seem to be at loose ends."

The principal turned in the direction Angela pointed, spotting this week's guest dance instructors standing at the door looking around. "Excuse me," Marla said, headed for the couple.

Angela snorted, patted her own expanding belly. "Only someone who'd never had a baby would say something that stupid."

"At least she gave up the idea of her parents giving dancing lessons," Finn said from behind his wife's chair. "Did you hear, the high school is building a new science lab with the money they earned from this summer's robot wars receipts?"

Angela rolled her eyes at Cass. "How could we forget, when you mention it every three days?"

Tyler fell to his knees in front of Cass. "You've got to dance with me. If I don't get away from those girls, there might be a homicide."

"I can't dance, Tyler," she replied. "I can hardly walk. I was supposed to have this baby four days ago."

Tyler whimpered, looking over his shoulder like a hunted man. "But I've got to get away from them. Angela?"

"Seven months pregnant, and I danced with you last time," Angela pointed out. "Go ask Paul."

"Or Cori," Cass offered.

"Or Maureen," Jason added. "I think she's in the nursery."

"Great. I'll try all three." Tyler stood up. "If one of them shows up, I went outside or something." He disappeared into the press of people.

Jason shook his head. "I told him not to tell them he would be here tonight."

Cass sighed. "He loves it. Besides, there's Laura with one of the tourists." She nodded toward where one of the latest beauty queen rivals was being led to the floor by a handsome young man. The guy looked like he didn't know what had hit him, and was probably right. Maybe he was an up and coming politician. Laura had been voted Most Likely To Be First Lady by her class last year. She was still miffed that June Kim had been voted Most Likely To Be President.

The summer after they married, Dan had taken over the operation of the campground, and Cori and Kady turned their attentions on him. They still hadn't settled who won. Cori got Dan, a wedding ring, and Cass's old house. Kady had shaken the dust of this little town off her feet and run to New York, from which she occasionally returned to rub in her *Sex In the City* lifestyle, her Kate Spade bag and Jimmy Choo heels. Neither would admit jealousy to the other, but they would to everyone else. They did admit jealousy for Cass who had the man, the ring, the big new house on the mountain as well as a house in California, the shoes, the bag and a great big yellow sapphire necklace that she wore whenever Jason asked.

The sapphire did seem an odd choice with the yellow cotton maternity dress, but she still looked stunning. She leaned against his side and closed her eyes.

"Are you okay?" he murmured into her hair.

"As okay as I can be, when I'm about to explode," she answered.

His mother appeared in front of them with Ben behind her. "You look tired, Cassie. You should go home."

"I'm fine. I'm tired of being at home." Cass summoned up a smile for her mother-in-law's benefit.

Mom shot him a threatening look, informing him in no uncertain terms he'd be at fault if anything went wrong. Then she took Ben's hand and led him away. The first tour he'd been separated from Cass, she'd taken it on herself to find out what happened to the missing Alfred Callisto. With Jason's sister Tessa's able help, she'd tracked him from the wife and two daughters he'd abandoned in Santa Fe, to a woman who had not married him and not given him any more children but had been cast off to a car accident that claimed his life in Idaho eight years ago. The woman in Santa Fe, Susan Callisto, had become fast friends with Jason's mother. One of her daughters was house-sitting his place in California while attending college on his dime. The other ran a B&B here in Potterville. The final Mrs. Callisto refused all contact with any of them. Eleanor thought it was only a matter of time before she, too, joined the bizarre extended family.

Jason looked around the room. *Bizarre and extended* about described the situation. In marrying Cass, he'd become part of the town family. Not caring that he was famous or his father had abandoned him, they'd accepted him. Andy had suddenly realized what he'd been missing in not having a son all these years. He'd taught Jason to fish and, when Brian and his kids visited, organized family fishing trips. Very little fishing was done, but there were lots of marshmallow and hot dog roastings and a good portion of singing campfire songs.

"Daddy," someone in front of him demanded in a little voice.

He looked down at his daughter. Sometimes he had to remind himself that the dark-haired, dark-eyed child who looked just like pictures of Annamaria at four was his daughter. It seemed too magical to be real, even though he'd been present for most of the pregnancy and the birth. He always expected to wake up one morning and discover he'd dreamed it all because his life couldn't be this good. Even when his wife was throwing dishes at him.

Andi put her little hands on her hips. "Momma's asleep."

"Momma is not asleep," Cass announced. "What do you need, swee'pea?"

"Can I stay with Mamaw and Papaw tonight?"

"Again?"

Andi stuck out her lower lip and gave her mother her best soulful expression. Cass narrowed her eyes, studying her child. Before the manipulation continued, he scooped Andi into his lap.

"Why do you want to stay with Mamaw and Papaw again?" he asked, smoothing her ponytails down her back.

"Papaw said he'd teach me to balance a spoon on my nose."

"Well, that is a vital skill, honey," Jason told Cass, who rewarded him with a patronizing smirk. "Okay. You can stay in town tonight. But you behave."

Andi twisted in his arms and gave him a loud smacking kiss on the lips, then vanished into the crowd.

Cass sighed. "Didn't we come down the holler tonight to pick her up from my parents?"

"Originally, but you might go into labor tonight, and if she's with your parents we won't have to worry about where she is while we go to the hospital."

"It makes sense, Cass," Finn said.

"Oh right, like I'm ever going into labor. I'm going to be pregnant forever. I feel like I've never *not* been pregnant. Do you ever feel that way?" she asked Angela.

"No." Angela smiled.

"She lies." Finn leaned over his wife's shoulder. "Every morning she wakes up and says *I am still pregnant. It wasn't a nightmare.*"

Angela whacked him, which caused him to stand up, rubbing his head. Then she grinned at Cass again. "I never say anything like that."

Cass laughed. "Okay. I get it. I think I've had enough of sitting here like a crow on a phone line tonight anyway. Take me home, Jason."

Jason rose and hoisted Cass out of her chair. He stood for a moment while she located her balance, and then escorted her to the door, past well-wishers, who all had a comment about her current overdue state.

"I feel like an elephant," Cass muttered as they walked through the muggy night air to the truck.

"You are a lovely elephant."

"You are a jerk." She flashed him a brilliant smile. "No kid tonight."

"What ever happened to *you are never touching me again*?"

"No kid tonight," she repeated.

"You are insatiable."

She slipped her hand behind his neck, tugged him down and kissed him, in the middle of the sidewalk, with people all around them. Her lips were soft and urgent. She tasted him like it was all brand new. Somehow that made everything brand new for him too. She shivered and the baby kicked. It probably felt a little smooshed.

She made an odd noise and tried to push him away. For a moment he resisted, but he relinquished her mouth.

"Water," she gasped.

"What?" As he took a step back, he felt dampness on his leg.

"It's time to go, Pop. Right now."

Meet the Author

Born in Northeast Ohio, I have lived on four different continents, including both sides of Asia, and traveled extensively. I have an extremely elaborate fantasy life and have forgotten that my bands don't really exist, to the extent that I have shopped for their albums on iTunes. I have met sheikhs, magnates, high ranking politicians and the guy who did the original production paintings for Raiders Of the Lost Ark, but I'm pretty sure the only celebrity who would make me completely tongue tied would be Randolph Mantooth of Emergency!

Join my mailing list http://eepurl.com/4VZuD

Turn the page for a special excerpt of Christa Maurice's

Satellite of Love

They love each other. Will the rest of the world let them?

Reluctantly on her way to a blind date, second grade teacher Maureen detours into her mechanic's garage because her brakes are squeaking. Her regular mechanic isn't there but his very intriguing brother Michael is. Michael tells her that he can't let her drive home with her brakes in that condition and offers to take her out to dinner in his 1972 Plymouth Satellite. Maureen can't believe how instantly and powerfully she's attracted to this grease monkey and neither can any of her friends, but since he's only going to be in town for a week, she doesn't want to waste an instant.

Except that grease monkey is no grease monkey. He's Bear D'Amato, rock n' roll drummer and in a week he's headed back to get ready for a world tour with his band, Touchstone. When he first meets Maureen, he just wants to go out with her a few times like a normal guy, but as the relationship deepens, he realizes he wants more than just a couple of dates. He wants a lifetime.

Maureen is shocked by his revelation, but she realizes she wants a lifetime too. Now all they have to do is convince the rest of the world.

On sale now!

Chapter 1

Maureen dropped her head to the steering wheel in front of Tony's Garage. She was not going to make that blind date, and depending on the repair bill, might be happy about that. One of these days she had to tell her friend Linda no when she came up with another man. So far they had all been wasted evenings.

She really needed to try to meet some decent men on her own. So far the strategy of school all day and sitting home all night planning for school the next day wasn't working so great for the social calendar.

At least the screaming brakes gave her a good excuse to cancel. The sign said closed, but when she pushed the door, it opened. The bay to the right was empty, but further back, in the bays behind the building, she could hear clanking and a radio playing. Tony must be working late.

"Hello?" Maureen peered through the short hallway from the obsessively clean waiting area to the back repair bays. The far door stood nearly closed so she could only see a sliver of the room. A tire, a black fender with a piece of masking tape on it, a work light, a black hood propped open. "Tony? Are you back there? It's Maureen Donnelly."

Feet shuffled and the radio's volume lowered. What if it wasn't Tony? Maybe one of his assistants had stayed late. Rusty or...the high school kid...Eric, that was his name. Did Tony trust his high school work-study assistant enough to leave him alone in the garage after hours? "I'm having some trouble with my brakes. They're making a lot of noise. You probably heard them when I pulled in."

What if it wasn't either one of them? What if it was some total stranger? What if it was somebody dangerous? She fumbled in her purse for her cell phone then stopped.

What was she going to do? Call 911 so they could listen to her screams for help without being able to do anything because they didn't know where she was? Tomorrow's headline could read: *Second Grade*

Teacher Slain In Garage, Too Stupid To Know Responders Couldn't Track Her Cellphone Signal. She should have gotten one of those apps that broadcast her every move. Then she could have just posted to Facebook. *Being murdered. Call Police. Tony's Garage.*

The door to the back bays opened and a bulky silhouette that didn't really fit Tony, Rusty, or Eric filled it.

She took a step back toward the outside door. "Hi, sorry I bothered you. I can come back in the morning." *Teacher's Body Found Rolled In Rug Behind Convenience Store, Cell Phone Still In Her Hand.*

"It's okay." The man walked through the dark hall and into the waiting area. His broad, friendly face seemed familiar. He wore his long brown hair in a ponytail and had a smudge of grease on his cheek. "I heard you pull in. You want me to take a look?"

"No." She bumped into the door. "I mean, you don't have to. I'll just leave it for Tony in the morning." The mechanic didn't look at all threatening, but adrenalin interfered with rational thought. *Memorial Service For Murdered Teacher Tuesday, Local Garages Offering Free Brake Checks. Says Tony D'Amato, owner of the garage where her car was found Friday, "If she'd just gotten that squeaking noise checked when she first heard it, all of this could have been avoided."*

"They sounded pretty bad. You might have worn down to the rotors. Let me take a look." He crossed the room.

Honestly, he looked about as threatening as the Easter Bunny. If the Easter Bunny had amazing shoulders. "It's okay." Before she announced that someone was picking her up, she stopped herself. The neighborhood wasn't the greatest and calling for a ride meant standing around in it, increasing her chances for ending up in that rug. Better the devil she had just met than the one who might be lurking in the dark. "Who are you?"

He had been reaching out, hopefully to grab the door because his hands were filthy, but pulled back when she asked. "I'm— I'm Michael, Tony's brother."

"Michael. No wonder you look familiar. Sorry. I wasn't sure." Too much caffeine and too many murder mysteries. She needed to lay off both for a while.

"That's okay." Michael pursed his lips. Nice lips they were too. Full, red, very kissable for the Easter-Bunny-slash-killer. "You want me to take a look at those brakes now?"

"Sure. Thanks. I know it's after hours, but they started to sound really bad." She held out her keys. "I guess you'll need to put it up on the lift or something."

Michael nodded, ripped some paper off the roll inside the door to protect the interior of her precious ten-year-old clunker and crossed the lot to her car. She wouldn't mind having that body in her driver's seat. The way he filled out his coverall was a sight. Broad shoulders, narrow waist, nice tight butt. Very nice.

She turned away from the window before he caught her staring. Good thing she wasn't going on that date in this frame of mind. From murdered and rolled in a rug to sweaty sex on the hood of a car in ten seconds flat, and all she'd needed was his name.

Oh. Date.

Her phone was still in her hand so she located the latest bachelor on her list of calls as she walked through the hallway to watch Michael pull her car in. Tony didn't like customers in the bay. He claimed it was dangerous. The only danger she could imagine was brain damage from the stench of oil, gasoline and exhaust. Brain damage be damned, she wasn't going to pass on the chance to ogle.

"Hello?"

"Hi—" Crud, what was this bachelor's name? "It's Maureen. I wanted to let you know I can't make it tonight."

"Sorry to hear that." He didn't sound sorry. Maybe Linda's sales pitch hadn't been that good.

"My brakes are making a horrible noise. I'm sure you can hear it." Michael had just pulled through the door and the squeals echoed beautifully on the cinderblock walls.

"That sounds pretty bad. Um... I guess you'll need a ride."

"No." That was it. No more of Linda's blind dates. "I'll be fine."

"Okay. I guess I'll talk to you."

Not if I recognize your number before I answer the phone. "Yeah. Okay. 'Bye." She closed her phone. At this very moment she could be at home watching TV in sweats, grading math tests and deciding to bring the car to Tony tomorrow. She'd washed her hair, shaved her legs, put on makeup and dressed up for whatshisname. The sexy dark blue jersey dress she'd selected needed somebody who'd appreciate her effort. Hands on hips to hold her coat open, she sauntered behind the car. Michael was operating the lift, but he gave her a once over when she passed.

"Well?" she asked.

"They aren't supposed to sound like that. I'll have to pull the tire off to see how bad it is, but it's not going to be good. Does Tony do all the maintenance on your car?"

"Most of it. He told me to go to the quick lube places for my oil changes." Lube, hehe. She really needed to mix with adults more often.

"Has your transmission fluid been clear?" Michael walked to the front driver's side tire, so she followed him.

"I guess so. The guy at the lube place said I needed to have it flushed next time I go in. Why?"

"Felt to me like your transmission was slipping." He popped the hubcap off and used a loud tool to loosen the lug nuts.

When she flinched away from the noise, she bumped into the car he'd been working on. It was black except for the trunk, which was orange. Just sitting there, hood up and orange trunk lid, it seemed to say, "Hey, baby, wanna ride?" She sidled toward the front. On the fender a strip of masking tape said *Satellite of Love*. "Is this your car?"

Michael looked over his shoulder, yanking the tire off as if it weighed less than a duvet. "Yeah. That's my baby."

"Satellite of Love?"

"My sister-in-law's idea of a joke. It's a '72 Plymouth Satellite."

As if that meant something to her. As far as she could tell, it was a car that might or might not run. She leaned on the Satellite's fender. Her car always looked so helpless up on the lift. More so now that it was missing a tire.

"You headed someplace tonight?" Michael asked.

"A date."

"Sorry."

"Naw, if I'd really wanted to be there I could have continued to ignore that squealing." She grinned, but he didn't turn around to see it. Another wasted effort. "So what are you doing here?"

"I'm visiting my brother and his family." Michael glanced over his shoulder frowning, clearly absorbed with the car thing in his hand. Men and their obsession with inanimate objects. "This is bad."

"What's bad?" She stepped forward.

"This piece?" He held up a dirty, holey piece of who knew what in his large, strong-looking hand. "This is the shoe. This is what stops your car and it works best when it isn't full of holes."

Her grimace, such an attractive expression, he did see. Of course. "Is it expensive?"

"Expensive?"

Why did he sound like money was no object to him? "Yes, is it going to cost a lot to fix?"

"It's not cheap, but it's a lot less expensive than plowing into a wall or another car." He shrugged. "Tony's pretty busy tomorrow, but if he can't get to it, I'm sure we can do it Sunday so you can have it back for Monday."

She clenched her fists behind her back. As if that would keep the money from flying out of her wallet. "Will somebody call me and tell me when to bring it in?"

"Oh no." Michael dropped the worn brake shoe on the floor. "You can't drive out of here like this."

"If you put the tire back on, I can."

"No, you can't." Michael folded his arms, which accented those fantastic shoulders and did incredible things to the muscles in his upper arms. "I can't let you drive this car in good conscience. You'd be a danger to yourself and anyone else on the road."

"Great." Maureen stared out the bay door into the waning light, thoughts of fantastic shoulders ebbing. She'd have been better off going on the stupid date. A whole weekend without a car? The price was too high. "How am I supposed to get home?"

"I can give you a ride or you can call a cab."

Her stomach growled. On the top of her To Do list for tomorrow was buying groceries. Until she could get out to the store, she was eating oatmeal and crackers with jelly. "Great."

"You know, if you're hungry we could stop for pizza on the way." Michael smiled. He had a warm, playful smile that gave her a glimpse of the little boy in this big hunk of man. "My treat since I know Tony is going to gouge you on the repair. I'll even kick in a ride in the Satellite of Love."

Well, that did make the bill a little more manageable. "You had me at pizza."

He nodded. "I'm known for overplaying my hand. Let me clean up and we'll get out of here." Switching off the work light hooked to the Satellite, he set it aside and closed the hood. Then he headed toward the little hallway. "It'll only take me a minute."

This had to be one of her more irrational moments. Fifteen minutes ago she'd been convinced he was going to murder her and dump her body in an alley and now they were headed out to grab a pizza? In his car yet. Insane much? "Hey, you aren't going to turn out to be a serial killer, are you?" she called after him.

He turned at the mouth of the hallway. "A what?"

"Never mind."

He chuckled, a deep rich sound. "Don't worry. I'm not a serial killer." Then he ducked through a door in the hall that was always closed.

She should probably be concerned about the way he emphasized the word *not*, but somehow couldn't summon the desire.

No, she was busy desiring something else.

* * * *

Bear stripped off his coveralls and hung them on the door of the extra locker. He'd been hoping to get a little more work done on the Satellite, but this was a lot more interesting. Pulling on the Tesla t-shirt he'd worn in this morning, he wished he'd dressed a little better. Of course, Maureen Donnelly thought he was an auto mechanic, so the old concert t-shirt and jeans might be a better way to sell the illusion.

His phone had five messages. One from Sandy, one from Candy, one from Jason and two from Marc. Sandy was probably mad he hadn't called in since last week. Going off the radar like he had, especially with a tour looming, must be driving Sandy nuts. Candy wanted him to do some publicity thing. Her job was getting them publicity, but she never had understood the word *vacation*. Jason, if Jason was still acting the way he had been for the past couple of weeks since he'd gotten dumped in *People*, was just calling to bitch. He called Marc and pinned the phone between his shoulder and ear while he scrubbed grease off his fingers.

"Yo."

"What?"

"Nothin'. When are you coming back?"

"Ten days." He checked his watch as if it measured days. Ten short days, until he was stuck in a room, and then a series of rooms, with the rest of the band and their melodrama.

"Good. Jason is selling the New York apartment."

"Beautiful, so he's going to be in Malibu all the time now?"

"I guess. Ty has taken up grass boarding."

"What the fuck is that?"

"Just like snowboarding, but on grass."

"He can still sing when he falls and fucks up his wrists. Did you call for a reason or just to give me a newsy update?"

"Why? You got a hot date or something?"

Bear didn't answer. He'd hoped to already be tooling down the road with Maureen Donnelly headed for a simple pizza between two people who'd just met. Two totally normal people.

"The suits just want to make sure everything is on track," Marc said. "The album is still moving up the charts but the single is slipping. The next single is coming out Tuesday and it would really help if you would pick up a little promo."

"I'm. On. Vacation."

"I know, but we owe the company a fortune and if this record tanks, we are never going to record another one. The label will drop us and we'll all end up managing a fast food joint."

"Yeah, I know. I took Rock Star 101 with you." His head started to throb. "We did all that promo when the album came out. The thing for MTV and that Canadian show. And we're doing that casino to kick off the tour. All I asked for was two fucking weeks."

"And all I'm asking you to do is take two hours out of your vacation and hit a radio station."

"Marc, they're getting the next ten months of my life."

"It's the job, man, and it's the best fucking job in the world." Marc's tone remained pleasant and even.

"I know. Is that what Sandy wanted?"

"No, Sandy wants to know where you are and that you're healthy."

"Tell him I'm right where I was the last time he talked to me and in about the same shape."

"Great. Jason has been busting his ass on promo."

The last thing he wanted to hear about was what a superhero Jason was. Not with a sweet thing like Maureen Donnelly waiting. "I gotta go."

"Oh, that's right. The hot date. See ya in ten days."

Bear snapped his phone closed as he pulled on his leather jacket. He should have skipped this whole music thing and gone into business with his brother.

Then both of them could be trying to scratch a living out of this little three bay garage.

He snatched the keys off the locker shelf and hurried out to see if Maureen Donnelly had hung around while he was getting scolded.

She stood in the filthy repair bay behind her car, holding her purse with both hands. Cocking her head, she gave him a little smile.

For about ten seconds, he couldn't take his eyes off her. The minimal makeup she wore accented the simple prettiness of her features instead of them being obliterated under raccoon eyeliner and some wild shade of lipstick. Her brunette hair was cut in a bob and pulled back off her face. He hadn't seen what with yet, but he bet it was a bow or some kind of flower. The dark blue dress crisscrossed over her perfect, unenhanced bust, creating some really intriguing cleavage.

Really intriguing. He couldn't see her legs around the bumper of the car, or her shoes. He wanted to check out her shoes and, more importantly, the legs that led into them. As he recalled, the hem fell right to her knees.

"Sorry I took so long." He tore his gaze away from where he could have seen her legs if he had x-ray vision, and met hers. She didn't seem to be on to him. "I had to make a call."

"No problem." She shook her head and her cute little bob bounced around her shoulders.

"I'll lock up and we can go." He ducked into the waiting room to lock the door and turn off the lights. The sooner he got out of here, the sooner he was going to get a look at her legs. "Which pizza place do you like better? Napoli or Mama Lena's? I like Napoli's."

"So do I, but I don't like to eat there." She sounded sorry as she followed him to the car door.

He glanced over his shoulder. Her pretty, small mouth was drawn into a frown. "Why?"

"They're always screaming at each other, did you notice? The food is wonderful, but the brothers who own the place are always arguing or yelling at the kids waiting tables." She shivered. "It just makes me uncomfortable."

"Tony always gets carry out. I guess there's a reason." He opened the passenger door of the Satellite. "Mama Lena's it is."

She sat down on the seat sideways and twisted forward like a lady. His mom used to get into cars that way when she wore a dress and he'd never seen any other woman do it. Swallowing at the unfamiliar rush of mixed heat and uncertainty, he opened the bay door so he could back out. This woman was not a score-seeking groupie. Maureen Donnelly qualified as a nice girl.

And he was already lying to her.

Not lying really, but not filling her in on a few details. Like he wasn't an auto mechanic and in a couple of weeks, he'd be off on the one ring circus currently known as the Bayonet Ball Tour. Like the next time she saw him after this, he'd probably be on MTV. If she even watched that. She struck him as a History Channel type.

Did it really matter? He was taking her out for a pizza, not marrying her. For one night, he could just be Michael, the guy who was buying her a pizza, taking her home and maybe getting a kiss on the doorstep instead of Bear D'Amato, drummer for Touchstone.

He backed the car out and closed the garage door. "So what is it you do?"

"I'm a teacher. I teach second grade at Wilson."

"Really?" Teacher. Little kid teacher yet. That fit. "You like it?"

"Yeah, it's great, but I'm looking forward to summer vacation."

"Oh?"

"February is kinda long and Spring Break is late this year so we've had this really long stretch with no days off. It gets a little tiring, for the teachers and the kids."

"I always thought the teachers were annoyed when we had days off." He glanced at her. She had half turned toward him with her purse in her lap, as if she were interested in the conversation, not as if she were amortizing him.

"Nope. We're all shooing the kids out the door and making plans for our days off."

"And what do you like to do on your days off?" What did regular people do on their days off? Most of his time was spent in the studio, on tour or in between and in between was only a couple of days here and there. Not that it was bad, he did have the greatest job in the world, but it was a twenty-four seven gig. Even last year's sabbatical had been spent analyzing what had gone wrong with the previous album so they could avoid it this time.

"The usual stuff. I read, watch TV, garden a little."

"Go out on blind dates."

She groaned. "Yeah. I should have given that up for Lent. My friend Linda means well, but she's not very good at it. I think next time I'm going to be washing my hair or something pressing like that."

"So it is an excuse."

"Like you've ever gotten it."

"Once or twice." A long time ago. Now all he had to do was pick a girl from the line up, which was frustrating in its own way.

Her laugh was light and musical. "So what do you do, other than fix cars?"

Damn. How to answer this question without flat out lying? "I travel and play music." That sounded good. Like they were two separate things.

"Travel. I've always wanted to travel, but never had the money. Where have you been?"

"All over." He clenched the steering wheel. He'd never seen much of the places he'd been. Travel, perform, sleep, repeat.

"That sounds wonderful."

Not the word he'd use. "So you have a garden?"

"Yeah. I bought a house last year so I spent last summer gardening. I'm really looking forward to my tulips and daffodils coming up this spring."

He pulled into the parking lot of Mama Lena's. The place was jammed. Great, now he had to use his fame to pull a few strings for a table, blowing his cover, or stand around like a jerk waiting for one. "Here we are."

"Wow, they're busy tonight." She checked her watch. "Let's hope the theater at the mall has a showing time soon so we don't have to wait long. I don't know about you, but I'm starved."

Oh yeah, she would *expect* to wait for a table. She wouldn't be disappointed when he couldn't magically make one open up for her. Man, he was so out of practice for this regular dating thing.

She climbed out without waiting for him to open her door and strode toward the restaurant, giving him the chance to fall back and check out the rear view, what he could see of it above and below her black raincoat. Her calves were slender and well shaped, practically insuring fantastic legs. The three-inch heels she wore put a beautiful glide in her stride. Her hair clip wasn't a bow or flowers. It was a gold Mickey Mouse. Mickey freakin' Mouse. This woman was so real, she was surreal.

He pulled open the door. Nobody lingered in the tiny waiting area and a blonde in a white t-shirt and black pants with a little red waitress's apron wrapped around her waist bounded over before the door even fell shut.

"Hi, Miss Donnelly, you need a table? Benny's clearing one now." The waitress's gaze shifted over Maureen's shoulder and her eyes went wide. He had about ten seconds before his cover went up in hysteria.

"Thanks, Tara. How's your sister doing?" Maureen scanned the restaurant. When she returned to the waitress, the girl's gaze pinged back to her, still wide eyed.

"My sister? Um, Ellie's fine. Um... I'll, um...check on Benny." The waitress spun around and all but sprinted for the back of the restaurant. Probably headed for the kitchen where she would tell the entire staff he was here.

"Tara's little sister was in my class two years ago." Maureen turned and frowned. "You have grease on your face."

"I do?" Bear watched over her shoulder for the kitchen staff to come boiling through the swinging doors to check out the visiting celebrity.

"Yeah. Do you want a Kleenex?" She dug in her purse.

"No, I'll just go wash it off in the bathroom." He lunged past her in the direction the waitress had gone, crossed the dining room without touching the floor and burst into the kitchen.

The entire staff huddled around Tara. They turned as a unit to stare at him. All of them in Touchstone's target audience range.

"I told you!" Tara shrieked.

"Hush," an older man hissed. The only one not in the crowd. "The customers will hear you."

"Listen, I just want to have a nice quiet dinner." Bear held up his hands. "I'll sign all the autographs you want in here, but out there I'd really appreciate it if you treated me like anybody else."

"But you're not anybody else," a girl with black hair and black rimmed glasses whimpered. "You're Bear D'Amato from Touchstone."

"You know Brian Ellis," another girl said.

"And Jason Callisto."

That broke their spell and they rushed him, order tablets out for autographs, babbling about how much they liked the album and the single and were they going to be doing a show anyplace close? He started signing. "I'm going to be in town for a few more days and I really want to keep it quiet. I just want to have dinner like anybody else. If everyone could just keep this between us until I leave, maybe I can talk the band into swinging by here while we're on tour. But seriously, if there's a breath of a rumor that I'm here, I can't promise anything."

The whole group gasped, exchanging conspiratorial glances. Hopefully, it would be as easy to arrange as it had been to promise. Sandy was going to murder him.

Tara stood in front of him with bright eyes. "Are you dating Miss Donnelly?"

"I'm having dinner with Miss Donnelly." Eventually. If he ever managed to get back to her. He'd been gone a really long time and still had grease on his face.

"I bet she doesn't even know who you are." Tara clutched her autograph to her chest. "She's so tragically unhip. I'll go seat her."

"Not a word," he cautioned as she scooted through the door. Now he was lying. Flat out, no doubt, lying.

But if he told her, she'd either run screaming or latch on tighter for all the wrong reasons. He just wanted one night. Not even the whole night. For the next three hours, he wanted to be nobody special.